E.M. Kelly

Murder By Symbols

A Detective Colton Baker Thriller

by

E.M. Kelly

Murder By Symbols

A Detective Colton Baker Thriller

Murder By Symbols
2024
Published by: Great Blue Hill Publishing
All rights reserved.

Cover design: Deranged Doctor Design

Murder by Symbols: A Detective Colton Baker Thriller is a work of fiction. Dr. Benjamin Church is a historical figure who lived back in the late 1700s. The Town of Stoughton, Massachusetts, is an actual town. Permissions obtained to use actual private business' names.

A very special thank you

Detective Dan Barber

For always responding, even all my late-night texts. This book would not be possible without you!

I remember going to the station and talking to dispatch and asking to speak with a detective regarding a book I was working on.

I thought for sure they'd just toss my request into the trash. Never in my wildest imagination did I expect to receive a callback, never mind hearing how interested you were in the project.

We first met on May 19, 2021, as Covid was winding down, so when we met at the station we still had to wear masks.

From the word *Go,* you were all in. You let me record all our conversations and even traveled around town with me to all the different locations where the fictitious bodies would be found.

You answered all of my questions as well as going deep into the inner workings of what a detective does. The ride-a-long with you was totally badass! Can we do another one?

I had the pleasure of speaking with your fellow officers and a common theme emerged. I constantly heard throughout the department how smart, professional and dedicated you are to the job.

I hope you know how much respect I have for you. I am both privileged and honored to call you a friend!

Stay safe out there!

Thank you to the men and women of the Stoughton Police Department

I had the pleasure of attending the Interactive Citizens Academy put on by the Stoughton Police Department. I found out about it at the last minute and, because of a certain detective, he made it possible for me to attend.

The course lasted twelve weeks, and we met twice a week on Tuesday and Thursday evenings. The class was very informative and provided the public with an opportunity to learn about a police officer's job. It is not an easy job, that's for sure.

It was there that I met Lt. Bonney (now Chief of Abington Police) and a host of other officers. Lt. Bonney has a great sense of humor and even came up with some nicknames for those in attendance. He dubbed me the 'Resident Author'.

We even had the pleasure of Deputy Chief Holmes (now Chief of Kingston Police) sitting in on several of the classes. At that time, there were some controversial topics in town and the Deputy Chief was very candid with the class. He even answered questions, and there were a lot of them.

The media often casts the police in a negative light, but that hasn't been my experience. They're good people doing a hard job.

I have nothing but the utmost respect for those who put on the uniform and protect us from evil in the world. And trust me, there is evil out there.

So, the next time you meet an officer on the street, say hello and thank them for their service. Remember, they're just people too!

May God watch over those who serve and protect us.

I'd also like to thank Charlie Gillis and the men and women of the Holbrook Regional Emergency Communication Center

I met Charlie when he coached my daughter's soccer team. Something he told everyone at the communication center when he introduced me around while giving me a tour of the facility.

Charlie is a dispatcher who worked for Stoughton out of the Stoughton Police Department. He now works at the Holbrook Regional Emergency Communication Center and dispatches for both the Stoughton Police and Fire Department.

In Loving Memory
David "Spanky" Sousa

David, or Spanky, to those who knew him, was a larger-than-life, one-of-a-kind guy. He was a family friend and someone that you could always count on. David and his wife, Maria both supported my efforts as an author. They bought my books, shared my social media posts, and David even helped me with this book. As a former Selectman for the Town of Stoughton, David met with me at Town Spa and told me what it was like to be in local politics.

David was a *doer*. He got things done. Years ago, we told him about an issue with the road in front of our house. Later that evening, there was a knock on our door. David had come out to look at the issue and the next day, the DPW was there to fix it.

My wife, Natalie, has known David all her life and grew up watching wrestling (WWF back in the day!) with him when he'd come over to a relative's home. Back then, she called him the *Big Kahuna*. David wasn't just larger-than-life in personality, he stood over six feet tall and was a gentle giant. When I asked David to meet and talk about his time as a Selectman, there was no hesitation. He simply said, "When?"

I told David that I wanted to base a character after him in this book and I wanted to call that character *Big Kahuna*. David looked at me for a long minute. Then he told me he wanted the character to be named Spanky. I was going to stick to my guns, but now that he is no longer with us, I decided to honor his request. It just so happens that night was the last time I saw him. Maria also joined us for dinner that night and I cherish them taking their time to help me. When we were getting ready to leave, David put his hand on my shoulder and told me how excited he was about this project.

So, for all you that didn't know Spanky, I hope you get a glimpse of who he was. For those who had the pleasure of knowing him, I hope this brings back fond memories.

To Maria and their kids, you have my heartfelt condolences. David will be missed by all that knew him.

For my mom, Elaine

Chapter 1

Stoughton, Massachusetts

Detective Colton Baker adjusted his tie in the bathroom mirror and hoped for an easy first day. It would be anything but.

Colton wasn't a big man. Most would consider him of average build. But he was strong. He worked out daily and took MMA fighting. He could scrap with anyone and had a grip like Superman. When he grabbed someone, they knew it. But his true talent was his intellect. Most people either had common sense or high intelligence. Colton had both.

Although Colton appeared young, he was almost thirty years old. His looks were deceiving. Many a criminal assumed he was inexperienced and naïve. He was anything but.

Colton graduated at the top of his class in the Police Academy and aced the detective test. He loved to read and had years of experience on the street as a patrolman. His ability to deduce situations and solve problems was a gift. It came natural to him.

He looked at himself in the mirror. His face was smooth after his morning shave. Some officers had facial hair, which Colton found unacceptable. He believed male officers should have a clean shave and keep their hair short. He did both.

Hayley, a seven-year-old poodle mix, darted between his legs, sat down on the tile floor and looked up at him.

Using the mirror, he looked down at her.

"Did she call?"

He exited the bathroom and headed over to the nightstand to check his phone. Hayley followed him, her tiny claws clicking on the tile. He checked his phone. No missed calls. Sprawled out on the bed was Roxy, his thirteen-year-old Shih

Tzu mix. She looked at him with sad eyes that pleaded, *Don't go to work. Come back to bed and snuggle.*

He reached out, scratched behind her ear, and kissed the top of her head. Roxy rolled over, exposing her belly, but Colton didn't have time to give her the attention she wanted. No tummy rubs this morning.

He picked up his phone and put it in his pocket. Then he clipped his new detective badge onto his belt.

A gun safe that appeared to be a large alarm clock with a phone charging station sat on the nightstand. He entered the code by pushing a few buttons, and the safe opened. Inside was a Glock 26. It was a compact weapon with a ten round capacity magazine. He picked it up, pulled the slide back, and exposed the brass round in the chamber. It was ready to fire.

Colton holstered his weapon and headed for the front door.

Hayley followed, right on his heels. Her tiny nails click clacking away. When they reached the door, he squatted down, rubbed the top of her head, then bent over and gave her a kiss. Having already made their morning pit stop outside, Colton made sure they had plenty of food and water. He grabbed his suit jacket and headed out the door.

Colton grew up in Stoughton and after graduating college, he joined the Stoughton Police Department. He'd started out as a patrolman and quickly got a glimpse of the side of town many didn't see. Most crimes take place behind closed doors and out of the public eye. It was a vast comparison to the small town he knew.

Colton's ability to adapt and get the job done caught the eyes of his supervisors, who encouraged him to take the detective's test. His uncanny knack for absorbing knowledge, combined with his love of reading and studying, made him the perfect candidate. As expected, he aced the detective's test.

On his ride to the station, Colton passed several yellow yard signs that said, *Keep 911 Local.* It was a hot topic around town, and the signs would surely only help fan the flames.

Colton wanted to get an early start and arrived at the station an hour before his shift started. He used his fob to gain entry through the employee's entrance.

He stopped at the front desk. Inside sat the Desk Duty Officer and two dispatchers. In Stoughton, both the police and fire were dispatched from the same location. They sat side by side, which led to faster communication between the two departments as they both worked on different frequencies. It was a win for the town and its residents. *Why would they want to split that up?* Colton wondered.

"Have you seen the signs popping up around town?" Colton asked.

"Don't even get them started, Detective," the Duty Officer said.

Colton looked at each of the dispatchers.

"The county wants to control all the 911 calls," the first dispatcher said. "They want to pull dispatchers from the police and fire stations and house them all in one location."

"Why?" Colton asked.

"Money. What else?" said one dispatcher.

"It just seems ... dumb," Colton said.

"Fucking stupid is my choice of words," said the other dispatcher.

"Welcome to small-town politics," said the Duty Officer.

Colton shook his head and walked away.

The Duty Officer leaned over the desk and yelled after Colton. "Small-town politics is everywhere, Detective. There's no escaping it. You'll see!"

Colton had responded to calls before, which led to heated debate around town, but he never had to investigate them. That had always been Detective Peterson's job. The small-town politics was one thing Colton wasn't looking forward to.

Colton walked to the detective's office and used his fob. Because the evidence locker was inside, only the detective and chief had access.

Once inside, he found a stack of case files on his desk waiting for him. After getting situated, he sat down and went through the files.

A few minutes later, the door lock clicked, and it swung open.

Chief Catherine McCormack stood in the doorway. She appeared to be around fifty and had a commanding presence. She wore glasses and had her blonde hair tied up in a bun.

Scandals had plagued the department for years. It was no secret that Stoughton had some bad cops in its ranks. Chief McCormack had made it publicly known she intended on weeding out all the corrupt cops and replacing them with good ones once she became chief. She was trying to right a ship that was way off course.

The economic downturn caused a rise in crime across the country, including Stoughton. Detective Peterson's death added to the already full caseload. The department urgently needed a detective. Public pressure mounted, and the Board of Selectmen and the Town Manager felt it. They couldn't wait another month and agreed to hire Colton earlier than planned.

"Good morning, detective," Chief McCormack said.

"Good morning, chief," responded Colton.

"Getting an early start, I see."

"Yes, ma'am."

"I'm sorry I had to bump up your start date. With Peterson passing away before he retired, I couldn't go without a detective. As you can see, his caseload was piling up."

"No worries, chief. I'll get through them as fast as possible."

"Are you getting settled in okay?"

"Yes, ma'am."

"Well, I'll leave you to it," the chief said, and closed the door.

Colton had some time to kill until roll call. He sat down at his desk and perused through the stack of open case files. In his summation, his predecessor was biding his time until retirement and had let his caseload lag. Colton was confident he could easily clear some cases and get them off the books. As he finished reading through each file, he jotted down notes for himself on a Post-It and stuck it on the inside of the folder. He looked down at his watch. It was 7:00am. Time for roll call.

Roll call was just starting when Colton walked in. Lieutenant Bonnett stood at the podium and addressed the patrol officers. Each one sat ready with a pen and notebook. Colton stood in the back corner as the Lieutenant spoke about a rash of home invasions and car break-ins. Like everywhere across the country, Stoughton had a drug problem too. Addicts would do anything for their next fix and once their money was gone, some turned to stealing to fuel their habit. "The chief has called for an increase of patrols through the hardest hit neighborhoods," Lt. Bonnett said. "Also, we've seen an uptick in overdoses again. We've added extra Narcan to each cruiser's med kit. Remember, Fentanyl is everywhere nowadays. Keep your gloves on at all times and be cognizant when searching anyone or their belongings. Just a whiff of that stuff can kill you."

Lieutenant Bonnett looked up and spotted Colton.

"As you all know, detective Peterson would have retired next month, but he suffered a massive heart attack and passed away. The poor bastard never got to enjoy a single day of his retirement. Detective Baker is taking over for him," Lt. Bonnett said, pointing to the back of the room.

There was a short applause.

After roll-call, Colton loaded up his cruiser and signed on over the air. His first stop would be a follow up to a breaking and entering case his predecessor started.

As Colton pulled out of the station parking lot, dispatch called him over the radio.

"Control to D-1."

"D-1," Colton said into the mic.

"Respond to the train station for a possible sudden."

Jesus, Colton thought. *A dead body in the first hour of the first day.*

"D-1 received."

"D-1 received."

Chapter 2

Train Station
Stoughton, Massachusetts

Colton arrived at the train station and found a swarm of onlookers standing by the South entrance. He glimpsed a body lying on the ground.

Two cruisers pulled in behind him as he exited his vehicle.

As the two officers approached, Colton pointed to the first officer.

"Push those people back."

Then he pointed to the second officer.

"Grab the yellow crime scene tape and cordon off this entire area."

Both officers did as instructed.

Colton walked over to the body. He expected to find someone who had overdosed. That's not what he found.

A man in his late fifties lay on the ground. A railroad spike protruded from the top of his head and a pool of blood surrounded it. Colton noticed what appeared to be a fresh tattoo on the man's forehead, which was a combination of letters, numbers, and strange symbols.

"D-1 to Control," Colton said into his radio mic.

"Control's on," replied the dispatcher.

"I have an active crime scene. Notify the MBTA (Massachusetts Bay Transportation Authority), the State Police CPAC Unit (Crime Prevention and Control), and the Medical Examiner."

"Received," the dispatcher said.

Colton composed his thoughts on what to do next.

"D-1 to Control."

"Go ahead, detective."

"Cancel fire and start me the Shift Supervisor."

"Received."

Colton went back to his cruiser and pulled out his crime scene kit. As a patrolman, he'd been on dozens of 'unattended deaths' scenes. Most were overdoses, suicides, and natural causes like cancer or extreme age. In those cases, he usually assisted Detective Peterson in rolling the body over for photographic purposes.

Now, he was the detective. He was in charge. As he walked back, he recalled his training. When he arrived back at the body, he took out his department-issued cell phone and began taking photos of the body and the ground surrounding it. Everything was evidence until proven otherwise. He'd supply the photos to the State Police and MBTA investigators.

The sound of approaching sirens cut off. The fire department had received word to cancel.

Colton continued taking photos when the two officers returned.

"What now?" asked the first officer.

"Keep everyone behind the tape. This happened on the train station property. It's an MBTA case."

Minutes ticked past and then Colton heard the faint sound of sirens growing closer.

Another minute later, three MBTA police cars pulled into the lot.

One cruiser had the word Supervisor written on the front corner panel. A woman got out. She appeared to be in her late thirties and had bright red hair, which was tucked up under her cap. She scanned the scene and walked over to Colton.

"Captain Morris," she said, holding out her hand.

They shook hands, and Colton introduced himself.

"What do you have, detective?" she asked.

"Homicide. Male. Possibly early fifties," Colton said.

Morris looked down at the body. "Wow, he pissed someone off."

"I'd say so," Colton replied.

"What do you need from us, detective?" Morris asked.

"What? This is your case," Colton said.

"How do you figure?"

"Oh, I don't know. Because he's on your property."

"Nope!" Morris said.

"What, you don't handle murders? You just chase turnstile jumpers?"

"Haha. Real funny. This is your case, detective," Morris said.

"Fuck you, it is," Colton said. "Get the Staties down here."

"They're gonna tell you the same thing, detective."

"Oh yeah, why's that?"

"Because the town of Stoughton owns this property."

"Since when?" Colton asked.

"Years ago," Morris said. "You new on the job?" she asked sarcastically.

Colton laughed.

"Actually, today's my first day," Colton said.

"No shit?" Morris said.

"No shit."

Morris stood there a moment, staring at him.

"I just made detective," Colton said. "Today is literally my first day."

"Damn!" she said. "You caught a body on your first day. That's just cruel."

"You sure it's mine?" Colton asked.

"If it was found on the tracks, it would be our jurisdiction," Morris said. "This is all yours."

Chapter 3

Stoughton Bakery
Stoughton, Massachusetts

Twenty minutes later, the Massachusetts State Police Homicide Detective arrived on the scene.

"Hey, detective!" the patrolman standing by the entrance yelled. "Staties are here."

The unmarked State Trooper vehicle pulled up to the tape. Detective Steve Barnes, a tall, bald black trooper with massive shoulders, stepped out. He wore black slacks and a Polo shirt with the Massachusetts State Police Logo on the left breast.

Barnes walked over and introduced himself to Colton and the MBTA Supervisor. Then he looked down at the body. "Well, I guess we can rule out suicide."

Colton nodded.

"Any ID on him?" asked Barnes.

"None," Colton said.

"Hey Detective!" the same patrolman yelled. "Chief is here."

Chief McCormack pulled up to the yellow tape and stopped next to Barnes' cruiser.

Colton walked over to meet her.

"Tell me what we've got, detective."

"White male, late fifties. Sharp force trauma to the head."

"Robbery?" the chief asked.

"Appears so," Colton said. "Bystanders saw a bum standing over the victim."

"Lots of transients around here. They use the tracks to move from town to town," the chief said.

"The MBTA supervisor is here, and she said the town owns the train station. Is that correct?" Colton asked.

"Yes," the Chief said. "The town purchased it a few years ago. They even filmed a scene for the movie Little Women here. The end scene at the train station, it took place right here.

"That's right," Colton said. "The one with Meryl Streep."

"Yup," she said.

"I forgot the town bought it," Colton said.

"Most people did," McCormack said. "Probably because it took forever and seemed like the sale wasn't going to happen, until it did."

Colton and the Chief walked over to Barnes.

"Hi Barnes," the Chief said. "Good to see you."

"Good morning, ma'am," Barnes replied.

"Detective Barnes here is one of the best," she said. "We worked together a few months back on a domestic abuse case where the husband violated the restraining order and killed his wife."

"Likewise, ma'am," Barnes said. "I'm sorry about Detective Peterson. He was a good man."

"Thank you, Barnes," the Chief said.

"I do have a few questions," Barnes said.

"Shoot," she said.

"Any reports of violence in this area?"

"No," she said. "Mostly just nuisance complaints about the homeless begging for change."

"I have the uniforms rounding them all up," Colton said. "Hopefully we grab the one responsible, or at least one that saw something."

"Any ID?" the Chief asked.

"None, ma'am. We believe the perp took the victim's wallet," Colton said.

"Detective, you said sharp force trauma to the head, correct?" asked the Chief.

"Yes, ma'am," Colton replied.

"With what?"

"Well, ma'am, someone drove a railroad spike into the top of his head."

The chief's eyebrows furled.

"Come look for yourself," Colton said.

They walked over toward the body. The Chief looked down.

"Holy shit!" she said, squatting down. "That's firefighter Bill McDonald."

"You know the victim?" Colton asked.

"Yeah, he's been on the fire department forever. He was getting ready to retire."

"You can cancel that retirement party," Barnes said.

"Jesus!" she said. "Bill never had that tattoo on his forehead."

"It looks new," Colton said.

The Chief stood up and scanned the parking lot.

"What is it?" Colton asked.

"I don't see his truck," she said. "He drives a huge black Dodge pickup. It's not here."

Colton walked over to the body and kneeled down next to it. He patted down both front pockets and then tucked his hand under the body, feeling the back pockets. "No keys," he said.

"What was he doing here?" Barnes asked.

"Probably came to grab breakfast from the Stoughton Bakery before starting his shift," she said.

"Where's the bakery?" Barnes asked.

The chief used her thumb to point behind her.

Barnes turned.

The bakery was less than fifty feet away.

"It's fairly new," she said.

"I'll go find out if he bought breakfast," Colton said.

A bell chimed when he walked in. Several staff members stood behind the counter.

"We're closed," said the young man behind the counter. "Per order of the police."

Colton flashed his badge. "Detective Baker, Stoughton P.D."

"Sorry, didn't know you were a cop. We get a lot of customers in suits every morning before they catch the commuter rail."

"I suppose you heard what happened out in the parking lot," Colton said.

"I can't believe it," the older woman behind the counter said. "He was such a nice man."

"Did you see what happened?" Colton asked.

"I was out back, making custards. I heard Maria, my mother-in-law, scream for help," said the man.

"And your name?" Colton asked.

"Kyle."

"Are you the owner, Kyle?" Colton asked.

"I own it with my sister-in-law, Lena, here and my mother-in-law, Maria."

"Any other employees?"

"No, just the three of us."

Colton turned his attention towards Maria.

"What exactly was it you were doing when you saw the body?" Colton asked. "Walk me through it. What you saw and heard."

"I was wiping down the table after a customer left," Maria said. "I looked out the window and that's when I noticed the body lying on the ground."

"You open at six. Is that correct?" Colton asked.

"Yes," Maria answered.

"Then what?" Colton asked.

"I saw a bum leaning over the body," Maria said. "He was touching Bill's face."

"Was he trying to help?"

"I don't know," Maria said. "Why run then?"

"He ran?"

"Yes," Maria said. "When he saw me, he took off."

Colton turned his attention back to Kyle.

"So ... you heard her scream, then what?" Colton asked.

"I came running out from the kitchen," Kyle said.

"Did you see anyone?" Colton asked.

"I saw a bum scurry around the corner," Kyle said, pointing across the street.

"When did you notice the body?" Colton asked.

"Maria had gone towards the body and came running back," Kyle said. "She said it was Bill McDonald. Said he was dead."

"Did you go over near the body?" Colton asked.

"Yes," Kyle replied.

"How close did you get to it?" Colton asked.

"Did we do something wrong?" Maria asked.

"No," Colton said. "The ground is pretty dirty near the body. We'll need to eliminate your shoe prints in the dirt."

"Oh, I understand," Maria said.

"Now, you know the victim by name. Is he a regular?" Colton asked.

"Yes, he comes in here every morning before his shift," Maria said.

"Have you had trouble around here before?" Colton asked.

"To be honest," Kyle said. "I thought it was one of those bums. Several live over there at the train station. They beg for money, but they never really bother anyone. They do sometimes fight with each other."

"Do you know what they fight over?"

"Money. Who has the better cardboard box? I really don't know."

"What else did you see?" Colton asked.

"That's it. I ran in to call 911."

"So, McDonald usually comes in for coffee, correct?" Colton asked.

"Usually," Maria said.

"Usually?" Colton asked.

"He usually comes in a little before seven and orders a hazelnut ice coffee, light, two sugars."

"But not today?" Colton asked.

"No," Maria said. "He must have gotten attacked on his way in."

"Do you know which vehicle he drives?" Colton asked.

"It's a big black truck," Maria said. "My late husband had one just like it."

"Do you have security cameras?" Colton asked.

"Yes, but only inside the store." Kyle said. "And another above the backdoor, so we can see when deliveries arrive."

"I'll need to see that footage, please."

Colton followed Kyle out back into a small office.

Kyle played the video from the time they arrived, which was 3:30 am. Nothing was on the video inside the store until 5:30 am. Maria could be seen bringing items from the kitchen and placing them in the display case. Maria unlocked the front door at 6:00 am. Shortly after, a slew of customers came in.

They walked back out front.

"Just to confirm," Colton said. "The victim didn't come into the store this morning, correct?"

"Correct," Maria said.

"Alright," Colton said. "Stick around in case we have any more questions." He turned and headed towards the front door.

"Excuse me, detective." Kyle said.

Colton stopped and turned around.

"Do you know if we'll be able to open today? I have all these fresh items just sitting here."

"I'll see what I can do."

Colton talked to the Chief and Barnes. He told them McDonald usually came in for coffee around seven and, like the Chief said, he drove a large black pickup truck. So not only was his vehicle not there but he also arrived an hour earlier than normal. He told them he had reviewed the bakery's camera footage and McDonald hadn't gone inside. They could eliminate the bakery, and it didn't need to be processed. Colton requested that the bakery be allowed to open. The chief agreed, but only after notifying McDonald's family. Last thing they needed was someone who grabbed a coffee and danish telling the family.

Colton walked back over to the bakery and informed Kyle that they could open. But, for obvious reasons, deliveries needed to go through the front door. He also asked them to refrain from discussing the incident with any patrons or posting anything on social media.

"Can we post that we're open?" Maria asked.

"Yes, but please don't mention the deceased."

When Colton returned, the State Police forensics team had arrived and begun processing the crime scene.

Colton told Barnes that he was going to go knock on doors to see if anyone heard or saw something. He'd scope out the area for any cameras that might have caught something.

Barnes agreed and said he was going to wait for the Medical Examiner.

An hour later, the medical examiner arrived and took the body away.

Chapter 4

Post Office
Stoughton, Massachusetts

Colton walked across the parking lot and stopped at the sidewalk. He began looking at all the buildings on Wyman Street. His eyes searched the corner eaves, overhangs, and above each door looking for cameras.

He spotted one across the street diagonally from the crime scene. He crossed the street and stood in front of the building, just below the camera. Turning around, he checked the camera angle to see if it captured the scene of the murder. No such luck. Either way, he'd still ask the owner to review the film. Maybe it caught the killer running down Wyman Street along the front of the train station.

Colton knocked on the door. No one answered. He wrote the address down and would come back later.

He turned right and walked behind the train station, parallel with the tracks.

The building was old and made from granite blocks. He passed the ticket window, which had been boarded up long ago. The actual station hadn't been used for decades. It sat dormant, although it was home to dozens of pigeons. They had found a way in through the top of the clock tower.

Colton continued making his way around the building. Beyond the tracks was a parking lot that was separated by a chain-link fence. After the lot was a strip plaza, which contained a hairdresser and other businesses. It was a good distance away. If there were any cameras, Colton doubted they'd capture anything at that distance. Still, he'd venture over later and look for cameras in case the perp fled in that direction.

Next, he turned and walked back towards the front of the building. A short distance later, he arrived back at the crime scene. In front of him was the bakery which abutted the Post Office. A federal building. They'd have cameras.

Colton crossed the parking lot and made his way along the chain-link fence that surrounded the Post Office property. Pieces of vinyl weaved horizontally through the link fence, making it difficult to see through. Weeds and vines had sprouted through cracks in the pavement and snaked their way upward, tangling themselves between the links.

Past the fence, Colton walked across the Post Office parking lot, took a left onto Porter Street and walked into the Post Office.

Once inside, Colton noticed the gate was down at the service window. The sign on the wall showed the Post Office didn't open for another thirty minutes. Colton heard voices on the backside of the window and banged on the gate.

"We're closed," shouted a voice from behind the gate.

Colton banged again, and said, "Stoughton P.D."

The voices behind the gate turned to whispers, and footsteps drew closer.

Colton heard a click, and the gate lifted.

An older man, mid-fifties, stood behind the window.

Colton flashed his badge.

"How can I help you, detective?" asked the man.

"Jerry, is it?" Colton said, reading the man's nametag.

"Yes, sir?"

"Is the postmaster here or a supervisor?" Colton asked.

"I'm the shift supervisor," Jerry said. "Is this regarding the police presence at the train station?"

"It is."

"What happened?"

"There was a homicide," Colton said.

"Oh, that's terrible!"

"I noticed you have cameras out back," Colton said. "I was hoping to review the footage."

"Of course," Jerry said. "I'll let you in."

Colton stepped over to the door. Jerry opened it and let him in.

Colton stepped in and looked around. There was a gigantic machine with a sorting table in front of it. He assumed it sorted the mail by street and route.

Jerry led Colton into a small office with a large monitor on the desk.

"Is this live?" Colton asked, looking at the different camera feeds on the screen.

"Yes."

"And these are all the cameras?" Colton asked.

"Every one."

Colton looked at each monitor. Some were inside the building and others were outside.

Colton pointed to the feed at the lower right corner. It was pointing down at the back lot. "Is that the only angle?"

"Yes, sir," Jerry said. "Probably not very useful. We have it pointing at the carrier vehicles out back. Being federal property and all, we don't get much trouble."

"I don't doubt that," Colton said. "No one wants to deal with federal charges."

"Sorry the video isn't helpful."

"What time did you start this morning?" Colton asked, stepping out of the office.

"I was here at 3:30 am. I unlocked the delivery bay door for the arriving mail. Once sorted, it'll get delivered later this morning."

Colton thanked Jerry and showed himself out.

There was no luck today of the incident being captured on film.

Colton walked back to the crime scene.

"How did you make out?" asked Chief McCormack.

"No luck," Colton said. "I just spent the morning searching for a ghost."

"Well, we need to notify McDonald's family," the Chief said. "We should start at the fire station. Inform the Fire Chief first. Hopefully, he can send some people over to comfort Mrs. McDonald and their children."

Chapter 5

Stoughton Fire Station 1
Stoughton, Massachusetts

"Good morning, Cap," Firefighter David Figgins said to Captain Smith as he walked into the station.

"Morning, Dave," Captain Smith replied.

"Have you seen McDonald? He was supposed to come in early and relieve me. I'm taking my boys fishing this morning down at the canal."

"No, I haven't seen him," Smith said.

"Did you hear the cops have a dead body up at the train station?" Figgins said.

"I did," Smith said. "Did you guys respond?"

"We did. But they canceled us before we arrived," Figgins said. "Must have been clearly dead."

Chief McCormack pulled into the fire station parking lot followed by two unmarked cruisers.

"The cops are here," a firefighter standing by the open bay door said.

Smith and Figgins walked over.

"This can't be good," Smith said.

Colton, Barnes, and McCormack walked into the fire station via the open bay door.

"Is the Chief in?" Colton asked.

"He's in his office," Smith said.

The three walked down between two fire engines. The driver-side door of one engine was open. A turnout coat hung from the door. Turnout pants and boots sat on the cement floor in front of the door. A bumper sticker on the backdoor window read: When seconds count, count on firefighters.

On the back wall was a door. The sign on it read Fire Chief.

They entered the door. Inside, a secretary sat behind a desk behind two computer monitors.

"We need to speak with the Fire Chief," McCormack said.

"What's this about?" the secretary asked.

"Firefighter Bill McDonald," Colton said.

"Is he in trouble?" the secretary asked. "He's such a nice man."

"It's of a personal nature," McCormack said.

"I'll let him know you're here," the secretary said, picking up the phone.

After a moment, she hung up. "The chief will see you."

The three stepped into the Fire Chief's office.

"What do I owe for this surprise visit?" Fire Chief Kenealy said, standing up behind his desk.

"Unfortunately, we have some bad news," McCormack said. "Bill McDonald was found murdered this morning."

"Jesus Christ!" Chief Kenealy said, sitting back down. His face flushed, then lost all color.

"This is Detective Baker and Detective Barnes. Barnes is with the Massachusetts State Police Homicide Unit," McCormack said. "They'll be handling the investigation. They have a few questions for you."

Kenealy, still in shock, nodded his head.

"Was Firefighter McDonald on duty last night?" Colton asked.

"I'm not sure. Let me ask Captain Smith."

The Fire Chief used the phone's PA system and called the captain to his office.

A moment later, Smith arrived.

"Pat, did Bill work last night?" Kenealy asked.

Smith looked around.

"That's not him up at the train station, is it?" Smith asked. "We heard over the radio that you have a dead body up there."

"I'm sorry to have to tell you this," Colton said. "But Firefighter McDonald was found murdered this morning."

"What?" Smith said. "How?"

"We can't go into details. It's an ongoing investigation," Colton said. "Do you know anyone who would want to hurt him?"

"No, Bill was the nicest guy," Smith said.

"Was he working last night?" asked Barnes.

"No, sir," Smith said. "He was supposed to be in early this morning to cover for Firefighter Figgins. But he never showed."

"Have you spoken with his wife, Wendy?" Kenealy asked.

"We haven't made the notification yet," McCormack said.

"I'd like to go with you, if that's alright?" Kenealy said.

"We were going to ask you if you'd join us," Colton said.

"Yes, of course," Kenealy said. He then picked up the phone and called his secretary. "Laurie, cancel all of my meetings this morning. Thank you."

The Fire Chief stood there a minute and then spoke. "Captain, pull out the black bunting, but don't put it up yet."

"Yes, sir," Smith said. "I'll lower the flag to half-mast as well."

"Hold off on that Cap'. Let us make the notification first. Once you lower the flag, the questions will start. I'll call you after we talk with Wendy."

"Yes, sir."

Chapter 6

Wendy McDonald
Stoughton, Massachusetts

Wendy McDonald was home folding laundry in the living room with the Price is Right on the TV. She wasn't watching it, but more listening.

She looked out the bay window of the living room as several unmarked police cruisers pulled up out front along with the Fire Chief.

Shock and disbelief washed over her face. She held the towel she was holding up to her face.

Wendy watched the individuals form up at the end of her walkway and head toward the house.

A moment later, the doorbell rang.

Wendy began to tremble.

She made her way over to the front door and opened it.

Tears formed in the corners of her eyes.

When the door swung open, Wendy looked into Fire Chief Kenealy's eyes, and she lost it. She crumpled to the floor and wailed. The sound cut right through them. It made bringing the news no one wanted to hear even harder.

McCormack opened the storm door and squatted down. Wendy buried her head into McCormack's shoulder and sobbed. Her chest heaved up and down.

After a moment, McCormack helped Wendy to her feet, and they moved into the living room. Chief McCormack used her foot to scoot the empty laundry basket out of her way and both women sat on the couch.

After a moment, Wendy composed herself and said, "I'm okay."

"I take it you know why we're here, Wendy?" Fire Chief Kenealy asked.

Wendy nodded her head as she wiped away the tears.

"How did you know?" asked McCormack.

Wendy used the towel she was still holding to wipe her eyes, followed by the snot dangling from her nose.

"I just knew something was wrong last night when Bill received that phone call," Wendy said.

"Do you know who called him?" asked Colton.

"He wouldn't tell me," Wendy said. "But he looked scared."

"Did you hear who was on the other end?" asked Barnes. "Was it a man or a woman?"

"I couldn't hear," Wendy said, wiping more snot from her nose with the towel.

"Every firefighter has a scanner in their house. They monitor the police frequency too. Most times, the cops arrive on scene first," Wendy said through her tears.

"You heard the call go out this morning?" McCormack asked.

Wendy nodded.

"As soon as I heard, I knew it was Bill," Wendy said. "It was the same feeling I had yesterday when Bill received that call."

"Bill didn't leave his phone here by any chance?" Colton asked.

"No," Wendy said. "It wasn't on him?"

Colton looked at Chief McCormack.

"We're still processing the scene," McCormack said.

"How did he die?" Wendy asked.

"We need to wait for the medical examiner's report," Barnes said. "They determine the cause of death."

"Was everything else okay at home?" Colton asked.

"Everything was great. Bill was looking forward to retiring soon. With the kids being older, we discussed so many plans," Wendy said. "We were going to get an RV and travel the country."

"Just curious," Colton said. "I noticed Bill had a lot of tattoos. Did he get any recently?"

"Oh gosh," Wendy said. "Bill loved his tattoos. He got his first one while in the military. He's been addicted ever since."

"But nothing new?" Colton asked.

"No," Wendy said. "Not that I'm aware of."

"Did Bill have a tattoo on his forehead, or mention getting one?"

"No," Wendy said. "Why?"

Wendy looked from Colton to Chief McCormack. "You don't think Ray, his tattoo artist, killed him, do you?"

"No," Colton said. "Nothing like that."

"If possible, can we get Ray's contact info?" Barnes asked.

Chapter 7

Stoughton Fire Station 1
Stoughton, Massachusetts

After they left Wendy's, Colton and Barnes followed Chief Kenealy back to the fire station. Colton had suggested they check McDonald's locker. It was possible he kept things at the station.

Chief Kenealy called Captain Smith on his way back and told him to put the flag at half-staff. He instructed Smith to have the men hang the black bunting on the station. The Chief also informed Smith that the detectives wanted to search McDonald's locker.

When Colton and Barnes arrived, the ladder truck was out front, and several firefighters were hanging the memorial bunting.

Smith met them at the open bay door. "How did that go?"

"About as well as expected," Chief Kenealy said. "I'm gonna call some off-duty guys and ask if they can go be with Wendy and the kids."

Smith looked at Colton and Barnes. "You want to search his locker, correct?"

"Yes, please," Colton replied.

"Follow me," Smith said.

As Smith passed Engine 1, he opened one of the side compartments. Inside were four Scott SCBA (Self-Contained Breathing Apparatus) airpacks and a variety of tools, including an axe and a Halligan which was used for opening doors and just about anything else. Smith grabbed the bolt cutters and headed for McDonald's locker.

Barnes got a laugh out of the bumper sticker on the outside of McDonald's locker. It was a picture of a fire pull alarm with the words: *Pull it, and I'll come.*

"I'll leave you to it," Smith said, after cutting the lock off McDonald's locker.

Colton and Barnes went through the contents. There was nothing there except a change of clothes and McDonald's dress uniform for special events and parades.

They thanked Smith and left the fire station. As they walked out, Colton's phone chirped. He pulled it out and looked at it.

"Patrol has rounded up five bums from the area," Colton said to Barnes.

"I'll meet you over there." Barnes said. He got into his cruiser and drove off.

As Colton pulled away, he noticed the firefighters had finished hanging the black bunting on the outside of the building.

Like the police department, the fire department was a brotherhood. It always came together during a time of crisis or loss of a member.

Colton stopped at McDonald's, the fast food chain restaurant, and ordered five meals. *You catch more flies with honey than vinegar.*

Colton returned to the station and found Barnes waiting in the lobby. The bums sat in the conference room with a patrolman watching over them.

One by one, Colton brought the men into the interview room. He sat across from them at a small interview table. Each man thanked him for the fast food and devoured the meal. Barnes stood in the corner listening as Colton asked each man about their whereabouts earlier this morning.

All five admitted to being at the train station. Four of them identified Henry, the bum seen standing over McDonald's body. He was not among those rounded up. Their stories all matched Maria's, the woman from the bakery.

The fifth bum said he didn't see Henry. Said he was too hungover. All he saw was a crowd.

Colton kicked the bums free.

"I wonder if the chief has spoken with the District Attorney yet," Barnes said. "They'll probably want to do a press conference later."

"Let's go find out," Colton said.

They walked over to Chief McCormack's office. Her door was open, and she sat behind her desk talking on the phone. She looked up and waved them in. A moment later, she finished her call.

"I just spoke with the District Attorney. He wants to plan a press conference for this afternoon," McCormack said. "Any leads?"

"We spoke with four bums, who all corroborated what Maria from the bakery said she saw," Colton said.

"We're assuming this is an isolated incident, then?" McCormack asked.

Colton looked at Barnes.

"I would say so," Barnes replied.

"And you?" McCormack asked Colton.

"I'm not sure, chief," Colton said. "My gut says no."

"Why?" Barnes asked.

"Because. We don't know if this bum, Henry, killed McDonald or not," Colton said.

"You're smart, kid. I'll give you that," Barnes said. "But this is your first homicide investigation. I've been doing this for years. Trust me. It's the bum."

"Well, find him," McCormack said. "And fast."

Chapter 8

Stoughton Police Headquarters
Stoughton, Massachusetts

"Before you go, detective," Chief McCormack said. "What made you ask Wendy about Bill's tattoos?"

"What person do you know that works in public safety gets a tattoo on their face?" Colton asked.

"But Colton, Bill's covered with tattoos," McCormack said.

"None on his hands, neck, or face, though," Colton said. "McDonald served in the military back in the late 80s and 90s. Back then, tattoos had to be covered. Not like it is today."

"Do you think the killer tattooed him?" McCormack asked.

"Yeah, I do."

"That's a first," Barnes said.

"What's your take?" McCormack asked Barnes.

"I bet he got drunk, asked for that stupid tattoo and when he sobered up and realized what happened to his face, he picked a fight with the tattoo artist. One thing led to another, and McDonald wound up dead."

"I disagree," Colton said. "What about the phone call Wendy said he received?"

"It was probably the tattoo artist," Barnes said.

"What about the bum?" Colton asked. "You've been doing this a long time. It's the bum."

"I don't like your attitude," Barnes said.

"Alright fellas," McCormack said. "Enough is enough. I have patrol searching for the bum."

"I'm heading over to the tattoo parlor now. Care to join me, detective?"

"I'll let you handle it," Colton said. "I want to look into a few cameras near the train station. Then I need to draft the warrant for McDonald's phone."

"Sounds good," Barnes said. "I'll check back in with you later."

Barnes left and went to chase down McDonald's tattoo artist.

Colton headed back to the train station to check out the camera diagonally across the street. He knocked on the door. The building manager said the camera hadn't worked in years. They left it up as a deterrent.

Next, Colton went over to the plaza beyond the train station parking lot to look for cameras. He found four facing the train station. He spent the better part of an hour reviewing camera footage. But the distance was too far away. Everything was too small to see. Another dead end.

Colton went back to the police station.

He drafted the affidavit and filled out the search warrant application for McDonald's phone.

The warrant requested the 'tolls' from the cellular carrier. Once approved, the phone company would provide all activity to and from McDonald's cell phone during that specific time period. It would include all texts and calls, incoming and outgoing, along with the timestamp and duration.

Colton completed the paperwork and headed for the courthouse.

It was a short ride. The county courthouse was in Stoughton.

Judge Cranshaw was in chambers and met with Colton. After explaining the details of the case, the judge signed the search warrant. He wished Colton good luck and congratulated him on his new position.

Colton returned to the station and scanned in the signed search warrant and sent it electronically to McDonald's cellular carrier.

Hopefully, by this time tomorrow, he'd have someone in cuffs.

Chapter 9

Stoughton Police Headquarters
Stoughton, Massachusetts

It was early afternoon when the District Attorney, Steve Harbor, arrived. He met with McCormack, Colton, and Barnes in McCormack's office. Barnes knew him well. He had worked with and reported directly to the man.

"Tell me what you've got, Detective," said Harbor, taking off his hat and sitting down.

Barnes brought him up to speed on the case and told him about the victim and the circumstances around his death.

"Any good leads or suspects?" asked Harbor.

"We're looking into a bum seen standing over the victim," McCormack said.

"And what about this tattoo?"

"I spoke with the victim's tattoo artist," Barnes said. "He told me McDonald hadn't been in to see him in a couple weeks."

"Told you it wasn't the tattoo artist," Colton said.

Barnes glared at Colton.

Colton had experienced interagency differences before while working with Peterson. It was just a job. But it was hard not to take it personally sometimes.

"Do we think the killer tattooed him?" asked Harbor.

"We're trying to figure that out," McCormack said.

"Well, I heard McDonald was a firefighter," Harbor said. "And a damn good one. Well respected in the community. The press is gonna be all over this one."

"We're scheduled to meet with the Medical Examiner in the morning," Barnes said. "Hopefully, we'll have some evidence to go on."

"Are we ready?" asked Harbor.

McCormack looked at Colton and then Barnes. Both nodded.

"Ready, sir," McCormack said.

Harbor turned toward Colton and Barnes. "When we get out there, the Chief and I will do the talking."

"Yes, sir," both Barnes and Colton answered.

"Then let's get this over with."

Chapter 10

Stoughton Police Headquarters
Stoughton, Massachusetts

David Monteiro was the owner and sole reporter of the Stoughton Times. He was tall with salt and pepper hair. Despite his age, he looked good for fifty-five. He'd grown up and spent his whole life in Stoughton.

He'd missed the boat with the digital news age. Like many in the newspaper business, David thought it was a fad. Newspapers were all he knew. They were around before he was born and he figured they'd be around after his death. How wrong he was. Sales declined with the wave of online news. Every year was worse than the previous one. Soon no one bought newspapers anymore and the Stoughton Times press came to a halt.

Sandra, David's ex-wife, had tried to get him to switch to digital news. She persisted, but David always assumed it would turn around. By the time David tried to switch, it was too late. People had found a new stream. He was behind the curve.

Eventually, the Stoughton Times all but closed.

The steep financial woes resulted in divorce. Sandra had had enough. She watched David drive the company into the ground and wanted no part of it. His unwillingness to change extended into their marriage. She had grown up poor and she told herself she wouldn't die poor. She divorced David and moved to California.

David's only saving grace was his daughter, Laynie. It broke his heart when she told him she wanted to go live with her mother in California after graduating high school. But it wasn't all bad. She'd been accepted to the University of Southern California journalism program.

Now, David dabbled in local online news. He didn't make much, but he got by.

Local media trucks lined the side of Rose Street with their satellite booms extended upward.

David stood outside his 2009 Toyota Camry, smoking a cigarette. He fiddled with his microphone recorder, ensuring it still worked which, thankfully, it did. It was old and outdated, like David. Some things die hard and one was David's love of capturing a story.

His phone chirped. It was his reminder that the press conference was about to start. He took one last haul off his cigarette, then dropped it to the ground and crushed it with his foot. He grabbed his antiquated equipment and headed inside the police station to get a seat.

Being a local reporter had its perks. David's name was on a seat in the first row. He'd written a fair article on McCormack when she became chief. Maybe she was returning the favor in hopes of some more fair press.

David sat in the aisle seat in the front row with his microphone recorder in his lap. All the other local news agencies had their microphones mounted to the podium. David seemed out of place.

He pulled his phone from his pocket and snapped a picture of the podium.

Then he opened his Messenger app, found Laynie's name and typed:

Wish you were here! He clicked send.

Next, he sent the picture he just took.

Three little dots appeared on the screen. A moment later, a message appeared.

Hey Dad! Where are you?

Covering a murder investigation.

In Stoughton?

Yes. Are you on assignment, honey?

Yeah. I'm covering another stupid political convention.

Call me later. Love you!

I will. Love you too, Dad!

David closed the app and tucked the phone back into his front pocket.

A moment later, Lt. Bonnett stepped up to the podium.

Chapter 11

Stoughton Police Headquarters
Stoughton, Massachusetts

Lt. Bonnett wore many hats in the Stoughton Police Department. One of those hats was the Media Relations Officer. It wasn't his favorite role, but it got his name in the paper and his face on the TV news. He noticed the Chief and others lined up in the hallway and informed the journalists the press conference was about to begin. He stepped away from the podium.

Chief McCormack led the group to the podium. She introduced herself along with Colton, Barnes, and the District Attorney.

"We are actively investigating a homicide that took place this morning at the Stoughton train station. At this time, we believe it to be an isolated incident," McCormack said. "We also believe there is no threat to the public."

"This morning at approximately six am, we received a call for an unconscious party at the train station. Upon arrival, it was determined that the victim was deceased. I'll now hand the podium over to District Attorney Harbor."

Harbor read a brief statement from a piece of paper and then opened it up for questions. "I'll hand it back to the Chief."

McCormack stepped back up to the microphone. As she did, one reporter shouted out a question.

"Is it true that the victim was a Stoughton firefighter?"

"Yes," she replied.

"How was he killed?" asked a different reporter.

"This is an ongoing investigation. We're not releasing details at this time," McCormack said.

"Do you have a description of the suspect?" another reporter asked.

"We're working on trying to obtain one."

The same reporter asked a follow-up question. "Obtain one. How?"

"We're reviewing camera footage in the area."

David Monteiro raised his hand.

"David," McCormack said, pointing to him.

"Was Bill McDonald the firefighter murdered today?"

McCormack paused. After a moment, she spoke.

"Yes, David. It was Bill McDonald," McCormack said. "I believe you knew him, correct?"

"Yes, Chief," David said. "He was a good man."

"He was," McCormack said. "Bill put his life on the line for this community. And sadly, someone took him from us."

Harbor stepped up to the podium and McCormack stepped aside.

"We'll have more information once the Medical Examiner finishes his report," Harbor said. "That will be all. Thank you."

Chapter 12

Nancy and Paul Baker's House
Stoughton, Massachusetts

It had been a long day. Colton returned home after the press conference to feed and let the dogs out. Both dogs greeted him at the door, each with their own routine. Hayley ran around in circles, excited to see him. Roxy barked. She had that cute, small dog bark that made Colton smile.

He bent over and patted and kissed the tops of their heads. Then he let them out. They ran out back and answered nature's call.

While they were outside, Colton filled their bowls. When they came in, they devoured their dinner.

"Hey girls, do you want to go visit grandma?" Colton asked them.

Roxy barked.

Once they finished eating, Colton loaded them up in his car and made the short trip across town.

When Colton arrived, he used the side door off the driveway. The dogs bolted into the house.

"Perfect timing!" his mom said. "Dinner is just about ready."

Colton gave her a kiss and followed the dogs into the living room.

"Hey dad," Colton said.

His father looked up at him. His eyes were glassed over, and his face held a confused look.

"Who are you?" his father asked.

The question and his dad's demeanor caught Colton off guard.

"That's Colton," his mom said from the kitchen. "Paul, you remember your son?"

"Oh, Colton!" his father said. A smile formed on his face, and the confusion dissipated. "Nancy, Colton is here."

Hayley jumped up into Paul's lap, and Roxy curled into a ball at his feet.

"It's good to see you, dad," Colton said. "And the girls are excited too."

Paul petted Hayley and began talking to her.

Colton returned to the kitchen.

"He's getting pretty bad," Colton said. "He didn't even recognize me at first."

"Some days are better than others," his mom said.

"Can I help you with anything?" Colton asked.

"Yes," she said. "Could you please bring in the grocery order from the front porch?"

"You order groceries online?" Colton asked.

"Had to," she said. "I can't always find someone to watch your father. So I learned how to shop online."

"If you ever need to go shopping, mom," Colton said. "Let me know. I'll come over and watch dad."

"I don't want to bother you," she said. "You're busy. Especially with your promotion."

"Mom, it will be no trouble," Colton said. "Please, call me if you need me to watch dad or go to the store for you."

"That would be great!" she said. "I don't like the meats the associates pick out. Most times, it expires that day or the next."

Colton retrieved the groceries off the porch and helped put them away while his mother served dinner.

"Wash up," she said, when he finished.

Nancy made a plate and brought it to Paul in the living room. Hayley and Roxy followed her back into the kitchen.

"Your father will only eat in his chair," she said, sitting down at the table next to Colton. The dogs sat under the table and got comfy.

"They're good dogs," she said.

"Dad seems to enjoy them," Colton said.

"I read some experts recommend small pets for patients with dementia and Alzheimer's," Nancy said. "The article said pets can help soothe and comfort them."

"I can leave them here with you for a couple days, if you'd like," Colton said.

"You wouldn't mind?" she asked.

"No," Colton said. "Not at all. You'd be doing me a favor."

"Busy first day, huh?" she asked.

"Unbelievable," Colton said.

"Susan called me," she said. "She was all excited. Told me you were on the news. I put it on in time to see you."

"I just stood there," Colton said.

"You looked handsome, though," she said.

"Thanks," Colton said.

"Susan also asked me if there's any word on if the town is keeping 911? Said signs are popping up all over town."

"I don't know," Colton said. "It's a hot topic down at the station."

"Well, hopefully the town will get to vote on it," she said.

Colton took a couple of bites and put his fork down.

"What is it?" his mother asked.

"I'm sorry, mom," Colton said.

"For what?"

"For not being around more," Colton said. "Figured I'd spend more time here helping you and dad. I thought being a detective would be a slower pace."

"Don't worry," she said. "How could you have known there'd be a murder? Besides, you'll catch them, and it will be all over."

"Yeah, until the case goes to trial," Colton said.

"When will that be?"

"At least six months to a year after we catch him," Colton said.

"Who knows if your father will even be around then."

"Mom, don't talk like that."

"God forgive me," she said. "But it might be for the best. It's not just his memory that's gone downhill. It's his health too."

Nancy stood up and walked over to the sink. She grabbed the sponge and began wiping down the counters.

"Your father is incontinent," she said, ringing out the sponge and putting it back in the holder in the sink. "We spend so much on his adult diapers."

"When did he start wearing diapers?" Colton asked. "I don't remember you telling me that."

"A few months back," she said. "When he wears the damn things!"

Colton looked at her quizzically.

"Your father takes the diapers off and walks around the house. He gets piss and shit everywhere. I swear, he's worse than a toddler."

"Are you serious?" Colton asked.

"Yes!" she said.

"I didn't realize he'd gotten that bad," Colton said.

"It's disgusting," she said. "I need to get the carpet replaced."

"Well, I'm here to help now."

"I know you are honey," she said and sat back down at the table. "But I think your father needs to go into a home."

"That's your decision, Mom," Colton said. "You have a life too."

"I'm afraid to tell your brother and sisters," she said. "They won't take it well."

"Then tell them to come over more often and help out," Colton said, his voice growing louder. "They always bitch but do nothing."

"I wasn't looking to make you upset," she said.

"I know, mom," Colton said. He reached across the table and rubbed her arm.

"Have you heard from Cindy?" she asked, placing her hand on top of his.

"I called her yesterday," Colton said. "But I haven't heard back from her."

They finished eating, and Colton did the dishes. After, he went to check on his parents. His father was asleep in his chair and his mom was relaxing on the couch watching TV.

"I'll swing by tomorrow after work with the dogs and bring over their leashes, bowls, and food," Colton said.

"Your dad will enjoy their company," she said. "Would you like to have dinner tomorrow?"

"I'd like that," Colton said.

"I'll make steak," she said. "I know it's your favorite."

Colton kissed his mother goodbye and headed for home.

Chapter 13

**Colton's House
Stoughton, Massachusetts**

Colton woke up early. Both Hayley and Roxy were asleep next to him. Roxy was snoring lightly.

He laid in bed thinking about the McDonald case. Something seemed off. He couldn't put his finger on it. His thoughts kept drifting back to the tattoo on McDonald's forehead.

Did the killer tattoo him? Colton thought. *What do those symbols mean?*

He laid there a minute longer. His mind shifted to the stack of home invasion cases sitting on his desk left by his predecessor, Detective Peterson.

Even though he was working the homicide investigation, he still had to work his caseload.

Colton's mind raced, and there was no turning it off. Well, a few drinks would stop it. But not at four in the morning. And definitely not before the start of his shift.

Now he was wide awake. He got up and dressed.

Both dogs were awake now. He gave them some love and attention, then let them out to do their morning business.

He fed them and made sure they had plenty of food for the day. The best part about living and working in Stoughton was it allowed him to check in on his parents and the dogs throughout the day.

He didn't have to be at the Medical Examiner's office until later.

Colton loaded up the dogs and their things and headed over to his parent's house. He ate breakfast with his mother while the dogs snuggled with his father.

After, he headed into the station to get started on Peterson's backlog of cases. Yesterday morning he had tried working on a case, but the McDonald homicide came in.

On his way into the station, Colton stopped at Dunkin's and grabbed a dozen donuts and a Box of Joe for the morning shift. They did good yesterday. Great teamwork and they did as asked.

Colton bought himself a Diet Coke. He gave up coffee years ago, and with good reason. Years back, when he was a patrolman, he responded to a fight at a construction site. Apparently, one worker didn't care for another guy on the job site and pinched a loaf into his coffee. The poor bastard drank most of the cup until he noticed the chunk of shit at the bottom. He had sent one man to the hospital to have his stomach pumped. The other he arrested.

Colton had made a mistake. He looked inside the cup. That was it. He swore off coffee and switched to bottled soda for his morning caffeine and hadn't had a drop of coffee since.

He arrived at the station and made small talk with the dispatchers and patrolmen. They welcomed the coffee and donuts. After socializing for a few minutes, Colton made his way to his office.

A lot had happened in the past twenty-four hours, so he reviewed Peterson's files to refresh his memory. All the home invasions happened during the day. That, in itself, wasn't abnormal. Most people worked during the day. Unfortunately, that was the only common denominator. The worst part was Peterson had no leads or suspects.

Colton contacted one of the victims. She said she'd be home for a little while this morning. He grabbed her case file and headed out.

A few minutes later, he turned onto Elizabeth Street. According to the case files, the robbers hit three houses on this street. *What was so appealing about this street?* Colton thought.

As he drove, he tried viewing the houses through the eyes of a thief.

It was a middle-class neighborhood. Most of the driveways were empty, meaning no one was home. Some houses had cameras, most did not.

Several landscaping trucks lined the side of the road. That meant some residents had money if they could afford landscapers. Most poor people mowed their own lawn.

Colton made a mental note. *Check with victims if they have landscaping services. If so, which day of the week?*

He pulled into the driveway and parked. Before he got out, he jotted down a quick reminder.

The sound of mowers zipping around yards and the smell of fresh cut grass filled the air.

Colton sneezed.

"Damn allergies," he muttered under his breath.

He headed up the walkway toward the front door and knocked. As he stood there, he noticed a camera above the door.

A woman in her late thirties opened the door. She had long, dark hair and wore a red dress. She had her head tilted to one side, attempting to put in her earring.

"Good morning, ma'am. I'm Detective Colton Baker," he said. "As I mentioned on the phone, I'm conducting a follow-up inquiry into the break-in you reported."

"Come on in, detective," she said.

Colton stepped into the front foyer.

"I gave my report to an older detective," she said, putting her earring in finally. "Is he no longer handling my case?"

"I'm sorry ma'am." Colton said. "Detective Peterson passed away suddenly. I'm taking over his caseload."

"Oh no," she said, working her foot into a tan high-heel shoe. "Wasn't he about to retire?"

"Sadly, he was," Colton said. "If you have a moment, I'd like to review your report. Find out if maybe you remember something."

"It's funny," she said. "I had called and left a message for Detective Peterson. Now I know why he never called me back."

"What was the reason for the call?" Colton asked. "Did you remember or discover something new?"

"Yes," she said, standing there with one shoe on. "That was exactly it. I discovered the set of silverware my mother left me was also missing, besides all the jewelry I reported stolen."

"Do you have pictures of it?" Colton asked.

"I do somewhere," she said.

"I have access to a pawn shop database where I can search for items that were pawned," Colton said. "Providing the pawn shop lists them."

"It'd be great if you found it," she said.

"I can't look everywhere," Colton said. "I need your help. Be diligent. Take a proactive stance in finding your property. Check Facebook Marketplace, Craigslist and other sites. If you spot your belongings, give me a call."

"I definitely will," she said.

"I noticed a camera above the door," Colton said. "Is that new?"

"Yes," she said. "My husband put it up last weekend."

"That's good," Colton said. "We call that target hardening. Criminals sometimes will return to the same location and victimize it again. But if they notice you've taken steps to protect your home, they won't risk the chance of getting caught."

"Detective Peterson recommended we get one," she said.

"In most cases," Colton said. "Not all, there's a connection between the victim and the suspect."

"Oh! Really?" she said.

"Knowing that," Colton said. "Off the top of your head. Who do you think is responsible?"

Her cheeks turned flush.

"I honestly don't know," she said. "What I can tell you is that I no longer feel safe in my own home."

"I'll have an increase of patrols through the neighborhood," Colton said. "Would that help?"

"Yes. Some," she said.

"I noticed several landscape trucks on your street," Colton said. "Do you have landscapers do your lawn?"

"Yes, we do."

"Which day of the week?" Colton asked.

"Today. Typically, on Tuesdays," she said. "You don't think it was them, do you?"

He flipped through her case file.

"No, ma'am," Colton said. "The incident took place on a Thursday. Is that correct?"

"Sounds right," she said.

Colton crossed the landscapers off his list.

"Do you remember anything else?"

"I'm sorry, detective," she said, slipping on her other shoe. "I'm just on my way out for an important business meeting. Can we talk another time?"

"Yes, ma'am. I understand. I'll leave you my card and if you think of anything, even a minute detail, please don't hesitate to call."

She thanked Colton for following up and showed him out.

Colton stopped by the local pawn shop. He'd known Randy, the owner, since middle school. He showed Randy pictures of the jewelry and asked about the silverware set. Randy said no one had brought any of it in, but he'd keep an eye out. Colton handed him a business card and left.

Chapter 14

Medical Examiner's Office
Boston, Massachusetts

Colton and Barnes arrived at the Medical Examiner's office in Boston.

"Good morning, Detectives," Medical Examiner Dr. Robert Hurst said.

"What can you tell us about our victim?" Colton asked.

"You were correct, Detective," Hurst said, looking at Colton. "It was a railroad spike."

Colton looked at Barnes and smiled.

"It was a six-inch spike with an offset head. The exact kind used on the railway," Hurst said. "It was driven straight into the skull. Death was instant."

"Ouch!" Barnes said.

"Ouch is right," Hurst said. "You're talking about a half-pound piece of steel being driven right into the top of the victim's head."

"Just covering all bases here, Doc," Colton said. "This wasn't a freak accident, right? It didn't fly off the tracks?"

"Not a chance, Detective," replied Hurst. "Here, let me show you."

Hurst walked over to the end of the metal table and pulled back the sheet, exposing McDonald's head.

"You see here," Hurst said. He pointed to the wound on top of McDonald's head. "This smaller wound here."

Colton squatted down, his eyes level with the wound. "What is it? What am I looking at?"

"Have you ever swung a hammer and missed, Detective?" Hurst asked.

"Of course," Colton said. "Who hasn't?"

"Your killer swung and missed once. That wound is from a missed hammer strike."

"God damn," Barnes said.

"Is that the official cause of death?" Colton asked.

"Yes," Hurst said. "A six-inch railroad spike driven into the top of the victim's head. A piercing brain injury is the official cause of death."

"Is there anything else?" Colton asked.

"Your firefighter here was covered in tattoos. His arms, legs, torso, they're just about everywhere. It appears he had a new one done recently on his forehead," Hurst said.

"I noticed that," Colton said. "I asked his wife. She said he didn't have any tattoos on his face."

"And I interviewed his tattoo artist," Barnes said. "He said he didn't do it."

"Then it's possible your killer tattooed your victim," Hurst said.

Barnes looked at Colton.

"That was my conclusion," Colton said. "The new tattoo on our victim's face doesn't match the style of his other tattoos."

"Good observation, Detective," Hurst said. "I compared the artistry of the forehead tattoo against the victim's other tattoos. I came to the same conclusion."

"Have you come across this before?" Barnes asked.

"A killer tattooing their victim?" Hurst said. "No. But in the ever-changing world we live in, I wouldn't put anything past anyone anymore."

"Anything else?" Colton asked.

"He had lung cancer. I'm assuming it's job related," Hurst said.

"Poor bastard," Barnes said. "Maybe the perp did him a favor and spared him the misery."

Colton looked up at Barnes.

"What?" Barnes said. "My mother-in-law had lung cancer. She suffered right up until the end. It was heartbreaking to watch."

Colton looked at Hurst and asked, "How far along?"

"Stage Four," Hurst said.

"How long did he have left?" Colton asked.

"It had metastasized," Hurst said. "Maybe six months, tops."

"Did he know?" Colton asked.

"I would assume so," Hurst said. "The question is, did he get it diagnosed?"

Barnes looked at Colton.

"You're not thinking he staged this to look like a murder. Are you?" Barnes asked.

"Cancer treatment can be expensive," Colton said. "The life insurance company might deny the claim, stating it was Workman's Comp related. It could take the insurance companies years of battling it out before they decided who was responsible. Meanwhile, the family doesn't receive any benefits until then."

"Jesus," Barnes said.

"Like you said, Detective. It was heartbreaking," Colton said. "Plus, it would explain how Wendy knew Bill was dead."

"I guess we pay Wendy another visit," Barnes said.

Chapter 15

Route 139
Stoughton, Massachusetts

Colton and Barnes left the Medical Examiner's office. Barnes told Colton he needed to stop off at the Milton State Police barracks to pick something up and would meet Colton in Stoughton.

Colton took the expressway, I-93 South, passing through the Braintree split before turning onto Route 24 South. As he approached the Stoughton exit, he slid into the right lane behind a weighted down dump truck. He looked to his left. Route 24 Northbound was a parking lot. Commuters heading up from as far south as Fall River made their way north. The congestion started at the top of Route 24 and continued for miles all the way down to Brockton. Massachusetts was known for many things, and its horrible traffic was one of them. It was a daily nightmare for local commuters.

The dump truck in front of Colton slowed as it entered the exit. The offramp snaked right, left, and right again before spilling out onto Route 139. Up ahead was a set of lights.

Both vehicles continued to slow for the light that had turned red. The loud staccato sound emanated from the truck when its Jake Brake engaged. It helped slow the truck by the sudden release of compressed air from the engine into the exhaust system. Combined with the regular brakes, the weighted down truck screeched to a halt. Rocks and dirt slid atop the uncovered load.

Colton pulled up behind the dump truck and stopped. He checked his phone. There was one missed call and a voice message from Cindy. He hit play.

I got your message. Sorry for the delay. I know you're nervous about your first day, but you'll do fine. You're incredibly smart. Don't let your head beat you. I'll call you later. I love...

Colton heard gunfire in the background, followed by a large explosion. Then the message ended abruptly.

Up ahead the light turned green. Thick black smoke shot from the dump truck's smokestack, and the sluggish truck started to roll. As the vehicle sped up, the truck bucked under the overloaded weight. The bucking and bouncing caused the uncovered load inside the truck's body to shift. Dirt and rocks spilled over the lip of the tailgate.

Colton's cruiser shook as an assortment of different size rocks and dirt rained down onto the roadway.

A fist-sized rock bounced off the street and smashed into the grill of Colton's cruiser.

"What the hell!" Colton shouted. Dirt and rocks continued to rain down. Another rock bounced up onto the hood and slammed into the windshield. The glass cracked and spidered.

The truck gained speed and drove away. Debris continued to fall over the tailgate.

"God damn," Colton said, watching the truck drive off. He activated his lights and siren.

Colton caught up to the truck. It pulled over and rumbled to a stop.

Colton picked up the radio mic. "D-1 to Control."

"Control's on," Dispatch replied.

"I'm out on Turnpike Street in front of Dunkin Donuts with commercial plate RSG-123."

"Received."

Colton stepped out of his cruiser, inspected the damage, and cautiously approached the truck's driver's side door.

The truck driver stuck his head out the window. "What seems to be the problem, officer?"

"A portion of your load spilled all over the intersection back there," Colton said.

"What? Are you serious?"

"Yeah, I'm serious," Colton said. "Step down with your license and registration."

"You sure it was my truck?" the driver asked. "Lots of trucks come through here."

"Yeah, I'm sure," Colton said. "I was behind you at the light and one of those rocks damaged my cruiser."

"Don't worry," the driver said. "My dad will take care of it."

"Your load is unsecured," Colton said.

The driver turned to the passenger. "You didn't cover the fucking load?"

"Step down," Colton repeated.

"Don't worry. My dad will take care of it," the driver repeated.

The driver popped the clutch. The truck shook as he tried to put it in gear.

"Turn it off and step down now!" Colton shouted.

The driver looked out the window. "Do you know who I am?" he asked, his face bewildered.

"No. And I don't care," Colton said. "Shut the truck off and step down." Colton placed a hand on his service piece.

"Can you believe this guy?" the driver said to the passenger. "The name is on the truck. Apparently, this jackass can't read."

"And, apparently, you don't understand simple commands. Step down! Now!" Colton ordered.

"Alright, alright. Don't get your panties in a bunch."

The truck door swung open.

Colton stepped to his right in case either man had a gun.

The driver climbed out. "Do you know who I am?"

"No," Colton said. "Should I?"

"You best find out who you're fucking with right now," the driver said.

"Look at me. I'm trembling," Colton said.

"Oh, you will be, pal. Trust me!" the driver said, hopping down off the last two steps. He landed on the ground and looked furious.

Colton sized him up. The man stood well over six feet tall and was solid muscle. A white tank top clung to his massive frame. His hair was brown and scruffy. He had a five o'clock shadow and a long scar under his left eye. Clearly, the man looked menacing and tried using it to his advantage.

Colton didn't show an outward ounce of fear. He'd arrested bigger and tougher men before. Yet, his training taught him to use caution and treat everyone as dangerous.

The driver approached Colton and began shouting again. "Do you know who my father is?"

"Put your hands on the truck," Colton ordered.

"You're so gonna regret this!"

"I assure you I won't. Now turn around and put your hands on the truck."

The man handed Colton his license and registration, then turned and faced the truck.

"For your protection and for mine, I'm going to pat you down. Do you have any weapons on you?"

"Look at me. Do I look like I need one? I can take care of myself."

Colton chuckled.

"What's so funny, asshole?"

"You know steroids kill brain cells and can shrink your penis, right?"

"You're gonna regret it once you find out who I am!"

"I'm sure I won't," Colton said again. "Anyone who has to ask if you know who they are speaks for itself. I'll fill you in. They don't."

The driver turned and took a threatening step toward Colton. He didn't flinch.

Colton grabbed his radio and requested backup. "D-1 to Control. Can I get another unit to my location?"

"Received," responded dispatch.

"My dad is gonna have a field day with you. It was a little spilled dirt."

"Oh, and here, I thought you were a tough guy. But come to find out you're just a daddy's boy."

"It must be your first day."

"Actually, my second."

"Well, it's also going to be your last."

The driver leaned forward in a dominating stance and stared at Colton.

Colton stared right back and didn't blink. Colton radioed dispatch again, his eyes still locked onto the driver's eyes.

"Control. Can I get the State Police Truck Team to my location?"

The driver threw his arms up. "You can't do that!"

"Received," dispatch said.

"Well, seeing how your unsecured load spilled all over Route 139, a state road, I sure can."

"They can yank my CDL on the spot. They'll kill my career. I can't drive without a license."

"You're in for a rough day. Unless maybe they know who you are," Colton said.

Backup arrived. A Stoughton cruiser pulled up.

The driver took a step back. He pulled out his phone and placed a call.

Two officers approached. Lt. Bonnett and Officer O'Sullivan.

"Whatcha got, Detective?" asked Lt. Bonnett.

"There's someone in the passenger seat. Can you pull them out and secure them?"

"You got it, Detective."

Colton radioed dispatch. He provided the driver's name, date of birth, and license number.

The two officers cautiously approached the truck. They removed the passenger, who appeared to be around eighteen years old. He had on a brand new company shirt and jeans. He looked petrified.

They patted the kid down and had him take a seat on the curb. Then they walked back over to Colton.

After Lt. Bonnett and O'Sullivan returned, Bonnett introduced Colton.

"Detective, this is our newest rookie, Officer O'Sullivan," Lt. Bonnett said. "She just completed her academy training and is now doing her probational training."

"It's a pleasure to officially meet you, Detective," O'Sullivan said.

"Likewise," Colton said. They shook hands.

"All the kid had on him was a cell phone, wallet, and keys," O'Sullivan said.

Colton thanked her.

"So, um ... let me ask you," Lt. Bonnett said. "Do you know who that is?" He nodded toward the driver.

Colton chuckled. "Yup. But I didn't let him know that."

"Apparently, I'm the only one who doesn't," O'Sullivan said. "Who is he?"

"That's Nino Romano. The son of Gino Romano, the mob boss," Colton said.

"Never heard of them," O'Sullivan said.

"Nino there is a supposed hitman for the mob. He's a very dangerous man," Lt. Bonnett said.

Colton chuckled, again. "You mean daddy's boy over there?"

Both Lt. Bonnett and O'Sullivan chuckled.

"I like you already, O'Sullivan," Colton said.

"I should keep an eye on the kid," O'Sullivan said. She went and stood next to him.

Dispatch radioed Colton and read back the driver's information. There were no outstanding warrants.

Nino hung up the phone and put it back in his pocket. He looked at Colton. "Buckle up, buttercup! My father is on his way down here."

"Still not scared," Colton said.

Colton looked at the kid sitting on the curb.

"Can you keep an eye on him while I talk to the kid?" Colton asked Lt. Bonnett.

"Sure thing, Detective."

Colton walked over toward the kid and asked, "What's your name?"

"It's Barry. Barry Knight."

"Why do you seem so nervous, Barry?" Colton asked.

"Am I going to jail?"

"Why? What did you do?"

"Because I didn't cover the load," Barry said.

"No, you're not going to jail."

"Am I in trouble?" Barry asked.

"Maybe with your boss, but not us," Colton said.

"Oh, good!"

"He's the driver, so he's responsible for his cargo," Colton said. "But I'm afraid if I write him a ticket, he'll take it out on you."

"He's scary," Barry said.

"Did you know this is a mob-owned company?"

"No, today's my first day."

"I'm assuming it's gonna be your last day, too," Colton said.

"Yeah, probably," Barry said.

Sirens grew closer and the State Police Truck Team arrived on scene.

Colton walked over to the state trooper, and they shook hands.

Nino watched them closely.

"Is it this guy's load I just passed back there?" the trooper asked.

"Yes, it is," Colton said. "And we've got ourselves a genuine badass over here."

"Oh yeah," the Trooper said. "Who?"

"Nino Romano."

"The mobster. This should be fun. I'll grab my clipboard."

The Trooper walked around the truck, inspecting it and wrote several violations down.

A bright red pickup truck pulled up and stopped. The name on the door matched the one on the dump truck. Romano Sand and Gravel.

An old man stepped out. A cigar dangled from his mouth. He wore a flannel shirt and faded jeans with black suspenders holding them up. He was bowlegged and walked with a limp. The man had a cell phone pressed against his ear, and he headed straight toward the trooper. As he approached, the man glanced over at the trooper's truck. He read the three identifying digits on the front corner panel of the trooper's cruiser to the person on the other end of the phone.

"You can stop your inspection, son," the old man said.

"Excuse me?" the Trooper said.

"You'll be getting a call in a minute."

The old man hung up. He headed toward Colton.

"Excuse me, Detective Baker?"

Colton turned around.

"None of this will be necessary," the old man said. "I already spoke to the Town Manager, and I'll pay for the damage to your vehicle. I have a crew coming to clean up the intersection."

A moment later, the trooper received a call over the radio telling him to call by phone. The trooper pulled out his cell phone.

A silver BMW pulled up. A man in his late fifties stepped out. He had a round face, red, rosy cheeks, and a huge gut. He had thinning brown hair that was combed over, hiding his balding head.

The old man walked toward the BMW.

"Hi Frank," the old man said.

"Hey Gino."

Colton moved closer to Lt. Bonnett. "Let me guess, Gino Romano."

"You got it," Lt. Bonnett said. "And that's the Town Manager. They're two peas in a pod."

The trooper hung up the phone and walked over to Colton. "Someone has some pull. That was my Colonel. He told me I best not write a ticket if I want to keep my job. Said to get back on the road. Sorry I couldn't be of more assistance."

"Not your fault. Small town politics," Colton said. "Thanks though. Stay safe out there."

Colton and the State Trooper shook hands again.

"Roger that. You too!" The trooper climbed into his truck and drove away.

Dispatch called Lt. Bonnett. Asked if they could clear and respond to a well-being check.

"Another overdose, probably," Lt. Bonnett said, and started for his cruiser.

"Thank you for the assist," Colton said.

"No problem, Detective," Lt. Bonnett said.

Both officers climbed into the cruiser and drove off.

Gino and Frank watched the cruiser activate its lights and siren and speed off. After, both men approached Colton.

"Detective Baker, it's a pleasure to meet you," the man with the big gut from the BMW said. "I'm Frank Langer, the Town Manager."

"Pleasure to meet you, sir," Colton said.

"I'm glad we were able to get your paperwork approved and pushed through so quickly," Frank said.

"I appreciate it," Colton said.

"This here is Mr. Romano," Frank said, putting his hand on Gino's shoulder. "He's a well-known businessman here in town and we'd hate to see his insurance go up because of a traffic citation. There's no need to issue a ticket or write a report. I'll handle it at the town administration level."

"Yes, sir," Colton replied.

"Thank you, Frank," Gino said, and then turned toward Colton. "Thank you, Detective."

Several trucks with the Romano name on them arrived. A work crew got out and started cleaning the roadway.

Gino walked over to his son.

"We all set, Pop?" Nino asked.

"All set. See you back at the yard."

Nino turned toward Barry Knight. "Let's go, kid."

Nino headed for the driver's side door and stopped. He turned and waved at Colton. "Have a great day, Detective," Nino said sarcastically.

Colton stood there, stoic.

Nino climbed up into the dump truck. A second later it rumbled to life. Colton watched the dump truck drive off, followed by the red pickup and the BMW.

Colton stood there a moment, watching the crew cleaning the street. Once finished, he turned and headed for his cruiser. As he reached the SUV, a call came over the radio for him.

"Control to D-1."

"D-1," Colton said into the mic.

"Make your way to 62 Ledgebrook Ave for the reported homicide."

Chapter 16

Romano Sand & Gravel
Stoughton, Massachusetts

Romano Sand & Gravel was hard to miss. It sat just off Turnpike Street and had an enormous pile of crushed rock that protruded into the sky. Large earth movers shuttled materials around the yard. The crushed stone was processed and turned into asphalt. They sold everything from loam to mulch, but their bread and butter was asphalt. They had multiple contracts with different towns, but their biggest customer was the State of Massachusetts. Highway and state road resurfacing contracts paid millions.

The Romanos sold to everyone. Contractors and the public. They'd drive in, stop at the scale house and tell the scale operator what they wanted. The operator would radio the front-end loader driver. The customer would drive onto the scale and be weighed. Once loaded, they'd stop on the scale again. The operator would charge them based upon the weight difference times the product cost.

Next to the scale house, tucked back into the trees, was a small trailer with a blue Porta Potty next to it. Parked out front was a red pickup truck, a silver BMW, and a dump truck.

"Why the fuck did you hire that guy, Frank?" Nino asked.

"I didn't know he was going to be a hothead," Frank replied.

"Nino, calm down. You did spill your load in the street, not to mention you were way overloaded," Gino said.

"I don't give a shit, Pop," Nino said. "That Detective... what's his fucking name ... humiliated me in front of the new kid."

"Baker," Frank said.

"What?" Nino said.

"His name is Detective Colton Baker."

"Thirteen."

"What?"

"Like a fuck'n baker's dozen."

"Are you alright?" Frank asked.

"How about I stomp your fuck'n brains out," Nino said.

"Really, Nino? You're gonna go after a fucking cop now? You know how much heat that will bring down on us? The Feds are already snooping around. Kill a cop and they'll climb right up your ass, cauterize it shut and make sure you never shit again," Frank said. Then he looked at Gino and said, "His ass needs to calm down."

"Nino, Frank's right," Gino said. "Calm down."

"We're lucky they're not looking into us for the death of Peterson," Frank said.

"You think I killed Peterson?" Nino asked, surprised.

"Didn't you?"

"No!"

"No one killed Peterson. He died of a heart attack," Gino said.

Nino and Frank exchanged glances.

"Can we get back to business?" Gino asked.

Both Frank and Gino nodded in agreement.

"Good," Gino said. "Now Frank, did you secure the Route 24 resurfacing project?"

"Yes. I had to grease a few hands in the Highway Department. Plus a few state troopers. We'll need to go over on the daily hours," Frank said.

"Those troopers love to rake in the overtime," Gino said.

"No one ever looks into that shit?" asked Nino.

"Yes," Frank said. "But that's why we pay people. So they won't. And then we have you for those who say no or ask too many questions."

"I like it when they say no," Nino said.

"Enough!" Gino yelled.

"What about Baker, the doughnut boy?" asked Nino.

Gino looked at Frank. "Well?"

"Don't worry about Baker. There's a reason I promoted him. I'll handle him. Just stay outta his way," Frank said.

"Fuck that. He can stay out of my way," Nino said.

"Nino!" Gino said. "We have a lot of big money contracts coming up. We don't need any issues, especially with the local PD. Stay out of Baker's way. You understand me?"

Nino nodded his head.

Gino's face flushed. "You understand me?" he yelled.

"Yes, Pop," Nino said.

"And the next time you pick up a load, clean off the tailgate. And make sure it's covered," Gino said. "You know better!"

"I'm sorry, Pop!"

"There are laws against it. And us owning a gravel pit makes you look stupid. Which makes me look stupid."

"It won't happen again, Pop. I promise."

Chapter 17

62 Ledgebrook Ave
Stoughton, Massachusetts

Colton found the house easily enough. It was the one with all the police cruisers and fire apparatus out front. It was a plush home in the nice part of town. The rich side. Not the Section Eight housing side. That was the high drug and crime section part of town. That part saw a constant police presence. This section rarely saw any. But not today. Today, something evil had happened on this side. Something that claimed the life of one of the town's elite.

Larry Fuller. The president and CEO of the largest bank in town.

Once inside, a patrolman directed Colton downstairs.

Colton descended the metal spiral staircase, which ended in a luxurious room. It was incredible. Most men had a room in their home where they watched sports or played video games. Most called it a Man Cave. But this Man Cave was on steroids. Large TVs lined the front wall and a lone recliner sat on a turntable. On one side was a small fridge. On the other, a rack of snacks. Wherever the chair turned, the drinks and snacks followed. With the use of their feet, they could swivel the chair and face the TV of their choosing.

There was a dance floor beyond the chair. Against the wall was a DJ station and large speakers.

In the left corner was a bar. A fully-stocked bar complete with a mirror and rows of bottles of booze. Colton counted the number of seats in front of the bar. Twelve. It was bigger than some dive bars he'd sat at.

This was the ultimate party room, minus the rich, dead banker sitting behind the bar.

In the right corner sat a jewelry store type glass container. It had been smashed open and pieces of glass covered the floor.

Colton stood there and scanned the crime scene.

Scattered across the floor and bar were dozens of cardboard trays with tiny circles in them.

Colton walked behind the bar and examined the body.

The man was propped up on a barstool. His back was to the mirror. Arterial spray covered the mirror, bar and even a portion of the ceiling. Dried blood covered the victim's chest and collected in the chair around his groin. His head was partially severed and dangled backwards over the chair. The only thing keeping it attached was a thin strand of neck muscles.

Lividity had set in. Once the heart stops pumping, blood sinks and pools in the lowest part of the body. The victim's buttocks and lower legs were a dark bluish-purple from where the blood had collected, minus what had spilled out from the man's neck.

Three sheets of paper towels, drenched in blood, lay straight on the floor in front of the man. An open laptop sat across from the victim on top of the bar. Next to it was a bottle of lube.

With a gloved hand, Colton examined one of the cardboard trays. He studied it.

The circles varied in size. Beneath each one was a description. It was a coin holder.

"Looks like a robbery gone bad," Barnes said from behind Colton.

"It appears so," Colton replied, turning around.

Colton nudged the computer mouse, and the black screen disappeared.

"Jesus!" Colton said, looking at the paused video on the screen.

"What is it?" asked Barnes.

"Sicko was into child porn."

Barnes moved to get a better view. On the screen was a naked young boy. He appeared to be ten or eleven years old. A man stood behind the boy. He appeared to be in the midst of a sexual act on the child.

"Looks like our victim here was pleasuring himself when the perp broke in," Colton said. "Hence the paper towels on the floor to catch his seed."

"Gross!" Barnes said.

Colton pointed to the laptop. "That could be our motive right there."

"What, you thinking someone found out about his little … fetish and killed him?" Barnes asked.

"Well, it's staring us right in the face," Colton said.

Barnes walked over to the smashed glass containers and inspected them.

Colton turned his attention back to the victim.

The head looked odd. It was anatomically incorrect and hung from the chair over the countertop. It was upside down in front of the bottles. Colton tried to view the face, but it was too close to the bottles.

He looked in the mirror. The man's face was visible between the bottles. He noticed something covering the man's eyes.

"Hey, Barnes! Check this out." Colton called.

"Whatcha got?" Barnes asked.

Colton positioned himself and got a better view of the victim's face.

"The killer placed coins over each eye," Colton said.

"Why?" Barnes asked.

"I don't know. Maybe he saw something he wasn't supposed to see," Colton said. "In Ancient Greece, they placed coins over the eyes of the deceased. It was payment for Charon to ferry the dead to the underworld."

"You know a lot of different shit, Detective," Barnes said.

"I like to read," Colton said.

"With all these coins missing," Barnes said. "I wonder if it was a planned robbery, and they weren't expecting old pud puller here to be home jacking one off. Caught the robber off guard."

"Maybe," Colton said. "But something feels off. I just can't put my finger on it."

"Well, my guess is it's the child porn," Barnes said.

Colton glanced in the mirror and noticed something on the man's forehead. He looked closer.

"Oh, shit!" Colton said.

"What is it?" Barnes said.

"Look at this," Colton said.

Colton and Barnes changed positions.

Colton moved so Barnes could look in the mirror.

"Well, I guess we don't need to speak with Wendy McDonald," Barnes said. "He didn't kill himself for the insurance money."

Carved into the victim's head were similar strange symbols to the ones tattooed on Bill McDonald.

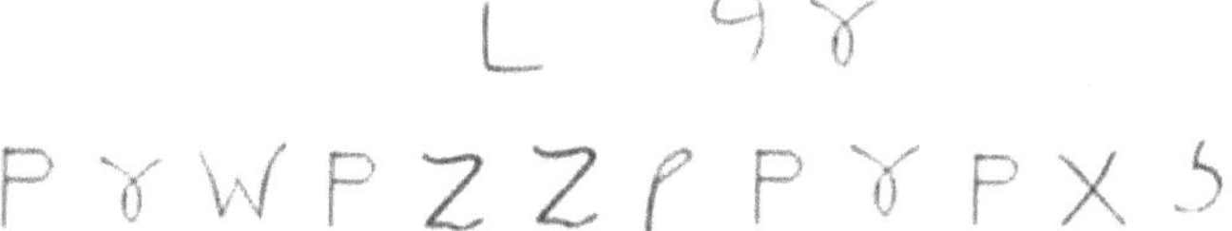

Chapter 18

62 Ledgebrook Ave
Stoughton, Massachusetts

Colton took out his department-issued cell phone and called the station. He asked for dispatch and put the call on speaker so Barnes could hear.

Colton asked what the nature of the call had been.

The dispatcher said someone from the bank called. Stated the victim didn't show for work, which was unlike him.

"Who was first on scene?" Colton asked.

"The responding officers were Lt. Bonnett and Officer O'Sullivan," the Dispatcher said.

"Can you pull the recording and put it aside for me?" Colton asked.

"Sure thing, Detective," the Dispatcher said.

Colton and Barnes headed upstairs and outside.

The first media truck had arrived. A reporter was interviewing several bystanders that had formed across the street. The boom in the news van was being raised.

"There," Colton said, spotting Lt. Bonnett and Officer O'Sullivan standing by the yellow tape down by the road.

Barnes whistled and got their attention. Colton waved them over.

"Is this the call you got when you were backing me up earlier?" Colton asked.

"Yeah," Lt. Bonnett said. "We came straight here from there."

"Nino Romano. He's a piece of work," Colton said.

"You got that right," Lt. Bonnett said.

"Who made entry?" Barnes asked.

"Officer O'Sullivan and myself," Lt. Bonnett said.

"Forced entry, correct?" Colton asked.

"Yes," Lt. Bonnett said. "We tried all the doors first, but they were locked."

"I ran the plate of the vehicle in the driveway," Officer O'Sullivan said. "It came back to this residence."

"Someone from his work was here," Lt. Bonnett said. "She called it in. She came over to check on him. Said they hadn't seen him in about a week. And no one heard from him. I told the fire department to wait outside, and we forced our way in through the front door. O'Sullivan and I searched the upstairs and then went downstairs."

"Did you approach the body?" Colton asked.

"No," Lt. Bonnett said. "I was halfway down the stairs when I spotted it. I stopped and went back up. It was apparent he was deceased."

"You got that right," Barnes said.

"We exited the same way we came in," Lt. Bonnett said. "Once outside, I called it in. Then O'Sullivan and I taped off the yard."

"Thank you, Lieutenant," Colton said. "And I assume you know the drill. We're going to need photos of the soles of your boots to exclude you from prints left in the upstairs carpet."

Just then, Chief McCormack pulled up.

Colton and Barnes walked over and met the Chief in the driveway.

"What'd you have, Detectives?" Chief McCormack asked.

"There's no doubt, Chief," Colton said. "Same killer as McDonald."

The Chief looked at Barnes.

"I agree, ma'am," Barnes said.

"What makes you think that?" Chief McCormack asked.

"This vic has similar markings on his forehead like McDonald," Colton said. "Except these were carved in. Not tattooed."

"Jesus!" Chief McCormack said.

"Bet you didn't realize Colton here was gonna be such a shit magnet when you promoted him," Barnes said, putting his hand on Colton's shoulder.

Colton smirked.

"Besides the symbols, any other apparent connections?" Chief McCormack asked.

"Both were robbed," Colton said.

"I know McDonald's wallet, phone, keys, and truck were missing," Chief McCormack said. "What's missing here?"

"Coin collection is missing," Colton said. "They were in a case which was smashed open. There are empty coin holders scattered everywhere down there."

"Plus, we don't know what else the killer might have taken," Barnes said.

"Any suspects?" Chief McCormack asked.

"We're still trying to locate that bum, Henry," Colton said. "I'll authorize overtime and increase the number of officers on patrol to assist," Chief McCormack said.

Chapter 19

Great Blue Hill Bank
Stoughton, Massachusetts

Hordes of media trucks flooded the street. The neighborhood buzzed with reporters and onlookers. Two murders, two days, one small town. The media whipped public interest.

The State Police forensics team arrived. They spoke with Colton and Barnes, then entered the house. The crime scene would take hours to process.

"Did you know this guy?" Colton asked Chief McCormack.

"Not personally," she said. "I've seen him at the bank before."

"This type of killing makes me wonder if it was revenge," Colton said. "Possibly for taking back someone's house through foreclosure."

"We should check with the bank," Barnes said. "See if they received any recent threats."

Colton and Barnes arrived at Great Blue Hill Bank a short time later. They spoke with a teller and identified themselves. The teller fetched the director of HR.

After a brief introduction, Colton informed her of Larry's death and asked if there was somewhere private to talk. She led them to her office.

"When is the last time you saw Larry?" Colton asked.

"The beginning of last week," she said. "He took off most of last week."

"And he was supposed to return yesterday. Is that correct?" Colton asked.

"Yes, that's correct," she said. "We had a big quarterly meeting scheduled this morning, and he didn't show again today either, which is very unlike him."

"What did you do?" Colton asked.

"We called him yesterday and then we called him several times this morning," she said. "We got worried something happened to him, so I had a teller drive over to his house."

"Was Larry personally overseeing any foreclosures?" Colton asked.

"No," the HR director said. "Our associates handle foreclosures."

"What can you tell us about Larry?" Colton said.

"Oh, Larry loved his coin collection," she said. "He told everyone about it. I guess he started it as a child with his father."

"Was he married? Any children?" Colton asked.

"No," she said. "Larry never married and never had children."

"Was he gay?" Colton asked.

"I don't know," she said. "He was a private person. But people assumed he was."

"Have you received any threats? Had any incidents here at the bank?" Barnes asked.

"Oh God, no," she said.

"May we see his office, please?" Colton asked.

"Yes, of course," she said. "Let me get the key."

She found the key and led them down the hall to Larry's office. The office was immaculate. There was nothing on the desk except a computer.

Colton pointed to the bookshelf behind the desk. "Look at this."

On the middle shelf sat three coins encased in thick plastic.

"I don't know shit about coins," Barnes said. "But they look old."

Colton looked at them. They were tiny and definitely appeared old. He took out his police-issued phone and snapped a few pictures of them.

"Will there be anything else?" she asked.

"That's all for now," Colton said. "If you think of anything, give us a call." He handed her his business card.

She closed and locked the office door and wished them a good day. Then she returned to her office and closed the door.

Colton and Barnes headed for the front entrance.

"I wonder if they knew their boss was a pedophile?" Barnes said.

"We should look further into it," Colton said. "But a part of me wonders if the killer staged it."

"You mean to send us down a rabbit hole?" Barnes asked.

"Exactly," Colton said. "I say we keep that info close to the vest. Don't want to ruin Larry's name in case the killer staged it."

"I agree," Barnes said.

They reached the front door when a bank employee rushed across the lobby toward them. The woman was older, in her late fifties.

"Is it true about Larry?" she asked in a whisper.

"I'm sorry," Colton said. "We can't discuss…"

The woman cut him off. "Did she tell you they were going to fire him?"

"Who?" Barnes asked.

The woman glanced around the bank.

"Larry," the woman whispered. "The Board was going to fire him."

"No," Colton said. "She didn't mention it."

"Larry's been meddling in customers' accounts," the woman said, her eyes darting around the bank.

"Is that normal for a bank CEO?" Colton asked.

"Hell no!" she said.

"And you have proof?" Barnes asked.

"Yes, of course," she said. "I'm not stupid."

An office door opened across the bank. The woman scurried away.

"What now?" Colton asked.

"I don't like being lied to," Barnes said. "That's for sure."

They stood there for a moment.

Barnes looked back at the HR director's door and started across the bank.

Colton followed.

Barnes didn't stop to knock. He walked right in.

The HR director was sitting behind her desk, talking on the phone. She covered the end of the phone with her palm.

"Excuse me," she said. "You can't just barge in here! I don't know who you think you are?"

Barnes slid his jacket to the side, exposing his shield clipped onto his belt.

"I'm a Massachusetts State Police Homicide Detective," Barnes said in a stern voice. "You are well aware of the fact that it's a felony to impede a homicide investigation?"

"W … What?" the woman asked.

"If I find out you just lied to me," Barnes snapped. "I will be back. And you'll be going to jail."

The color drained from her face.

"And guess what? I just found out that you lied to me," Barnes said.

"Pam. I'm gonna have to call you back," she said into the phone and hung up.

Barnes took a step into the room, allowing Colton to enter.

"Now, do you want to tell us the truth?" Barnes said with a growl. "Or do I need to come back here with a subpoena and haul your ass off to jail?"

"I was just trying to protect the bank," she said.

"What you need to do is start telling the truth," Barnes snapped. "Tell my partner here everything."

Barnes looked at Colton and winked.

Colton gave a slight nod.

Good cop. Bad cop.

The HR director informed them that they had caught Larry handling people's accounts. She explained that Larry was supposedly helping elderly customers with their finances and doing light shopping for them. In exchange, they were paying him.

"Sounds like he was just trying to be a nice guy," Colton said.

"Contrary," she said. "We discovered Larry had four elderly customers make him the beneficiary on their account."

"That's not good," Colton said. "What else?"

"He was taking bribes from people to slow down the foreclosure process," she said.

"And putting people further in debt?" Colton said. "What else?"

She looked down at her desk.

"What else?" Colton asked again.

The woman shuffled some papers on her desk.

"What else?" Barnes snapped, playing bad cop again.

The woman looked up at him.

Barnes glared at her.

"He was forcing people into foreclosure," she said.

"How the hell does one do that?" Colton asked.

"He'd stop payment transfers. Then he'd send out letters stating that their payment hadn't been received. He sent them demand letters. If they didn't pay, he'd force their accounts into foreclosure," she said.

"Jesus Christ," Barnes said. "No wonder the guy got murdered."

"I think he knew the board was onto him," she said. "He took the week off and…"

"Never came back," Colton said.

"Yes," she said, standing up. "I want you to know we did nothing wrong. Once we found out, we started an internal investigation. We have all the documents. We're going to notify the authorities, the Banking Commission and the FDIC, once our investigation is complete."

"Now we will be back with a subpoena," Barnes said.

Chapter 20

62 Ledgebrook Ave
Stoughton, Massachusetts

Colton and Barnes exited the bank and headed for their vehicles.

"We need to find that bum, Henry," Colton said.

"You think Fuller foreclosed on his house?" Barnes asked.

"Only one way to find out," Colton said. "We need to ask him."

They arrived back on Ledgebrook Ave and found the media trucks had doubled.

Colton met Barnes at the end of the driveway.

"Must be a slow news day," Barnes sarcastically chuckled.

Both men proceeded toward the house.

"Hey, listen," Colton said. "I think we look at this from two angles and avoid tunnel vision. First, we need to look into this foreclosure scam our victim was supposedly running. But we can't lose focus on the child porn we found on his computer, either."

"I agree," Barnes said. "Let's go talk with Trish. She heads up the State Police Forensic Team. I saw her arrive earlier."

Both men walked inside. They met with Trish downstairs and informed her of what they had discovered at the bank. Barnes instructed her to look for paperwork from the bank and to search Larry's computer as well. He told her they had seen child porn on the laptop upon arrival.

"Also," Colton said. "See if you can find a ledger detailing the vic's coin collection. No doubt they'll pop up in some coin or pawn shop."

Colton and Barnes searched the upstairs while the forensic team finished processing the downstairs.

Larry had an office on the first floor next to the kitchen. There was a desk, a couch, and artwork hung on the wall.

Larry's desk was immaculate, just like his desk at the bank.

Colton slid open the top drawer. Inside were a few pens and paper clips. He slid open the second drawer. Inside was a folded map of the town of Stoughton. Colton unfolded it. There was a yellow highlighted circle around the cemetery off of Central Street.

"Hey Barnes," Colton called.

"Whatcha got?" Barnes asked, stepping into the office.

Colton held up the map and showed it to Barnes.

"Why in the hell would he have that in his desk drawer?" Barnes asked.

"I don't know," Colton said. "Let me ask you, who keeps pens and paperclips in their desk, but no paper?"

"You think the killer took the papers?" Barnes asked.

Colton shrugged.

"Bag the map as evidence," Barnes said. "We'll look at it down at the station."

They continued searching the rest of the house.

"Did this guy just move in?" Colton asked. "Because this guy has nothing personal here. It's just furniture."

"No kids and never married," Barnes said. "I've got a wife and three kids. There's shit everywhere in my house."

They finished searching the first floor and moved upstairs. There were three bedrooms upstairs. Each room had a queen-size bed, a nightstand, and artwork on the walls.

"Bingo," Barnes said, from down the hall.

Colton made his way down to the master bedroom.

Barnes stood there holding a cell phone that was still plugged in.

Colton looked around the room. It was immaculate except for the pair of slacks on the floor and a tee-shirt on the bed.

Barnes tapped the screen, and it lit up.

"Damn," Barnes said. "It's locked. Facial recognition."

"Of course it is," Colton said.

"I'll bag it and see if they can't open it down at the lab."

They made their way back downstairs to the basement.

When they arrived, the Medical Examiner was getting ready to bag the body.

"I hate the headless ones," the Medical Examiner tech said.

"And he's a lot heavier than he looks," said the other tech, straining to lift the body.

"Yeah, probably an optical illusion. The missing head makes it look lighter," said the first tech.

They got the body bagged and onto the stretcher and removed it from the house.

On the way back to the station, Colton stopped by Roy's Coin and Stamps Shop. He spoke to Ben, Roy's son, who said his dad was off for the evening. Colton informed him about the theft of a valuable coin collection. He asked Ben to contact him should someone come in looking to sell some. After he left Roy's, he stopped by the pawn shop in the center of town and informed them as well. Colton left his business cards with both shops.

Hopefully, someone would try to turn in the coins.

Chapter 21

Stoughton Police Headquarters
Stoughton, Massachusetts

Colton arrived back at the station. He grabbed a folded cardboard box, assembled it, and put it on his desk. On it he wrote the date, case number and Larry Fuller's name. This was the second murder box he'd created in as many days.

The map he took from Larry Fuller's desk was still in the plastic evidence bag, which he placed inside the box. Then he carried the box over to the evidence locker. After unlocking the door, Colton placed Larry's box on the shelf next to McDonald's.

There was a knock on the door.

Colton opened it and found Barnes standing there.

"I called the D.A. and told him about Larry and the bank foreclosures," Barnes said, walking in. "His office is gonna handle it. Hopefully, we can get a subpoena for those bank accounts."

"Can you believe the nerve of that guy?" Colton said. "Using the bank to steal from people."

"If that's not motive for murder," Barnes said. "I don't know what is."

"Just think," Colton said. "If that woman didn't tell us, the bank would've covered it up."

"Thank God, there's still some decent people out there," Barnes said.

Colton chuckled.

"What?" Barnes asked.

"I didn't think that HR woman was gonna go for the good cop, bad cop routine, but it worked perfectly," Colton said.

"You weren't too bad yourself, Detective," Barnes said.

"Hey, listen," Colton said. "I'm sorry about giving you an attitude yesterday. You should have definitely checked with McDonald's tattoo artist."

"No worries," Barnes said. "Ultimately, you were right. But it doesn't mean we don't chase down leads. What if McDonald had paid his artist to tattoo his forehead?"

"True," Colton said.

"It wasn't a waste of time," Barnes said. "We either confirm or eliminate. One is as important as the other. And after finding those same symbols on Larry Fuller's forehead, we definitely know the two murders are connected."

"Speaking of which, let me check to see if we received McDonald's phone records yet," Colton said, walking over to his desk.

"Perfect," Barnes said. "Let's see if we can find out who called him."

Colton sat down and checked his email.

There it was. A response from the phone company. Colton clicked on it and opened the email. Inside was a pdf containing Bill McDonald's cell phone records. He opened the pdf.

The report listed all the incoming and outgoing calls. Each with its own timestamp. The first call listed was an incoming call. The time stamp matched the time Wendy said Bill had received the call. Five minutes earlier, Bill had placed a call to the same number.

Colton ran the number through ZetX, a website that's free for law enforcement. Instantly, it provided the subscriber's name and phone carrier.

"Am I reading that right?" Colton said.

Subscriber: Lawrence Fuller
Carrier: Verizon

"Holy shit!" Barnes said, looking over Colton's shoulder. "Our two victims called each other."

"Or the killer called Bill from Larry's phone," Colton said.

"We need to have his phone dusted for prints," Barnes said and pulled out his phone.

He called Trish at the State Police Forensic Lab. When she answered, Barnes instructed her to dust the cell phone he'd found upstairs for prints. He informed her that the two victims spoke with each other prior to their deaths.

Barnes hung up.

They looked at each other.

"We need to talk to Wendy again," Colton said. Find out how they knew each other."

Chapter 22

**Romano Sand & Gravel
Stoughton, Massachusetts**

Frank pulled in, parked in front of the trailer and hurried inside.

"You guys see the news?" Frank asked, walking in.

"No," Gino said. "What's up?"

"There's been another homicide," Frank said, looking at Nino.

"You think I killed somebody?" Nino said.

"I take it you know who it is, Frank?" Gino asked, putting an end to the nonsense before it escalated between the two.

"Yeah," Frank said. "Larry Fuller."

"CEO of the Great Blue Hill Bank?" Gino asked. "Are you serious?"

"I just drove past his house. It's definitely him," Frank said.

"Well, I guess that's one less problem we have to deal with," Nino said with a chuckle.

"It was you!" Frank said. "Wasn't it?"

"What? It wasn't me," Nino said, glaring at Frank. "Why would I kill him?"

"How do you know it was a homicide?" Gino asked. "Larry wasn't in the greatest of shape."

"Yeah, he had that big fumper on him," Nino said.

"Fumper?" Frank said. "What the hell is a fumper?"

"You know, a front bumper," Nino said, holding out his hands and acting like he had an enormous belly that hung down over his crotch.

"That thing was huge!" Gino said with a chuckle.

"And he'd hike his pants up over it," Nino said. "He looked fucking ridiculous."

The men all laughed.

"So, Frank, where do we stand with the resurfacing projects?" Gino asked.

"Obviously, I secured the Route 138 project here in town. That was easy enough to get," Frank said.

"And what about the Route 24 contract?" Gino asked.

"That one's proving a little trickier," Frank said. "Apparently, there's been several bids."

"Are you greasing the right wheels?" Gino asked.

"I am, but so are the other bidders," Frank said.

"Give me the name of the guy we've been paying," Gino said.

Frank told him.

Gino looked at his son.

"Go pay him a visit. I'm not paying this piece of shit for no reason. We're getting what we're paying for and that's that."

"With pleasure, Pop," Nino said.

"I'd hate to see him end up in one of our asphalt grinders," Gino said. "Then mixed into a resurfaced roadway somewhere."

Nino looked at Frank and smiled.

"Gotta love the power of persuasion," Nino said.

Both Gino and Nino laughed. Frank stood there with a horrified look on his face.

Chapter 23

Stoughton Police Headquarters
Stoughton, Massachusetts

District Attorney Harbor arrived at Stoughton Police Headquarters. He met with Barnes, who asked about Colton. How he was doing? Could he keep up?

Barnes told him that Colton had a good head on his shoulders. Said Colton had a knack for homicide. The gruesome scenes didn't deter him. He joked Colton was better his first day than some detectives with years of experience that he'd worked with in the past. When they finished speaking, they headed over to Chief McCormack's office to meet with her and Colton to see if they'd made any new discoveries.

"What do we know?" Harbor asked, taking a seat.

"We know Larry took time off last week," Barnes said. "Our forensic team checked his computer, and he had no vacations planned. We checked his bank account, and he hadn't purchased tickets anywhere."

"Was it a staycation?" Harbor asked.

"Not sure," Barnes said.

"Thoughts?" Harbor asked.

"Well, there was a bum seen standing over our first victim," Barnes said. "Then our second vic is a banker who we found out is conducting a foreclosure scheme. My guess is this bum lost his house to Fuller, and this was a revenge killing."

"But … how does Fuller's scheme tie into McDonald?" Colton asked. "He was a firefighter. Not an employee at the bank."

"I don't know," Barnes said. "But we can connect them through phone records."

"The phone company sent over McDonald's entire call history," Colton said. "It was in a pdf format which is searchable. I entered both Fuller's phone number and the numbers from the bank. Nothing. If they spoke, it wasn't from those numbers."

"What's your point?" Barnes asked.

Harbor turned toward Colton.

"Do you think our second victim planned a vacation? What are your thoughts, young man?" Harbor asked Colton.

"No sir, I do not."

"Barnes here tells me you have a good head on your shoulders," Harbor said. "Tell me what you think."

Colton looked at Barnes, who winked at him.

"I think there's more to it," Colton said.

"Go on. Speak freely," Harbor said.

"Well, we know both victims spoke on the phone. But we're not sure if they knew each other. We're trying to find the connection," Colton said. "We're going to meet with Wendy McDonald tomorrow morning. Hopefully, she can shine some light on the connection. But, to your question regarding the vacation, I think the bank suspended him. I think they don't want that known because it means they knew what he was doing prior to finishing their supposed investigation."

"Continue," Harbor said.

"I think our killer found out the bank suspended Fuller," Colton said. "And that means someone from the bank told him."

"Are you thinking who I'm thinking?" Barnes asked.

"Yup!" Colton said. "That woman from the bank. The one who told us about Fuller when we were leaving."

"Bingo!" Barnes said.

"Do you think both murders are connected to the foreclosure scheme?" Harbor asked.

"I don't know," Colton said. "My gut says no."

"I agree," Harbor said. "That's why, as of right now, I'm starting a task force. I want you and Barnes running point."

Harbor looked at McCormack. "You okay with that?"

"Yes sir," McCormack said.

"My office has been in touch with the bank. The Board of Directors has agreed to meet with us tomorrow afternoon. I promised not to press charges if they fully cooperate."

Barnes turned to Colton.

"Tomorrow morning, we meet with the Medical Examiner. After, we meet with Wendy McDonald," Barnes said. "The forensics team is going through Fuller's phone. They're checking his calendar, emails, and anything on it. Hopefully, they'll have something for us by tomorrow."

"What about the symbols?" Harbor asked.

"Nothing yet," Colton said. "We're going to focus on them next."

Harbor looked at each of them.

"I want to make this abundantly clear," Harbor said. "We do not discuss the symbols with anyone not working on the investigation. We keep that close to the vest. I don't want to see it on the six o'clock news."

"Speaking of which," McCormack said, looking at her watch. "It's time for the press conference."

Chapter 24

Stoughton Police Headquarters
Stoughton, Massachusetts

David Monteiro stood outside the Stoughton Police Headquarters. Press vans lined Rose Street and the municipal parking lot next door was full too. The sun was still in the sky. It was a beautiful New England warm summer's evening.

The press conference was being held outside. They set the podium up on the sidewalk. There were no seats. David would have to stand holding his recorder.

Like the previous press conference, the local media had their microphones hooked up to the podium. Wires spidered across the cement out to the different cameras that were set up.

Behind him, reporters checked in with their stations while others rehearsed their reports.

David arrived early and parked in the Post Office lot and walked over. He stood in the front row.

Lt. Bonnett walked out to the podium. He noticed David and nodded.

David nodded back.

Lt. Bonnett spoke to the reporters. He informed them Chief McCormack and District Attorney Steve Harbor would be out soon to address the media.

One reporter asked how to spell the Chief's name. Lt. Bonnett spelled it out.

After a few moments, Lt. Bonnett glanced at his watch. A minute later, he glanced over his shoulder at the front door of the police station. The press conference was set to start.

David pulled out his phone and snapped a photo of Lt. Bonnett standing at the podium outside. Then he opened his text app. He found Laynie's name and began typing.

Hi honey!

He waited.

A minute later, he received a reply.

Hi dad! Sorry I wasn't able to call the other night. By the time I got home it was too late to call.

David sent the picture he had just taken.

Did they make an arrest in the murder case?

David chuckled to himself as he typed.

I wish!

David watched the three little dots appear. Then her text came.

What's going on?

David typed out his response and hit send.

There's been another murder.

Within seconds, there was a response.

Dad, are you serious?

David responded.

Bank CEO found murdered. My source says it was brutal.

Another instantaneous response.

Are the two murders related?

David looked up. Chief McCormack and District Attorney Harbor walked out the front door.

Don't know. Hoping to find out now. Love you!

David's phone vibrated. He read the text and smiled. Then he slipped the phone into his pocket.

Keep me posted, Dad. You know I love a killer story!

McCormack walked out to the podium, followed by Harbor, Barnes, and Colton.

"As you probably know," McCormack began. "We discovered a body this morning in a home on Ledgebrook Avenue. We're investigating this as a homicide. At this time, we believe this is an isolated incident, and that there is no threat to the public. I'll now hand over the podium to District Attorney Harbor."

Harbor stepped up to the mic and, once again, read a prepared speech. Once he was done, he opened it up to questions.

"How did the victim die?" asked the reporter from Channel 7.

"That's something we're not disclosing," Harbor said.

David raised his hand.

Harbor pointed to him.

"Are the two murders connected?" David asked.

"Yes," Harbor said.

"Can you elaborate?" David asked.

"Not at this time," Harbor said.

"Did the two victims know each other?" David asked.

Harbor looked at McCormack. She stepped up to the podium.

"Hi David," McCormack said. "Nice to see you."

David smiled and nodded.

"To answer your question," McCormack said. "We're trying to find that out. And if so, how?"

The reporter for Channel 5 raised her hand. McCormack pointed to her.

"Was the victim stabbed or shot?"

"We're not disclosing that at this time," McCormack said.

Other reporters raised their hands. They all seemed to ask the same question, just phrased differently. They all seemed focused on how the victim died.

David looked around at his fellow journalists. Today's reporters weren't like they were before. Years ago, reporters asked hard questions. They were persistent. Wouldn't take no for an answer. If they smelled blood, they went after it. They'd dig in. Now, reporters ask soft questions and accept whatever response they're given. They don't challenge or push back.

If Laynie were here, she'd dig in like a tick. She's the living definition of unrelenting.

Chapter 25

Nancy and Paul Baker's House
Stoughton, Massachusetts

Colton returned home after a long day. Both Hayley and Roxy greeted him at the door. He gave them some much needed attention. Plus, they were a great distraction for him.

He let them out and stood there. The events from today played out in his mind.

The visual of the banker's posed body and the crime scene plagued Colton's mind. *Was it a robbery? Was it a vigilante pedophile hunter picking off prey?* Whatever the case may be, the image was now seared into his mind.

He shook the thoughts from his mind and contacted his mom. She texted him a list of items she needed from the grocery store.

He let the dogs in and gathered a few dog toys together, along with their food and bowls, and packed them up. Then he hopped in the shower.

After, he went to the store and grabbed the items his mother had requested. He picked out the best-looking meats and made sure to check the date. He stopped back home and grabbed the dogs.

Colton arrived at his parents' house a few minutes later. He carried everything in and helped put the groceries away.

"Oh!" Nancy said. "These steaks look good. You did a good job picking them out. And look at that, they don't expire tomorrow. How wonderful!"

She put them on the counter and pulled out a bowl.

"I'll marinate them first," Nancy said.

"I can't stay, Mom," Colton said. "Can I get a rain check?"

"Oh sure, honey," Nancy said. "That'll give them a chance to marinate longer."

Colton went to check on the dogs. They'd assumed their positions with his dad. Hayley sat in Paul's lap, and Roxy was curled into a ball at his feet. His dad was sound asleep in the chair.

He returned to the kitchen to find his mother had made him a sandwich.

"You need to eat," she said, handing him the paper plate.

Colton thanked her and kissed her goodbye.

"Come by tomorrow night," she said. "I'll cook the steak."

"I will," he said, taking a bite of the sandwich, and walked out.

Chapter 26

Medical Examiner's Office
Boston, Massachusetts

Colton and Barnes arrived at the Medical Examiner's office first thing in the morning. Hurst sat in his office. He spotted them and came out. They followed Hurst into the exam room.

The body of Larry Fuller, the bank CEO, was on the metal table. A sheet covered his body. Only his head was exposed.

"What can you tell us?" Colton asked.

"I've been doing this for close to thirty years," Hurst said. "And this was a first for me."

Colton and Barnes exchange glances.

"Well, now you've got my attention," Barnes said.

"Cause of death?" Colton asked.

"Decapitation," Hurst said. "But you're not gonna believe this!"

"He ate the coins," Colton said.

"How did you know?" asked Hurst.

"The killer turned him into a human Pez dispenser," Colton said.

"What?" Barnes asked.

"Head flips back and candy comes out. Except the candy is coins," Colton said.

Colton held up his left hand. Then he moved his thumb, mimicking the motion used to flip open a Pez dispenser.

"Oh yeah, I remember those," Barnes said. "My kids had them."

Hurst turned and opened a plastic container. He pulled out a jar of coins and placed it on the examination table next to the victim's body.

Colton looked at the jar.

"How many coins did you pull out?" Barnes asked.

"We removed forty-seven coins from the victim's stomach," Hurst said.

"God damn," Barnes said. "How do you get a person to eat one coin, never mind a stack of them?"

"That's not my job, Detective," Hurst said. "You'll have to ask the killer."

"I remember how grimy and tainted my fingers used to become back in the day at the casinos," Barnes said. "Imagine that on the inside?"

"Exactly, Detective," Hurst said. "Except your victim's body absorbed it, causing a serious infection. His body produced a ton of white blood cells to attack the coins."

"Jesus," Barnes said.

"How long did that take?" Colton asked.

"My guess, a couple days," Hurst said. "It was a slow, painful death. Your killer wanted him to suffer before he died."

"So ... torture?" Barnes asked.

"You could call it that," Hurst said.

"Murder weapon?" Colton asked.

"My guess, a hatchet," Hurst said. "After he sliced the victim's throat, it appears he slid the blade into the slice. Then, using brute force, worked it back and forth with a seesaw motion, wedging it deeper into the neck."

"So, our killer is strong?" Colton asked.

"And tall," the Medical Examiner said. "Or he stood on something. Because the wound is downward, not upward."

"How about the coins covering his eyes?" Colton asked. "Any significance there?"

"They're not coins," Hurst said. "They're medallions."

"Medallions?" Barnes said. "Really?"

"Here, let me show you," Hurst said, pulling out a small plastic container from the larger container. He opened it and inside were two of the same medallions. He took one out and held it in his gloved hand.

"We dusted it for prints and didn't find any. Your killer must have wiped them clean."

"He's smart," Colton said.

"See this right here," Hurst said. He pointed to the medallion in his hand. "That's the bail. It's the part the chain slides through."

Colton looked at the medallion. "Is there something on it?"

"There is," Hurst said. "There's actually something on both sides." He flipped it over in his hand.

"Any clue what it is?" Colton asked.

"I haven't had the chance to research it," Hurst said. "I had pictures taken for you."

"Great," Colton said. "I'll look into it."

"Thanks," Hurst said. "I'm swamped this week, so I appreciate the help."

"No problem, doc," Colton said. "What about his forehead?"

"Your killer used a razor blade to carve the symbols into the skin," the Medical Examiner said. "My guess, an Exacto Blade."

"Like the kind used on model cars?" Colton asked.

"Exactly," Hurst said. "That's why it's so precise."

Barnes chuckled. "I see what you did there, doc."

"Any idea what the symbols mean?" Colton asked.

"They appear to be random symbols to me, but I bet they have meaning to your killer," Hurst said. "You've got your work cut out for you to determine that."

"Anything else you can tell us?" Colton asked.

Hurst picked up his clipboard and skimmed through it.

"There is one more thing," Hurst said. "Your killer tattooed a tiny **W** onto your vic's right thumb."

"That's odd," Colton said.

"That's because there's nothing normal about this case," Barnes said.

"Can you compare the ink on McDonald's forehead to the ink on Fuller's thumb?" Colton asked.

"I already did," Hurst said. "It's an exact match."

They thanked Hurst and left.

Outside in the parking lot, Colton and Barnes spoke briefly.

"That's the damnedest thing," Barnes said. "In all my years working homicide, I never had someone tattoo a body."

"Maybe we pay McDonald's tattoo artist another visit after we visit Wendy," Colton said. "See if McDonald used another artist."

Chapter 27

Wendy McDonald
Stoughton, Massachusetts

Colton and Barnes arrived at the McDonald residence.

The community of Stoughton had a tight bond, as did the fire department.

When they arrived, Wendy let them inside. They stood in the living room. Colton noticed three off-duty firefighters in the kitchen. The men all wore Stoughton Fire tee shirts. Two were preparing breakfast, and the third was replacing a lightbulb in the kitchen chandelier.

"They just showed up," Wendy said.

"They're good men," Colton said.

"Yes, they are," Wendy said. "Bill loved the guys he worked with."

"Can we talk with you in private?" Colton asked.

Wendy led them down the hall to her bedroom.

Colton observed three more firefighters down the hall, fixing little things around the house. Things Bill would never get to.

Once they entered the bedroom, Wendy closed the door behind them.

"Any updates?" she asked.

"We're following up on some leads," Barnes said.

Wendy's eyes began watering. She pulled a tissue from her sleeve and blotched her eyes.

"I assume the Medical Examiner told you Bill had lung cancer," Wendy said.

"Yes, he did," Colton said.

"I should have told you," she said.

"It's okay," Barnes said. "We understand."

"The other morning, when I heard a body had been discovered, I assumed Bill had committed suicide," Wendy said.

"Why would you assume that?" Colton asked.

Wendy looked down. After a moment, she looked back up. "Bill had tests done late last week to see if the cancer has spread," she said. "I assumed it was his doctor who called with bad news. He usually went for a drive after those calls. Said he liked to absorb the info and plan out his next move."

"Could you please provide me with his doctor's number?" Colton asked. "I need to verify the number."

"You don't think that whoever called him had anything to do with his death?" Wendy asked. "Do you?"

"We just need to verify," Colton said.

Wendy walked over to the dresser. She shuffled around a few papers and picked one up.

"I found his doctor's number," she said, handing the paper to Colton.

Colton tucked it into his notepad.

"Did Bill know a Larry Fuller? Lawrence Fuller," Barnes asked.

Wendy thought about it for a moment. "Doesn't sound familiar," she said. "Is that who killed him?"

"No," Barnes said. "Just following up on a lead. Most are nothing, but we check them anyway."

"Did Bill have a laptop?" Colton asked.

"No," Wendy said with a snort. "Bill was a lot of things, but tech savvy wasn't one of them. He could barely use a cell phone."

"I can relate," Barnes said.

"Detective, did Bill get a new tattoo?" Wendy asked. "You mentioned it the other day."

Colton looked to Barnes.

"Had he gotten anything lately?" Barnes asked. "It looked new to us."

"Bill loved tattoos," Wendy said. "He started getting them shortly after joining the Army. He got one every couple of years until being diagnosed with lung cancer."

"I'm sorry." Colton said.

"It's not your fault," Wendy said. "Shit happens, as Bill used to say."

Colton chuckled. "Very true."

"Bill started getting tattoos again after his diagnosis. He stopped taking his medication. Said it wore him out. He didn't want to jeopardize his crew when on shift. He decided to get tattoos and combat the pain with pain."

"Tough as nails," Colton said.

"Like you wouldn't believe," Wendy said.

Barnes and Colton thanked her for her time and gave their condolences again. Colton handed her his card and told her to call if she remembered anything. Then they left.

Chapter 28

Great Blue Hill Bank
Stoughton, Massachusetts

Barnes, Harbor, and Colton arrived at Great Blue Hill Bank. They met with the board members and their team of lawyers. The ranking board member read a prepared speech. In it, they confirmed Larry was going to be removed as president and CEO. Apparently, he'd had an argument with several customers over their property being foreclosed. It seemed Larry was involved in a bunch of shady things. The bank was still discovering evidence. They had hired a legal firm to assist them. The Lead Attorney sat across from District Attorney Harbor.

"He was basically running a shakedown," Harbor said. "But why?"

"We're still trying to figure that out," said the Lead Attorney.

Colton flipped through Larry Fuller's file.

"He was well off. Wasn't he?" Colton asked.

"He's been the CEO for the last fifteen years and makes roughly $125,000 a year," the Lead Attorney said.

"Is that normal?" Colton asked. "I thought it would have been higher."

"Great Blue Hill Bank is a small bank," the Lead Attorney said. "The average salary of a small bank CEO is between $75,000 and $100,000."

"So, Larry was making more than average," Colton asked.

"Yes, but with fifteen years of employment," the ranking board member said. "That includes yearly raises and bonuses which account for his larger than average salary."

"Plus, he worked hard at maintaining business with the bank, correct?" Colton asked.

"Yes, that's correct," the board member said.

"Were his bonuses affected by the dollar amount in the bank?" Colton asked.

"Excuse me?" the board member snapped.

"If the amount of money within the bank dropped below a certain amount, would that affect Larry's bonus?"

The bank's legal team looked at each other. No one answered.

District Attorney Harbor leaned back in his chair. He tapped his index finger on the table.

"I'd like to remind the board and its attorneys that my office has extended an olive branch. We're here under the condition of full disclosure and, in exchange, my office and the weight of the Commonwealth will not prosecute this bank and its board members."

The bank attorneys huddled and whispered to each other.

"I strongly suggest you answer my detective's questions before I have you all arrested and charged," Harbor said. "This all happened right under your nose."

The legal team appeared to be squabbling.

"Oh, and did I mention I'm meeting the Attorney General of the United States this weekend?" Harbor said. "I bet he'd love to throw the support of the federal government my way and assist in the investigation."

Several board members turned a shade of white.

"We'll be cooperating one hundred percent," the Lead Attorney for the bank said.

"Perfect," Harbor said. "Now please answer my detective's question."

"Yes," the ranking board member said, glaring at Colton. "It would affect his yearly salary."

"And if it dropped below that number?" Colton asked.

"He'd be terminated," the ranking board member said.

"Great!" Barnes said. "These assholes drove him to do it."

"It's not like that," the ranking member said.

"Sure, it's not," Barnes said. "Do you understand the ramifications of what you've done?"

"We provided people with mortgages to buy their own homes," another board member said.

"No," Barnes said. "You terrorized people."

"Enough," the Lead Attorney said.

"I want a list of all the clients Larry shook down," Barnes said.

"We can provide that," the lead attorney said.

"Actually," Colton said. "I'd also like a list of all open mortgages with the bank. And any foreclosed ones dating back to when Fuller started at the bank."

The ranking board member leaned over and conversed quietly with the Lead Attorney.

"We're gonna need some time," the Lead Attorney said. "That's thousands of accounts we need to review."

"How long do you need?" Harbor asked.

The Lead Attorney looked around at his co-council.

"At least a month," he said.

"I expect the account information within a week."

Colton, Barnes, and Harbor stood up and walked out.

Chapter 29

Stoughton Police Headquarters
Stoughton, Massachusetts

After they left the bank, they all met back at McCormack's office.

McCormack sat behind her desk. Harbor stood in between Colton and Barnes.

"How did that go?" McCormack asked.

"These two," Harbor said, using his thumbs and pointing at Colton and Barnes. "They just landed an investigation of a lifetime down at the bank. Never mind the murder investigation that goes along with it."

"Fuller was that involved with the foreclosure scheme?" McCormack asked.

Barnes stood there, noticeably pissed.

"Are you seriously going to give them a pass?" Barnes asked, looking at Harbor.

"Let's see what the bank provides. If they're lucky, Fuller only tried to shake down a handful of clients," Harbor said.

"If it's more?" Barnes asked.

"I never promised them anything in writing," Harbor said. "Plus, I can rescind the offer at any point."

Harbor put a hand on Barnes' shoulder. "Don't worry. We'll get them."

"So, what do we know?" McCormack asked. "Have we found any connection between Bill McDonald and Larry Fuller?"

"Only the phone call between the two the night McDonald went missing," Colton said.

"We visited McDonald's wife, Wendy, again this morning," Barnes said. "She confirmed he had cancer."

"Any explanation for why she knew her husband was dead?" McCormack asked.

"She said she thought the call Bill received was from his doctor. Apparently, Bill had more tests done, and she thought the doctor called with bad news," Colton said. "Bill usually went for a drive after receiving not so good news. Then he didn't come home. So, when she heard the call on the police scanner, she thought Bill had committed suicide."

"Suicide?" McCormack said. "Bill didn't seem the type."

"Wendy said Bill didn't take any pain medication," Barnes said. "He didn't like how it made him feel. Didn't want it to affect his job. Wanted to be there for his guys. Said Bill started getting tattoos to battle the pain. Fight pain with pain."

"Jesus!" McCormack said. "Stage four cancer with no pain meds. That's brutal. I can see why she thought he killed himself."

"Now, what's interesting," Colton said. "McDonald received a phone call which Wendy thought was the doctor. Then he went for a ride, like he did after receiving bad news. The next morning, we discovered his body."

"Your point, Detective?" Harbor asked.

"McDonald had a new tattoo," Colton said. "Like the killer knew Bill's pattern of life."

"So, it's someone close to him," McCormack said. "Someone who knew his routine."

"Exactly," Colton said. "They replicated it and then murdered him."

"What about Fuller?" Harbor asked.

"We don't know Fuller's day-to-day business," Barnes said.

"But," Colton said. "We know the killer had to have learned that the bank suspended Fuller."

"How did it go at the Medical Examiner's this morning?" Harbor asked.

"You're not gonna believe it," Barnes said.

"What?" Harbor asked.

"The killer made Fuller eat the coins," Barnes said.

Harbor looked at Barnes.

"How many?"

"Forty-seven coins," Barnes said.

McCormack sat upright.

"Did you say forty-seven coins?" McCormack asked.

"You heard right," Barnes said.

"And the killer marked Fuller with the same symbols?" Harbor asked.

"Yes, and no, sir," Colton said. "Some symbols were the same. And there were new ones, too."

"Do we know what they mean?" Harbor asked.

"No," Barnes said. "But the killer used an Exacto knife to carve them into Fuller's forehead."

"We're talking torture here?" McCormack said.

"Appears so," Barnes said.

"This is one sick individual," Harbor said.

"This is personal," Colton said. "Revenge."

"Any leads on the bum seen standing over McDonald?" Harbor asked.

"None yet, sir," McCormack said. "We have patrol searching for him."

"Have you looked into the coins?" Harbor asked.

"Not yet, sir," Colton said. "It's on my list of things to do."

"Well, you have your hands full," Harbor said. "I'll leave you to it."

Chapter 30

Nancy and Paul Baker's House
Stoughton, Massachusetts

It had been a long day. After the meeting at the bank, Colton stopped off at his parents' house.

He had a quick bite to eat. Leftovers from the other night.

Nancy put the tupperware away and sat down next to him.

"I can't believe it," she said. "Another murder?"

Colton mentioned Larry Fuller by name to see if she knew him. His mother used to be involved with different community programs around town until Colton's father came down with dementia. She knew almost everyone. Paul, Colton's father, jokingly used to call her the *Mayor of Stoughton*.

"Is that who was murdered?" she asked.

"Did you know him, Mom?" Colton asked.

"That old snake in the grass," she said. "Yeah, I knew him."

"How?"

"We used to have our mortgage at his bank," she said. "But we kept getting foreclosure notices after we made our monthly payment."

"When was this?" Colton asked.

"Probably ten years ago," she said.

"Really?"

"Your father was furious," she said. "It didn't happen just one time, mind you. It happened month after month. And they tried hitting us with fees, too."

"What did you do?"

"We ended up refinancing with a different bank."

Colton finished eating and gave Hayley and Roxy some attention. They seemed to like spending time with his parents.

"Your father loves having them here," Nancy said, standing in the doorway between the kitchen and the living room. "I haven't seen him smile that much in years. They climb up in his lap and he pats them for hours."

Colton smiled.

"Will you be back for dinner?" Nancy asked.

"I'll try," Colton said. "I'll let you know either way."

Colton said goodbye to his father and the dogs. He walked into the kitchen and gave his mother a kiss on the cheek.

"Good luck," she said. "I hope you catch the sick bastard."

Chapter 31

Stoughton Police Headquarters
Stoughton, Massachusetts

Colton arrived back at the station. He wanted to check something out. He wanted to compare Bill McDonald's and Larry Fuller's social media pages against one another. See if their lives overlapped or crossed.

Colton walked into the station and found Barnes waiting for him in the lobby.

Barnes was holding a TownSlice pizza box.

"I see you found *The Slice*," Colton said.

"Who doesn't get their pizza when in town?" Barnes asked.

"Touché."

"Where did you go for lunch?" Barnes asked.

"I went to my parents' house," Colton said. "They're elderly and my dad has dementia. I try to check in on them when I can."

"Aw! Look at you," Barnes said, with a twang of sarcasm. "A good son."

"You're more than welcome to join me next time," Colton said. "My mom is a social butterfly and would love the company. Plus, she's a phenomenal cook."

"Sure, why not," Barnes said. "I'm not one to pass up a home-cooked meal."

They walked back to Colton's office. Colton filled Barnes in on his plan to cross-reference the victim's social media pages.

Once inside the office, Colton sat at his desk.

Barnes sat down across from him and started eating pepper and onion pizza. It smelled delicious.

Barnes offered Colton a slice. He declined.

Colton began his search on the computer.

"What system do you use in Stoughton?" Barnes asked. Cheese dangled from his lip. "Do you use CLEAR by Thomson Reuters?"

"No," Colton said. "Some feel there's too much controversy surrounding it."

"Do you?" Barnes asked.

"I'm on the fence," Colton said. "I can see both sides, though. It's a powerful tool that combs through an absurd amount of data. Then it sorts it and makes it searchable. It brings everything about that individual right to your fingertips."

"What's wrong with that?" Barnes asked.

"Some consider it an invasion of privacy," Colton said. "They don't just scour the internet, they buy data from utility providers, social media and a ton of other sources. Plus, it's a very expensive subscription-based program."

"What are your thoughts on the Commonwealth Fusion Center?" Barnes asked.

"We use the Commonwealth Fusion Center," Colton said. "But that's different. That's data compiled through law enforcement databases and used to prevent or identify specific individuals of terrorist activities. Plus, it has analytics on Organized Crime, Identity Theft, Gangs, Narcotics Trafficking, Financial Crimes and Crime Patterns and Mapping."

"You already know all this, and you just made detective?" Barnes asked.

"Like I said before. I like to read," Colton said. "Plus, I assisted Peterson a few times."

"Then you know the Commonwealth Fusion Center won't provide you with a cross-comparison of McDonald's and Fullers' social media pages, right?" Barnes said.

"I know that," Colton said. "But it will tell me if they've been involved in any financial crimes. Plus, they're two men in their fifties. Chances are they don't have much of a social media presence. It shouldn't take long to comb through their pages."

Colton checked the Commonwealth Fusion Center site first. There was no mention of either McDonald, Fuller, or Great Blue Hill Bank. They most likely never got caught or had charges filed against them.

Colton moved onto Facebook and started with McDonald's page.

He scrolled through the feed. McDonald hadn't posted in years. Most of the posts were from his wife, Wendy, of their children. Bill wasn't even in the pictures. Wendy just tagged him.

Colton typed Bill's name into the search bar and hit search. Then he tapped posts.

Multiple posts came up of Bill at different fire department events and situations that took place in town.

The Stoughton Fire Department tagged McDonald in multiple posts. He was present at last year's town annual Touch -a-Truck event. Another post tagged him as helping teach a free public CPR class. There were pictures of Bill standing behind a booth handing out stickers and plastic helmets to kids at the town's summer carnival. He was present at the public awareness event that reminded residents to change the batteries in their smoke detector. The posts went back years. Bill took part in parades and different activities around town during his career.

There was nothing negative about McDonald on social media.

Colton repeated the same process for Larry Fuller. Fuller had a page, but no posts. Unlike McDonald, Larry wasn't married and had no children. Colton searched by name and then posts.

Like McDonald, Larry's work tagged him in posts. The bank had its annual float in the Fourth of July parade, where they handed out candy to the kids and pens and different swag to adults. It was a great marketing technique that hit directly to their customer base, local families and businesses. The bank tagged Larry in other posts, which spanned back years. The posts advertised different promotions the bank ran back then.

Colton found a post that caught his attention. It was by an individual who posted to one of the Stoughton news type pages.

This individual tagged the bank and posted about her negative experience with Great Blue Hill Bank. The post accused the bank of shady practices and running a foreclosure scam. Her post had one-hundred-and-nineteen comments, most of which agreed with her. The others were diehard Stoughton residents. They wouldn't allow negative things said about the town, even if they were true. They were the *Karens* of the internet.

Colton took screenshots of the thread. He clicked on the different usernames who left comments. Then he took screenshots of their home pages. Any of them could be the killer.

Barnes finished the last slice of pizza and used a napkin to wipe his hands and mouth.

"Should we go inquire about the coins found inside Larry?" Barnes asked.

"Sure," Colton replied, and grabbed the folder containing the pictures of the coins.

Chapter 32

Roy's Stamps and Coins
Stoughton, Massachusetts

Colton and Barnes arrived at Roy's Stamps and Coins.

A bell above the door jingled as they walked in. A strange but sweet smell hung in the air.

"Can I help you?" asked a man from behind the counter. He looked about fifty years old and had on a navy-blue shirt and wore wire-rim glasses. He had his salt and pepper colored hair combed back with some kind of hair gel.

"Are you Roy?" Colton asked. He flashed his badge and introduced himself and Barnes.

"Yes, I'm he," Roy said. "Welcome back, Detective. My son Ben told me you stopped by the other day. No one has brought in any coins."

"Thank you for keeping an eye out," Colton said.

"Anything to assist law enforcement," Roy said. "My brother is a cop down in Connecticut."

"Oh yeah," Barnes said. "What part?"

"Windsor Locks," Roy said.

"Beautiful down there," Barnes said.

"Do you know it?" Roy asked.

"I do," Barnes said. "My cousin lives there."

"Small world," Roy said. "I wonder if they know each other?"

"Possibly," Barnes said.

Colton placed his briefcase on the glass case.

"Do you have a minute?" Colton asked. "Can I show you some photos?"

"Sure!" Roy said.

Colton pulled out a stack of photos and laid them out on the glass.

"Oh, my!" Roy said, picking up a photo. "Where did you find this?"

"It's part of an ongoing investigation," Barnes said.

"I assume you know what that is?" Colton asked.

"Yes, I do," Roy said, picking up a magnifying glass and examining the photo. "This is a rare find. It appears to be an original. I'd need to see the actual medallion though to confirm it's not a knockoff. There are lots of fakes out there."

"What is it?" Colton asked.

One side has a tree depicted on it with the words, *Liberty Tree*, beneath it. The other side is of an arm holding a pole surmounted with a cap of Liberty with the words, *Sons of Liberty*, beneath it.

"This is a Sons of Liberty medallion."

"Okay," Barnes said. "What does that mean?"

"This has huge historical importance to the formation of our country," Roy said.

"How so?" Barnes asked.

"Have you ever heard of the Boston Sons of Liberty?" Roy asked.

"No," Barnes said. "But something tells me my partner here has."

"I have," Colton said, looking at Barnes. He then looked at Roy. "Go on."

"Sam Adams founded the group," Roy said. "Each member wore one of these medallions. It's how they identified other members of the group."

"Like colors used by gangs today?" Barnes said.

"Exactly. But my knowledge of its history is limited," Roy said. "But Stan over at the Stoughton Historical Society should know. He loves talking about history."

Colton showed Roy pictures of the coins removed from Larry Fuller's stomach.

"How about these?" Colton asked. "Do you know anything about them?"

Roy studied the photos for a minute.

"You don't, by chance, have one on you, do you?" Roy asked.

Colton removed a plastic evidence bag from his inside coat pocket.

"What kind of coin is it?" Colton asked, placing it on the glass.

"They're 1776 Continental coins," Roy said.

"What are they worth?" Barnes asked.

"Well, there are several kinds," Roy said. "Some were made of pewter. Some brass. And some silver. They can range in price from ten thousand dollars to over a million. Like the medallion, there's a bunch of knockoffs."

"A million dollars!" Barnes said. "Imagine that."

Roy walked over to his desk and grabbed his coin magnifier.

He brought it back and held it over the coin and bent over.

He studied it for a moment.

"Can you turn it over, please?" Roy asked.

Colton flipped it over.

Roy looked at it.

"Are they all like this?" Roy asked.

"Exactly," Colton said.

"Where did you find these?" Roy asked.

"You don't wanna know," Colton said.

Barnes chuckled.

"Is it real?" Colton asked.

"Oh, yeah!" Roy said. "It's real alright."

"What's it worth?" Barnes asked.

"Just curious," Roy said. "How many coins do you have?"

"Forty-seven," Colton said.

The color exited Roy's face. He staggered and took a step back.

"What?" Barnes said.

"If they're all like this one," Roy said. "Then you have close to fifty million dollars' worth of coins."

"No shit," Barnes said.

"No shit, Detective," Roy said.

Colton put the coin back in his pocket and collected the photos.

"Thank you for your help, Roy," Colton said.

Then they left.

Chapter 33

62 Ledgebrook Ave
Stoughton, Massachusetts

Colton and Barnes walked through Fuller's house again.

They stood downstairs in the room where Fuller's body was located.

"What are we missing?" Colton asked, looking around the room.

"You mean why our killer made Fuller eat forty-seven million dollars' worth of coins?" Barnes said.

"Yes," Colton said. "That changes things."

"Ya think!" Barnes said.

"Is it possible this has nothing to do with the foreclosure scheme?" Colton asked.

"Foreclosure scheme seems more plausible," Barnes said. "Plus, it connects Fuller to McDonald."

"Does it? How?" Colton asked. "Or are you just interpreting it that way?"

"We know for a fact that Fuller was running a foreclosure scheme," Barnes said. "Then combine that with the bum seen standing over McDonald. It directly connects the two murders."

"I know they're connected," Colton said. "But technically, only through the symbols. We can't make any other connection between the two victims."

"Once we find that bum, Henry," Barnes said. "You'll see. They're connected."

"This case is so convoluted," Colton said. "Child porn, rare coins, foreclosure scheme, homeless bums. None of it makes sense, especially when combined with one another. It feels like white noise. Like it's supposed to distract us."

"I agree," Barnes said. "In all my years as a State Police Homicide detective, I've never worked such complex cases."

"Let's review what we know," Colton said. "Fuller was watching child porn and about to pleasure himself when the killer entered."

"Right," Barnes said.

"What if the killer didn't know?" Colton said. "Didn't know the coin's value. What if he was so disgusted by what he found Fuller doing that he made him eat the coins?"

"That's a possibility," Barnes said. "Then it's not about the coins... It's about the foreclosure scheme."

"Or is it about the child porn?" Colton asked.

"Maybe the killer knew their value," Barnes said. "And that's why he made Fuller eat them."

"We need to learn more about Fuller," Colton said. "Any word from your friend Trish over at the Forensic Team? Were they able to get into Fuller's phone?"

"Let me call," Barnes said.

Barnes took out his phone and placed the call.

Colton walked around the crime scene. He tilted his head and looked at things from different angles. Then he squatted down to get a different point of view.

After a moment, Colton stood and walked upstairs. A minute later, he came back down.

Barnes hung up.

"Trish said they weren't able to get into Fuller's phone. They couldn't get past the facial recognition," Barnes said.

"We can swing by the forensic lab and grab the phone," Colton said. "Then head over to the Medical Examiner's office. See if we can't unlock it using Fuller's face."

"Good idea," Barnes said. "Guess what else Trish said?"

"They didn't find any child porn on Fuller's computer except the website we saw," Colton said.

"How did you know that?" Barnes asked.

"Because Fuller took off his clothes in the second-floor bedroom," Colton said.

"So?" Barnes asked.

"Most people don't strip naked on the second floor. Then go down to the basement and jerk off," Colton said. "The killer made him undress upstairs. Then he entered the child porn site onto Fuller's laptop."

"Holy shit!" Barnes said. "He's deliberately trying to throw us off."

"Exactly," Colton said. "Hence the white noise."

"But why?" Barnes asked.

"He wanted to mold our perception of Fuller," Colton said. "Wanted us to perceive him in a different light. To see him as a predator."

Chapter 34

Nancy and Paul Baker's House
Stoughton, Massachusetts

After they left Fuller's house, they returned to the station.

"Any good restaurants around here?" Barnes asked.

"Do you like steak?" Colton asked.

"Love it," Barnes said.

Colton picked up the phone and made a quick call. He hung up and invited Barnes to his mother's house for dinner.

Barnes put his hand up, not wanting to impose.

"My mom's a phenomenal cook. I bet you haven't had a better steak," Colton said. "Plus, she's a social butterfly and would love the company."

Barnes agreed.

"But I have to warn you," Colton said. "My dad has dementia."

"My dad had it too, before he passed," Barnes said. "I understand."

"You'll be a welcome distraction for her," Colton said.

"Let's go," Barnes said.

They arrived at Nancy and Paul's five minutes later.

When they walked in, the smell hit Barnes. His face lit up. "My God!" he said.

Nancy smiled.

"If you think it smells good, wait until you taste it," Colton said.

Hayley and Roxy came running into the kitchen to meet them.

Colton gave the girls some love and introduced Barnes to his mother.

"This is Detective Steve Barnes," Colton said. "He works for the State Police."

"Nice to meet you, ma'am," Barnes said.

"It's a pleasure to meet you, Detective," Nancy said.

"Wanna beer?" Colton asked.

"I'd love one," Barnes replied.

Colton pulled two cold bottles from the fridge.

Nancy stood scooping french fries from the FryDaddy. She looked over her shoulder at Barnes. "How long have you been a cop?"

Barnes leaned against the kitchen counter and took a sip of his beer. "Twenty-two years."

"I bet you've seen a thing or two," Nancy said.

"You can say that," Barnes said.

Colton slipped into the living room to say hello to his dad.

Nancy flipped the steaks and added a little more seasoning. She put the fork down and turned toward Barnes. "So ... how's he doing? I know he was nervous about the promotion. But Jesus ... two murders in a row?"

"Your son has a good head on his shoulders," Barnes said. "He's a natural. One of the best I've ever worked with."

"Really? Thank you," Nancy said. "He's always been so smart. But sometimes he doubts himself."

"Doesn't everyone?" Barnes said.

"Touche!" Nancy said. She turned and shut the stove off.

Colton walked back into the kitchen.

"Wash up," Nancy said. "Dinner is ready. Help yourself."

She plated her husband's dinner and brought it out to him.

Nancy engaged in conversation with Barnes throughout dinner. He kept telling her how delicious he thought the steak was. He must have liked it, because he had thirds and cleaned his plate.

"Coffee?" Nancy asked.

"Yes, please," Barnes replied.

Nancy was mid-pour when Barnes' cell phone rang. He excused himself to the other room and returned a minute later.

"That was Trish," Barnes said. "She said they found a ledger detailing all of Larry's coins. Said there was just over two hundred million dollars' worth of coins listed."

"Two hundred million," Colton said. "We only found forty-seven million. Where's the other one hundred fifty plus million?"

"Great question," Barnes said. "We'll have to go back to Larry's house and check the bank."

Chapter 35

Romano Sand & Gravel
Stoughton, Massachusetts

Gino Romano got into his red pickup truck and left his house. He arrived at the sand and gravel pit a few minutes later. He had a meeting scheduled with his son, Nino, and his friend and business partner, Frank.

Gino pulled up to the front of the trailer and parked next to Nino's dump truck. As he stepped out, Frank pulled in next to him.

They exchanged pleasantries and walked in together.

Nino sat inside on an old brown couch. It looked old. Like it was from the 1970s. He sat eating a bowl of cornflakes.

Gino took a seat behind his desk, and Frank stood in the middle of the trailer.

"Where are we at with the Route 24 resurfacing project? Did you talk with our friend?" Gino asked, looking at Nino.

"Yes, Pop," Nino said. "I paid the guy a visit yesterday. Problem resolved."

"What was the issue?" Gino asked.

"The guy said he has college tuition due soon for his kid. Said he was hoping to get a little extra by having a bidding war."

"What did you tell him?" Gino asked.

"I told him if we didn't get the bid, he wouldn't have a kid to send to college," Nino said.

"Jesus!" Frank said.

"Did you hear from this guy, Frank?" Gino asked.

"Oh, yeah!" Frank said. "Received the call last night. He told me we won the bid. Kept asking me to pass it along to the big guy who had shown up."

"Perfect!" Gino said. "When does the project start?"

"Next month," Frank said.

"Put Rourke on it," Gino said. "Tell him to start moving the equipment and get it into place."

"Don't forget," Frank said. "We need to go over on the daily hours. We promised the troopers they'd get their overtime."

"Tell Rourke eleven-hour days," Gino said. "He knows how to split up our guys' time so we're not shoveling out overtime. Let the Staties have it. We're not paying for it."

Outside, flashing blue lights caught Gino's eye. He stood up.

"What the fuck!"

Chapter 36

Romano Sand & Gravel
Stoughton, Massachusetts

Nine-One-One. What's your emergency?
Hi! There's a dead body at Romano Sand & Gravel.
How do you know they're dead?
Because it's covered with flies.
Where's the body located?
In the porta potty next to the trailer. Near the big excavator.
What's your name?
There was a click and the line went dead.

A white unmarked van sat across the street from Romano Sand and Gravel. Inside was a middle-aged man with salt and pepper hair. Next to him sat a young woman, early twenties, with olive skin and black hair.

"Here he comes," the young woman said.

A red pickup truck turned into Romano Sand & Gravel. A moment later, a silver BMW pulled in. Both parked next to a dump truck.

"We've been here for over a week. Any word yet?" she asked.

"Yeah. Braxton wants us to sit on the old man," the middle-aged man said.

"Really? Did you just hear what Nino said?"

"I did," the man said, putting his Dunkin' Donuts coffee cup on the dashboard.

"They bribed a state employee and threatened his family," she said.

"Did they?" he asked. "Or did Nino just say he did? We need the state employee to corroborate. Otherwise, the higher-ups are just gonna toss it."

The sound of approaching sirens filled the air. A moment later, a Stoughton Police cruiser appeared. Followed by another. Both cruisers turned into Romano Sand & Gravel.

More sirens filled the air.

A minute after, a fire truck and ambulance appeared and turned in.

"What the hell is going on?" he asked.

"The fire department's here. Probably a work-related injury," she said.

Another Stoughton cruiser appeared and pulled in.

"That's quite the response for an injured worker," he said.

Two minutes later, both the ambulance and fire truck pulled out.

Then two unmarked cruisers appeared and pulled in.

"That second cruiser is an unmarked State Trooper," he said.

"Do you think the local and state cops have a wire up?" she asked. "Think they heard what we heard?"

"We better get over there and find out," he said.

They exited the van. Both put on their blue windbreakers. The ones like you'd see on TV with the big three golden letters on the back.

FBI.

Chapter 37

**Romano Sand & Gravel
Stoughton, Massachusetts**

The two FBI agents crossed the street and entered the sand and gravel pit.

A patrolman who was rolling out crime scene tape spotted the two agents approaching. He used his radio and called Colton.

"897 to D-One," the officer said into the mic.

"D-One," Colton responded.

"Detective, are you expecting the Feds?"

"No," Colton said.

"Well, there's two of them approaching on foot. And they don't look happy."

Colton turned to Barnes. "Did you call the Feds?"

"Hell no!" Barnes said.

Colton responded to the patrolman. "I'll be right there."

Colton and Barnes made their way out front.

As they approached, the middle-aged man, and the young woman pulled out their credentials.

"I'm Special Agent Wolf of the FBI," the middle-aged man said. "And this is Agent Diaz."

"How can I help you?" Colton said.

"First of all. You can tell me what you're doing on my stakeout scene?" Special Agent Wolf demanded.

Before Colton could answer, Special Agent Wolf went on a diatribe. "Your career is over, detective. Why would you interfere with a federal case? Do you think you can just swoop in and steal our case? Are you stupid or something? You'll be lucky if you get hired as a security guard after this!"

Colton looked at Barnes who looked just as surprised.

"Well, I have to compliment you on the great job you're doing," Colton said sarcastically. "Letting a homicide take place right under your nose. Great surveillance!"

"What are you talking about?" Agent Wolf asked angrily.

"We got a call for a dead body," Colton said.

"Are you serious?" Agent Wolf asked.

"No," Colton said. "We figured we'd send the whole department down here just to blow your investigation."

"I don't like your tone, detective," Special Agent Wolf said.

"Really?" Colton said. "Well, this is my third body in as many days. And they all seem to be connected."

Both FBI agents looked at each other.

"Mind if I look?" Agent Diaz asked.

"By all means," Colton said. "Just don't disturb anything."

Barnes handed her a pair of gloves.

"Over there," Barnes said. "In the shitter."

Agent Diaz put the gloves on and walked over to the Porta Potty.

She opened the door and looked inside. She turned around and covered her mouth. Her face was green.

After a minute, she composed herself. She used her foot to hold the spring-loaded door open. Then she leaned in and examined the body.

Inside was a white male, late fifties, balding and shirtless, sitting on the toilet. His pants were around his ankles. The man's body slumped over to one side. His head and shoulder leaned up against the wall. A red-like rash covered the man's upper torso. It appeared the killer used sandpaper on him. His lips were split open and swollen. Dried blood covered his mouth and chin. Medallions covered each eye.

The same rash was on his forehead. Except it wasn't everywhere. It was precise. It was the killer's calling card. More strange symbols.

Once done, Diaz stepped out and let the door swing closed.

She removed her gloves and then bent over, sucking in big breaths of air. She used the sleeve of her coat to wipe the sweat from her brow.

Once composed, she stood up and adjusted herself.

She walked over to Colton and Barnes.

"My God!" Agent Diaz said. "It looks like someone used sandpaper on his skin."

"I'm thinking sandblaster," Colton said.

"Have all your bodies had those strange markings?" Diaz asked.

"Yes," Colton said. "The first victim had them tattooed on his forehead. The second victim had them carved into his forehead with an Exacto blade."

"And these appear rubbed on," Diaz said.

"Exactly," Barnes said.

"Do you know what these markings mean?" Diaz asked.

"No," Colton said. "A quick Google search indicates they're all just common symbols. We've found nothing tying them together, except they're left on each of the victims while still alive."

"So, torture?" Diaz said.

"That's what the Medical Examiner thinks," Colton said.

"Well, obviously," Special Agent Wolf said. "It's the work of some sick and deranged individual."

"Why dump the body here?" Diaz asked.

"Probably because it's secluded and just off the highway," Special Agent Wolf said.

"Doubt it," Colton said, pulling a piece of gum from his pocket.

"Wanna enlighten us, Detective?" Special Agent Wolf said.

"Because he dumped his first victim in broad daylight over at the train station at six in the morning."

"And the second?" Diaz asked.

"Inside the victim's home," Colton said.

"What makes you think it's a man?" Diaz asked.

"I'm sorry?" Colton said, questioning the question.

"You said, *His* first victim. What makes you think it's a man?"

"Based upon the size of the victims. The brutality. And the ability to dump them with speed suggests it's a male."

"What if it's two women?" Diaz asked.

"Well, that would be something, Agent Diaz. Since most serial killers work alone," Barnes said.

"What I want to know," Colton said. "How'd this body get dumped right under your nose?"

"I don't like your tone, Detective," Special Agent Wolf said.

"Oh, it's my tone, again," Colton said. "Here I thought it was the question."

Chapter 38

Romano Sand & Gravel
Stoughton, Massachusetts

They all stood looking out the window.

Two cruisers pulled in, followed by the Fire Department.

"Did one of our workers get hurt?" Gino asked.

"I don't know, Pop," Nino said. He picked up the radio sitting on the table. He tested the volume. "If someone got hurt, they never called it in."

"Go find out," Gino said.

Nino walked over to the door, opened it, and stepped out.

A moment later, he returned.

"What's going on?" Gino asked.

"There's a dead guy in the Porta Potty," Nino said.

"One of our guys?" Gino asked.

"No," Nino said. "It didn't look like one of our guys."

"Some junkie musta used the porta potty to shoot up," Gino said. "Probably overdosed."

"But who called it in?" Nino asked. "No one told us."

Frank started pacing the trailer.

"What is it, Frank?" Gino asked.

Frank stopped.

"It's not the…" Frank said, but Nino cut him off.

"No!" Nino said. "I didn't touch a hair on his or his kid's head. Plus, he called you after I visited him."

"Thank God!" Frank said.

"Do you actually think I'm stupid enough to drop a body in our backyard? Literally," Nino said.

Gino stood in front of the window.

"Great," Gino said. "More cruisers."

"Are you serious, Pop?" Nino said.

Both Frank and Nino walked over to the window.

Nino looked out the window.

The two unmarked cruisers pulled up and parked in front of the trailer.

"The whole fucking police station is out there."

"I know," Gino said.

Colton and Barnes stepped out of their cruisers.

"Hey! Isn't that Baker boy?" Nino said, pointing out the window at Colton.

"Yeah," Frank said. "That's him."

The three of them stood watching out the window as a uniformed officer cordoned off the area with yellow crime scene tape.

"Frank," Gino said. "Should you go out and say something?"

"Like what?" Frank said.

"Like, find out what's going on. You are their boss after all," Nino said and sat down on the couch.

"True," Frank said.

"Just go find out," Gino said.

Frank took a step toward the door and stopped.

"Oh, shit!" Frank said.

"What?" Nino asked.

"The FBI is here!" Frank said.

"You're lying," Nino said.

"Fuck!" Gino said, looking out the window.

"What is it, Pop?" Nino asked.

Gino stood next to Frank, looking out the window.

"Did you see them?" Frank said, stepping further into the trailer. "Did you, Gino?"

"Yes, Frank," Gino said. "I see them."

"I tried warning you!" Frank said. "But you just wouldn't listen."

"Calm down, Frank," Nino said.

"Calm down!" Frank said. "The FBI is standing right outside and you want me to calm down? What if they bugged this place? We're fucked!"

Nino looked over at his Dad.

Gino grabbed a pen and paper from his desk.
He wrote something down. Then held it up.
There were two words in big capital letters.
DON'T SPEAK!
Suddenly, there was a knock on the door.

Chapter 39

Romano Sand & Gravel
Stoughton, Massachusetts

Colton and Barnes stood at the bottom of the steps for the trailer.

The door opened.

Nino Romano stood there, stoic. He tensed his body, flexing his muscles. "Can I help you?"

"I'm Detective Baker and this is Detective Barnes," Colton said.

"Yeah, we've met," Nino said, looking at Colton.

"Did you know there's a dead guy in your Porta Potty?" Barnes asked.

"Nope, but thanks for letting us know," Nino said.

"Do you know who it is?" Barnes asked.

"Maybe ... an associate?" Colton asked.

"Sorry," Nino said. "Don't know, doughboy."

Barnes looked at Colton. Then back at Nino.

"Ah, I get it," Barnes said. "A play on words. It's a baker's joke."

"Impressive," Colton said. "He tells kindergarten jokes. Explains why he's still playing in the sandbox." Barnes laughed.

"I see what he did there," Barnes said, looking at Nino.

"Did you get it? Because your Daddy owns a sand pit."

Nino's face grew red, and a big vein bulged in his neck.

"Gino, go deal with that," Frank said, ushering Gino toward the door. "Before they start throwing punches."

"Can I help you?" Gino asked, stepping in front of Nino.

"Bye, Popeye," Colton said. "It's time for the adults to talk."

Barnes had to control his laughter.

Nino walked over to the table inside the trailer. He grabbed the back of the plastic chair and gripped it tight. Nino's face was burning red and his muscles tightened. The chair couldn't withstand the intense pressure being applied, and it started to crack and splinter.

Frank watched Nino practically destroy the chair. "Calm down," Frank said. "They're gonna want to come in here and snoop around. Don't want them thinking that chair was used to kill the dead guy out there."

Nino cooled his jets and sat down.

"Good," Frank said. "Stay calm. Give them no reason to think we're involved in the death of that person out there."

"What?" Nino said. "I thought you said they overdosed?"

Frank looked at Nino. "I didn't say that. Your Dad did."

"You think they'll want to come in here?" Nino asked.

"I'm willing to bet bottom dollar," Frank said. "And knowing your Dad, he'll probably invite them in."

Frank was correct. Gino invited them inside. "Feel free to look around, detectives."

Colton and Barnes did just that.

The two FBI agents took advantage of the situation and poked their heads in.

Colton walked around. The trailer was smaller than he thought. Inside was a desk and a table with chairs. No sandblaster or anything suspicious. Colton was positive that the murder didn't take place here.

Colton and Barnes left and met back in front of the Porta Potty. They waited for Trish and the State Police forensic team to arrive. After the crime scene was processed, the Medical Examiner took the body away.

Barnes asked Trish and her team to process the trailer. Gino had granted them permission. Before Trish entered the trailer, Special Agent Wolf pulled Barnes aside and asked to speak with him. After, Barnes spoke to Trish again.

The forensic team entered the trailer and exited a few minutes later. It was the fastest processing of a scene Colton had ever seen. Something was up, he was sure of it.

Chapter 40

Stoughton Police Headquarters
Stoughton, Massachusetts

Colton pulled up to the intersection of Pleasant and Park Streets and stopped at the red light. He took a sip of his soda.

Two black SUVs with tinted windows passed in front of him. He didn't notice if there were red and blue lights tucked into the grill.

But most likely they were Feds.

The light turned green.

Colton turned right. He pulled up behind the SUVs. FBI agents out in the field don't use government license plates. They use civilian plates, same as Colton's own unmarked cruiser.

He ran the plate.

It came back *No Matching Record.*

Just as he suspected.

Feds.

After the run-in this morning, they were probably heading to the station to meet the Chief. Colton radioed dispatch and put his location over the air. Told them to expect company. He wanted to provide the Chief with a heads up. Hopefully, she was listening.

The three vehicles rolled through the center of town. They turned right onto Rose Street.

The two black SUVs slowed and pulled up in front of the police station. Colton turned into the detective's parking lot just before the building.

He grabbed his keys and soda and got out. Colton used his magnetic keycard to gain access to the south side of the building. He was standing in the Chief's office before the FBI agents even cleared the front door.

"Feds are here," Colton said, walking into the Chief's office.

McCormack adjusted her uniform and fixed her hair.

"Thanks for the heads up," McCormack said.

The phone on her desk rang. She answered it and then hung up.

"They're at the front desk," McCormack said.

McCormack led Colton out into the hallway and closed her office door.

Together, they walked down to dispatch.

Two FBI agents wearing suits stood in the lobby outside the dispatch office. Both stood with their shoulders back, displaying confidence.

McCormack invited them inside.

Once inside, Special Agent Wolf introduced himself, along with Agent Diaz.

Chief McCormack introduced herself and said, "I believe you know Detective Baker."

"Yes, we've met," Wolf said. There was a distinct, disdained tone in his voice.

"I guess you're here regarding the body found this morning?" Chief McCormack asked.

"Yes," Wolf said.

"Great," Colton said. "Here to fuck up our investigation, you mean?"

Wolf took a step closer to Colton.

They were almost standing nose to nose.

"Listen, son," Wolf said. "You're lucky we're not taking over this entire thing."

"On what grounds?" Colton asked. "And what were you doing at Romano Sand and Gravel, anyway?"

Wolf didn't answer. He just stared at Colton.

"Well?" Colton said.

Wolf continued to stare at him.

Colton stood there stoically. His eyes locked onto Wolf's. Neither one blinked.

After a moment, Wolf looked from Colton to the Chief. "Is there going to be a problem?"

"Yeah," Colton said. "I watch the news. The FBI can't seem to solve anything. But you're really good at political intimidation and persecution, though."

Wolf's cheeks turned bright red.

"There's no problem," McCormack said, stepping in between the two men. "None at all."

"I didn't think so," Wolf said.

McCormack turned around. The interaction had played out in front of the civilian dispatchers and other police officers. Worse was that District Attorney Harbor and Barnes had walked in.

"Detective Baker, can I see you in my office, please?" McCormack said.

By the tone, it wasn't a question, but an order.

McCormack then looked at Harbor. She nodded her head, indicating for him and Barnes to follow.

Colton led the way down to the Chief's office.

McCormack opened the door and held it open for them. Once through, she stepped in and closed it.

"Colton," Chief McCormack said. "We have three bodies. All with the same strange symbols. You had to expect a visit from the FBI."

"Except the latest body was dumped right under their nose," Colton said. "And what exactly is it they're investigating?"

"It's no secret the Romano's are part of the mob," McCormack said. "They're most likely investigating them. That's my guess, anyway."

"I agree," Harbor said.

"This is our town," Colton said. "It's our investigation."

"I agree with that, too," Harbor said.

"Colton wasn't wrong in what he said," Barnes said.

"I know," McCormack said. "I don't like the fact that it took place in my house. Right in front of me."

Harbor looked at Colton.

"You've got brass balls, kid," Harbor said. "I'll give you that."

Barnes chuckled.

"What do we do now?" Colton asked.

"We talk to them," Harbor said.

"And what happens if they want to take over the investigation?" Colton asked.

"There's nothing we can do. Our hands are tied," McCormack said. "We can't just tell the FBI to back off. It doesn't work that way."

Chapter 41

Stoughton Police Headquarters
Stoughton, Massachusetts

Colton and Barnes returned to Colton's office.

Special Agent Wolf wanted to officially notify the Chief that the FBI was working on a case in town which overlapped the homicide investigation. He wouldn't say exactly what they were working on. But then again, the feds weren't known for laying their cards out on the table.

Wolf told the Chief and Harbor that they were requesting to be kept in the loop regarding the homicide investigation. He also said they'd like to attend all press conferences as well.

McCormack had looked at Harbor, who nodded. "But we ask that you inform us if you find anything out about our homicide," McCormack had said.

Wolf agreed, and then left.

"This shit keeps getting weirder and weirder," Barnes said, taking a seat.

"Tell me about it," Colton said.

"We have no clue who the guy in the porta potty is," Barnes said. "And neither do the Romanos. Which I find hard to believe."

"None," Colton said. "He had no ID on him."

"Watch," Barnes said. "The killer probably threw the guy's wallet into the shitter."

"That's just gross," Colton said. "Thankfully, he didn't stuff the body in there."

"Hopefully forensics can identify him through fingerprints or dental records," Barnes said.

"I'll check missing persons," Colton said. "See if our victim matches any missing reports."

Colton ran a check. There was no one missing that matched the victim's age or description.

"Why does this feel like one of those books that when you reach a certain point, it has you choose which path to follow?" Colton said.

"I remember those books," Barnes said. "I always chose wrong and had to start over."

"That's what we should do," Colton said. "Start over and ignore the stuff we know is false. Just like in the books."

"Can't hurt," Barnes said.

"Let's start with the symbols," Colton said. He flipped open the Medical Examiner's report on the first victim. He pulled out the picture of the symbols tattooed on Bill McDonald's forehead.

He went and placed the photo on the whiteboard. Colton then made some index cards with McDonald's age, occupation, how he died, and other pertinent information.

Next, he went through Larry Fuller's folder and pulled out the picture of the symbols carved into his forehead.

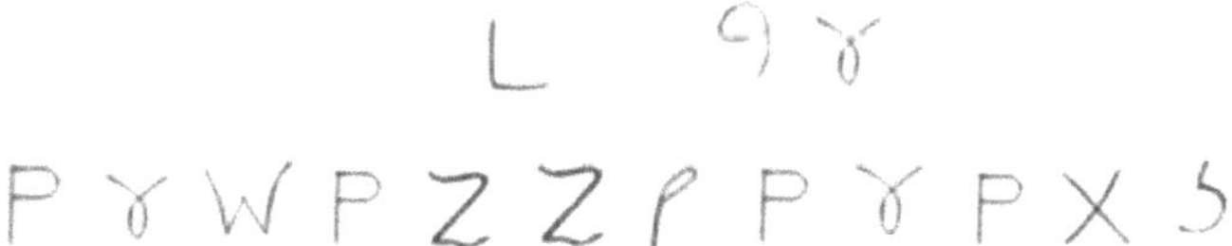

He made an index card for Larry and placed it and the picture on the whiteboard next to McDonald.

While Colton did that, Barnes used his cell phone to research the symbols on the internet. After a few minutes, Barnes became visibly frustrated.

"I hate technology!" Barnes said. "I can't find a damn thing on these symbols. Shit, most of them are on the damn keyboard!"

Colton couldn't help but laugh. He thought the same thing, except for a few of the markings. *If we only knew the cypher, we could decipher what the killer is saying.*

Chapter 42

Stoughton Police Headquarters
Stoughton, Massachusetts

David Monteiro arrived at Stoughton Police Headquarters. There was a buzz in the air. Reporters swarmed about. The press briefing was about to begin. Earlier, David had tuned into several of the different media channels' reports. Their coverage was all the same. They kept regurgitating what the police chief and district attorney said in the prior two briefs. None of the news outlets were digging into the story. It seemed they were just waiting for the info to be dished out to them. No one was conducting any actual investigational journalism. If Laynie were here, she'd be tearing into these murders. After all, her expertise was covering serial killers and homicides.

David often wondered where she got that from because he always hated covering homicides. Thankfully, back in his day, he didn't cover many. The few they had were murder suicides or crimes of passion. The police solved them that day.

Now it seemed murders nationwide were still going unsolved. With advanced technology, how were crimes going unsolved?

McCormack, Harbor, Colton, and Barnes came out, followed by two people in suits. An older man and a younger woman. Both stood off to the left.

David did a double take. He recognized the older man in the suit. He was an FBI agent. David searched his memory, trying to remember the man's name. It was coming back to him. 9/11 popped into his head. David thought back to that time. There'd never been a news story like that before. Not in his lifetime, anyway. It was hard to forget the horror that the world witnessed that day.

Slowly, a memory came crawling back to him.

Security concerns popped into his head. Security was tight after 9/11, especially in Massachusetts. Two planes departed from Logan airport in Boston that day. Both hit the World Trade Center buildings.

In the weeks following came the anthrax attacks on senators and the news media. Local police and fire had their hands full responding to perceived anthrax scares. Thankfully, the local cases were just scares. It was during that time that David met FBI Agent Wolf. David had done a story on the scares and requested to interview an FBI agent to get a perspective on the federal government's response to the incidents. David remembered walking away impressed with Wolf. Wolf was very competent and highly motivated. Plus, Wolf was the first and only FBI agent David had ever met.

That same man that David had interviewed all those years ago now stood to the left of the podium. Wolf had aged some. His hair was now gray, but that face was undeniable. It was Agent Wolf.

David couldn't believe it. This was the third murder in as many days. And now the FBI was involved. He needed to tell Laynie.

He turned off his antiquated recorder and pulled out his phone. He filmed the press conference and captured the two FBI agents.

Chief McCormack stepped to the podium, followed by District Attorney Harbor. Both gave brief statements. They didn't mention the FBI agents, nor did they answer questions.

Once the briefing concluded, David made a brief commentary and stopped filming.

He opened his text messaging app and began typing.

Hey Laynie! You're not gonna believe this. There's been another murder! The press conference just ended. And guess what? The FBI is here. I even know one of the agents. His name is Wolf. I met him years ago while covering a story on the anthrax scares right after 9/11. Anyway, the agents didn't speak, which is odd. Why bring them out? This smells of a coverup! I'll send you the video I took. Wish you were here! Love you!

David hit send.
Then he sent Laynie the video.

Chapter 43

Washington Dulles International Airport
Fairfax County, Virginia

Laynie sat at the Dulles International Airport terminal waiting for her flight. She bought her ticket and breezed through security, which rarely happens. She sat slouched in one of the hard, uncomfortable plastic chairs. The ones sat on by thousands of travelers per day.

An hour ago, she had received a text and video from her father. Two FBI agents were in her hometown at a press conference for a third murder victim. She pulled out her phone and watched the video again. She couldn't believe what was happening back home.

Laynie grew up in Stoughton, born and raised. She had spent most of her childhood at the Stoughton Times, which her parents owned. She was there every day after school with her mom and dad. They'd bring her with them on interviews and follow-ups for quotes on stories they were working on. She'd accompanied them as they covered events around town. She'd talk to local business owners who came in to run ads and people looking to list their upcoming events.

On Saturday mornings, she went in early with her father. He'd set the plates on the press while Laynie helped fill the ink. Soon the press was humming and cranking out paper after paper. She loved that sound. It was incredible to see the stories her parents worked on in black and white.

As she got older, David allowed Laynie to write her own column. They called it Laynie's Corner. She went out and conducted interviews, tracked down leads, and wrote her own stories. Laynie felt like part of the community.

At the start of her junior year, Laynie's mother told her she was divorcing her father and moving to California. Her mother wanted her to come with her, but Laynie's whole life was in Stoughton. She wanted to graduate with her friends and work at her father's newspaper. Her mother told her the paper was a dying business. Laynie was young and didn't understand what that meant. As any child would, she perceived it as an attack on her father. Plus, there was no way Laynie was leaving her avó (Portuguese for grandmother). Her avó was a loving woman who loved her family and loved to cook. If you came to her house, you ate. No one was ever hungry under her roof. She had been a pillar in the Stoughton Portuguese community.

Shortly after her parents divorced, her mother relocated to Los Angeles for work. Then the unthinkable happened. Her avó became sick. Within a month, she was gone. Her passing crushed Laynie. She'd lost the two strongest women in her life.

Laynie decided she needed a change of pace. She applied to the University of Southern California journalism program. She received her acceptance letter that spring. After she graduated from high school, Laynie moved to California to live with her mother while she attended college.

During her junior year of college, Laynie got a part-time gig at NBC Los Angeles. It didn't take long for her bosses to notice her knack for a story and her relentless pursuit of it. She chased down every lead. No matter what, she always uncovered a story. She had a knack for it. Laynie didn't care what the story was, she wanted to tell it. But, even more, she cared about telling the truth. People connected with the truth. They knew when they were being fed a line of bullshit. Laynie's stories never had a whiff of stink on them.

Laynie loved being a reporter like her dad, except she didn't want to use a pencil to tell her story. She wanted to use a microphone and camera. The truth came naturally, and the camera loved her. It was easy to see.

Once she graduated college, Laynie worked full-time at NBC Los Angeles.

In March 2014, Laynie covered the death of a prostitute. She became fascinated with the case. It was a surprise when the police discovered there were two killers. The pair had killed three women in late 2013 and another in February 2014. The police captured both suspects in April 2014. Laynie dug deep into both killers' past. They had previous arrests and convictions for kidnapping, and lewd and lascivious acts on a child. She followed and reported on the case through the trial. One killer accepted a plea deal, and the court sentenced him to life without parole. The other pleaded innocent, but a jury found him guilty and sentenced him to death.

Laynie loved covering the case, and her coverage impressed her bosses. They assigned her to cover homicides across Los Angeles. She crushed it. Laynie dug into the stories and came up with info the police hadn't. She made connections that were missed. Most detectives despised her. A handful respected her. Some even met with her. They listened to what she'd found. Sometimes her info panned out, which helped build her credibility.

People become enthralled with serial killers and the media knows it. When there's a serial killer story, it dominates the news cycle. Her tenacity and drive to find the truth, no matter where it went, led to her covering serial killers across the country.

Over the years, Laynie covered sixteen serial killers who were all captured and convicted. She still reports on the Little Rock serial stabbings, which claimed the lives of three people. To this day, the police have made no arrests. The case remains unsolved.

Laynie ended each assignment with a saying. *I'm not here to judge. I'm here to tell the truth. You judge for yourself if they're guilty or not.*

Laynie adjusted in her seat. If the story back home didn't pan out, at least she could turn the trip into a family reunion. She opened her laptop and brought up Facebook. She scrolled through photos on her family's social media pages. It'd been a while since she'd been back. She'd returned several times over the years for graduations, weddings and the occasional funeral.

She missed the culture and especially the food. L.A. had a lot to offer, but she missed that small-town feeling, that sense of community. Having been so busy lately with work, it would be nice to see family, rest and relax, and enjoy some good ole Portuguese food. That would be worth the trip alone.

She continued to scroll through Facebook and explored some Stoughton pages. The town she grew up in seemed the same, but also different.

One thing she remembered was her father always driving slowly around Stoughton. He complained about cops being dirty. One of his favorite lines, he'd say when talking about the cops in Stoughton, *they'd pull over their own mother and write her a ticket.*

She recalled something about the police chief being fired over corruption and a coverup. There was even a town recall involved. She remembered the Stoughton Police were always in the news when she was a kid. But it was never for a good reason.

As a reporter for the Stoughton Times, her father covered the stories. Apparently, some cops didn't care that much for his coverage.

Laynie hoped things had changed. She did a quick Google search and found the current Stoughton Police Chief was a woman. Not only that, she was apparently cleaning house and weeding out the bad cops.

Her phone dinged, and she pulled it from her purse.

There was a new message from her cameraman, Dan.

Leaving NYC now. Meet you at Logan Express in Braintree. Safe travels.

Chapter 44

WTFH News Studio
Los Angeles, California

WTFH Senior Producer Hank Willis stood in the Los Angeles production booth running down a checklist before they went live. He wore a headset and pressed the talk button to speak directly with Steve, the cameraman on site at the national convention in Washington, D.C.

On the wall hung dozens of TV screens, each with a different location. Each one was a live feed taking place across the country. Several people were in the booth overseeing various news reports. They pushed buttons to queue up different segway pieces and footage.

"Are we ready to go?" Hank asked.

"No," came the response through his earpiece.

Hank looked up at the large screen and found Steve's location. "What seems to be the problem, Steve?"

"Laynie."

"What about her?" Hank asked.

"She's not here."

"What do you mean she's not there?" Hank snapped. "Where is she?"

"I saw her catch a cab about twenty minutes ago."

"A cab? Where?"

"I don't know."

"She didn't say where she was going?" Hank asked.

"Nope."

"You just watched her leave?"

"Hank, you have met Laynie, right?" Steve said. "She does whatever she wants and there's no stopping her."

"Yes, I've met her. She's my goddamn fiancée!" Hank shouted into the headset before ending the call.

Hank tilted his head back, took a deep breath and slowly exhaled before reaching into his pocket. He pulled out his cell phone and opened his *Favorites* list. Laynie's name sat at the top. He tapped her name and held the phone up to his ear.

It began to ring.

"Hello, Hank," Laynie said.

"Why aren't you at the convention?"

"Well, I love you too, Hank."

"Laynie, I'm not in the mood. Where are you?"

"I'm sitting in Dulles airport."

"Why are you at the airport?"

"A killer story dropped into my lap."

"Jesus, Laynie!"

"Literally."

"Where?"

"Boston. Well, Stoughton actually," Laynie said.

"Stoughton? Why does that sound so familiar?"

"It's my hometown."

"What the hell is going on there?"

"Hank, it's a serial killer."

Hank rustled through some papers containing the major stories off the national wire. "I'm not seeing anything about a serial killer on the wire."

There was a brief pause.

"Check your messages," Laynie said.

Hank pulled the phone away from his ear and looked at the screen. There was a new message from Laynie.

It was a video file.

Hank clicked on the video and began watching it. After a moment, he hit pause. He put the phone back up to his ear. "Okay, it's a press conference regarding the latest of several recent murders."

"Watch it until the end," Laynie said.

Hank continued watching the video.

"Jesus! Your dad shot this video?"

"Keep watching, Hank," Laynie said.

Hank watched until the end.

"Is your dad right? Are those two FBI agents?"

"Yes, Hank."

"Why didn't they speak?" Hank asked. "Hell, they didn't even get mentioned."

"I know. That's why my father sent it to me."

"The FBI is involved, and it's not on the wire?" Hank asked.

"That's exactly why I'm going, Hank. My father thinks this is a coverup."

"A coverup?" Hank said.

"He texted me and said he could use me on this one. Said something felt like a coverup. You know my dad's gut is always right."

"Laynie, you know I love your dad. He's who you get that Masshole (a sarcastic term of endearment that combines Massachusetts and asshole together) spitfire attitude of yours from, but you can't just jump on your own assignments and leave."

"This could be an exclusive, Hank."

"It doesn't matter, Laynie!"

"Well, Hank," Laynie said with an angry tone. "You know I'm an investigative journalist, yet you've stuck me in the political ring and won't let me dig in and do any investigating."

"You know why."

"Yes, I know. Because we're a chicken shit newsroom that's too afraid to dig up dirt on politicians in case they're friends with our bosses."

"Laynie, if you keep talking like this and the wrong people hear, you can kiss your career goodbye."

"I don't care who hears me! It's the truth. Maybe I should turn my investigational abilities on WTFH. How about that, Hank! It probably wouldn't take me long to discover who's banging whom and who the sexual perverts are on the board. Birds of a feather flock together and cover up for each other."

"Alright Laynie, you win."

"I knew you'd see it my way, Hank."

"Okay, Laynie. Do what you do best. Bring me the story."

"I will."

"I want daily progress reports," Hank said. "Understand?"

"Yes, Hank," she said. "But before you hang up … there is one thing."

"What?" he asked through a long breath.

"I need a cameraman."

"I'll send you Steve, since he doesn't have an assignment now, thanks to you."

"Well, I was thinking about Dan."

"Dan's already on an assignment."

"He's in Boston. I just spoke to him. He'll be in Stoughton by the time I arrive."

"And what about Steve?"

"Give him Dan's assignment. You know Steve and I don't get along."

There was a long pause.

"Fine," Hank said. "You better bring me an exclusive!"

"I will. Love you!"

"Love you too," Hank said and clicked off.

Chapter 45

Logan Express
Braintree, Massachusetts

Laynie's flight landed at Logan Airport. She made her way downstairs and through the terminal. When she reached the baggage claim, she took a left and exited outside. Signs led the way to the Logan Express bus stop. Every few minutes, a Logan Express bus approached. She watched closely, looking for the one bound for Braintree. Logan Express had several terminals on the North Shore and out west. Those not paying attention could find themselves heading in the wrong direction. Braintree was south of the city. The locals called it the South Shore.

Her bus arrived. She boarded but didn't have a ticket. Bus stops didn't sell tickets, only the terminals did. She sat in the back. Her seat was on the passenger side, next to a window. When they arrived at the terminal, those with tickets could exit. Those without would wait for the cashier. Once onboard, the passengers would purchase a ticket before exiting.

After a thirty-minute ride, the bus pulled into the terminal. When the bus came to a stop, she noticed Dan waiting for her. He stood next to a man holding a small metal container. The cashier. Dan smiled and waved. Laynie smiled and waved back. Dan pointed to Laynie and handed the cashier a ticket. The cashier motioned for to get off. She did.

Laynie and Dan hugged. It felt good to see each other.

Dan and Laynie went to journalism school together and hit it off on day one. They both loved what they were doing and were dedicated to their craft. Dan's family had died when he was young. Back in college, when Laynie found out Dan didn't have any family, she invited him to stay at her mother's in California during school breaks. When Laynie came to Massachusetts, Dan came along too.

David and Dan got along great. Years ago, David had expressed he hoped Laynie and Dan would get together. Unfortunately, that never happened. Dan eventually found a nice woman and married her. They have two kids and live in California.

Massachusetts traffic is brutal. The highways are worse. Laynie had Dan take back roads through Randolph and Canton over to Stoughton.

On the ride, Laynie filled Dan in on what she knew so far. She told him her father had expressed that a coverup was taking place because the FBI was involved.

"You know what that means," Dan said. "Serial killer."

"My thoughts exactly," Laynie said.

Ten minutes later, they entered Stoughton.

"What's this *Keep 911 Local* about?" Dan asked after passing the third yard sign.

"I don't know," Laynie said. "I'll have to ask my dad."

They arrived at David's house a few minutes later. He was standing on the front porch, waiting for them.

David gave Laynie a long, loving embrace. The joy was evident on his face.

David invited them in.

Laynie went to put her stuff in her childhood bedroom.

"I hope you don't mind the couch again," David said to Dan.

"I love this couch," Dan said. "I've been crashing on it since college."

Laynie came back out. "We're exhausted, Dad," she said. "We've been up all night."

"Get some sleep," David said. "I have some errands to run, anyway. We can catch up over dinner."

Chapter 46

Medical Examiner's Office
Boston, Massachusetts

Colton and Barnes pulled into the Medical Examiner's office parking lot.

"Is that your friend over there?" Barnes said, pointing to the black SUV with tinted windows.

"Is that them?" Colton asked. "What the hell are they doing here?"

Colton parked, and they stepped out. As soon as they did, Wolf and Diaz exited their vehicle.

"Guess you were right," Colton said. "Good eye."

Wolf and Diaz crossed the parking lot.

"Figured we'd join you this morning," Wolf said.

"If you're here, who's watching the Romanos?" Colton asked.

Wolf's face hardened, and he shot Colton a glare.

"Play nice, buddy," Barnes whispered to Colton.

"We want to find out who the victim is," Diaz said. "Like you said, the body was dumped on our stakeout."

Colton softened a little. He wasn't expecting honesty from a Fed.

"Well ... let's go find out who he was," Colton said.

Once inside, Colton introduced Dr. Hurst.

Wolf and Diaz introduced themselves.

"The FBI?" Hurst asked, raising his eyebrows.

"Colton here is trying to see how many boxes he can check off in his first week," Barnes said jokingly. "It took me years before I first worked with them."

"What can you tell us about the victim?" Colton asked Hurst.

A body lay covered on a steel examining table. Hurst walked over and picked up a file from the table.

"We ran the prints, and this is fifty-seven-year-old Alex Torres," Hurst said, and handed the folder to Colton.

"What kind of rash is that all over his body?" Diaz asked.

"A sandblaster," Hurst said. He drew back the sheet, exposing the man's head and upper torso. He pointed to the rash. "I found sand consistent with a sandblaster inside the wounds."

"How?" Diaz asked.

Hurst looked at Colton and Barnes, then at Diaz.

"By a sandblaster," Hurst said.

"I know that," Diaz said. "I mean how? Aren't sandblasters inside a box to protect the user? My dad used to work at an auto body shop when I was a kid. They had one there."

"They have portable sandblasters nowadays," Colton said. "You can even get them on Amazon."

"That must have been painful," Barnes said.

"Excruciating," Hurst said.

"The killer used it on one of the man's eyes,"

"What a sicko."

"Next, he used it on the mouth. It split the lips open and blasted right through the tongue. Finally, your killer stuck it inside the mouth. He held it there up against the back of the victim's throat until it ruptured a vein," Hurst said.

"Jesus!" Diaz said.

"The amount of blood that poured down his throat would have muffled his screams. The victim swallowed and inhaled the blood. We found a large quantity of sand in the victim's lungs and stomach."

"Is that the cause of death?" Colton asked.

"The official cause is a ruptured esophageal varices," Hurst said. "Your victim bled to death."

"One last thing," Hurst said. "Your killer tattooed another tiny **W** onto your vic's right thumb. Same as the last victim."

Chapter 47

David Monteiro's House
Stoughton, Massachusetts

Laynie slept like a baby. It felt great to be home. She went out into the kitchen. There she found her father sitting at the table talking to Dan.

"Hey, you're awake," David said.

Laynie smiled. It was nice to see her dad finally and not just read his texts or hear his voice over the phone.

"You guys hungry?" David asked.

Both Laynie and Dan said yes.

"TownSlice?" David asked.

"Dad, do you even need to ask?" Laynie said.

TownSlice or the "Slice" as it's known to the locals is a pizza joint that serves barroom pizza. A barroom pizza is an individual-sized pizza. They're a big thing on the South Shore of Massachusetts. TownSlice was a huge restaurant. One side is a bar and lounge. The other is sit down dining. Then, on the backside, there was a large takeout area. High school students getting their feet wet in the workforce mostly staffed this side.

People came from all around. They even had large floor-to-ceiling freezers with all kinds of frozen pizzas inside. Customers traveling through Stoughton would stop to order a pizza. They'd buy frozen ones too and toss them in a cooler. They'd eat the to go pizza they ordered on the ride home and heat up the frozen ones later. People even trekked from other states to eat a *Slice* pizza and bring the pizzas home.

Anytime you drove past the place, it was always packed. It was also one of the last places in town that was cash only. But they have multiple ATMs for those that don't have cash on them.

"I suppose you want your usual?" David asked.

"Bacon with buffalo chicken, crispy," Laynie replied.

Dan liked the traditional cheese pizza.

David ordered the pizzas and picked them up. They ate them with a few beers.

Over dinner, Dan asked about the *Keep 911 Local* signs around town.

"You saw those, huh?" David asked.

"What's that all about?" Laynie asked.

David explained that some town residents were upset. The county had built a brand-new dispatch center two towns over in Holbrook. The goal was to centralize the dispatch for all the surrounding towns.

"What's wrong with that?" Laynie asked.

"Some people are upset," David said. "They wanted it to go before the town so they could vote on it. Others are upset that the town will lose the federal stipend for not having both dispatchers under one roof in town."

"How was it approved then?" Dan asked.

"The town manager, he had the only say," David said. "People didn't like that. They feel that they should have a say in their own safety. After all, it's their tax dollars paying for it."

"That's understandable," Laynie said.

"Well," David said. "Some people believe the Town Manager was bribed and paid off. They fear their public safety was bought and paid for. To make matters worse, Avon, the town between Stoughton and Holbrook, voted it down. Unlike Stoughton, the citizens in Avon had a say."

"What can you tell us about the murder victims?" Laynie asked.

"I don't know all the details surrounding their deaths, but I can tell you what I know," David said. "The first two were both town employees."

"I thought the second victim was the CEO of a bank?" Laynie said.

"He was," David said. "But, years ago, he was a selectman and also the interim town manager. For a brief period."

Laynie sat there, staring off into space. Processing.

"Oh boy," David said. "I see your wheels turning."

After a minute, Laynie reached for another slice of pizza and took a bite. She washed it down with a swig of beer.

"Let me ask you this," Laynie said. "Do you think there's a connection between the murders and the 911 dispatch issue?"

David thought for a moment.

"To be honest," David said. "I never thought about it that way. I'm not sure I see how they're connected."

"You said people are upset." Laynie said. "Upset to the point they made signs and placed them around town."

"People are upset," David said. "For some, it's about the money, taxpayers' money. Especially since a few years back the town paid to upgrade the dispatch system."

"Where is the current dispatch located?" Laynie asked.

"It's inside the police station. Both the police and fire dispatch from that location. In fact, they sit side by side."

"Interesting," Laynie said.

"So, it basically boils down to money and votes," Dan said. "Or is there more to it?"

"It's more than that," David said. "We also have a shortage of dispatchers. The ones we have are constantly working overtime and are getting burned out."

"That's not good," Laynie said.

"I think the hope is that with a large dispatch center, they'll be enough dispatchers to cover," David said.

"What if there's a shortage there, too?" Laynie asked.

"There very well could be," David said. "But there was an incident that took place. It riled up a lot of people," David said.

"What's the incident?" Laynie asked.

"The way I heard it," David said. "A woman moved here from down south. She moved to escape her abusive husband. Apparently, her husband found out where she was staying. He somehow got inside the apartment and not only assaulted her but raped her as well."

"My god, that's horrible," Laynie said.

"I guess she had a young daughter with her, who went and hid when the father arrived. The little girl heard what was happening to her mother and called 911. Being a child and having just moved here, she didn't know the area. The dispatcher asked if she was near a window. She was. They asked her to look outside. She did. They asked her to describe what she saw. She told them she saw a set of traffic lights and a school. They asked her if she was in a large apartment complex, which the girl confirmed. Because the dispatchers lived in Stoughton, they knew where she was, the Sto Apartment complex. It's across from Hansen Elementary School, which is the only school with traffic lights."

"That was smart thinking on the dispatcher's part," Dan said. "Having her look out the window."

"Yes, it was," Laynie agreed.

"So, what happened?" Dan asked.

"The dispatchers sent cruisers to the Sto Apartments. They informed the officers of the situation and had them slowly circle the buildings. The dispatcher told the girl to watch for the blue lights. She did. A minute later, she saw them. The dispatcher asked where she saw the blue lights. She said right below her. Dispatch relayed to the responding officers that they were in front of the building. Now they needed to know which floor. The dispatcher had the little girl quietly step out into the hallway. They instructed her to wait for the officers. Eventually, they located the girl on the fourth floor. When the police entered the apartment, the father was actively raping the mother."

"Jesus!" Dan said.

"The police arrested the man," David said. "That little girl was brave. She possibly saved not only her mother's life, but her own as well."

"After hearing that story," Dan said. "I can see people's concerns. The fear of potentially having someone not familiar with the town dispatching."

"Fear," David said. "It spreads like wildfire. Especially in a small town."

"But," Laynie said. "Is it enough to kill over?"

Chapter 48

Stoughton Police Headquarters
Stoughton, Massachusetts

Colton spent most of the day looking into Alex Torres, the latest victim.

Torres was a mechanic at his brother's garage. He'd worked there for the past thirty years, ever since it opened.

Colton and Barnes made the trek down to Taunton. They checked in with the Taunton Police Department first. Apparently, the Torres family had several friends in the Taunton Police Department. They sent a detective and two uniformed officers to accompany them to make the notification. Colton didn't mind. He'd done one too many notifications this week already.

They met at the family garage. Jorge, Alex's older brother, almost fell over when he found out that his brother was dead. The two were close. Maria, Alex's sister-in-law, held her husband as he wept.

Maria told them that Alex had never married, but he had two daughters. Both were in their early thirties. Maria described Alex as a workaholic. Told them Alex worked seven days a week and hardly took a day off.

They discovered that Alex had recently connected with an old friend. Back when they were younger, the pair loved to go camping together. Alex and his friend planned to canoe the Saco River in Maine this week. The family encouraged him to go. Thought it would be good for him to get away. Clearly Alex didn't make it. Which led to the question, where was Alex's friend?

They tracked down Alex's friend. He'd just moved back to Taunton and worked as a bartender. He told them Alex cancelled at the last minute. Mentioned going to Stoughton, something about an old car.

Colton was back in his office, staring at the three case files. Torres was a mechanic, McDonald a firefighter and Fuller, a bank CEO. He found nothing tying the victims together. Nothing. No connection. Or at least that he could find, minus the symbols, the killer left.

Both Bill McDonald and Larry Fuller lived in Stoughton, Torres did not. He lived in Taunton, which was about twenty miles south. The only connection Colton could find was Route 138. It ran straight through the middle of both places. Other than that, nothing.

Colton thought back to something Diaz had said at the Medical Examiner's office. She mentioned her dad worked at a garage and said he had a sandblaster at his shop. Alex's friend said he cancelled the trip to look at a car. Did his job play a part in his murder? Was that it? Was it their professions? Did the killer have an axe to grind with certain businesses?

If that was the case, there'd be no connection between them. Now Colton's brain hurt.

He needed to get out of his office. Maybe a change of scenery would help.

Colton stepped out of his office as Barnes was coming around the corner.

"You ready for the press conference?" Barnes asked.

"Already?" Colton said. "I lost track of time."

They walked up front to meet with Chief McCormack and District Attorney Harbor.

"What have you been working on?" Barnes asked as they walked.

"I've been trying to find a connection between our victims," Colton said.

"Any luck?"

"None," Colton said. "I'm starting to wonder if there is no connection."

"What about the symbols?" Barnes asked.

"Maybe they're just the killer's calling card," Colton said. "No connection to one another."

"You know," Barnes said. "It could just be that simple."

Chapter 49

David Monteiro's House
Stoughton, Massachusetts

David's phone chirped. He picked it up and looked at it.

"They're holding another press conference down at the police station," David said.

"When?" Laynie asked.

"Soon," David said. "You wanna go?"

Laynie looked at Dan. "How many beers have you had?"

"Just the one," Dan said, holding up the can.

"Me too," Laynie said. "But we just arrived. I haven't had time to research or investigate."

"You know, Laynie," David said. "Let's just go down there. Listen to the brief. Talk to some of the other reporters. See what they think."

"Dad," Laynie said. "They're just gonna regurgitate the same talking points."

"Their network is probably telling them to," Dan said. "Just like ours does."

"Touché," Laynie replied.

They quickly got dressed and made it down to the station as the press briefing started.

It didn't take long for the other reporters to spot Laynie.

It started out with whispers, which turned to pointing. Finally, a young reporter mustered up enough nerve and walked over.

"Excuse me," she said. "Are you Laynie Monteiro?"

"I am," Laynie said with an enormous smile. She remembered what it was like meeting a big-time journalist when she first started out.

"Are you here to cover the murders?" She quickly realized how dumb that was. "Of course you are. Stupid question."

"What's your name?" Laynie asked.

"I'm Scarlett," the reporter said.

"Hi Scarlett," Laynie said. "It's a pleasure to meet you." Laynie held out her hand.

The woman's face lit up, and she shook Laynie's hand. "This is so cool!"

"What do you think about these murders?" Laynie asked.

"They're horrible," Scarlett said. "But a bit odd."

"What's odd?" Laynie asked.

"Because it's a small town," Scarlett said. "I mean, what are the chances? Three back-to-back murders. Really?"

"Yet, no one seems to be asking that question," Laynie said. "You should ask that."

"Oh, I can't," Scarlett said. "My producer gave me a list of questions to ask. He doesn't like it when we deviate. He doesn't want to rock the boat with law enforcement."

"Oh," Laynie said.

Lt. Bonnett stepped up to the podium. He announced the briefing was about to begin.

McCormack spoke. She identified the third victim. When she finished, Harbor spoke. Then McCormack stepped back up to the microphone. Said they'd hold another briefing once they had more information to share.

"One question if I may before you leave," Laynie shouted, her hand raised in the air.

McCormack turned. She spotted the woman with her hand raised. Then she noticed the woman was standing next to David Monteiro.

"Shit," McCormack muttered under her breath.

"Stoughton is a small community," Laynie said. "You've found nothing connecting the victims together?"

"No," McCormack said. "There isn't."

"I find that hard to believe," Laynie said.

"You're entitled to believe whatever you want," McCormack said.

"Then why is the FBI involved?" Laynie asked.

McCormack stood there for a moment with a blank expression.

Harbor nudged McCormack out of the way. He stepped up to the mic.

"The FBI is here in a supportive role," Harbor said. "They're lending their expertise."

"Why would the Bureau send a counter-terrorism agent to support a homicide investigation?" Laynie asked.

Special Agent Wolf's face turned a dark shade of red.

"No more questions," Harbor said. Then he stepped away from the podium and walked into the police station. Colton and the others followed.

Laynie turned around and found Scarlett standing behind her.

"That was amazing!" Scarlett said.

"A word of advice, Scarlett," Laynie said.

"Yes, of course. Anything."

"Don't be afraid to ask questions," Laynie said. "Even if your boss tells you no. You're a reporter, not a puppet. Shake the tree and see what falls out."

Chapter 50

Stoughton Police Headquarters
Stoughton, Massachusetts

Colton sat in McCormack's office. Barnes and Harbor were present, along with Agents Wolf and Diaz.

"Who was that reporter?" Wolf asked.

"That was Laynie Monteiro," McCormack said. "She's a reporter out in Los Angeles. Her father is a local reporter here in Stoughton."

"Which station?" Wolf asked.

"I'm not sure," McCormack said. "One of the big affiliates."

"Well … it looks like this story is gonna go national," Harbor said.

Chief McCormack's phone rang. She answered it. "Tell him I'll call him later. I'm in a meeting right now."

A moment later, someone pounded on the door.

Colton opened the door.

Standing there was Frank Langer, the Town Manager.

Frank barged in, obviously mad.

"What the hell is going on here?" Frank asked. "Why am I finding out on the news that these murders are connected?"

McCormack looked at Harbor.

Frank turned towards Wolf.

"Who are you?" Wolf asked.

"I'm the town manager. I run this town," Frank said.

"Well," Wolf said. "This is now my investigation."

"Are you serious?" Colton said.

"Let's hold on here a minute," Harbor said.

"Right now, this is a murder investigation. The state has already formed a task force. Are you telling me the government is taking over my task force?"

"I'm telling you, the FBI is taking the lead on this investigation," Wolf said.

"On what grounds?" Barnes asked.

Wolf went to answer, but Colton cut him off.

"Maybe we should have this conversation in private," Colton said, nodding toward Frank.

Frank's face turned a bright red. He had a few choice words for Colton. He then said, "Who do you think you are?"

Colton stood there, staring back, no emotion on his face.

Frank looked at McCormack. "Your career is over!" He then stormed out.

"Please tell me you're joking about taking over this investigation?" Harbor said.

"No, I'm not," Wolf said.

"On what grounds?" Harbor asked.

"Because the town manager is poking his nose around," Wolf said. "I played stupid for him, but I know who he is."

"Well ... he is the town manager," McCormack said.

"Yes, he is," Wolf said. "I shouldn't be telling you this, but he's involved in the case we're working."

"Really?" Harbor asked.

"I personally witnessed him at a murder scene," Wolf said. "Now he's barging into the police chief's office, demanding to know about an investigation. Who knows what she would have told him if we weren't standing here?"

"You're out of line!" Harbor snapped. "Chief McCormack has more integrity than anyone in this room."

"That might be so," Wolf said. "But no other police department would allow someone to just walk down to the police chief's office. Especially after telling that officer no over the phone. That man uses his position of authority to intimidate police officers, allowing him to do whatever he pleases."

"Do you care to tell us more about your investigation?" Harbor asked.

"No," Wolf said. "Not at this time."

"How convenient," Colton said. "You're gonna take over our investigation but not tell us about yours or how they're connected."

"That's right," Wolf said.

"Do you know what I think?" Colton asked. "I think you got called out by that reporter and now you're pissed. So, you walk in here and rain on our parade."

"Speaking of that reporter…" Wolf said.

"Her name is Laynie Monteiro," McCormack said. "She covers national murder cases and serial killers. So you better bring your best game, gentlemen. Because she's going to fact check and dig deep into everything you say."

"Isn't she that reporter who helped catch a serial killer out in LA?" Barnes asked.

"That's her," McCormack said. "She's so good that some detectives go to her to help solve the case."

"Let's be clear about one thing," Wolf said. "We won't be going to her. We're keeping this investigation as close to the vest as possible."

Chapter 51

Faxon War Memorial Park
Stoughton, Massachusetts

Colton shot down Pleasant Street, his siren blaring. He straddled the double yellow line as he approached the intersection for Central Street. With a push of a button, the sound of the siren changed from the hi-low pitch to the annoying repeating scatter sound. Cars on both sides of the road pulled over. They parted like a wake left by a boat's hull cutting through the water.

The light in the center of town was red. Posted signs prohibited a left turn onto Park Street.

Traffic stopped, and Colton turned left.

Up ahead were two cruisers. Both had their emergency lights on and blocked traffic from going past the town green.

Colton pulled up behind the cruisers and parked.

A uniformed officer ran yellow tape around a telephone pole in front of the memorial.

Colton stepped out.

"Hell of a first week, Detective," the uniformed officer said, continuing to cordon off the area.

Faxon Memorial Park is a triangle-shaped green which contains two separate war memorials. Park Street, also known as Route 27, runs along the top of the small piece of land. Walnut Street and Walnut Avenue run down along the sides. Walnut Avenue turns into Walnut Street, creating the V-shape of the triangle.

The smell of fresh cut grass filled the air and the flowers surrounding the war memorial swayed in the slight breeze. What appeared to be white dandelion pieces floated around the area. One wafted towards Colton and landed on his coat lapel. He looked down. It wasn't a piece of that annoying weed, but a feather. Pinching it with his fingers, he blew it away.

Colton stepped up onto the curb. Two uniformed officers stood further down on the sidewalk near the second memorial.

Colton walked past the first memorial. It was a tribute to the Stoughton residents who had served in the military. A walkway made from cement pavers led from the sidewalk to the memorial. Mulch beds ran along both sides. They contained red, white and blue flowers and trimmed shrubs. A flagpole stood in the center of each flower bed. Both poles flew the American flag with the Prisoner of War (POW) beneath it. At night, lights inside the mulch beds illuminated the memorial and flags. Behind the memorial was a large yew, a type of shrub, which hid the electrical box that powered the lights.

Also inside the park were two Civil War cannons and a Howitzer from the Vietnam era. Benches surrounded the perimeter of the green. In the middle of the park was a huge flowering tree. Behind it was a large gazebo where bands played in the summer. Several benches provided seating near the gazebo.

Colton continued down the sidewalk. Lt. Bonnett and Officer O'Sullivan stood near the second memorial. It was a granite stone that stood by itself. Mounted on it was a plaque which read:

Roll of Honor: Dedicated to those who died for peace and freedom.

The plaque listed each of America's wars, from the Revolutionary War up to Vietnam. Beneath each war were the names of Stoughton residents who died during combat in that war.

A large concentration of white feathers lay on the ground near the officers' feet.

A small gust of wind caused the feathers to swirl and scatter about.

Both officers looked down.

Immediately, Lt. Bonnett turned and stepped away. Officer O'Sullivan turned her head, put her hands on her knees, and dry heaved.

Colton made his way closer.

"Real fucking sicko, Detective," O'Sullivan said, wiping her mouth with the back of her hand.

Colton looked down at the body.

"Jesus Christ," Colton said, trying to contain the contents of his own stomach.

Sprawled out before him was a woman's body. Feathers stuck to the thick black tar that coated the corpse. They flickered in the breeze like a candle. Flies buzzed and circled around. Some had landed on the tar and became stuck. The victim's mouth gaped open. Horse manure filled the void. Two large medallions covered her eyes, the same Sons of Liberty medallions found on Larry Fuller.

Strands of the woman's gray hair stuck out through the tar that covered her head.

Colton squatted down and removed a pen from his shirt pocket. Gently, he lifted some feathers, exposing spots of bare skin. He didn't see any clothing on the body. She was naked when whoever did this applied the tar and feathers.

The black coating made it hard to guess the woman's age.

The weight of it hit him all at once. It was his job to find out who she was. More importantly, he was responsible for catching whoever did this to her.

Taking a moment, Colton composed himself, and his mind went to work examining the crime scene. He didn't know her or how she had died, but he would find out.

"Do you think she was alive when they did it?" O'Sullivan asked from behind.

"Not sure," Colton said. "Once she's on the table, the Medical Examiner will be able to tell."

Lt. Bonnett made his way back over and stood next to Colton.

"Why would someone dump a body in plain sight?" asked O'Sullivan.

Both Colton and Lt. Bonnett looked at her.

"Never mind. Rhetorical question. Because they wanted the body to be found," O'Sullivan said.

"Bingo!" Lt. Bonnett said.

Colton stood up and circled the body, examining it. After a moment, he radioed dispatch and asked them to contact Barnes, and to notify the task force.

Behind the scenes, dispatch began calling in additional officers and notified both the District Attorney and Medical Examiner's office.

"The Chief is here," O'Sullivan said.

Colton looked up and saw the Chief coming toward him.

"What do we have?" McCormack asked as she approached.

"A woman," Colton said. "She's covered in tar and feathers. Unable to approximate her age. I don't see any gunshots or stab wounds, but I haven't moved the body."

"Same guy?" McCormack asked.

"Appears so," Colton said. "He covered her eyes with the same medallions we found on Larry Fuller."

"Any symbols?" McCormack asked.

"None that I can see," Colton said. "The tar is pretty thick in some places. We should know more once the Medical Examiner gets her cleaned up."

"Have you called Barnes?" she asked.

"He's on his way," Colton said. "I told dispatch to notify the task force as well."

"I'll leave you to it," McCormack said, and walked away.

Colton made his way into the middle of Park Street. He stood there looking at the crime scene and beyond.

Sirens filled the air.

Additional cruisers arrived. Colton instructed them to block off the streets around Faxon Park.

Colton looked at all the surrounding houses.

"Several of those homes have security cameras," Colton said to Lt. Bonnett and O'Sullivan. "Can you go knock on their doors and ask them if we can review their footage?"

"Sure thing, detective," said Lt. Bonnett.

The two uniformed officers walked away.

Colton headed back to the body and pulled out his department-issued cell phone and started taking photos of the scene.

Sirens fill the air again. Barnes' undercover State Trooper SUV pulled up, and he stepped out.

Barnes lifted the yellow tape and made his way towards Colton. "Same guy?"

Colton nodded.

"Pretty brazen, dropping a body out in public like this," Barnes said.

"I have my people knocking on doors to see if anyone caught something on their home security cameras."

Barnes walked over to the body. "Jesus! They tarred and feathered her. That must've hurt."

Chapter 52

Faxon War Memorial Park
Stoughton, Massachusetts

"What are you thinking?" Barnes asked Colton.

"Something the rookie said. Why dump a body here?" Colton said. "Why tar and feather her?"

"This guy is sick and twisted," Barnes said. "That's your reason."

Colton relaxed his body and cleared his mind. He looked at the body. He let words appear in his mind based upon what he saw. It was an old writing trick to kick start ideas.

Woman
Tar
Feathers
Sons of Liberty medallions

Colton looked around at the surroundings. He stood in place and slowly turned. He took everything in, making a mental note of what he saw. He started by searching across the street. Colton looked at the furthest things first and brought his eyes closer.

Lawyer's office
Houses
Walnut Street
Grass
Trees
Park benches
Two old cannons
Gazebo
Howitzer
Large war memorial

Colton had turned one hundred and eighty degrees.

Houses
Dentist office
Center of town
Historical Society
Bank
Houses
Small war memorial
Park Street
Intersection (Park Street and Walnut Street)
Library

Colton arrived back where he started.

He started moving the words around in his mind, trying to see if anything connected?

He eliminated grass, trees, houses and park benches.

The list shortened.

He concentrated on the remaining words.

After a moment, Colton's eyes drifted toward the smaller war memorial.

"There," Colton said, pointing to it. He started walking toward it. Barnes followed.

Colton went over to the memorial and scanned it with his eyes. "Bingo!"

Barnes looked at the memorial.

Barnes turned and looked at the body. Then looked back at the plaque. "Jesus!"

"I know, right," Colton said. "Back during the Revolutionary War, they tarred and feathered people."

"Do you remember anyone specific or of importance who was tarred and feathered?" Barnes asked.

"Yeah, I do," Colton said. "John Malcom, a customs official back in 1774. A mob dragged him from his home and dumped hot tar on him. They tore open pillows and covered him with feathers. Then they paraded him around the city for all to see, beating him as they went."

"God damn," Barnes said. "I was right, sick and twisted."

"Our guy did the same thing," Colton said. "He tarred and feathered her. Then dumped her in a highly visible location for all to see."

Chapter 53

Walnut Ave
Stoughton, Massachusetts

Officer O'Sullivan slipped under the yellow crime scene tape and headed toward Colton and Barnes. "Excuse me, detectives."

Both Colton and Barnes turn around.

"We found a gentleman who has footage of the park this morning."

"Where?" asked Colton.

O'Sullivan pointed to a triple-decker across from the park. "Right over here."

They walked over. Several cars were parked out front. A wrap-around porch led to a parking lot with more cars. Next to the front door was a sign mounted on the wall. It contained a picture of a camera with the words, *Surveillance Camera In Use.*

O'Sullivan led them inside and down a set of stairs to a small office. There they found Lt. Bonnett speaking with an elderly man sitting at a desk with two large monitors.

"Sir, this is Detective Baker," Lt. Bonnett said. "He's investigating the incident across the street."

Colton introduced Barnes, and they shook hands.

"Is it true they found a body over in the park?" the old man asked.

"Unfortunately, so," Colton said.

"I hope you're able to catch whoever did it. It's terrible what's happening to this town."

"So, you have twenty-four-hour surveillance. Is that correct?" Colton asked.

"Yes."

"Have you had trouble in the past? What made you install the cameras?"

"My wife and I live on the first floor and my kids live upstairs with my grandkids. We had an issue with people breaking into our cars. Someone even came up onto the porch and stole our packages that we had delivered. We installed them and put that big sign up as a deterrent."

"Did it help?"

"Oh, yes."

"Are they digital cameras?"

"Is there any other kind nowadays?"

Both Colton and Barnes exchanged smiles.

"I suppose you want to review the footage?" the old man said. He pushed a button, and two front porch cameras appeared on the screen.

"Where to?" the old man asked.

"Let's start at five this morning," Colton said.

The man clicked the video and dragged the time-bar back. They watched for a moment. Feathers swirled near the memorial.

"Can you rewind it slowly?" Colton asked.

The old man clicked the mouse, and the video scrolled backwards. Dawn turned to starlight. The homeowner explained the cameras have a sensor which switch to starlight when it becomes dark. The stream of commuter head and taillights becomes less and less. White specks swirled around the memorial. Colton noted the time. It was 4:25 am. The head and taillights of passing cars became less frequent the farther back the film went.

Suddenly, everything on the screen turned black.

"What happened?" asked Colton.

"I don't know," the man said.

"Go forward, please."

The man hit a button. After a few seconds the blackness disappeared, and the video returned.

"Okay. Go back again. But go slow."

The video moved backward, and at 3:58 am the video went black.

"What now?" asked the man.

"Keep going back, please."

Seconds turned into minutes. At 3:52 am, the video appeared again. Nothing. No feathers, no body, and no one dumping it.

"Whatever happened, it happened in those six minutes," Colton said.

"I don't know what happened," the man said. Maybe the power went out."

"Can you send me a copy of this video?" Colton asked.

"Sure. I'll just need your email address."

Colton pulled out one of his business cards and handed it to the man.

"I appreciate all of your help. I'll be in touch. If you think of anything else, please give me a call."

Chapter 54

Faxon War Memorial Park
Stoughton, Massachusetts

Colton, Barnes, and the two officers left the old man's house.

"That was odd," Barnes said as they walked back to the crime scene. "How did the video go black for six minutes? Do you think it was a power outage?"

"Doubt it," Colton said.

Down the street, beyond the yellow tape, Colton noticed the satellite boom of a news truck.

Chief McCormack was talking to an officer when she noticed Colton and Barnes had returned. She made her way back to the crime scene.

"The press is here," McCormack said.

Out of the corner of his eye, Colton caught a silver BMW drive up to the crime tape and stop.

"Frank Langer is here," Colton said.

McCormack sighed.

Frank was yelling at one of the uniformed officers, who finally let him through.

"Probably threatened to have him fired," McCormack said.

As Frank approached, he began yelling. "Are you serious? They dumped the body right here, out in the open."

"Wow, with that keen sense of deduction, he should have been a detective," Colton joked.

McCormack smiled.

As Frank grew closer, he tried to approach the body.

"Whoa! What do you think you're doing?" Colton said. "This is a crime scene."

"I'm the Town Manager…"

Colton cut him off.

"I don't give a shit who you are. Get the fuck out of my crime scene."

Frank stopped. His face turned beet red, and he looked at McCormack.

"Don't look at me," McCormack said. "It's his crime scene."

Frank looked back at Colton.

"I don't know who you think you are," Frank said, pointing at Colton. "But your first week is gonna be your last!"

"Not the first time I've heard that this week," Colton said.

Barnes stepped forward. "Is there a problem here?"

"I don't know you," Frank said. "But I'm the Town Manager, and this is a local issue. So please butt out!"

"Well ... I'm Steve Barnes, a Massachusetts State Police Homicide Detective assigned to the Norfolk County DA's office."

"Well, this isn't your crime scene," Frank said. "It happened in my town, which I'm in charge of."

"Actually, this is my crime scene," Barnes said, and looked at his watch. "As of right now."

"Under who's authority?" Frank said.

"The Norfolk County DA and the State of Massachusetts," Barnes said. "In case you didn't know, all unattended deaths get assigned to the DA's office."

"Since when?" Frank asked.

Barnes turned and looked at Colton and McCormack. "Is this guy for real?"

"Afraid so," Colton said.

Barnes turned back toward Frank.

"Oh, I don't know. Since the 1800s. Now get out of my crime scene before I arrest you."

Frank stood there for a moment. Then he turned and walked away.

"Well ... that pissed him off," McCormack said. "He's not used to being told off."

"What's his issue?" Barnes asked.

"He thinks because he's the Town Manager he can do whatever he wants," McCormack said. "Plus, he's best friends with Gino Romano and his son Nino."

"Aren't those the guys from the Porta Potty crime scene? The mob guys?" Barnes asked.

"Yup," Colton said.

"And the same guys you had a run in with a few days ago?" Barnes asked.

"Correct," Colton said. "Bunch of assholes!"

"Frank's probably snooping around to find out what we know," McCormack said.

"Changing gears," McCormack said, turning toward the body. "I know it's early, but do you have any leads yet?"

"No," Colton said. "We can't even ID the victim. The tar is covering her face and fingers."

"The medical examiner is gonna have a field day with this one," Barnes said. "That tar is gonna be a bitch to get off."

"Alright, I'll leave you to it," McCormack said. "Check in with me later. I need to prepare a press release. They're gonna be all over this one."

Chapter 55

**Faxon War Memorial Park
Stoughton, Massachusetts**

A black SUV with tinted windows pulled up to the tape and stopped.

FBI Special Agent Wolf and Agent Diaz stepped out. Both wore their standard black suits and dark sunglasses.

"The Feds are here," announced a uniformed officer.

"That didn't take them long," Barnes said.

Both agents walked over.

"Same symbols?" asked Diaz.

"Can't tell," Colton said.

"Can't tell?" Wolf said. "I know you're new and all, but you can't tell?"

"Oh, I'm sorry," Colton said. "I can't see through the thick coat of tar and feathers they covered her with."

"Really?" Diaz asked. "May I take a look?"

"Sure," Colton said.

Diaz walked over to the body and squatted down next to it. Colton went over and stood next to her.

"Wow," Diaz said. "I wasn't expecting that."

"Looks like our killer took a play from the Revolutionary War playbook," Colton said.

"I guess so," Diaz said, standing up. "You find anything out about those symbols?"

"Not yet," Colton said.

"My bet it's Nino Romano," Wolf said. "These vics probably wouldn't play ball with the Romanos, so they killed them and are trying to make it look like a serial killer to cover their tracks."

Colton and Barnes exchanged glances.

"You might be right," Barnes said. "His crony was just here?"

"Who?" Wolf asked.

"Frank Langer, the town manager," Barnes said. "Prick tried to walk right up to the body?"

"Seriously?" Diaz said.

"Had to threaten to arrest him to get him to leave," Barnes said.

"I think you're putting the cart before the horse," Colton said. "We don't even know who she is. Never mind if she's connected to the Romanos."

"Trust me, kid," Wolf said. "If you knew half of what they've done, you'd assume the same thing."

"Is that why you're here?" Colton asked. "Are you working a RICO (Racketeer Influenced and Corrupt Organizations Act) case against the Romanos? Do you have evidence that directly ties them to these murders?"

"We're not discussing any case we may or may not be working on," Wolf said.

"Well ... I hope you're not impeding a homicide investigation in order to make a big mob boss arrest," Colton said.

"Again ... I don't like your tone," Wolf said.

"What's with you and my fucking tone?" Colton asked. "It's never the question, just my tone."

"Time for us to leave," Wolf said. "Come on, Diaz."

Just then, Officer O'Sullivan returned.

"Detective," O'Sullivan said. "Lt. Bonnett and I spoke with the bank manager. She said the bank's ATM has direct sight of the park. She's queueing up the video from this morning now."

Chapter 56

Stoughton Center Bank
Stoughton, Massachusetts

Lt. Bonnett opened the bank door as they approached, and they filed inside. The bank manager met them halfway across the lobby. She was a middle-aged woman wearing a business dress with high-heel shoes, which clacked on the tile floor. She greeted the group and shook their hands.

"I understand you have security footage of the park," Colton said.

"Yes," the manager said. "The ATM camera faces the memorial. If you follow me, I pulled the footage for you."

They followed her into her office. She sat down at her desk and turned her computer monitor so everyone could see it.

"I can't believe someone was killed over there," she said. "It's such a beautiful park. I sometimes sit over there and eat my lunch."

"A real tragedy," Chief McCormack said.

The manager clicked the mouse, and the video from the ATM appeared.

"Can you please go to 3:50 am this morning?" Colton asked.

The manager pressed a couple keys, and the video jumped to that moment. They all looked at the monitor. It was 03:51 and one car passed by. At 03:52, the video went black. They watched six minutes of blackness. At 3:58, the video resumed.

"Same as the old man's footage," Barnes said.

Colton pulled out a business card and handed it to the manager. "Can you please send me a copy?"

Colton thanked her, then turned and exited the bank.

"What did I miss?" McCormack asked.

Diaz chased after Colton.

She caught up to him halfway back to the crime scene.

"You didn't seem surprised," Diaz said. "Did you know that was going to happen?"

Colton stopped in the middle of the street. The others caught up.

"I figured it would," Colton said. "It happened to another recording."

"Where?" Diaz asked.

"Right there," Colton said. He pointed to the elderly man's house seventy-five yards away.

"What would cause that to happen on multiple recordings?" asked McCormack.

"I've heard of it before," Colton said. "But I've never seen it."

"What?" Barnes asked.

"Jammers," Colton said.

"I'm going to be fifty-four," Barnes said. "I've never been tech savvy. My kids are, though. What kind of jammer can knock out video?"

"Military," Colton said. "They developed jammers to stop IEDs in Iraq and Afghanistan."

"So, the bad guys couldn't use cell phones to detonate the bombs, correct?" Barnes said.

"Exactly," Colton said.

"But how does that affect video?" Barnes asked. "Plus, can't we just use that fencing thing?"

"Geofencing," Colton said.

"That's it," Barnes said.

"How does it work again?" Barnes asked. "I wasn't kidding. I'm not tech savvy at all."

"Remember January 6th?" Colton said. "And how they arrested people who stormed the Capitol later?"

"Yeah, it was all over the news."

"Well … all cell phones have a GPS built in. Google and your apps use that GPS to track where you are. Hence how businesses and certain places pop up on your social media. If something happens in a specific area, we request the geofencing data for that area. The phone companies provide us with every cell phone customer in that area at that time."

"By request, you mean a warrant, right?" Diaz asked.

"They won't give it to us any other way," Colton said.

"But how does a cell phone jammer affect video and this geofencing?" Barnes asked.

"Well, there's other types of jammers," Colton said. "There's Wi-Fi jammers that block the Wi-Fi signal. Most of these home security cameras are all Wi-Fi, so the video goes black or turns to snow."

"And the geofencing?" Barnes asked.

"GPS jammers," Colton said. "They're illegal in most countries because aircraft use them to navigate and land safely. The military uses them to knock down drones. They also jam the GPS in cell phones, so there's no more signal for the apps to track. A person using multiple jammers together can basically move undetected and leave no digital trace."

"I'm impressed, Detective," said Special Agent Wolf.

Colton turned and stared at Wolf.

"So, there's no point in getting a warrant then," said Barnes.

Colton didn't answer. He continued to stare at Wolf, his eyes like lasers.

"I believe Detective Barnes asked you a question," Wolf said, staring back.

"Is that why you're here?" Colton asked. "Are the Romanos selling jammers?"

"I'm not at liberty to discuss any investigation we may or may not be working," Wolf said.

McCormack's mouth fell open.

Barnes looked from Colton to Wolf then back again.

Colton stared at Wolf for another minute, then turned toward Barnes.

"Sorry," Colton said. "To answer your question, yes. I'm still going to get the warrant to prove my theory. Plus, there could have been a brief power outage that caused it. But, I doubt it. That's a big coincidence, the power going out at the same exact time our suspect is dumping the body. I'll request a report of outages from National Grid just to rule it out."

Technicians with the State Police Crime Lab arrived and began processing the scene.

Lt. Bonnett and Officer O'Sullivan stood by their cruiser, directing traffic.

"Why don't we do that?" asked O'Sullivan, nodding toward the Lab Technicians.

"We're a small town," Lt. Bonnet said. "We don't have the budget to keep technicians on the payroll, never mind a lab."

"So, this is it? We just stand around."

"Isn't it glorious?" Lt. Bonnett said. "We knock on all the doors and chase down the leads. Meanwhile, the Staties have the big expensive crime lab with all the technicians and gadgets. The real kicker is they get all the credit for our hard work."

The Medical Examiner arrived, and they waved him through.

Chapter 57

Wendy McDonald
Stoughton, Massachusetts

Laynie knocked on Wendy McDonald's door.

It opened.

Laynie identified herself.

"I know who you are," Wendy said. "My husband and I have seen you on the news."

"Then you know why I'm here?" Laynie asked. "Yeah," Wendy said. "You want to do a story on my husband."

"Not just that," Laynie said. "I want to help catch who did this to him."

Wendy invited Laynie, David and Dan in.

Moments later, Laynie was sitting on the couch next to Wendy. Laynie noticed Wendy's red eyes. It was obvious she was still in mourning.

David offered his condolences.

"Thank you, David," Wendy said.

"Do you know each other?" Laynie asked, surprised.

"Yes," Wendy said.

"Wendy and I dated briefly after high school," David said.

Dan pulled out his tripod and started setting up the camera.

"Oh gosh," Wendy said. "I look horrible."

Laynie reached over and took Wendy's hand. "You look like someone who just lost the love of their life. No one will judge. I promise," Laynie said.

Out of the corner of her eye, Laynie caught Dan giving her the thumbs up, indicating the camera was ready to roll.

"Wendy, I'd like to ask you a few questions about Bill," Laynie said, scooching closer.

"Bill was a firefighter, is that correct?" Laynie asked.

"Yes," Wendy said. "For thirty-six years. He was going to retire next year."

"Wow," Laynie said. "That's a long time. Sounds like he was dedicated to the job."

"He loved that job," Wendy said. "Over the years, he won several awards for saving people. Just last winter, he rescued a small child. Some kids were playing hockey, and one child fell through the ice. Bill's engine was first on the scene. He told me he saw the other kids going out to try to rescue their friend. Said his heart leapt into his throat. He feared they'd fall in, too. Bill being Bill, he jumped into action and went out onto the ice without the proper equipment. Thankfully, he was able to save the boy."

"Your husband was a true hero," Laynie said.

"Yes," Wendy said. "Yes, he was."

Tears welled in Wendy's eyes. Laynie handed her a tissue from her purse.

"How did you two meet?" Laynie asked.

Wendy looked at David. "Well," she said. "After your father dumped me, his best friend asked me out."

Laynie looked over at her father, who diverted his eyes down to the floor.

"And you have children?" Laynie asked.

"Yes," Wendy said. "We have two girls. They're both in college."

"Can you think of any reason why someone would've murdered your husband?" Laynie asked.

"I think he was at the wrong place at the wrong time," Wendy said. "The town needs to do more about the homeless situation and the growing violence."

Laynie wanted to ask Wendy to elaborate, but she noticed Wendy was becoming emotional. Instead, Laynie jotted down a note to look into the homelessness and violence.

"Final question," Laynie said. "Was Bill for or against keeping 911 local?"

"No. Bill was dead set against it," Wendy said. "I know Bill said the Fire Chief wanted it though."

"Really?" Laynie said.

"Yes," Wendy said. "Bill told me it was the Fire Chief pushing it. Said the Chief was coming down hard on the firefighters to push it."

Chapter 58

Stoughton Bakery
Stoughton, Massachusetts

Laynie and Dan drove over to the Stoughton Train Station. The lot was full. People took the commuter rail into Boston. Most for work. Some for pleasure.

Laynie scoped out the area. She recognized the crime scene from news media reports. She turned and noticed the bakery window, which had a full view of the crime scene.

"I wonder if they saw anything," Laynie asked.

"Let's go find out," Dan said, grabbing his camera.

They walked over to the bakery.

Dan hit record as they walked in.

Laynie opened the door. A bell chimed. Once inside, the sweet smell of bread filled her nostrils. Childhood memories of her Avo's house fluttered back. A warmth washed over her as she remembered her grandmother's face.

Laynie looked up at the menu, surprised. It was a Portuguese bakery. Every item had the English translation next to the Portuguese word.

"Can I help you?" an older woman said from behind the counter.

"Good morning," Laynie said. "May I get a coffee and a dozen *papo Seco* (type of Portuguese roll)."

"What kind of coffee would you like, dear," the older woman asked.

"Medium regular," Laynie said. The woman looked very familiar, but Laynie couldn't place her finger on it.

The older woman poured the coffee. Then she retrieved the rolls. "Anything else, dear?" the woman asked.

Laynie eyed the case. "I'll take some *Pasteis de Nata* (type of Portuguese dessert)."

"Which ones?" the older woman asked.

"Those ones, please," Laynie said, pointing to the ones in the middle.

A younger woman exited the kitchen area carrying a tray of assorted pastries to be placed into the display case and set the tray down atop the case.

"Laynie!" the younger woman screamed.

Laynie looked up to see her best friend from high school staring at her, her face beaming with a smile from ear to ear.

"Oh, my God! Lexi!" Laynie said. "How are you?"

Lexi began screaming and ran into the kitchen. The scream grew dull once inside the kitchen, but intensified when Lexi came scurrying into the cafe.

The two women met and embraced.

"When did you get back?" Lexi asked.

"I landed the other day."

"Are you here to cover the murders?"

"Yes," Laynie said.

"Do you want to talk to my mom?" Lexi asked.

"About what?"

"You don't know?"

"Know what?" Laynie asked.

"My mom found the body," Lexi said, pointing out the window. "Right there."

Laynie looked out the window. "Bill McDonald?"

"Yes," Lexi answered. "Did you know the killer tattooed strange symbols on the poor guy's forehead?"

"No," Laynie said. "Are you serious?"

"Yeah, my mom walked over to the body. A bum was standing over it. When he saw my mom, he took off running."

"Did the bum kill McDonald?" Laynie asked. "How did McDonald die?"

"The killer drove a railroad spike through the top of his head," Lexi said.

"Wow," Laynie said. "That's intense."

Lexi called her mom out of the kitchen. When she arrived, Lexi asked, "Do you remember my mom, Maria?"

"Yes," Laynie said. "I remember. She was friends with my mom and avó."

"Come around out back," Maria said. "We can talk there."

Maria filled Laynie in on everything she had witnessed that morning, including the bright black tattoo.

Chapter 59

**Faxon War Memorial Park
Stoughton, Massachusetts**

They were driving back to David's house when they heard about the fourth victim. David had a police scanner in his car and the thing was squawking non-stop.

"Where?" Laynie asked.

"They haven't said yet," David said, sharing his focus between the road and the scanner.

They didn't need to hear where. David rounded the corner and there was a swarm of police cruisers up ahead.

"Found it," Dan said.

David pulled up and parked. Laynie reached into her bag and pulled out her press credential lanyard.

It wasn't her first time dealing with a crime scene.

David followed Laynie and Dan up to the yellow crime scene tape. Laynie had her microphone out, and Dan had his camera on his shoulder.

"Over there," Laynie said, pointing to the body.

Dan swung the camera around and started filming.

"Let's try to get a better angle," Laynie said.

They walked the perimeter of the tape. The way the cops had parked the cruisers limited their view from that angle.

On the corner of Park Avenue and Walnut Street was an attorney's office. The front door faced Park Avenue. The parking lot was out back off Walnut Avenue.

Laynie walked up the walkway and tried the front door. It was open. She stepped inside. A moment later, she waved Dan inside. At the other end of the hallway, there was a glass door. It led out to the parking lot.

Laynie walked through the building and out the back door as she held the door for Dan. They crossed the parking lot and stopped at the sidewalk.

"Nice thinking," Dan said.

They now had a direct view of the body.

"You ready?" Laynie asked Dan.

He gave her a thumbs up.

She adjusted her hair and turned her back to the crime scene.

Dan used his free hand and pointed her to the left. He then gave her another thumbs up, letting her know he had a great shot of her and the body in the background.

Laynie held the microphone up and began doing what she did best.

"I'm here at Faxon Park in the small, sleepy town of Stoughton, Massachusetts. Behind me you can see the latest body. We're waiting for confirmation of the cause of death. I've been covering murders for a long time and it's highly unlikely to have four back-to-back murders like this in such a small community. Just to be clear, at this time we cannot confirm the body behind me is the victim of a murder. I will go out on a limb though and say I believe they were murdered. I'd even go further and say we're looking at the work of a serial killer. I base that assessment upon the press brief I attended last night for the third victim. When I was there, I noticed two FBI agents. When I asked why the FBI was here, District Attorney Steve Harbor said, and I quote, "The FBI is here in a supportive role. They're lending their expertise." I can tell you from years of experience, the FBI is called in to help catch a killer. The question here is why? Usually, the FBI makes a formal statement regarding their involvement. That has not happened. Also, why is the lead agent on the FBI's counter-terrorism task force here? Are these murders somehow related to a terrorist attack? I plan to find out, so stay tuned."

"We've got company," Colton said, spotting Laynie.

Barnes turned around.

"Is that the reporter from last night?" Barnes asked.

"It is," Colton said. "I'll be right back."

Colton made his way across the grass and crossed the street.

Chapter 60

Walnut Street
Stoughton, Massachusetts

Colton walked across Faxon Park and crossed Walnut Street. Then he turned and headed toward Laynie.

"Listen," Laynie said. "I'm behind the yellow line."

"I'm not here for that," Colton said.

"Well, don't think for one minute you're going to move us," Laynie said. "I'm with the press." She held up her press credentials that hung on the lanyard around her neck.

"Not gonna move you either," Colton said.

"Then what are you doing here?" Laynie asked.

"I'm politely asking you to refrain from airing footage of the body," Colton said. "We haven't ID'd the victim yet. I'd hate for their loved ones to see them like that."

"Oh," Laynie said. "I thought for sure you were going to tell us to leave."

"Nope," Colton said. "Believe it or not, I believe in the freedom of the press. I just wished sometimes you guys showed a little restraint, especially with those who've perished."

"I'm not like that," Laynie said. "I try to provide a voice for the victim. I even try to help catch the killer."

"I respect that," Colton said. "But it's my job to catch their killer."

"Well..." Laynie said. "You know that once the FBI gets involved, they take over the case. They'll tie your hands and screw you over. Trust me. I've seen it happen."

Colton just stood there for a moment.

"Any details you'd like to share?" Laynie asked.

"Sorry. I'm not the sharing type," Colton said.

"You know I can help you, right?" Laynie said.

Colton looked over at Barnes. "I have enough help. But thanks for the offer."

"I'm gonna do my own investigating," Laynie said. "Maybe we can compare notes sometime?"

"Sorry," Colton said. "Like I said, I'm not the sharing type."

Laynie looked at Colton. She studied his face.

"You look familiar," Laynie said. "Did you grow up here?"

"I did," Colton said. "Over off Lakewood Drive."

"Do you have an older sister?" Laynie asked.

"I do," Colton said. "How about you? Did you grow up around here?"

"Yes," Laynie said. "Off Plain Street. Over by TownSlice."

"Your last name is Monteiro, right?" Colton asked.

"Yes," Laynie said. "My Dad is David Monteiro. Yes, he's a reporter. And yes, he owns the Stoughton Times."

"Following in your Dad's footsteps," Colton said.

"Wow," Laynie said. "Now I know why you're a detective."

"Game on," Colton said. "Show off those investigational journalism skills. Maybe you can live up to your own reputation."

Dan chuckled from behind.

Laynie's face turned red.

"We've got our footage," Laynie said. "Lets go talk to one of the victim's family and coworkers. See what we can find out."

She turned around.

"Come on, Dan. We're leaving."

Chapter 61

Great Blue Hill Bank
Stoughton, Massachusetts

Laynie and Dan left Faxon Park and arrived at Great Blue Hill Bank a few minutes later. They entered through the front lobby. Laynie had her microphone in hand, and Dan had the camera on his shoulder.

Before they had walked across the lobby, a woman met and stopped them.

"I'm sorry," the woman said. "There's no recording in the bank. Of any kind. It's prohibited."

"And … you are?" Laynie asked.

"The HR Manager," the woman said. "And please tell him to stop filming."

Dan took the camera off his shoulder.

Laynie introduced herself.

"Yes," the woman said. "I know who you are."

"Would you be willing to talk to us about Larry Fuller?" Laynie asked.

"I'm sorry," the woman said. "The bank prohibits us from speaking about other employees."

"You know he's dead, right?" Laynie said.

"I know," the woman said. "It's such a tragedy. Now I'm going to have to ask you to leave."

"Sure," Laynie said. "No problem."

They turned and headed for the door.

"That was odd," Dan said once outside.

"Please tell me you got that on film," Laynie said.

"I took it off my shoulder," Dan said. "But I never stopped recording. I got the whole interaction."

"What company doesn't want free publicity by being on the news?" Laynie said. "Or to say something nice about the deceased."

"Maybe she was sleeping with Larry," Dan said.

"That crotchety bitch?" Laynie said. "No, I didn't get that vibe from her. It's something else."

"What now?" Dan asked.

Laynie looked at her watch. Then she looked around the parking lot.

"The bank closes in less than an hour. And there's only four cars here," Laynie said. "I say we sit and wait. Grab an employee as they leave work. See if they'll talk to us."

They spotted the first employee coming out. Laynie rushed over with her microphone in hand. She introduced herself and asked if they could speak for a moment.

The woman held up her hand. "No comment," she said and continued walking to her car. The next employee steered clear of Laynie and Dan. She walked at a brisk pace, her head down as she went.

A timid older woman exited the bank.

"Third times a charm," Laynie said. She approached the older woman and asked her for a comment on Larry Fuller.

The woman looked over her shoulder. "Not here."

"We can talk in private, if that's better for you," Laynie said. "Meet me at TownSlice," the woman said. "And you're buying the drinks."

"Sure thing," Laynie said. "I'll follow you."

"No! Don't," the woman said. She glanced over her shoulder at the front door of the bank. "Meet me there in twenty minutes, but don't follow me."

"Okay," Laynie said.

The woman scurried to her car.

Laynie stood in the parking lot and watched the older woman drive off. Once the car was out of sight, Laynie turned toward

Dan's car. As she walked, she noticed Sherri, the HR woman, standing in the bank window staring at her.

Laynie waved.

The HR woman flashed a scowl and disappeared back into the bank. It was obvious the older woman feared reprisals if she spoke to a reporter.

Laynie continued walking to the car and got in.

"No luck?" Dan asked.

"How about a drink?" Laynie asked.

Chapter 62

**Stoughton Police Headquarters
Stoughton, Massachusetts**

After the Medical Examiner left, Colton headed to the station. He wanted to look into something. First on his list was to check the cameras around town. Several years ago, the department had applied for a grant which was approved. The grant specified that the department must use the money on technical equipment. Someone suggested they buy cameras and place them around town to monitor certain locations. So they did. They placed cameras in the center of town, Halloran Park, and a few other locations.

It was a great asset to dispatch. If someone called from one of those locations, they could bring it up on the screen. It provided them with immediate eyes on the area. They could relay what they saw to the responding units.

Colton logged into the camera system and brought up the footage from this morning. As he suspected, everything was black during that time period.

Just to rule it out, Colton called the power company. No outages this morning.

His hunch about jammers was looking more plausible. Plus, the fact that the FBI was so interested in the case warranted its own suspicion.

Colton knew someone he could call, but would she answer his questions? He needed to call her back anyway. He grabbed his phone and placed the call.

It rang once and went to voicemail.

"Hey Cindy, it's me. I have a tech question and was hoping you could answer it for me. Call me back. Love you."

Colton sat at his desk. Dozens of questions swirled around in his head. One kept rising to the surface. *How did the FBI not notice someone dumping a body? Did they have constant surveillance? Could that be it? Did they leave and miss it? They have egg on their face and don't want to admit it?*

Questions without answers brought more questions.

Then the answer hit him. It was so simple. *The killer used the same jammers at Romano Sand and Gravel. That had to be it. Now it made sense. The FBI was poking around because the killer jammed their equipment.*

He'd ask Agent Diaz. She'd been honest with him before at the Medical Examiner's office.

There was a knock on the door. It was Barnes. Colton let him in.

"Any luck with the cameras?" Barnes asked, taking a seat.

"No," Colton said. "Same thing with our cameras. Six minutes of blackness."

"What about the bum?" Barnes asked. "What's his name?"

"Henry," Colton said. "You think he could pull this off?"

"I don't know," Barnes said. "Maybe he's not even a bum. Maybe he dresses like one to deceive people. No one wants to get close to a bum."

Colton sat there for a minute, pondering the idea.

"What about that reporter?" Barnes asked, changing topics. "She picked up on Wolf being FBI without him being mentioned."

Colton did a quick internet search.

"Damn," Colton said. "She's the real deal."

"Who?" Barnes asked. "The reporter?"

"Yeah," Colton said. "She's covered a lot of serial killers. One article says her research helped detectives catch a killer. Says some welcome the help with cold cases."

"Jesus," Barnes said. "We should use her."

"I may have already put her in motion," Colton said.

"When? This morning?" Barnes asked. "I was wondering why you went to talk to her. What happened?"

"She said she was the best at what she did," Colton said.

"And she asked to share notes."

"What did you say?" Barnes asked.

"I told her no," Colton said. "Told her to live up to her reputation and show off those investigational journalism skills."

"So … you poked the bear," Barnes said.

"I guess we'll find out," Colton said.

Chapter 63

TownSlice
Stoughton, Massachusetts

Laynie and Dan walked into TownSlice. The older woman waved to them from a booth. She was in the upper section of the lounge behind the bar.

They made their way past the bar and through the lounge.

Laynie tried to introduce herself, but the woman cut her off.

"I know who you are," the woman said. "I knew your Mom, and I used to read Laynie's Corner."

Laynie smiled.

"This is Dan. He's my cameraman," Laynie said, sitting down.

"Nice to meet you, Dan," the woman said. "I'm Gina."

The waitress came over and Gina ordered a Long Island Iced Tea. Laynie and Dan ordered beers.

"I suppose you want to know about Larry," Gina said.

"What can you tell us?" Laynie asked.

"Larry was dirty as the day is long," Gina said.

Laynie and Dan glanced at each other.

After the first drink, Gina opened up. She told them about Larry's foreclosure scheme and how the bank caught him.

"A man came in one day. He stood there shouting and shaking a piece of paper over his head," Gina said. "The guy was really upset."

"About what?" Laynie asked.

"He had received a foreclosure notice in the mail," Gina said. "The man was furious. He was screaming about how someone had cancelled his transaction for his mortgage payment. Then he pulled out his phone. He had screenshots of the transfer and of the bank cancelling the transfer."

"Really?" Laynie said.

"Yes," Gina said. "Someone at the bank had cancelled his payment. The money was still sitting in his account."

"Jesus," Dan said.

"That's not all," Gina said. "The bank was charging him late fees on top of the foreclosure process."

"What happened?" Laynie asked.

"Of course, the bank was full of customers. They all turned around and listened. The guy rambled on. The back office staff came out too."

"How did the bank handle it?" Laynie asked.

"Larry came out and apologized. Said it was some sort of computer glitch. Larry calmed the man down and brought him into his office. The man walked out smiling. He had one of Larry's coins in his hand."

"One of Larry's coins?" Laynie asked.

"Larry had an eclectic coin collection. He showed it off to everyone. He'd throw work parties at his house and invite us all over. Once he told me it was worth millions."

"He was murdered in his home, correct?" Laynie asked.

"Yes," Gina said. "I wonder if whoever killed him took his coin collection?"

"We'll look into that," Laynie said.

"We sure will!" Dan said.

"Can we go back to the bank for a minute?" Laynie asked. "Did other customers complain?"

"A lot did," Gina said.

"What's a lot?" Dan asked.

"Well, someone posted on Facebook about the incident at the bank," Gina said. "The last I saw, there were one hundred and twelve comments on the post. Multiple people were complaining. Said the same thing happened to them. People closed their accounts and moved their money to a different bank."

"And that post prompted the bank to look into it?" Laynie asked.

"Oh yeah," Gina said. "Especially since the person who created the post not only tagged the bank but tagged some board members too."

Gina could drink. She went on and on about Larry. Said no one liked him. He was a know it all. Apparently, he would stick his hand in a community bowl of chips and then lick his fingers. Then he'd reach back in. It grossed everyone out.

Two hours later, Laynie and Dan left TownSlice. They headed for Roy's Coin Shop.

Chapter 64

Stoughton Police Headquarters
Stoughton, Massachusetts

A press brief was scheduled for this evening. Prior to the meeting, Wolf met with Harbor and McCormack.

"Well, now that I've been called out by that reporter," Wolf said. "I'll be speaking at this evening's press brief. I want our time at the podium limited. Say what we need to say, then head back inside. Especially where we don't have much."

Both Harbor and McCormack agreed.

The time came for the press brief to begin. They all walked outside to the podium.

McCormack went first and gave a short speech. She stated that there were no new developments. Harbor was up next. But before McCormack finished, Laynie had her hand in the air. She didn't wait to be called on. She called out her first question.

"Now that the FBI is taking a more predominant role, who is officially in charge?" Layne asked.

McCormack looked at Harbor and he stepped up to the mic.

"Thank you for the question," Harbor said. "The FBI informed us that they are taking the lead in this investigation."

Harbor looked at Wolf and smiled. Wolf glared at him and stepped up to the podium.

"Agent Wolf," Laynie said. "Since you're heading up this investigation, I have a few questions for you."

"Wolf adjusted his tie. "Okay," he said. "Go ahead."

"What can you tell us about Larry Fuller?" Laynie said. "We've learned through our investigation that he was running a foreclosure scheme at Great Blue Hill Bank. Are you looking into this as a possible motive for his death?"

"I'm going to defer that question to District Attorney Harbor," Wolf said.

Harbor stepped back up to the podium.

"Yes," Harbor said. "We're looking into his employment as a possible motive."

Laynie looked around. All eyes were on her.

"Final question," Laynie said. "Is there any connection between the efforts to keep 911 local and these murders?"

Colton and Barnes looked at each other.

Harbor looked at McCormack, who shook her head no.

"I'm being told no," Harbor said. "That will be all for tonight. Thank you."

Chapter 65

Stoughton Police Headquarters
Stoughton, Massachusetts

After the press brief, they met back in McCormack's office.

"How did she know about Larry Fuller?" Harbor asked, furious.

"I'd guess she spoke to the woman down at the bank," Barnes said. "She's how we found out."

"There's a reason detectives want to work with her," McCormack said. "She digs in."

"Well, I don't like her snooping her nose around here," Wolf said.

"Why?" Colton asked. "Got something to hide?"

"I'm really growing tired of your mouth," Wolf said.

"Oh, I thought it was my tone," Colton said.

"Now if you don't mind. I'd like to speak to the chief and DA for a moment," Wolf said.

Barnes was first out the door followed by Colton and Diaz. Wolf closed the door behind them.

"I'm sorry," Diaz said, following Colton. "My boss can be a real dick sometimes."

"No worries," Colton said. "We know it's not you."

Colton opened his office door and they walked in.

Diaz looked around.

"Don't mind the mess," Colton said. "It's my first week and I haven't had a chance to decorate."

Barnes chuckled.

"What do you think they're talking about?" Barnes asked.

"Whether or not they should pull me from this case," Colton said. "Obviously, Wolf has it out for me. They'll probably use my lack of experience against me."

There was a knock at the door. Barnes opened it.

It was Wolf, Harbor and McCormack.

They walked in.

"After speaking with Special Agent Wolf," McCormack said. "We'd like to split up into two teams."

Colton sat up in his chair.

"Barnes," Harbor said. "You'll be working with Special Agent Wolf. You'll be following up on the Alex Torres murder and looking into the Romanos."

"Okay, boss," Barnes said.

"We think it best to divide and conquer," Harbor said. "Especially with the number of victims now."

"So, Colton," McCormack said. "That leaves you and Diaz."

"Colton," Wolf said. "You know the lay of the land, so you'll be point."

Colton's eyes bulged.

"Yes, sir," Diaz said.

"We'll check in each morning and evening," Wolf said. "Go home. Get some rest. Tomorrow, we dig in and find this killer."

Chapter 66

Roy's Stamps and Coins
Stoughton, Massachusetts

Laynie and Dan walked into Roy's Coin Shop. The bell hanging above the door chimed.

Roy stepped out of his office.

Laynie approached the counter and introduced herself.

"Hi, I'm Laynie Monteiro and I'm an investigative journalist with WTFH. This is Dan, my cameraman," Laynie said. "Are you the owner?"

"Hi Laynie," he said. "I'm Roy. Yes, I'm the owner."

"We're here doing a story about the recent murders."

"Okay," Roy said. "What does it have to do with me? Will my store be in your story?"

Laynie flashed Dan a smile.

"Of course. Both you and your store. But," Laynie said. "Only if you help us out."

Roy's face was beaming.

"What do you want to know?"

"Well, we heard the second victim, Larry Fuller, was an avid coin collector," Laynie said. "Do you know anything about his collection?"

"No," Roy said. "But there was a detective in here asking questions."

"What kind of questions?" Laynie asked.

"He had some pictures," Roy said. "He wanted to know what kind of coins they were," Roy said.

"And what coins were they?"

"There were several kinds," Roy said. "One was a medallion, not a coin."

"What kind of medallion was it?" Laynie asked.

"It was a Sons of Liberty medallion," Roy said. "But it wasn't one of those knock-offs. It was a real one." Laynie wrote it down and noted to look into it.

"What other kinds of coins did the detective ask about?" Laynie said. "Were they rare?"

"Oh yeah," Roy said. "They're rare alright."

"What were they?" Laynie asked.

"They were 1776 Continental Coins."

"What's that? What are those?"

"They're coins made by the Continental Congress prior to the Revolutionary War," Roy said.

"Are they valuable?"

"Extremely."

"What are we talking here?" Laynie asked. "A thousand dollars? Hundred thousand dollars?"

"Try a million," Roy said.

"That's an expensive collection. A million dollars."

"No," Roy said. "A million per coin."

Laynie's eyes widened.

"How many coins?" Laynie asked.

"According to the detective, there were close to fifty coins."

"Did the detective leave their name?" Laynie asked.

"Yeah," Roy said. "He left his card. Let me grab it." Roy disappeared into his office and returned a moment later.

He put the card down on the glass countertop and slid it over.

"Detective Colton Baker," she said. "Funny. I just met him."

"I think he's new," Roy said.

"New?" Laynie asked.

"Detective Peterson recently passed away," Roy said.

"I remember him," Laynie said. "My dad was friends with him."

"Well, they hired this Baker guy to replace him, but he looked really young."

Laynie looked over her shoulder at Dan with wide eyes. She then looked back at Roy.

"So, they have a new detective investigating multiple murders?" Laynie asked.

"Do you mind if we get some shots of your store?" Laynie asked.

"Not at all," Roy said. "To be honest, I could use the publicity."

"We can't make any promises regarding sales, but you and your store will definitely be in the news piece," Laynie said.

"When will it air?" Roy asked.

"Hard to say," Laynie said. "We still have some investigating to do. If you have a business card, I can contact you before it airs."

"That would be wonderful," Roy said.

"Would you be interested in a follow-up interview?" Laynie asked. "Once we uncover more of the story."

"Of course!" Roy said. "Stop by any time."

Roy handed both Laynie and Dan one of his business cards.

Chapter 67

Nancy and Paul Baker's House
Stoughton, Massachusetts

After the press brief, Colton stopped by his parents' house. With so much going on, it felt like it had been forever since he'd been back.

When he walked in, the dogs came running. Hayley ran circles around him. Roxy let out a few barks.

"Is that you?" came his mother's voice from the living room.

Colton walked out to see her. The dogs followed.

"Howdy stranger," Nancy said.

"I know. I'm sorry, Mom," Colton said. "How have you been? How's Dad?"

"Oh, he's the same," she said. "I had to flip the mattress last night. He pissed the bed so badly it went everywhere. Soaked right through the sheets. And, of course, I hadn't zipped the mattress protector all the way. So it bled through. Room stinks like piss."

"Geez … I'm sorry, Mom," Colton said. "Sorry I wasn't here to help."

"Could you do me a favor?" she asked.

"Anything," Colton said. "What do you need?"

"Your father is out of his Depends diapers," Nancy said. "If he'd been wearing one last night. Well … you know."

Colton offered to go buy some. Nancy texted him a picture of the front of the box.

"Have you eaten?" Colton asked.

"No, not yet," Nancy said.

"I'll grab something on my way back."

Colton left and returned a short time later. He bought three packs of adult diapers and KFC for dinner.

"It's good to see you," Nancy said, touching Colton's face.

"You too, Mom."

"How's the investigation going?" Nancy asked.

"Slow," Colton said. "We need to catch a break."

"I saw Laynie on the news," Nancy said. "That's David Monteiro's daughter, you know. He owns the Stoughton Times. Laynie used to write for the paper back when she was a kid. She had the knack back then. That girl had a way about her. She can get anyone to talk. I guess that's good for a reporter."

"One would assume," Colton said. "Since her job is to literally hold a microphone in peoples' faces and have them talk."

"She's about your age," Nancy said.

Colton glared at her.

"I'm friends with her father," Nancy said. "I could set you up on a date."

"Thanks, but no thanks, Mom," Colton said.

"Mmm ..." Nancy said, licking her fingers. "I haven't had Kentucky Fried Chicken in years. It's delicious. I forgot how good it was."

"A bit expensive," Colton said. "But good."

"Have you heard from Cindy?" Nancy asked.

"No," Colton said. "We've been playing phone tag."

Chapter 68

David Monteiro's House
Stoughton, Massachusetts

They arrived back at David's after grabbing takeout for dinner.

They were sitting around eating when Laynie brought up David dating Wendy.

"I can't believe I didn't know you dated Wendy McDonald," Laynie said.

"Her last name wasn't McDonald back then. It was Simpson," David said.

"Whatever Dad," Laynie said. "You still dated her, and I never heard about it."

"Why are you acting so surprised?" David said. "How many boys did you date in high school? It was the same thing."

"Wait," Laynie said. "So you used to be best friends with Bill McDonald?"

"I was," David said. "Until he stole my girlfriend."

"What was he like?" Laynie asked.

"It was over thirty years ago, Laynie," David said. "People change. We were in high school."

Laynie sat there for a minute.

"Dad," Laynie said. "Did you know the other victims?"

"Yes," David said. "I knew Larry. Back when I had the paper. He'd place ads in the Stoughton Times for the bank. He'd list job postings, offers the bank was running, things like that."

"How about the other victims?" Laynie asked.

"Well, I knew Graziele Alves. She was the tax collector, so most of the town knew her. I didn't know her personally the way I knew Bill."

"And what about Alex Torres?" Laynie asked. "Did you know him?"

"I can't say that I did," David said.

"Hmm…" Laynie said.

"What?" David asked.

"I just realized that all the victims are roughly the same age," Laynie said.

"Don't most serial killers target victims of the same age or profession?" Dan asked.

"Yes," Laynie said. "But I've never covered one that kills all older people. I wonder if it's their age that has something to do with why they're being targeted and not their profession. I'll look into that."

Just then, Laynie's phone rang. It was Hank. He wanted an update.

Laynie told him that they'd had a productive day, and they'd had several interviews. She told him about the foreclosure scheme Larry Fuller was running.

"Dan sent me the footage from the press brief," Hank said. "You did great. Keep digging."

"Oh, trust me," Laynie said. "I will."

"Don't I know it," Hank said. "Well, I just called to check in on you. Say hi to your dad for me."

"Will do," Laynie said. "Love you."

"Love you, too," Hank said.

Chapter 69

**Medical Examiner's Office
Boston, Massachusetts**

Colton and Barnes arrived at the Medical Examiner's office. This time, FBI agents Wolf and Diaz followed them.

Once inside, a lab technician led them into the autopsy room where a sheet covered a body that lay on a steel gurney.

Agent Wolf stood in the back while the other three stood near the table.

A moment later, Dr. Hurst walked in. He pulled back the sheet.

Colton couldn't believe it. The woman looked different. Twenty-four hours ago, she was unrecognizable. Today the tar was gone. Now she looked like a woman. Not something out of a horror movie. Well, except for her eyes and the symbols on her forehead.

"Totally different, huh?" Hurst asked.

"You ain't kidding," Barnes replied.

"I had four techs in here working all night," Hurst said. "Two removing the feathers and two removing the tar. I had them start with her hands. They cleaned them up enough to lift prints."

Hurst picked up the clipboard off the table and reviewed it.

"Meet Graziele Alves. Fifty-five," Hurst said. "I provided her info in the folder."

Hurst handed it to Colton.

"As you can tell, your killer left more symbols. He branded them on."

"Branded?" Barnes said. "Like they do to cattle?"

"Yes sir," Hurst said.

"So, he killed her and then branded her?" Colton asked.

"No," Hurst said. "She was alive."

"Jesus!" Barnes said.

"It was excruciating," Hurst said.

"What else can you tell us, Doc?" Colton asked.

Hurst pointed to several clear bins behind him on the counter. Some contained feathers and others tar.

"We'll start with the feathers," Hurst said. "At first, we thought they were from a pillow, but they're real seagull feathers. I'm not sure where one goes to get seagull feathers. So, you'll have to look into that."

Colton made a note. *Check for any reports of dead seagulls being found.*

"Then there's the tar," Hurst said. "I want to preface that it was sticky as hell."

"You don't say," Barnes said sarcastically.

"What's the official cause of death?" Colton asked.

"You're dealing with a real sicko here, Detective," Hurst said. "He poured hot tar all over her, which left second and third-degree burns. We found tar inside both nostrils. Then he packed her mouth with horse manure. We found it deep inside the trachea. She suffocated to death."

"Holy shit," Barnes said. "No pun intended."

Hurst cracked a smile.

"What can you tell us about the tar?" Colton asked.

"This wasn't your everyday kinda tar," Hurst said. "It's rare."

"No offense, doc … tar isn't rare," Barnes said.

"You're correct," Hurst said. "But this tar is."

"What kind of tar is it then?" Barnes asked.

"Pine tar," Hurst said.

"What is it used for?" Barnes asked.

"Well, tar has a lot of uses," Hurst said. "From roads to roofs. But this kind is used on…"

"Rigging," Colton said, before Hurst could finish.

"That's right, detective," Hurst said. "They would apply it to the ropes in the rigging of old sailing vessels. Back then, rope would quickly rot when exposed to water. They covered it in tar as waterproofing to preserve the rope."

"Do people still tar ropes?" Barnes asked.

"I believe most rope, not all of course, is now synthetic," Hurst said. "They're made from nylon, polyester and polypropylene. It's cheaper, easier to make, and stronger."

"Who around here still uses hemp rope and tar?" Barnes asked.

"Two ships come to mind," Colton said. "The U.S.S. Constitution in Boston Harbor and the Mayflower Two, down in Plymouth."

"Mayflower Two?" Diaz asked.

"Yes," Colton said. "It's a replica of the original ship that brought the Pilgrims to Plymouth."

"It's docked down next to Plymouth Rock," Barnes said. "You should check it out sometime. Not the rock, though. It's tiny and embarrassing."

"Tiny?" Diaz said.

"Over the years, visitors chipped off pieces," Colton said. "They built a well-type structure over it to keep people away. It's rather unfortunate looking for such a historical site."

"Are you done with the history lesson?" Wolf asked from behind them.

The three looked at each other.

"Anything else you can tell us?" Colton asked.

"I took the liberty of printing out her fingerprints and the symbols for you," Hurst said. "They're in that folder."

"Thanks, doc," Colton said.

"I hope you catch the bastard, Detective," Hurst said.

The four of them left and walked out to their vehicles.

Once in the parking lot, Wolf said, "Agent Diaz, you're with Detective Baker. Barnes, you're with me."

Chapter 70

Stoughton Police Headquarters
Stoughton, Massachusetts

Colton and Diaz arrived back at the station and stopped by Chief McCormack's office. Her door was open. They poked their heads in.

"We've ID'd the tarred and feathered woman," Colton said.

"Who was she?" McCormack asked.

Colton looked at his notepad. "Her name is Graziele Alves."

The chief stood up.

"The Town Clerk?" McCormack asked.

"Did you know her?" Colton asked.

"Yes," McCormack said, sitting back down. "We grew up together. You could say we were two peas in a pod. We'd run into each other every so often. Usually while grabbing lunch around the corner. We'd sit and talk. Sometimes we'd go out to dinner together and catch up."

"Should we do the notifications together?"

"It's pointless," McCormack said. "She never married. She has no children, and both of her parents are dead."

"Any siblings?"

"None. She was an only child."

"I'll grab a warrant and then head over to her place," Colton said.

"Yes. But do me a favor," McCormack said. "Keep it off the airwaves. Laynie Monteiro is probably listening. She'll be all over you."

"Can you call a press conference?" Colton asked. "Keep her off my back?"

"I'd love to," McCormack said. "But the FBI is lead now. That's their call."

Colton looked at Diaz.

"Would you look at that?" Colton said. "We have an FBI agent right here."

McCormack looked at Diaz.

"Call the press conference," Diaz said.

"Are you sure?" McCormack asked.

"Yeah," Diaz said. "I doubt Special Agent Wolf wants to deal with that reporter again. Never mind her being on scene of an active investigation."

"Get the warrant," McCormack said. "And I'll get Harbor to schedule a press conference for today. I'll list the time as to be determined.

"Will do, Chief," Colton said.

Chapter 71

Graziele Alves' House
Stoughton, Massachusetts

McCormack notified Harbor about the fourth victim's identity. He agreed to call a press brief.

Colton obtained the search warrant for Graziele Alves' house. Diaz accompanied him along with a patrol unit. She called Wolf on the way and told him about the press brief. She failed to mention she had provided authorization for it.

Shortly after, they arrived. It was a pleasant house in a quiet neighborhood. A car was in the driveway. Colton ran the plates. It came back to Graziele Alves. They searched the outside of the house first. There were no broken windows or forced entry. Colton noted that there were no cameras, either.

Once they had finished outside, they searched inside. Colton forced the door open.

The inside was clean. Ms. Alves was what Colton would call a neat freak. Maybe that's how older people without kids lived. Clean.

They searched the premises. There was no sign of a struggle. No blood. Whatever happened to Graziele Alves it didn't happen here.

On the kitchen table, they found a printed airline ticket. They also found a printed hotel and rental car reservation.

Colton called the airline. Graziele never made her flight. Next, he called the hotel. She never checked in. He called the car rental company too. He couldn't leave any rock unturned. As suspected, Graziele never rented the car.

While Colton made the calls, Diaz checked the house and closets again. No suitcase.

"Let's check the bathroom," Colton said. "See if she took her toiletries."

They checked the sink and underneath. No toothbrush or toothpaste.

"Odd," Diaz said. "She left her tickets here but took her suitcase."

"I think the killer printed them. Then left them for us to find," Colton said.

"But why?" Diaz asked.

"He's trying to throw us off," Colton said. "Trying to send us in a different direction. He tried the same thing with Larry Fuller. Made it look like Fuller was a pedophile watching child porn. We discovered the killer added it to Fuller's computer at the time of Larry's death."

"What do we do now?" Diaz asked.

"We notify Barnes and get the State Police Forensics Team down here to process the house. Have them go through her laptop," Colton said. "Then we pay a visit to Stoughton Town Hall and talk to her coworkers. See if she had a trip planned."

"And if she did?" Diaz asked.

"I doubt it," Colton said. "But if she did, then our killer probably knew about it. My guess, he posed as an Uber driver and caught her off guard."

Chapter 72

Stoughton Police Headquarters
Stoughton, Massachusetts

Wolf and Barnes arrived at the station. McCormack and Harbor were already at the podium, giving the brief. They walked over and stood off to the side. Laynie was there. She looked disappointed by the brief. It was short and provided nothing new.

After the brief, Wolf and Barnes met with Harbor and McCormack in her office.

Wolf wanted to know who authorized the press brief. McCormack told him Diaz had. Wolf looked pissed.

"Where is Agent Diaz now?" Wolf asked.

"She's with Colton executing a search warrant on Graziele Alves' house," McCormack said. "They should be back shortly."

They waited.

Colton and Diaz returned thirty minutes later and McCormack called them into her office.

Wolf started right in on Diaz.

"Who do you think you are? You do not have the authority to speak for the FBI. You are neither a Special Agent nor an Agent in Charge," Wolf said.

"And shame on you," Wolf said, pointing at McCormack. "For listening to an agent fresh out of the academy."

"Don't you blame her," Harbor injected. "It was your idea to split up into teams. You knew Detective Baker was new to his role. Same with Agent Diaz. That's on you!"

"Alright, alright," Wolf said. "Let's all just calm down."

"For what's it's worth," McCormack said. "I think Agent Diaz made the right call. Imagine if we hadn't called the press conference? Laynie Monteiro would have been all over Graziele Alves' house. Can you imagine her standing there, live, drilling my officers or Colton and Diaz? What a shitshow that would have been."

Wolf turned to Diaz.

"You made the right call," Wolf said. "But please, next time, run it past me first."

"I will," Diaz said.

"Where are we with the investigation?" Wolf asked. "What did you find at the house?"

Colton told them what they'd found.

"I received your message, Colton," Barnes said. "I've contacted Trish. She and her team are on their way over."

"We have nothing on the killer?" Wolf asked. "Zero leads?"

"What do you want us to do?" Colton asked.

"I wanna sit on the Romanos," Wolf said.

"You think they dumped a body on their property and thought we wouldn't investigate it?" Colton asked.

Wolf didn't even look at Colton.

"I believe Nino is the killer and Gino is orchestrating it," Wolf said.

"I'm sorry," Colton said. "But why do you think the Romanos have anything to do with these murders?"

"I don't know why," Wolf said. "That's your job to find out."

"Yeah," Colton said. "I would if you'd let me do my job."

"Barnes and I will sit on Gino," Wolf said. "You and Diaz sit on Nino."

"For how long?" Colton asked.

"We're going to sit on them for a few days," Wolf said.

"This is gonna be a waste of time," Colton said. "We should be digging into the victims' past," Colton said. "We should be looking for a link between them."

"I'm in charge of this task force," Wolf said. "So you'll do as I say or I'll have you replaced."

Colton looked to McCormack.

"Sorry, Colton," McCormack said. "It's the chain of command."

"We should be looking for the actual killer," Colton said.

"You've got a real chip on your shoulder," Wolf said. "For someone with your lack of experience. You should sit back and watch how things are done."

"Are you gonna show me?" Colton asked. "Because the last time I checked, the FBI hasn't had the greatest track history lately."

Wolf's face turned bright red.

"Fine," Wolf said. "You and Diaz look into the victims' past."

Chapter 73

Town Hall
Stoughton, Massachusetts

Colton and Diaz arrived at the Stoughton Town Hall. It was an old brick building with a granite block foundation. On the first floor was the Tax Collector's Office. They walked in.

Colton introduced himself and asked to speak with some of the staff.

"Isn't it just awful what happened to Graziele," an older woman said.

"It is," Colton said. "We'd like to ask you some questions."

"Come on inside," the woman said. "I'm Mary."

Colton and Diaz walked through the swing door at the end of the counter.

"Stephanie," Mary said to a fellow employee. "Can you watch the counter while I speak with the detectives?"

Stephanie nodded.

Colton told Stephanie that he'd like to speak with her too, after.

Mary led them down to a small break room. They sat at the table next to the microwave.

"What can you tell us about Graziele?" Colton asked.

"She was the best," Mary said. "She was a great boss. I really enjoyed working for her."

"Was there anything different about her?" Colton asked. "Anything at all?"

"Not that I recall," Mary said. "Although she was excited about her trip."

"Her trip?" Colton asked.

"Yes," Mary said. "Graziele was supposed to be in France now. She'd taken two weeks off for her trip."

"When was she slated to leave?" Colton asked.

"I thought she was leaving last week," Mary said. "She'd taken off last week and this week. I was surprised to hear she hadn't left."

"Was she travelling with anyone?" Colton asked. "Husband? Boyfriend?"

"No," Mary said. "Graziele was single. She never married and never had children."

Colton made a note.

"She was going alone," Mary said. "But there was something. It happened the last Friday she worked."

"What was that?" Colton asked.

"She received a phone call," Mary said. "She seemed shaken up."

"Did you ask her about the call?" Colton asked.

"I did," Mary said. "She said it was nothing. Wrong number. The call was too long for a wrong number. I asked her if someone had threatened her."

"Why would you ask that?" Colton asked.

"We're tax collectors, Detective," Mary said. "Have you ever met someone who enjoys paying taxes? People are upset. Some people owe thousands. Sometimes people lose their homes because of nonpayment of back taxes."

"Has anyone recently lost their house? Or is there anyone about to lose their home?" Colton asked.

"None that I can think of," Mary said. "But Graziele handled those cases."

"Can we get a copy of those, please?" Colton asked.

They finished speaking with Mary and then spoke with Stephanie. She had little to offer as she had started two weeks ago.

Mary made copies of the files of the homes that owed back taxes. She handed them to Colton as they left.

"We'll look at these when we get back to the station," Colton said. "But first I want to stop by the scene again and look around. Maybe we missed something."

Chapter 74

Stoughton Public Library
Stoughton, Massachusetts

Colton pulled up against the curb and stopped. He stepped onto the grass and looked around.

The police cars and crime scene tape were all gone. A slow trickle of cars proceeded through the green light in front of the library.

The distant sound of a running lawn mower echoed in the square.

Diaz got out and stood next to him.

"What am I missing?" Colton asked.

Diaz looked around.

"Nothing," she said. "The crime scene techs already processed the area."

"I know," Colton said. "But something's missing. I just can't place my finger on it."

Colton turned, taking a second look around. Nothing jumped out to him.

"What's that building over there?" Diaz asked.

Colton turned and saw her pointing toward the set of lights.

"That's the library," Colton said.

The library was a large two-story gray building set atop a hill. The front of the second floor hung over the entrance. Six large pillars held up the overhang.

"Hmm…" Colton said. "I bet there's a great vantage point of the park from the second floor. Let's check it out."

They crossed the street and walked up the ramp to the front door.

Yellow and blue flowers swayed in the light summer breeze. The petals were open, accepting the warm sunshine.

The library didn't open for another thirty minutes, but the lights were on. Colton walked up to the window and peeked inside. An older woman was scanning the books in from the overnight drop-box.

Colton tapped on the window. The woman looked at her watch. Then she looked up.

"We don't open for another thirty minutes," she mouthed and went back to scanning the books.

Colton tapped on the window again. The woman looked up, annoyed. This time, Colton held his badge up to the window. He pointed to the door.

The woman smiled. Her entire demeanor changed, and she headed for the door.

"May I help you?" she asked, opening the door a crack.

Colton identified himself and Diaz.

"Is this about that awful murder at the park?" she asked.

"Yes," Colton said. "May we come in?"

"Oh sure," the woman said. "Come on in, Detective."

"I assume you want to go upstairs," she said. "The park view is beautiful up there."

Colton told her she was correct. The woman pointed to the stairs.

Colton and Diaz made their way across the library. They took the stairs up to the second floor.

"Libraries have such a unique smell," Colton said, ascending the stairs. "I love it. All the old books."

Diaz looked out at the book-filled rows.

"Each book is like a magic key," Colton said. "When you read them, they open your mind's eye and the words on the page come alive in your imagination."

"I guess you like to read," Diaz said.

"Love it," Colton said. "Ever since I was a little boy. Growing up, my mother brought me to the library every Saturday morning. Do you like to read, Agent Diaz?"

"Not unless I have to," she said.

They reached the top of the stairs, and Colton looked around.

A janitor, emptying a small wastebasket into a trash barrel, looked up, surprised, clearly not expecting to see someone before the library opened.

They reached the window in the far front corner and looked out. It provided them with a bird's-eye view of the crime scene and all of Faxon Park. From this vantage point, they could see both memorials, the cannons, howitzer, and park benches. They could even see the gazebo. Which was tucked in the back.

Still, nothing jumped out at him.

"Maybe this was a waste of time," Colton said.

They stood there for a moment longer. They were about to leave when movement inside the gazebo caught Colton's eye.

Colton pointed.

"There's someone in the gazebo," he said.

"Where?" Diaz said.

"Inside," Colton said. "Lying on the bench."

The person inside the gazebo sat up.

It was a man.

Colton looked closer. The man matched the description of Henry, the bum seen standing over McDonald's body at the train station.

Colton turned and bolted for the stairs.

Chapter 75

Stoughton Public Library
Stoughton, Massachusetts

Colton bolted out of the library and sprinted across Park Street. Diaz was right behind him. They dodged cars as they ran through the intersection.

They ran into the park and headed straight for the gazebo. When they arrived, the man was gone.

"He was just here!" Colton said.

"He couldn't have gotten far," Diaz said.

Colton turned and scanned the area.

"There!" Colton shouted. The man walked from behind a car. More of a hobble than a walk. He was on Walnut Avenue, heading toward the center of town.

Colton gave chase.

In a matter of seconds, Colton was behind him and gaining fast.

The man looked over his shoulder and started hobbling faster.

Colton caught up to him and tackled him to the ground. The man stunk of piss and booze.

"I didn't do nothing," the man said.

"You're Henry? Aren't you?" Colton asked.

"Yeah, but I didn't do nothing."

Colton cuffed him. Then he radioed dispatch and requested a patrol car.

Sirens filled the air and, a minute later, two cruisers came bombing up.

They placed Henry in a cruiser.

"Jesus," one officer said. "He stinks."

Colton and Diaz walked back to their car.

They arrived at the station. Henry was in the interview room.

Colton called Barnes to tell him that he had tracked down Henry. Barnes was around the corner and said he'd be there shortly.

Colton knocked on the interview room door. The patrolman opened it and stepped out. Once in the hallway, Colton pulled a twenty-dollar bill from his wallet. He handed it to the patrolman and told him to go to McDonald's and grab a bunch of burgers, fries and a large Coke.

Barnes arrived along with Wolf.

The patrolman returned with a large bag of McDonald's.

Barnes looked through the interview room window and smiled. "How many burgers do you think you'll have to eat before he confesses and asks for one?" Barnes asked.

"He's not gonna confess," Colton said.

"You wanna bet five bucks?" Barnes said.

"Sure."

"I bet he confesses after one burger," Barnes said.

"Let's go find out," Colton said.

Both men entered the interview room.

"You're a hard man to track down," Colton said, putting a bag of food and drink from McDonald's on the interview table.

Colton sat down at the table. Barnes stood in the corner.

"Is that for me?" Henry asked.

"Would you like some?" Colton asked, pulling a burger from the bag.

Henry licked his lips.

Colton unwrapped the burger and took a bite.

"Tell us why you killed Bill McDonald?" Colton said.

"I didn't kill that man," Henry said. "If that's what you think."

"What did you do with his wallet and keys?" asked Barnes.

"I didn't take his wallet nor his keys," Henry said, staring at the McDonald's bag.

"We have eyewitnesses who said they saw you standing over the body," Colton said, wiping ketchup from the corner of his mouth.

"I didn't kill anyone," Henry said.

Colton pulled a long French fry out of the bag and ate it. "Still hot," Colton said. "Tell us what happened, and I'll give you a burger. Hell, you can have the fries and drink too."

Henry hung his head low. After a moment, he spoke.

"He was already dead," Henry said. "I didn't take his wallet or keys. I swear. I just took the coins."

Colton and Barnes exchanged glances.

"The ones from his pocket?" Colton asked.

Henry shook his head.

"What coins then?" Colton asked.

"The ones covering his eyes."

Chapter 76

Stoughton Police Headquarters
Stoughton, Massachusetts

Henry told Colton he saw a big black truck drive off after dumping the body. Said he didn't see the driver. Colton asked what happened to the coins. Henry said he pawned them at the pawn shop on Seaver Street. Told them he went on a four-day binge with the money he made.

They left Henry sitting in the interview room. Colton gave him the bag of McDonald's to eat.

Both Barnes and Colton exited the interview room.

"You owe me five bucks," Colton said, closing the door behind him.

Barnes smiled.

Colton went to his office to check the status of McDonald's truck. No hits on the APB.

"Take a ride over to the pawn shop?" Barnes asked.

"Let's go," Colton said.

Colton and Diaz drove in one car with Barnes and Wolf in another. They headed to the pawn shop.

"Hey, Detective," Randy said as Colton walked in. "Still haven't seen any of that jewelry or silverware set."

"Thanks for keeping an eye out," Colton said. "But I'm here regarding something else."

Randy looked at Barnes, Wolf, and Diaz.

"Is this about the recent murders?" Randy asked.

Colton pulled out a picture of the Sons of Liberty medallions. "Have you seen these?"

Randy looked at the picture. "Yeah," he said. "I bought two off some bum the other day."

"Do you still have them?" Colton asked.

"Yes, sir," Randy said. "Did he steal them? I didn't know he stole them."

"We're gonna need those," Barnes said. "They're part of a murder investigation."

"They're out back," Randy said. "Let me go get them."

Randy retrieved them and put them on the counter.

Colton pulled out two evidence bags and slid the medallions into the bags.

"What about my forty bucks?" Randy asked.

"What?" Barnes said.

"I paid forty bucks for those," Randy said. "Twenty each."

Colton pulled out his wallet and opened it. He took out two twenty-dollar bills and tossed them on the counter.

They walked out.

"Well, this changes things," Colton said. "Here we thought the killer took them from Fuller and used them as a calling card. Turns out he already had them."

"What if Fuller was the first victim?" Barnes said. "Not the second."

"You could be right," Colton said. "McDonald's phone records show Fuller called him. We'll need to confirm the time of death with the medical examiner."

"Do you want to fill us in?" Diaz asked.

"McDonald was our first victim," Colton said. "His wife said he received a phone call and went out but never returned."

"McDonald is the victim you found at the train station?" Diaz asked.

"Correct," Colton said. "We pulled McDonald's phone records to see who called him that night."

"The number belonged to Larry Fuller, your second victim," Wolf said, getting into the conversation.

"Right," Colton said.

"So, you're able to tie the first victim to the second victim via phone call," Diaz said.

"Yes," Colton said. "But we haven't found anything else linking them together."

"What about Alex Torres?" Diaz asked. "The guy in the porta potty at Romano Sand and Gravel. No connection with the other three?"

"Correct," Barnes said.

"And no connection between Graziele Alves and the others," Colton said. "None. Except the strange markings on their foreheads."

Chapter 77

Stoughton Police Headquarters
Stoughton, Massachusetts

They held another press brief. McCormack took the podium first. She asked the public for help.

"If you saw anything," McCormack said. "Please contact us here at the station."

Laynie was present. She started firing questions off as soon as McCormack was done speaking.

"Do you actually have any new info to share?" Laynie asked. "Or is this brief another waste of time?"

"When we have more information, we'll share it," McCormack said.

"Is it true you have a suspect in custody?" Laynie asked.

"No," Wolf said, stepping to the podium. "That is not true."

"Do you have any leads?" Laynie asked. "Any suspects?"

"None at this time," Wolf said.

"So, to be clear," Laynie said. "You have four bodies. No connections. No leads. And no suspects. Is that correct?"

"Yes," Wolf said through clenched teeth.

"We've spoken to members of the public and they're scared," Laynie said. "They're scared to go out. Scared to let their children play outside. What are you doing to ease the public's fears? Also, it being an election year, has the Town Manager or Board of Selectman put any pressure on you to catch the killer?"

"That's all the questions for today," Wolf said.

As Harbor and McCormack walked away from the podium, they told Colton he better catch the killer soon.

"Political pressure is mounting," McCormack said.

"It's an election year," Harbor said. "So expect everyone and their uncle to come out of the woodwork. Each with their own two cents. They'll all know best how to run this investigation."

Chapter 78

Stoughton Police Headquarters
Stoughton, Massachusetts

Colton and Diaz stood watching the different reporters wrap up. Some reviewed their notes, while others recorded segments to be used for the ten and eleven o'clock broadcasts later tonight. Cameramen took their microphones off the podium and wrapped up electrical cords.

Laynie spotted them standing alone and headed over to ask a few questions.

"Are they always such pigheaded assholes?" Laynie asked, walking up to them.

"Off the record. Yes," Diaz said.

"I've covered cases like this before. They always step on their dicks."

Colton chuckled.

Diaz snorted and covered her face.

"Present company excluded," Laynie said.

"Of course," Colton said.

"How does your chief put up with it?" Laynie asked.

"She's one of the good ones," Colton said. "They're all pulling rank on her."

"Probably the best thing. If things go sideways, they'll be the faces everyone remembers and not hers," Laynie said.

Colton nodded.

"They'll probably still try to screw her," Laynie said. "Based upon my personal experience."

Laynie's phone rang. She answered it.

Colton and Diaz turned away.

"I like her," Diaz whispered.

"Me too," Colton replied.

"Should we invite her to dinner?" Diaz asked.

"I don't recommend we invite her," Colton said. "But … maybe we mention where we're going. See if she picks up the hint."

"Sure," Diaz said. "If she shows up, we can pick her brain. Hell, if they don't want to listen to her, maybe we should. Can't hurt to get a different perspective."

"Sorry about that," Laynie said. "It was my Dad."

"No worries," Colton said. "We were just discussing dinner. We're heading over to the Gorettie's Grille."

"Great food," Laynie said. "Enjoy."

Colton and Diaz headed for their car and got in.

"Did she take the bait?" Colton asked, driving away.

"Well, she's running to her car, so I'd say so," Diaz said.

Diaz continued to watch over her shoulder. "Here she comes."

A few minutes later, they turned into the Gorettie's Grille parking lot. Laynie turned in right after them.

"Are we really going to do this?" Diaz asked. "Are we sitting down with a reporter?"

"I guess so," Colton said.

"Does this violate our investigation?" Diaz asked. "I mean, is it legal?"

"We'll just feel her out. See what she has to say," Colton said. "If other departments use her, it can't be illegal."

"Okay."

"We don't give her anything new," Colton said. "We simply reiterate the info given at the press briefs."

Diaz looked at him. "Do you really expect that to fly with a veteran reporter?"

"I don't know."

"She has years of experience dealing with this type of thing," Diaz said. "She's gonna see right through us novices."

"What if we tell her the truth?" Colton said.

"Are you serious?"

"We tell her off the record," Colton said. "Put an ace in her pocket. She'll have all the facts other news agencies are scrambling to verify. It's a prime lead."

"Is there a but?" Diaz asked.

"Yeah," Colton said. "She needs to tell us what she thinks and what she uncovers."

"You know we could lose our jobs because of this?" Diaz said.

"Nothing ventured, nothing gained," Colton said.

Chapter 79

Gorettie's Grille
Stoughton, Massachusetts

Colton and Diaz walked up the ramp to Gorettie's Grille with Laynie a few steps behind.

"Fancy meeting you here," Laynie said, stopping next to them while they waited for a table.

"Hi, Detective Baker," the maitre d' said.

Colton smiled and said hello.

"What is this place, Cheers?" Diaz asked, nudging Colton with her elbow playfully.

Colton looked at her questioningly.

"Come on!" she said. "You live like twenty miles from Boston."

"What am I missing here?" Colton asked.

"*Norm!*" Diaz said playfully. Maybe a little too loud. She caught the attention of the bartender and patrons at the bar.

"I have no clue what you're talking about," Colton said.

Blushing, Diaz sang the little jingle. "*Where everyone knows your name.*"

Colton's eyebrows raised.

"You seriously don't know Cheers? It was a TV show back in the eighties," Diaz said. "My dad loved it. That and the A-Team."

"Of course I know Cheers," Colton said with a huge smile. "I just wanted to see if you'd sing it."

Laynie laughed.

"Right this way, *Cliff*," the hostess said, laughing before leading them to their table.

The waitress came and they placed their order. They made small talk over drinks.

Once the food arrived, Laynie jumped right in.

"Tell me about the victims?" Laynie said. "Have you made any connections? Did the killer leave anything on them?" Her questions came like rapid fire.

Colton and Diaz exchanged glances.

"That's a yes," Laynie said. "Especially how you two just looked at each other. Speaking of which, are you guys a couple? You look cute together."

"No, we're not a couple," Colton said. "Can we stay on topic, please?"

"Right," Laynie said. "You guys realize how the media works? We arrive and stick a camera in people's faces. Everyone's looking for their fifteen minutes of fame. Plus, I've covered dozens of serial killers. Some like to leave things behind. Taunt the police. So, am I right? Did the killer leave something behind?"

Colton put down his fork and leaned back against the booth seat.

"Don't worry," Laynie said. "I won't be releasing any information until I have confirmation."

Colton sat there. He rubbed the stubble on his chin.

"I heard the killer left some sort of strange symbols on the body. Do you care to comment on that?" Laynie asked. "Because everyone loves a good Zodiac Killer story."

"I'm not ready to disclose any information about the case," Colton said. "At some point. But not yet. I'm not ready to put my career on the line. First, you'll need to prove yourself to me. But I'll do you a solid in the meantime."

"It's something about the killer?" Laynie asked.

"Sort of," Colton said. "But before I do this. I want to know everything you've heard."

"All of it?" Laynie asked.

"Yes," Colton said. "Listen. There's no doubt you're one of the best reporters on the planet. You find the facts and tell the entire story. People trust you. They see themselves on the news and open up to you. When people see us, they think they're going to jail."

"There's truth to what he's saying," Diaz said, picking apart a dinner roll.

Laynie twirled her fork in the spaghetti.

"If what you give me pans out, I'll even sweeten the deal," Colton said.

"How so?" Laynie said.

"I'll share new details of the case with you when they come in," Colton said. "You'll have a leg up on everyone else."

"You'd do that?" Laynie asked.

"I looked into you," Colton said. "I made some calls. You're the real deal. You actually help and hold back details to not interfere with the case. I respect that."

Laynie hoisted the fork of spaghetti and put it in her mouth. She slurped in the last strands, sending a splotch of red sauce twirling onto the table. She covered her mouth with her free hand, embarrassed.

"Okay," Laynie said. She sat there for a moment. "With any criminal enterprise, they can't pull anything off without help. They'll need a few outsiders, some willing participants and some not knowing they're being played," Laynie said.

"Are you talking about the Romanos?" Diaz asked.

"No?" Laynie said. "Who's the Romano's?"

"What criminal enterprise are you talking about, then?" Colton asked.

"Small town corruption," Laynie said.

"Are you serious?" Diaz said. "Baker. This is a waste of our time."

Colton's eyes shifted from Laynie to Diaz. He reached out and touched her arm.

"I want to hear more," Colton said.

Laynie turned to Diaz. "Think about this." She then turned her attention back to Colton.

"Those victims have no connection besides working for the town," Laynie said.

"What about the banker?" Diaz asked.

"Good point," Colton said, earning a nod from Diaz.

"You're a detective," Laynie said. "Did you not look at the bank?"

"Of course we spoke with the bank," Colton said.

"No," Laynie said. "Look at the bank."

Colton glanced at Diaz again.

"You seriously never looked at your paystub?" Laynie asked.

"What are you saying?" Colton asked.

"The town uses Great Blue Hill Bank," Laynie said. "It has its money there."

Colton looked at Diaz again, which Laynie noticed.

"Oh," Laynie said. "Did you think I meant the foreclosure scheme Larry Fuller was running? Yeah, I know all about that. I spoke with Gina down at the bank. A few Long Island Iced Teas and she opened right up. I'm talking about the bank itself, though."

"I don't think we know," Colton said. "Fill us in."

"Well, four dead bodies can make you overlook things," Laynie said.

Colton took a sip of his drink. "Okay, I see a connection with the firefighter and tax collector. Both were employees of the town. But how does a bank CEO and car mechanic tie into it?"

"You don't know?" Laynie asked.

"No," Colton said.

"Larry Fuller wasn't always a banker," Laynie said. "A long time ago he was a Selectman for the town. At one point, he was also the Acting Town Manager."

"Seriously? I didn't know that," Colton said.

"And the mechanic?" Diaz asked.

"Alex Torres was friends with my Dad years ago. He used to live in Stoughton. He also used to work for a garage and that garage had the tow contract with the town."

"How did we miss that?" Colton asked.

"The fire department does inspections and signs off on permits for construction," Laynie said. "I'd find out if your dead firefighter ever did building inspections and cross reference those with buildings either owned by the town or mortgaged through that bank," Laynie said, twirling another fork full of spaghetti. "Maybe the bank foreclosed on them."

"We looked into a bum," Colton said.

"The one seen standing over Bill McDonald?" Laynie said. "Yeah, I heard about him. Is he homeless because of Larry Fuller's mortgage scheme?"

"That's what we thought," Colton said. "But we've ruled him out as a suspect. And no, him being homeless had nothing to do with Larry Fuller."

"Thank you for that," Laynie said. "It will save me time chasing down the bum."

"Tell me about the symbols?" Laynie said. "What do they look like?"

"I don't know what you're talking about," Colton said.

"Clamming up tight I see," Laynie said. "My source said there were symbols."

"I've got nothing," Colton said.

"Forehead," Laynie said. "Tattooed."

Colton and Diaz just sat there. Silent.

"Okay then," Laynie said. "You won't budge on the symbols. But what about the medallions and coins?"

"Where did you hear that?" Colton asked.

"From Gina," Laynie said. "She told me Larry had an impressive coin collection. I wondered if his murder was a home invasion gone bad. I spoke with Roy, down at the coin shop. He told me you were in there asking about the medallions and coins and he told me what they were."

Again, Colton and Diaz sat there. Silent.

"I've told you everything I know so far," Laynie said. "What can I get from you for my story?"

"I'll tell you what," Colton said. "I can walk you through the McDonald crime scene in the morning," Colton said.

"You'd do that?" Laynie asked.

"Meet me at the Stoughton Bakery at seven," Colton said.

"I'll meet you there," Laynie said. Then she pulled out her wallet and dropped some cash on the table. She took a sip of her drink and left.

Chapter 80

Gorettie's Grille
Stoughton, Massachusetts

"Did you really make a phone call inquiring about Laynie?" Diaz asked once the reporter left.

"Hell no," Colton said. "I wouldn't know who to call. I said it to puff up her ego. Good ole human nature. I made her aware that we knew who she was and what she was capable of. She didn't deny it. So, she had to uphold her reputation. And she told us everything she knew."

"She gathered a lot of info in a short time," Diaz said.

"True," Colton said and sat there, thinking for a minute.

"What is it?" Diaz asked.

"Laynie asked us several times about the symbols," Colton said.

"So," Diaz said.

"I couldn't tell her anything. Even if I wanted to," Colton said. "We've been so busy I haven't even looked into the symbols."

"Do you think she knows more than she's letting on?" Diaz asked. "And what about the victims being connected? Have they all worked for the town? Is any of it true, or is she sending us on a wild goose chase?"

"Could be," Colton said. "Once I'm back at the station, I'll look into the symbols more."

"Well, we're here at this great restaurant with an incredible meal," Diaz said. "We should at least pretend to enjoy it."

"There's no pretend here," Colton said, cutting into a steak tip and taking a bite. "These are the best tips around."

"Let's talk about something else," Diaz said. "Taking a break sometimes helps."

"Sounds good to me," Colton said. "What do you want to talk about?"

"Are you married?"

Colton looked up from his plate.

Diaz smiled.

"No," Colton said, chewing his steak.

"Girlfriend?" Diaz asked.

Just then, Colton's phone that was on the table rang.

Diaz glanced at the phone. She saw the name Cindy displayed on the screen.

Colton answered. It was a woman's voice.

"I need to take this," Colton said. He got up and walked away.

Chapter 81

Gorettie's Grille
Stoughton, Massachusetts

"Hey sis," Colton said, walking outside the restaurant.

"How you are doing, little brother?" Cindy asked.

"I'm okay."

"Just okay?" she said.

"Yeah," Colton said.

"Ever since we were kids, you always said, *I'm good*. And you only said *I'm okay* when things weren't. You wanna tell me what's really going on?"

"My first day I landed a murder case."

"Oh wow. No worries, you'll catch the perp." Cindy said, trying to cheer her brother up.

"Well…"

"Well, what?" Cindy asked.

"I have four bodies now."

"Are you serious?" Cindy asked. "I know Stoughton was taking a turn for the worse, but Jesus, I didn't know it was that bad. Is it all drug related?"

"I wish," Colton said. "Serial killer."

"Holy shit!" she exclaimed. "How do you know it's the same guy?"

"Who says it's a guy?" Colton asked.

"Because most serial killers are men, little brother," came her reply. "How are the bodies connected?"

"The killer is leaving strange markings on the victims."

"So, he's a sicko," she said.

"I guess."

"Sounds like a sicko to me," she said.

"He's outsmarting us at every turn," Colton said.

"How? Aren't there cameras everywhere nowadays? Plus the geofencing. Or is he not using a phone?"

"I think he's using jammers," Colton said.

"Plural?"

"Yeah," Colton said. "He's knocking out cellular, Wi-Fi, and GPS. He's putting himself in a blackout bubble."

"Follow the bubble both ways," Cindy said. "From when it starts to where it stops."

"The feds tried. Nothing," Colton said.

"The FBI is involved?" she said.

"Unfortunately," Colton said. "The Special Agent in Charge is a real dick."

"Be careful, little brother. Don't ruffle the federal feathers."

"I won't. Well, maybe a bit," Colton said. "You talked to Mom? She's been asking about you."

"No," Cindy said. "It always turns into a fight. She hates what I do."

"Yeah," Colton said. "You being a spook for the CIA doesn't sit well with mom. Constantly in foreign countries. In harm's way. She's always worried about you."

"Worried about me?" Cindy said. "You're a cop."

"But I'm here," Colton said. "I get to stop by. Which, by the way, Dad's gotten worse. Mom's considering putting him in a home."

"That bad, huh?" Cindy said.

"Yeah," Colton said. "Maybe you can call and talk to her. She's afraid of what you guys are going to say."

"I hate to do this, but I gotta go," Cindy said.

"Okay," Colton said. "Call Mom. And stay safe out there."

Chapter 82

Gorettie's Grille
Stoughton, Massachusetts

Colton walked back to the table and sat down. "Sorry about that."

"Girlfriend?" Diaz asked.

"No," Colton said with a chuckle. "That was my sister."

Diaz's face lit up.

"My dad has dementia," Colton said. "My mom and sister don't talk much. So she calls me for info on my dad."

"I'm sorry about your dad," Diaz said.

"Thank you," Colton said. "How about you? Are you married or have a boyfriend?"

Diaz blushed. "No one," she said. "I'm single."

"Tell me about yourself," Colton said. "Where did you grow up?"

"I grew up in a small town in New Mexico, right on the Texas border," Diaz said. "My dad was in the Air Force. He was stationed at Holloman Air Force Base as an aircraft mechanic. That's when he met my mom. Now he works on cars. I always dreamt of becoming an FBI agent. My mom's favorite movie is Silence of the Lambs. Ever since I saw that movie, I wanted to become an FBI Agent."

"Agent Clarice Starling," Colton said. "Great movie!"

"After high school I joined the Air Force," Diaz said.

"Following in your dad's footsteps, I see," Colton said. "What did you do in the Air Force?"

"I was with the 341st Security Forces Group," Diaz said.

"Oh," Colton said. "You provided security for the missile silos."

"How did you know that?" Diaz said. "Were you in the Air Force?"

"No," Colton said. "I never joined. I like to read, though."

"After the Air Force, I applied to the FBI. A few weeks later, I received confirmation that I'd been accepted," Diaz said. "I trained at Quantico and I recently graduated. The Lakeville Office is my first assignment."

"Lucky you," Colton said. "You got stuck with Wolf."

"He's not that bad," Diaz said. "He's rough around the edges. But I'm used to that type. My dad's that way."

"Let me ask you," Colton said. "Why is the FBI looking at the Romano's?"

"I'm not at liberty to say," Diaz said.

"Correct me if I'm wrong," Colton said. "But I'm guessing your surveyance equipment got jammed the night Alex Torres' body showed up in the Porta Potty at the Romanos. That's why Wolf has such a hard-on for this case."

Diaz moved a piece of chicken around on her plate with her fork. After a minute, she looked up.

Colton saw the look in her eyes.

"I understand. You can't say," Colton said. "No worries."

The waitress returned with the check.

"Maybe we can grab a drink sometime," Colton said, changing the subject. "Once the case is over."

"I'd like that," Diaz said, smiling.

Chapter 83

Stoughton Police Headquarters
Stoughton, Massachusetts

After dinner, Diaz went to her hotel and Colton went back to the station. Laynie's question at dinner about the symbols got him thinking. He needed to look deeper into them. They were the one thing he'd spent little time on. Yet the symbols were key to cracking the case. He knew it.

Colton sat at his desk, perplexed. It had been days with no new leads. Just more bodies. He needed to figure out what the symbols meant. Wolf's crack team down at Quantico hadn't come back with anything either which was odd in itself. They're some of the smartest techs on the planet down there.

He walked out into the kitchen to grab a drink.

Lt. Bonnett was in the kitchen pouring himself a cup of coffee. "How's the investigation going? Any leads into the symbols?"

Colton sighed and shook his head.

"That good?" Lt. Bonnett said.

"Can't seem to crack them," Colton said. "They're just random letters and symbols. Hell, most are on every keyboard. What I need is the killer's cypher to figure them out."

"You're a brilliant detective, with a good head on your shoulders. You'll break it," Bonnett said.

"The only thing I found was one small internet article from fifteen years ago. It was about a doctor from 1775. It listed a few of the symbols and specifically mentioned Stoughton."

"Really?" Bonnett asked.

"I can't find anything else pertaining to it. It's probably nothing. I'm just chasing another rabbit down the hole."

Bonnett stood there for a moment.

"You should talk to Stan," Bonnett said.

"Who's Stan?" Colton asked.

"He's the town historian. He works over at the Stoughton Historical Society."

"That's the old building on the corner of Pleasant and Park?" Colton asked.

"Yeah," Bonnett said, looking at his watch. "If you head over now, you might catch him before he leaves."

Chapter 84

Stoughton Historical Society
Stoughton, Massachusetts

Colton drove over to the Historical Society. It was a tall brick building with a long brick walkway. A black iron rail separated the walkway and large granite steps led up to the building. Large white pillars stood on each side of the front door.

There was no parking lot. Just spaces out front along the curb.

Colton walked up and pulled the old, heavy, olive-green door open and entered the building. It was massive inside. The smell reminded him of museums he had visited as a child on school field trips.

"Sorry, we're closed!" came a voice from out back.

"Stan?" Colton called out.

"We're closed," came the voice again. Followed by the ding of a microwave. "Damn, that's hot!"

Colton made his way further into the building. He passed an information desk with pamphlets and historical trinkets for sale.

He crossed the wide atrium and into the next section. Along the walls were long glass cases filled with historical artifacts. Some had old garments inside. One had a musket from the Revolutionary War. Others had maps which listed historical locations throughout town. Another had weapons inside that were passed down through the centuries.

Colton continued on. He heard a fork and knife scraping across a plate.

He turned the corner. An elderly man sat at a table. His hair was white as snow. The man was eating his dinner.

"Stan?" Colton asked.

The man glared up at him. He had daggers for eyes. They screamed, *why are you bothering me while I eat my dinner? Didn't you hear me?*

"I'm sorry, young man, we're closed," the man said. You'll have to come back tomorrow."

"Are you Stan?" Colton asked, holding up his badge. "I'm Detective Colton Baker."

"I'm sorry," the man said. "Yes, I'm Stan. How can I help you, Detective?"

"I have a few questions, and I was hoping you could help me," Colton said.

"What about?" Stan asked.

"I'm looking for info on a..." Colton flipped open his notepad. "A Dr. Benjamin Church," Colton said.

"Ah ... America's first traitor," Stan said. "What do you want to know?"

"Everything!"

Chapter 85

**Stoughton Historical Society
Stoughton, Massachusetts**

"It must be important if you're coming in after hours," Stan said.

"Is it a bother?" Colton asked.

"No bother at all. I usually eat dinner and putter around after we close. How can I help you, Detective?"

"Please, call me Colton."

"So, what led you here, Colton?" Stan asked.

"I have some symbols I'd like you to look at," Colton said. "See if they mean anything to you or have historical relevance to the town. I did a Google search, and it mentioned Dr. Church and Stoughton. Mentioned something about the Resolves."

"Sure. Let's take a look," Stan said.

Colton laid the manila folder down on the desk and removed several large photos.

"Is that what I think it is?" Stan asked.

"Yes, they're carved into a body."

Stan put his fork down and turned his head away, covering his mouth with his hand.

"I'm sorry," Colton said. "I should have told you they were sensitive photos."

"It's not a bother," Stan said. "I saw my share of bodies in Vietnam. I just wasn't expecting it is all."

"While I was checking the internet, I came across an article. It was about a doctor from 1775. It included some symbols in the story. But the interesting part is it mentioned Stoughton specifically. Unfortunately, there wasn't much content in the article. I was speaking with Lt. Bonnett about it and he suggested I come see you," Colton said.

"Ah ... Lt. Bonnett," Stan said with a chuckle. "He was a little shit growing up. But he turned into a great man."

"He's one of the good ones," Colton said. "Dedicated to the job."

"Let me recall," Stan said, rubbing his chin. "The doctor in your article is Dr. Benjamin Church, Jr. If memory serves me correctly, he was a surgeon in Boston. A damn good one, too. You said the article mentioned the word 'resolves'. I'd need to doublecheck, but I believe he helped write the Suffolk Resolves."

"Do you know anything about the symbols?" Colton asked.

"Not much," Stan said. "But I have a book at home about him. He was one of America's very first founding fathers. Unfortunately, he was our first traitor, too."

"How come I've never heard of him before?" Colton asked.

"History has a way of expunging certain people and events. Dr. Church was one of them."

"What can you tell me about him?"

Stan stood up. "Let me put on a pot of coffee. This may take a while."

"Dr. Benjamin Church, Jr. was a surgeon in Boston," Stan said, putting a fresh filter into the coffeepot. "In 1750, he went to Harvard along with John Hancock. They both graduated in 1754. In college, Church was quite the poet. It was there that he wrote the poem, The Choice. Years later, his friend John Draper, who owned a printing press in Boston, published it. After college, Church was a surgeon on The Prince of Whales. It was a sloop of war, a type of naval warship. He served for five months. When his enlistment was up, he applied to study in London. Payment for his time at sea wasn't enough to cover the cost, so he sold the poem from college to help cover his costs to travel to London. There he studied under the famous surgeon, Dr. Charles Pynchon. I believe that was what his name was. But don't quote me on it.

It was there that he married his wife, Sarah. She was the sister of a classmate. Once he finished his studies, they returned to Boston with drugs and medications. Here, Church opened a drug shop next to his friend John's printing press.

Colton looked uninterested.

"Is this not what you wanted?" Stan asked. He got up and poured himself a cup of coffee.

"I thought his life story was going to be different," Colton said. "It doesn't really seem to tie into my investigation."

"Oh wait, Detective," Stan said. "It gets real good. And you said everything."

"I did," Colton said. "Please continue."

Stan offered Colton a cup of coffee.

"I'm good," Colton said. "Can't stand it."

"Where was I?" Stan asked, taking a seat along with a sip of coffee.

"Church returned from London," Colton said.

"Yes, that's right," Stan said. "I'm not sure how much you're caught up on your American History. But after Church returned from London, things changed here in the colonies.

Parliament had enacted the Sugar Act in April of 1764. It put a tax on molasses to help raise revenue. Boston merchants stopped buying the taxed molasses, which led to smuggling.

The following year came the Stamp Act of 1765. The French and Indian War was coming to an end. It had been an expensive war. To offset the cost of the war, Parliament enacted the Stamp Act which put a tax on paper goods. It forced the colonists to buy stamped paper from London. Those goods were things like newspapers, legal documents, playing cards, magazines, and other uses. This angered the colonists, and many considered it a violation of their rights. It was this act that coined the phrase, *No taxation without representation.*

Oliver Andrew was the Stamp Act Distributer here in Boston. On August 14th, 1765 a crowd hung an effigy of Andrew on an elm tree in Boston. The Lieutenant Governor, Thomas Hutchinson, ordered the sheriff to remove the effigy. But a large crowd had formed and prevented it from being removed. Some of those in attendance included Samuel Adams, John Hancock, Joseph Warren, Paul Revere, and Dr. Benjamin Church, Jr. That day marked the foundation of the Boston Sons of Liberty. And that elm tree that the effigy hung from became known as the Liberty Tree.

Later, an angry mob cut down the effigy and paraded it through the streets of Boston. They stopped at Oliver Andrew's house, where they beheaded the effigy and burned it. Then they burned Oliver's stable house and looted his home. Andrew Oliver resigned the next day. The following year, in 1766, Parliament repealed the Stamp Act."

"Can I stop you there?" Colton asked. He pulled out some pictures and slid them across the table.

"Oh," Stan said, looking at them. "A Sons of Liberty medallion. Its members wore them to identify themselves out in public. Like I said, Dr. Church was a member."

"A lot of what you're telling me is coming back," Colton said. "It's been a long time though."

"It's not just you," Stan said. "It happens to a lot of people. They forget their history."

"And what about Stoughton and the resolves that I found online?" Colton said. "How do they tie into Dr. Church?"

"On March 5th 1770, the Boston Massacre happened," Stan said. "An incident took place between a crowd and nine redcoats. The crowd taunted the soldiers and threw objects at them. One soldier fired, followed by others. When the smoke cleared, eleven men lay shot. Four died on the spot. Now regarding Dr. Church, it's reported that he tended to the wounded. It's not clear if he was present at the site of the shooting or not. I assume it was after in the hospital. But not only that, he helped perform the autopsy on Crispus Attucks, a mulatto man.

The nine soldiers faced charges in the death of the colonists. In a turn of events, John Adams represented them at the trial. Church testified to his autopsy findings and they found six soldiers not guilty. They found the others guilty of manslaughter. Luckily, they escaped the death penalty. But there is a unique bit of information. The Suffolk County Sheriff tattooed those found guilty."

Colton sat straight up.

"Tattooed how?" Colton asked.

"The sheriff tattooed an M for murder on their right thumb," Stan said.

"Holy shit," Colton said, standing up.

"What is it?" Stan asked.

Colton looked at his watch. It was late.

"I need to check on something," Colton said. "Will you be around tomorrow?"

"I'm here every day," Stan said. "I'll find that book on Church."

Colton bolted out of the building.

Chapter 86

Stoughton Police Headquarters
Stoughton, Massachusetts

Colton raced back to the station. He needed to look at the autopsy photos. All along, they thought it was the letter *W* the killer tattooed on the victim's thumbs.

He called Diaz once he arrived back at the station. She was at the hotel. It was just up the street. She'd be there shortly.

Once at his desk, Colton pulled out Bill McDonald's file and flipped through the pictures until he found the one of his right hand. The one with the tattoo.

Colton stared at it for a long minute. It was definitely an *M*.

He then pulled out the folder for Larry Fuller, Alex Torres, and Graziele Alves. Next, he went through the photos. He pulled out all the ones of the victim's right hand. Then he laid them out on his desk.

When he finished, there was a knock on the door.

It was Diaz.

"What's the big rush?" Diaz asked. "Did you find a big break in the case?"

Colton stood there.

"Holy shit," Diaz said, looking at Colton's face. "You did! Didn't you?"

Colton walked her over to his desk and showed her the pictures.

"Look at these," Colton said. He pointed to the M in the photos.

"Okay," Diaz said. "We already know the killer tattooed a W on their thumbs."

"Except it's not a *W*," Colton said. "It's an *M*."

"Okay," Diaz said. "It's an M."

Colton picked up a photo.

"It's not just an M. It's M for murder," Colton said.

"What?" Diaz asked, looking at the picture.

"I was looking into the symbols after our conversation with said reporter," Colton said. "And I came across an article. It's about a doctor from the late 1700s. There were a few matching symbols, and it mentioned Stoughton. I was talking to Lt. Bonnett, who suggested I go see the town's historian over at the Historical Society."

"I take it you went," Diaz said.

"Yes," Colton said. "And thank God I did."

"What did this Town Historian have to say?" Diaz asked.

"Well, it turns out the doctor mentioned in the article is Dr. Benjamin Church, Jr. He was a surgeon in Boston. But not only that, he was a member of the Boston Sons of Liberty."

Diaz sat up in her chair. "Like the medallions used to cover the victim's eyes?"

"Exactly," Colton said. "Do you remember the Boston Massacre?"

"Yeah, of course," Diaz said. "The shot heard 'round the world."

"Right timeframe. Wrong event," Colton said. "That's the Battle of Lexington and Concord."

"Oh, that's right," Diaz said. "So much happened back then, it gets confusing."

"Well, here's the interesting part," Colton said. This Dr. Church not only tended to the wounded of the Boston Massacre. He also helped conduct the autopsy on one victim. Not only that, but he also gave a sworn testimony at the British soldiers' trial. Do you know what the sheriff did?"

"No," Diaz said. "What did he do?"

"The sheriff had an M tattooed on the guilty soldiers' thumbs. M for murderer."

"Holy shit," Diaz said.

"I know, right," Colton said. "So, it's not just the medallions. But the medallions and the tattoos."

"What else did this historian say?" Diaz asked. "Are there any other connections?"

"I don't know," Colton said. "He's going to check his books. I'm going to meet with him tomorrow."

"What do we tell Wolf and Barnes?" Diaz asked.

"We wait," Colton said. "We need more time."

"I agree," Diaz said.

"We find out more on this Church character and see how he ties into our cases. Just because we made a connection doesn't mean it'll hold water. We need more info to find the killer. Hopefully, tomorrow we get that info."

Chapter 87

Stoughton Bakery
Stoughton, Massachusetts

It was early and the streets were damp from the overnight rain. Laynie pulled up to the curb and parked. The light from the bakery shone out onto the sidewalk.

She got out and looked around. Across the street, she noticed a camera above the door.

Laynie stopped and fixed her hair using the reflection in the Stoughton Bakery window.

She walked in and a bell above the door jingled.

Lexi was behind the counter. She looked up. "Hey! You're back."

"I'm meeting someone," Laynie said, walking up to the counter.

"Can I get you something?" Lexi asked. "Medium regular, was it?"

Just then, the door chimed.

They both looked.

Colton walked in.

"Is that who you're meeting here?" Lexi asked.

"Yes," Laynie said.

"I've seen your stories. You're an incredible journalist," Lexi said.

"Thank you," Laynie said. "I appreciate you saying that."

"Are you helping him?" Lexi asked.

"Sort of," Laynie said. "He just doesn't know it. Please don't tell anyone. His bosses will kill him."

"What can I get you, Detective?" Lexi asked as Colton approached the counter.

Colton ordered a soda.

"Have a seat," Lexi said. "I'll bring out your drinks."

Colton pointed at the table in front of the window that overlooked the train station.

"Poignant view," Laynie said and sat down. "Isn't that where McDonald was killed?"

"It is," Colton said, taking a seat.

"Well … you've kept your end of the bargain so far," Laynie said. "A lot of cops don't. They hear what I have to say. But never show up or reciprocate."

"I'm a man of my word," Colton said.

Lexi brought out their drinks.

Laynie blew on her coffee and took a sip.

"So … what happened to McDonald?" Laynie asked.

"As you know," Colton said. "McDonald was found over there near the train station. Someone drove a railroad spike into the top of his head and left his body. You know about the symbols. I'm not going into detail about them. Yes, tattooed."

"By the killer?" Laynie asked.

"Yes," Colton said.

Laynie jotted down a few notes.

"Were symbols left on the other victims?" Laynie asked.

"What do you think?" Colton asked.

"I know there are four bodies so far and I suspect there'll be another one soon."

"And why do you say that?" Colton asked. He never took his eyes off of her, studying her face.

"Call it a hunch," Laynie said. "I'm willing to bet on it. And I believe that's how you know it's the same killer."

"Where did you hear that?" Colton asked.

"A good reporter never divulges their sources," Laynie said, picking up her cup and leaning back in her chair.

"Maybe you're the killer," Colton said.

"You know that's not true," Laynie said. "I was in Washington D.C. covering a political convention. I have tons of witnesses. Plus, I was live on WTFH News."

"I know," Colton said.

"You're just trying to get under my skin is all," she said.

"Maybe."

"Well, Detective Baker, I'll have you know I've sat across from convicted serial killers and interviewed them for hours. So nice try, but it's not gonna work."

"Alright," Colton said. "Relax."

"I am relaxed," she snapped.

"Let's start over again."

"Fine," she said and plopped her cup on the table.

"Here's what I propose," Colton said.

"I'm listening," Laynie said, crossing her arms.

"You ask me a question. If it's false, I'll say false."

"Okay."

"And if it's true, I won't say anything."

"What do I get?" she asked.

"Well, for starters, you'll eliminate any falsehoods in your story. Other news agencies won't have that."

"Can you sweeten the deal?" Laynie asked, uncrossing her arms.

"I'll provide you with one thing neither you nor any other news outlet have," Colton said.

A smile flashed across Laynie's face. She pulled a notepad from her pocketbook and said, "Deal!"

Laynie held her notepad in one hand and a pen in the other. She scanned down the list of things she'd obtained during her investigation and now she had the chance to confirm the facts.

"All the victims have strange markings on them?" Laynie asked.

Colton just sat there and took a swig of his soda.

"Fact," Laynie said, and put a check mark next to it.

"Are they all tattooed on?"

"No," Colton said.

"How then?" Laynie asked.

"Next question," Colton said.

"Is there any connection between the victims besides being town employees?"

"We're still looking into that," Colton said.

"So … the only connection is the symbols?" Laynie asked.

Colton took another swig of his soda.

"Is it plausible that's the only connection?" Laynie asked.

"What makes you say that?" Colton asked.

"Well," Laynie said. "Most serial killers go after a certain type of people. Like prostitutes, for example. There's no connection between the victims other than they all worked the street. Do you think this guy is just picking town employees at random? I mean, if you can't find any other connection between them, is it possible that's the only connection?"

"It could be," Colton said.

"I know cops use local cameras to locate vehicles. Were you able to catch the suspect's vehicle on camera?"

"No," Colton said.

"Really?" Laynie said. "I noticed one across the street when I came in this morning."

"It doesn't work," Colton said. "But you can confirm that with the owner."

"Do you think the killer knew the camera wasn't working?" Laynie asked.

"I don't know."

"Any others?" Laynie asked.

"Yes. One more. Behind the bakery. Above the back door," Colton said. "It only looks straight down, though. Again, you can confirm that with the bakery."

"Why is the FBI truly involved?" Laynie asked. "And not only that, but Agent Wolf who is a counter-terrorism agent."

"How do you know what Wolf does for the Bureau?" Colton asked.

"My dad's a reporter too," Laynie said. "He interviewed him after 9/11 happened."

"I was unaware of that," Colton said. "I thought he was a regular field agent. You'd have to ask the FBI that question."

"And what's this one thing no news agency has?" Laynie said.

"Medallions," Colton said. "They were placed over McDonald's eyes. The bum, Henry, seen standing over him, took the medallions. He pawned them."

"That's how you excluded him as a suspect?" Laynie asked.

"Correct," Colton said. "We went to Roy's Coin Shop to determine what they were. Now we're trying to determine if they have any significance to the murder."

"And do they?" Laynie asked.

"I'm not sure," Colton said. "We're still investigating."

"And these medallions. Were they left on all the victims' eyes?" Laynie asked. "Is that what no one else knows?"

"You're an Investigative Journalist," Colton said. "I think you can figure it out."

Chapter 88

Corner Cafe
Stoughton, Massachusetts

Colton called Diaz once he left the bakery. She told him she was starving and asked about good breakfast cafes nearby.

"There's a great place down the street," Colton said. "I'll text it to you."

The Corner Cafe is a quaint little breakfast spot just outside the center of Stoughton. It's nestled on the right side of a small strip mall.

They pulled in at the same time.

When they walked in, Diaz's face lit up.

The cafe had a rustic feel to it. There was a countertop to the right. Patrons sat on stools in front of it. Several old timers sat eating and talking. Beyond the counter was the grill. A large mound of seasoned diced potatoes sat on top. The chef worked the spatula. She continuously flipped bacon, taking some off and adding more. She poured eggs and added ingredients per each order. She flipped and folded them, making perfect omelettes every time. A chalk board hung on the back wall. Written on it were the daily specials. A dozen tables sat in the middle of the cafe. Most of them were taken. Along the left wall was a row of booths. And tucked in the back left corner was the waitress station. Piled high were plates and cups. Multiple pots of coffee percolated on burners. When combined all the aromas instantly made one's mouth water and stomach grumble. It smelled incredible.

A waitress waved to Colton. "Sit wherever you'd like, Colton," she said.

"Jesus," Diaz said. "Everyone does know your name."

They sat down at a booth along the side wall.

A minute later, the waitress came over.

"Good morning, Cinzia," Colton said.

"Hey, Colton," Cinzia said, putting down a glass of Coke in front of him. She looked at Diaz. "Coffee?"

"Yes, please," Diaz said.

Cinzia placed a coffee mug down in front of Diaz and filled it from the coffeepot she was holding in her other hand. She then pulled two menus from her apron and placed them on the table. "I'll give you a minute," she said and walked away.

"No coffee?" Diaz asked.

"Can't stand it," Colton said. "Tastes like someone crapped in a cup and added water."

Diaz looked the menu over. A minute later, Cinzia returned.

"What can I getcha?" Cinzia asked.

They ordered breakfast, and it arrived a few minutes later.

"How did it go with the reporter?" Diaz asked.

"She's a little firecracker," Colton said. "Definitely good at her job. She brought up the victims all working for the town again. Figured it's worth looking into. I'll check when we get back to the station."

"When are you meeting the historian again?" Diaz asked.

"I'm gonna swing by tonight before they close," Colton said. "Care to join me?"

"I'd love to," Diaz said.

"You didn't mention it to Wolf?" Colton asked. "Did you?"

"No," Diaz said. "See where it leads. He wanted to split us up. Fine. Plus, he said you're running point for our team."

"Hopefully, it pans out," Colton said. "And the historian can provide us with some more useful information."

Colton's phone buzzed. It was the Chief.

He answered it.

"Where are you?" McCormack asked.

"Grabbing some breakfast," Colton said.

"Get your ass back here," McCormack said. "The killer sent us a letter."

Chapter 89

Stoughton Police Headquarters
Stoughton, Massachusetts

Colton stood up and put his phone in his pocket. He looked around and spotted the waitress.

"Hey Cinzia," he called out. "I gotta go."

"What is it?" Diaz asked.

Colton pulled out his wallet and dropped two twenty-dollar bills on the table. More than enough to cover the bill.

"That was the Chief," Colton said. "The killer sent us a letter."

"Are you serious?" Diaz said, wiping her mouth and hands with a napkin.

"I guess so," Colton said.

They ran out to their vehicles. Colton activated his lights and siren and headed for the station.

When they arrived, Wolf was standing in McCormack's office. He was reading the letter, which was on McCormack's desk.

"Come on in," McCormack said. "Have a seat."

Diaz sat down.

"Did he really send in a letter?" Colton asked.

Wolf looked up from the letter. "No. He dropped it off."

"Where?" Colton asked. "Here?"

"Yup," McCormack said. "Just walked in and slid it under the window at the front desk."

"Are you serious?" Colton asked. "Did dispatch get a look at him?"

"Unfortunately, no," McCormack said. "He came in wearing a hood and a mask."

"What kind of mask?" Colton asked.

"The type we all wore during the pandemic," McCormack said.

"Damn!" Colton said.

"There's still a lot of people wearing them," McCormack said. "Probably will for a long time. He took advantage of that."

"Tell me we caught him on camera?" Colton said.

"No," McCormack said. "He must have used a jammer."

"So, we didn't catch a car or plate number?" Colton said. "Nothing?"

McCormack shook her head.

"Where's the letter?" Colton asked.

"Agent Wolf is reading it now."

"Well, it appears the killer has taken a real liking to Detective," Wolf said, holding up the letter.

"What?" Colton said.

Wolf handed the piece of paper to McCormack.

The Chief picked her glasses up off the desk and put them on. She read the letter and looked over her glasses at Detective Baker. "Why is he calling you *Norm*?"

"I don't know," Colton said.

"Did you and Agent Diaz go out to dinner with that reporter from WTFH?" McCormack asked.

Colton's face flushed. "Can I see that?"

McCormack handed Colton the letter.

Colton's eyes widened as he read it.

"Did you go to dinner with Laynie Monteiro?" McCormack asked again. This time with a tone in her voice.

"No, I did not," Colton answered with a tone of anger in his voice. He continued reading.

"Why were you at dinner with that reporter?" snapped McCormack. "That woman humiliated us in front of the cameras."

Colton stood up. "I didn't go to dinner with her. Agent Diaz and I were there. She came over to our table and sat down."

"Colton, I can't believe you!" McCormack said. "What did you tell her?"

"I didn't tell her anything," Colton said. "She went on about how all the victims were at one point town employees."

"Alright Colton," Wolf said. "But you had dinner with Agent Diaz, though, correct?"

"Yes," Colton said. "It was strictly professional. But you're missing the bigger picture."

"And what's that?" McCormack snapped. "Laynie Monteiro is going to slander this department again on the nightly news?"

"No," Colton said, sitting down.

"What is it then?" Wolf asked.

"Have you ever seen Cheers?" Colton asked.

"What? Are you serious?" McCormack snapped.

Wolf held up his hand towards McCormack. "Yes, I've seen Cheers."

"When Agent Diaz and I arrived, the maitre d' said hi to me by name," Colton said. "Agent Diaz referred to the TV show Cheers. You know the jingle part, *Where everyone knows your name.*"

"Yes, I know it," Wolf said.

"Well, Agent Diaz referenced the show and called me Norm. She did it like the patrons on the show. She said it loud enough it caught the attention of the bartender and patrons at the bar."

"Oh my God," McCormack said. "The killer was in the bar."

Chapter 90

Gorettie's Grille
Stoughton, Massachusetts

A sea of police cars rushed to Gorettie's Grille. Colton and Diaz were the first ones to arrive.

They walked in just after eleven.

The hostess was someone Colton didn't recognize. But then again, he usually came for dinner.

The hostess picked up two menus. "Two for lunch?"

Colton pulled out his badge. "I'm Detective Baker and this is Agent Diaz. We need to talk to the manager immediately."

The horde of police cruisers pulling in caught the hostess's attention through the window.

"He's out back," she said. "I'll go get him."

The young woman turned and scurried past the bar. She entered through two swinging doors that led to the kitchen.

Wolf and Barnes arrived. Wolf was instructing a patrolman to tape off the driveway's entrances to the restaurant. Barnes was talking to Trish, head of the State Police Forensic Team.

A moment later, the hostess returned with the manager in tow.

"What's going on?" the manager asked, watching the events unfold outside.

Colton introduced himself and Diaz. "We're investigating a string of homicides," Colton said. "We believe the killer was here last night. I'm going to need to see all of your surveillance video."

Wolf walked in behind them.

"We're gonna need to see all the receipts from last night too," Wolf said.

"Sure," the manager said. "The office is out back."

Barnes walked in with Trish and her team.

"Dust every table," Barnes said. "Start with the bar first. They've probably all been wiped down, but who knows? Maybe we'll get lucky."

"Yes sir, Detective," Trish said.

"And don't forget the bathroom," Barnes said. "Even the toilet handles."

Barnes and McCormack met them in the back office. They all huddled in. The manager sat at his desk. He pulled last night's video up.

"Jesus," McCormack said, looking at the video. "The bar is full. How are we going to find him?"

"Most restaurants have their tables numbered," Colton said. He looked at the manager. "I assume you do, correct?"

"Yes," the manager said. "We can match the table number with the time and pull the receipts."

"Providing they paid with debit or credit card," Wolf said. "We can get their identity."

"We talk to the waitstaff," Colton said. "We show them the tables and ask if anyone stuck out. Did they get a vibe from anyone? We can use it as a starting point."

"I'm impressed," Wolf said.

McCormack turned to the manager. "We're gonna need to talk to all the staff working last night."

"I'll call them in," the manager said.

Colton pulled McCormack aside.

"Ask the manager for that employee list," Colton said. "We need to watch what we say. We can't exclude an employee from being the killer. Maybe they were working and overheard Diaz last night."

McCormack turned to the manager again. "We're gonna need that list."

Chapter 91

David Monteiro's House
Stoughton, Massachusetts

Laynie sat at the kitchen table doing research. She was looking into the Sons of Liberty medallion. Dan was on the couch reviewing the film he'd shot. He was getting it ready to be edited and sent to the network.

There was a loud knock on the door.

Laynie got up and answered it. When she opened the door, she screamed. "Oh, my God!"

Dan bolted to Laynie's side.

Standing in the doorway was her cousin, David, known as Spanky to most. He stood well over six feet tall. He looked like a football player with his wide shoulders. But he was a gentle giant. Everyone knew him and you couldn't miss his booming voice. He'd grown up and lived in Stoughton his whole life and was a 'Townie', as he put it. He was the sweetest and kindest yet tough as nails guy you'd ever meet. A true friend. A family man. Always willing to help. He was bigger than life. A one-of-a-kind guy.

"I heard you were back in town," Spanky said, with a huge smile.

Laynie jumped up and wrapped her arms around his big neck and gave him the biggest hug.

"Geez ... are you trying to kill me?" he said, hugging her back.

"It's great to see you, Spanky," Laynie said.

"You too, kiddo," Spanky said.

Laynie put her hand on Dan's shoulder.

"Spanky, this is my friend and cameraman, Dan," Laynie said.

They shook hands. Dan's hand was dwarfed compared to Spanky's baseball mitt-sized hands.

"Come on in," Laynie said. "Dad should be home soon."

"Speaking of which," Spanky said. "Your dad said you wanted to talk to me."

"I do," Laynie said, leading him over to the table.

"You covering the murders?" he asked.

"That's what I wanted to talk to you about," Laynie said. "Dad mentioned you were a Selectman here in Stoughton."

"I was," Spanky said. "The town's changed. Lots of shady characters."

"Really?" Laynie said. "I always thought this was a great town."

"It is," Spanky said. "Don't get me wrong. The people of Stoughton are great. The people running it, not so much. Hell, some don't even live here. I got rid of a lot of them. I cleaned the trash out. But then they had me forced out."

"What do you mean?" Laynie asked. "I don't understand."

"Lots of outside influence," Spanky said. "For example, a package store closed. Certain people wanted the liquor license moved. They wanted it moved to the other side of town. I said no. They offered me ten thousand dollars to move it. I told them, go fuck yourself!"

"My dad said you were great," Laynie said. "Said you were handling the town's problems. I even heard you went to people's houses and spoke with them. Is that true?" Laynie asked.

"It is," Spanky said. "I loved that job. It gave me the ability to get things done. You know me, I'm a people person."

"I assume that was a problem for certain people," Laynie said

"Yes, it was," Spanky said. "They even had Nino Romano take a run at me."

"I literally just found out about the Romanos the other day," Laynie said. "You're lucky you're still alive. I heard he's the muscle."

"Did your dad tell you that?" Spanky said with a chuckle.

Laynie smiled.

"Tell me about the Romanos," Laynie said. "I don't remember the name."

"They moved to town about ten or twelve years ago," Spanky said. "Probably right after you moved to LA with your mom."

"They own a sand and gravel company. Is that correct?" Laynie asked.

"Yeah," Spanky said. "They do a lot of paving."

"Asphalt, right?"

"Yeah, hot top," Spanky said. "Pavement. Blacktop. Whatever you want to call it."

"My dad says the Romanos landed some big highway resurfacing jobs right out of the gate. I thought Tillers had all the highway jobs locked up." Laynie said.

"Your dad's right," Spanky said. "Tillers had all the highway repaving contracts until about ten to twelve years ago."

"What happened?" Laynie asked.

"Story goes, one of Tillers' trucks was travelling down Route 3 and a rock fell from the tailgate," Spanky said.

"That's not good," Laynie said.

"Oh, it gets better."

"Did the rock hit someone?" Laynie asked.

"Bingo!" Spanky said. "But that's not the worst part."

"Oh, God," Laynie said.

"Yup!" Spanky said. "It bounced off a car and hit a State Trooper's windshield."

"Did the Statie get hurt?" Laynie asked.

"Minor injuries," Spanky said. "Glass in the face. But what happened next was even worse."

"What happened?"

"Of course, the Statie pulled the truck over and the driver denied it. Gave the trooper an attitude."

"Then what happened?"

"Story goes, Tillers wouldn't apologize. They backed the driver."

"That's it?" Laynie asked.

"Oh no," Spanky said. "The Troopers Union went after Tillers. They started pulling over every Tillers truck and wrote tickets. The Troopers union put pressure on the department that handed out contracts and soon enough, Tillers started losing bids."

"My dad always told me never to mess with a trooper," Laynie said.

"That wasn't the end of it," Spanky said. "The Troopers Union went to the legislature and persuaded them to pass a law that requires cleaning off all dump truck tailgates."

"That's good, right?" Laynie asked.

"Yeah, it is," Spanky said. "Before, dump trucks had bumper stickers on them that said they weren't responsible for damaged windshields from falling debris. There were a ton of cars with dinged hoods and cracked windshields. The law changed that."

"So," Laynie said. "Something good came out of it."

"Now, if your car gets damaged," Spanky said. "You get the truck's plate. Then you call the police. Tell them where the incident took place."

"Changing gears," Laynie said. "What can you tell me about the *Keep 911 Local?*"

"The county wants a new dispatch center," Spanky said. "They're already building it over in Holbrook. Kicker is the town doesn't want it. We just spent a couple of million dollars a few years back updating the dispatch system over in the police station. But certain people, outside people, want it. There's money to be made."

"My dad said the town doesn't even get to vote on it. Said only the Town Manager gets to decide."

"It's bullshit," Spanky said. "The town should have a say."

"Yeah," Laynie said. "Especially when it's the taxpayers footing the bill."

"The Town Manager, Frank Langer. Let me tell you, he's a piece of work," Spanky said. "Him and his buddy Gino Romano."

"Did you know Larry Fuller?" Laynie asked.

"That snake in the grass," Spanky said. "He got what was coming to him."

"Are you talking about the foreclosure scheme he was running?" Laynie asked.

"Bingo," Spanky said. "You need to look into the land where they're building the new fire station."

"Let me guess," Laynie said. "The bank foreclosed on the property."

"You got it," Spanky said.

"And that bank was Great Blue Hill Bank?" Laynie asked.

"Some real shady shit going on," Spanky said. "Worst part. Most people don't even know."

"Where are they building this new fire station?" Laynie asked.

Spanky gave her the address and told her she should go check it out.

"Larry Fuller and Frank Langer orchestrated the sale to the town," Spanky said. "The Romanos got the contract to clear the land and dig the foundation. They get to sell the timber, loam, rocks and whatever else they dig up."

"Did you know the other victims?" Laynie asked.

"Yeah," Spanky said. "Funny thing. They all used to be best friends in high school. Ask your father. He'll remember."

Chapter 92

Nancy and Paul Baker's House
Stoughton, Massachusetts

Colton received a call over the radio asking him to call dispatch.

"Are you serious?" Colton asked. He activated his lights and siren. "When did he leave the house? No, tell my mother to stay at the house. I'm on my way."

Colton raced down his parents' road. As he drove, he was looking between houses for his dad. Apparently, he'd gotten out when his mother was taking a shower.

Up ahead, Colton spotted someone walking down the sidewalk. He sped up.

As he got closer, he recognized the older man walking. It was his dad.

Colton pulled over and got out.

"Dad!" Colton shouted.

"Who, me?" his father said, turning around.

Colton grabbed his father by the shoulders and looked him up and down.

His dad had no socks on and was wearing two different shoes. His diaper was sopping wet and leaked through to his pants.

"Dad, what are you doing out?"

His father had a confused look in his eyes. "I'm going to see my sister."

"Dad," Colton said. "Aunt Marie moved to Florida twenty years ago."

"No, she didn't," Paul said. "She lives over on Pine Avenue."

"Come on dad. I'll take you home."

Colton steered his dad towards the car.

"Am I under arrest?" Paul asked. "I've never ridden in a police car before. The lights are bright."

Colton got him inside and buckled up.

He drove him home.

When Colton arrived at his parents' house, his mom was crying. She was still wearing her bathrobe and had her hair up in a towel.

"Paul, are you okay?" Nancy asked.

"I'm okay," Paul said.

Nancy looked him over. "Jesus! He needs to be changed again. I just changed him before I got in the shower."

"That could have gone a lot worse," Colton said.

"It's getting so hard, Colton," Nancy said.

"Mom," Colton said. "There's no shame if you need to put dad in a home. You need to worry about yourself. If you get sick, who'll take care of dad?"

Nancy turned and covered her face with her hands and began sobbing.

"Putting dad in a home doesn't mean you're giving up on him. It just means you're getting the care he needs." Colton said.

"Your brother and sisters won't like it," Nancy said.

"When's the last time they came over?" Colton asked.

Nancy just stood there. Silent.

"Your silence speaks volumes, Mom," Colton said. "And did Cindy ever call you?"

Nancy shook her head no.

"Well, until they come here and take care of him, they can keep their mouths shut," Colton said.

Colton left and headed to Walmart. He bought a four-pack of door alarms and mounted them on all the doors.

Chapter 93

David Monteiro's House
Stoughton, Massachusetts

"I appreciate you coming over," Laynie said.

"No problem," Spanky said. "It's my pleasure."

"Hey," Laynie said. "I just remembered something Dad told me. He said you started the Winter Parade of Lights. Is that true?"

"Guilty," Spanky said. "It started out like any parade the police and fire departments led. We took all the town vehicles and decorated them with lights. I mean, we used dump trucks, trash trucks, front-end loaders. We even had the high school band march."

"That is so cool!" Laynie said.

"Now it's grown," Spanky said. "Bands from other towns come. There's antique cars, politicians, and even the local tree company. We have floats with kids who toss candy. Stoughton businesses have floats and hand out swag. It's really turned into a huge event that everyone seems to love."

"And you play Santa in the parade?"

"Every year," Spanky said. "I love being part of the community and helping those less fortunate. To see those kids' faces light up ... man, it makes my heart swell."

"You're a good person, Spanky," Laynie said. "There's a special place in heaven for you!"

Just then, David walked in carrying a stack of pizzas.

"Hey, Spanky," David said. "I'm glad I didn't miss you. TownSlice was packed tonight. I hope you don't mind. I grabbed you a pizza."

"What kind?" Spanky asked.

"Hamburger, pineapple, ham, well done with a sprinkle of BBQ sauce."

"Check out the memory on Pops," Spanky said.

They sat down and ate and they discussed everything Stoughton related. It became apparent that Spanky knew a lot of people.

"Is there anyone you don't know?" Laynie asked.

Spanky sat there for a moment.

"Of course there is, but I plan on meeting them," he said.

"Dad," Laynie said. "Before you came home, Spanky was telling me about the new fire station. He said Great Blue Hill Bank foreclosed the property and sold the land to the town. Now they're building the new fire station on the land."

"So, we have a fire fighter murdered. The banker who foreclosed the land murdered and the tax collector murdered. Then there's the movement to keep 911 local. The town can't vote on it. Only the Town Manager can, and he also happens to be best friends with the Romanos who've won the contract to clear the land and dig the foundation. What's the common denominator here?"

"The fire station," David said.

"You could be onto something," Spanky said.

"What else can you tell me about the issue with the dispatchers?" Laynie asked.

"I remember a few years back when I was Selectman," Spanky said. "The Police and Fire Department did an active school shooting drill. They had actors play victims in the hallways. It was impressive to watch how great a job the Police Department did. The officers didn't hesitate at all. They cleared the school."

"I remember that," David said. "I did a story on it."

"Well, looking back, I remember the Fire Chief being so excited, as he should have been. Both the Fire and Police Department did a phenomenal job. But what's funny is the Fire Chief commented on how effective the dispatchers were. Said how great it was having both agencies' dispatchers sitting next to each other. They could instantly relay information. He was proud that day."

"So, the Chief was for it before. But now he's publicly against it?" Laynie asked.

"Yes," David said. "They recorded the whole thing. You can find the video on YouTube."

"You should talk with Charlie," Spanky said. "He's a dispatcher. Let me get his number."

Spanky found Charlie's name in his phone and texted his contact info to Laynie.

"Well, I should probably get going," Spanky said. "Thank you for the pizza, cuz."

They said their goodbyes and Laynie hugged Spanky.

He put his hand on her shoulder. "If you need anything else, just call."

Chapter 94

**Holbrook Regional Emergency Communication Center
Holbrook, Massachusetts**

Laynie started digging right into the Keep 911 Local controversy. Like any reporter worth their weight in salt, she went straight to the horse's mouth.

She contacted Charlie, the dispatcher for Stoughton. The one Spanky had told her about. Charlie agreed to meet with her.

"We have a huge problem here in Stoughton," Charlie said. "There's a dispatcher shortage."

"A shortage?" Laynie said.

"There's only three dispatchers," Charlie said. "One is on medical leave. That only leaves two of us. I haven't had a day off in weeks."

"Oh, my lord," Laynie said.

"To make matters worse," Charlie said. "The other dispatcher came down with Covid. I worked seventy-two hours straight. A patrol officer was kind enough to watch the desk for me. I grabbed a few hours' sleep out back. Thankfully, no incidents took place. It ended up being a quiet night, which rarely happens."

"You must be burnt out," Laynie said.

"You can say that again," Charlie said. "I literally had to go home because I was exhausted."

"I hope you got some sleep," Laynie said.

"I wish," Charlie said. "Chief McCormack came to my house pleading with me to return to work."

"Are you serious?" Laynie asked.

"I felt bad for her," Charlie said. "She was in a pickle. She had no coverage for the dispatch desk."

"Couldn't the Chief put a patrol officer on the desk?" Laynie asked.

"She can't," Charlie said. "They're not properly trained. Here in Stoughton, the dispatchers cover both the Police and Fire Departments. They wouldn't know what to do if there was a fire. Which station is the closest? How many engines to send? Who to contact if mutual aid was required?"

"What about a firefighter?" Laynie asked. "Couldn't they cover the desk?"

"Again, they're not properly trained," Charlie said. "Which tow company to call after a car accident? How to run someone's plate or license. How to check the Bureau of Prisons. Find out if they're on parole. And the worst part is that our Dispatch Center is less than two years old. It's all new equipment with no one properly trained on how to use it except the current dispatchers."

"Let me ask you this," Laynie said. "How do you feel about the new County Dispatch Center?"

"To be honest," Charlie said. "I welcome it."

"Really? Why's that?" Laynie asked.

"The Center will cover a bunch of towns," Charlie said. "The new Center will hire all the current dispatchers. If someone is out, they have a pool of dispatchers to cover. The best part is that each dispatcher can cover another dispatcher's town with the click of the mouse. They're using the same state-of-the-art equipment that they've been trained on."

"And you're all for that?" Laynie asked.

"Yes," Charlie said.

"What about those who opposed it?" Laynie asked. "I've heard the story about the woman who left her abusive husband."

"Are you talking about the incident at the Sto Apartments?" Charlie asked. "The little girl who called 911?"

"Yes," Laynie said. "That's the one."

"I'm aware of it," he said.

"What do you say to those people who want the dispatchers to know the town they work for?" Laynie asked.

"That's easy," Charlie said. "The new Dispatch Center is hiring all the current dispatchers from the town they're currently employed with. So that won't be an issue. The only difference is they'll be dispatching from a different location."

"Interesting," Laynie said.

"Would you like a tour?" Charlie asked.

"You have access to the new Dispatch Center?" Laynie asked.

"I do," Charlie said. "I'm doing my training there."

"So … Is this a done deal already?" Laynie asked.

"Yes," Charlie said. "The Town Manager just approved it. I and the other dispatchers have started our training."

Laynie and Dan followed Charlie over to Holbrook, where the new Dispatch Center was.

"Are you ready to be amazed?" Charlie asked, unlocking the door.

Laynie and Dan stepped inside, and their eyes widened.

On the back wall was a movie theater-sized screen. It was enormous. On the screen was the map of the current towns the Center dispatched for.

On the floor, there were close to a dozen dispatch stations. Each one had several large monitors.

"Are you getting this?" Laynie asked Dan.

"Oh yeah," he said, holding the camera on his shoulder. "This place is incredible."

Charlie brought them over to his station.

"Check this out," Charlie said. Under his desk was a foot pedal that raised and lowered the desk. "I found that I actually like to stand while dispatching." He then showed them how the dispatch station worked. When a 911 call came in, the caller's location appeared on the map. It provided accuracy to within a certain footage. It also showed fire hydrants as well. The dispatcher can tell the arriving engine company exactly where the closest hydrant is.

They left the Dispatch Center and headed for Stoughton Town Hall. Once inside, there was a somber mood in the air. It was understandable after the death of Graziele Alves.

Laynie found the building records of where the new Fire Station was being built. It was previously a bar. It had a long history of trouble. The town revoked their liquor license and shut the bar down after learning the owner was selling cocaine and other drugs to patrons. Laynie wondered if that was the liquor license that someone tried bribing Spanky to have moved, or the package store that closed. So far, Spanky was right.

After further digging, Laynie discovered Gino Romano had bought the bar for short money after being foreclosed by Larry Fuller's bank. Gino made a pretty penny by flipping the land and selling it to the town.

After, Laynie and Dan returned home, Laynie used her laptop and searched the Stoughton Media Access Corporation website. She found archive video footage from town meetings with Town Manager Frank Langer discussing the new Dispatch Center. After touring the facility, Laynie understood why Frank went with the County Dispatch Center.

She also found videos of Frank pushing the new Fire Station on the foreclosed land. The land on which Larry Fuller's bank had foreclosed. There was definitely a conflict of interest given Frank's association with both Larry Fuller and the Romanos. It was all done in the open. The question at hand, was it worth killing for?

Chapter 95

Stoughton Bakery
Stoughton, Massachusetts

Wolf and Barnes parked in front of Stoughton Bakery.

Barnes was on the phone talking with his wife.

"You want something?" Wolf asked.

"Hold on, honey," Barnes said. He pulled out his wallet and took out a twenty-dollar bill and handed it to Wolf. "I buy, you fly?"

Barnes told him what he wanted and then went back to the conversation with his wife.

Wolf went into the Stoughton Bakery and placed his order.

"Excuse me!" came a voice from behind him.

Wolf turned around.

Standing there was a middle-aged man wearing wire-rimmed glasses.

"Are you Special Agent Wolf?" the man asked.

"I am," Wolf said.

"I'm Paul Brown," the man said and held out his hand. "I'm the Chair Selectman here in Stoughton."

"It's a pleasure to meet you," Wolf said, shaking his hand.

"Let me ask you," Paul said. "How is the investigation going?"

"We're working diligently," Wolf said.

"Is there anything I can do?" Paul asked. "Do you need anything?"

"I think we're good for the time being," Wolf replied.

"I have another question, if you don't mind," Paul said.

"Sure," Wolf said.

"How's Detective Baker doing?" Paul asked.

"He's a little wet behind the ears," Wolf said.

"The reason I ask is because I have serious doubts about him," Paul said.

"Really?" Wolf said. "Why?"

"Let's just say there was an incident when he worked patrol," Paul said.

"Do you care to elaborate?" Wolf asked.

"I think he's buddy buddy with the Town Manager," Paul said. "Frank Langer."

Wolf looked at him quizzically.

"Last year there was an incident at a gas station," Paul said. "It was a large fight. Officer Baker was the first on scene. He couldn't get control of the situation and had to call for backup."

"That's not abnormal," Wolf said. "Officers request backup all the time."

"Did I mention there was a gun involved?" Paul said. "Officer Baker seized the weapon and placed it on the back of his cruiser."

"Again, that's not abnormal," Wolf said.

"Well … he messed up big time," Paul said. "He never ran the weapon or the suspect. Later that night, that same suspect was arrested in Brockton for brandishing a firearm."

"Mistakes happen," Wolf said.

"Except that weapon was used to commit a murder," Paul said.

"How do you know it was the same suspect if Officer Baker never ran the suspect's info?" Wolf asked.

"Because the sergeant who responded with the other officers to assist Officer Baker saw it later on the news. He even called over to Brockton Police to confirm it was that same man."

"The department reprimanded Officer Baker," Paul said. "He then threatened the sergeant."

"Wow," Wolf said. "That shouldn't have happened. I can say this, Detective Baker can get a bit mouthy at times."

"You're in charge of this investigation now," Paul said. "You shouldn't take any guff from Detective Baker."

"I do have a question for you, though," Wolf said. "Why do you think Detective Baker is buddy buddy with the Town Manager?"

"Why else would he promote Baker from officer to detective if he wasn't?"

"I don't know," Wolf said.

"Oh, by the way," Paul said. "I'm going to hold a Special Selectman's Meeting and demand the removal of Detective Baker from this case. He already let a murderer go once."

"Thank you for the heads up," Wolf said.

Wolf received his order and headed back out to the car.

Chapter 96

Town Hall
Stoughton, Massachusetts

Frank Langer called Chief McCormack. He told her she needed to come to Town Hall. The Board of Selectman wanted to speak with her.

McCormack met Frank out front of the Town Hall. They entered through a side door. A negative vibe filled the room. The board members didn't look happy.

Frank and McCormack sat at a small table in front of the selectman.

"We appreciate all the hard work you've put into fixing the department," Paul Brown, the chairman said. "But we have some serious concerns. Especially about how this case is being handled."

"My department is doing the best it can," McCormack said.

"That's our concern," the selectwoman said.

"Is Detective Baker the right person for this case?" another selectman asked. "He's new and inexperienced."

"Listen," McCormack said. "Detective Baker has a good head on his shoulders. Four bodies in his first week is unprecedented."

"I agree with the Chief," Frank said. "When we promoted him, I figured it would be day-to-day stuff like robberies. I never imagined a serial killer."

"Imagined or not," the Chairman said. "We have a serial killer running around. The town is panic-stricken."

Frank leaned forward into the mic. "I'd like to remind the Board that the Stoughton Police Department is no longer running this investigation," he said. "The FBI is."

"We're aware of that," the Chairman said.

"Why'd you drag us down here, then?" Frank asked.

"Well, Frank..." the Chairman said. "I need not remind you that this is an election year. If people don't feel safe in their own town, how do you think that's gonna translate at the polls? Not good. That's how."

"You'll be fine, Paul," Frank said.

"You'll address me as Mr. Brown or Mr. Chairman."

"Sorry," Frank said.

"You will be if this killer isn't caught," the Chairman said. "Speaking of which ... that Detective Baker already let a murderer get away once before."

"Paul," Frank said before correcting himself. "I mean, Mr. Brown. We've been over this in great detail. There's no need to rehash old events."

"We'll see about that," the Chairman said.

It felt like they were in the hot seat for eternity. But the meeting finally ended.

McCormack and Frank walked out together.

"Colton's not a bad guy," McCormack said.

"I know that," Frank said. "There's a lot of pressure on us right now. I just hope he has the chops to find the killer."

"Well, the State Police and FBI are involved. So hopefully we'll catch them soon."

Frank blew out a long breath.

"I know," Frank said. "But they're both plagued with scandals."

"Oh, and like this department hasn't had its fair share," McCormack said.

"True," Frank said. "But we live here. This is our community. We're tasked with taking care of it. But what if we can't? What does that say about us?"

"Do you want me to fire Colton?" McCormack asked. "He's still on probation."

"No," Frank said. "I don't want him to lose his job."

"He won't technically be fired from the department," McCormack said. "He'll just go back to patrol. But I don't have anyone else who's taken the detective's exam. So, I can't hire anyone else."

"Which brings us back to why we hired Colton to begin with," Frank said.

"Well," McCormack said. "Back then we could have hired from outside the department. If we do that now, it's gonna take weeks to interview and hire."

"No," Frank said. "We hired Colton. We'll keep him."

Chapter 97

Stoughton Police Headquarters
Stoughton, Massachusetts

"I was told about your little incident with the gun," Wolf said.

Harbor and Barnes looked at McCormack.

"What incident with a gun?" Harbor asked.

"Where'd you hear that from?" McCormack asked. "Let me guess, Paul Brown?"

Wolf turned to Colton.

"Do you deny it?" Wolf said. "You didn't run a suspect who was wanted for murder? Not only that. You let him walk away with the gun?"

"That's not what happened," Colton said.

"Care to enlighten us?" Harbor said.

"Back when I was new to patrol," Colton said. "I was dispatched to a large fight at the Mobile gas station. When I arrived, there were eight males fighting in the parking lot. I called for backup before I got out. Back up arrived almost immediately. We broke up the fight and separated the fighting parties."

"So, what about the gun?" Harbor asked.

"One suspect had a gun," Colton said. "I ran him. He came back clean and had a legal LTC (License to Carry). Stupidly, I didn't run the gun."

"So what about the gun?" Barnes asked.

"Apparently, later on that night," Colton said. "The same suspect pulled the gun on someone over in Brockton. Brockton Police arrested him and ran the gun's serial number. It came back as being involved in a murder. The person I ran was not the suspect in that murder. Nor the person Brockton arrested."

"That was you?" Harbor said. "I remember hearing about that. But Brockton is in Plymouth County and we're in Norfolk. I didn't hear anymore about it."

"Did you threaten the sergeant who reprimanded you?" Wolf asked.

"He called me out in front of all my fellow officers during roll call," Colton said. "He belittled me in front of my peers."

"That shouldn't have happened," McCormack said. "Praise in public, reprimand in private."

"After roll call, I followed him into his office. I told him if he ever did that again, I'd knock his lights out."

"I would have too," Barnes said. "We need our fellow officers to trust us. Doubt is dangerous out on the streets. The last thing you want is doubting the officer coming to help you."

"Well ... I also heard you're buddy buddy with Frank Langer, the Town Manager," Wolf said.

"No," Colton said. "I barely know the guy."

"You were lied to Special Agent Wolf," McCormack said. "You see, Paul Brown's son is a Stoughton Police Officer. He's been on the force for just over a year. His father, the chairman of the Board of Selectman, believed his son should have been promoted to detective and not Colton here."

"The same selectman you told me about in your office?" Harbor asked. "The one who wanted you to fire Colton."

"Yes, sir," McCormack said. "That's the one."

"Maybe we should look into him for trying to interfere with a homicide investigation," Barnes said.

"That's something we can always look into later," Harbor said. "But first, we need to catch this killer."

Chapter 98

Maxx Training Center Martial Arts
Stoughton, Massachusetts

It had been a while since Colton had worked out at the gym. The back-to-back murders had zapped him of his gym time. And after the meeting today, he needed to blow off some steam.

Colton headed across the street to the Maxx Training Center and Martial Arts. He'd been going for years. Staying in shape was necessary as a cop. You never knew when you'd get into a physical altercation with a suspect.

The gym was located diagonally across the street from the Station. Most of the officers worked out there. Mike Varner, the owner, was a world-class fighter with numerous wins under his belt. After he left the fighting circuit, he started his own gym. Having nothing but respect for law enforcement, Varner offered a discount to the men and women of the Stoughton Police Department.

Varner always had a smile. In fact, he was known for it. He was a pillar in the community. He always went out of his way to help people, especially those less fortunate. He supported most causes in Stoughton. Varner believed in being a positive role model to the young. He knew that discipline combined with the right mindset could accomplish anything. He used his gym for special events that were open to the public. A town favorite was Varner's Nerf gun fight nights. It was a huge hit with the kids and the parents. Varner even provided pizza. He always gave back to the community.

Varner had taken an instant liking to Colton. He trained Colton in MMA fighting. Colton could stand on his own in the ring. For a smaller guy, Colton could scrap.

Colton was working the heavy bag when Varner walked in. He spotted Colton and headed over to hold the bag.

Colton was landing heavy hits and hard kicks to the bag and Varner had to lean into the bag.

"Tough case you got, huh?" Varner asked.

"You can say that again," Colton said, stopping to catch his breath.

"I believe in you," Varner said. "You'll catch him." Varner then turned and walked into his office.

Colton stood there for a moment. Varner was a man of few words. Some men are all talk and no action. Varner was the opposite. But what little he had just said was exactly what Colton needed to hear. Those few words energized Colton. He showered and headed back to the station.

Chapter 99

Stoughton Police Headquarters
Stoughton, Massachusetts

Colton sat at his desk, going through the crime scene photos, trying to find a connection between each location where the bodies were found. First, there was firefighter Bill McDonald, a town employee.

The fourth victim was Graziele Alves, the town clerk. Another town employee.

"Bill McDonald was Irish. Graziele Alves was Portuguese. Two totally different cultures and languages. They didn't have any of the same friends and didn't run in the same circles. The only connection was they both worked for the town," Colton said.

"That's gotta be it," Diaz said.

"Is it though?" Colton asked.

"What do you mean?"

"Is it really that simple?" Colton asked. "Just because they work for the town? I don't buy it."

Diaz furrowed her brow.

"You still think it's connected to the Church guy?" Diaz asked.

"I do," Colton said.

"To be honest, I'm having a hard time making the connection. How is this Church guy from 1775 connected to our victims?" Diaz asked. "Between the town hall, school system and Department of Public Works, there's got to be several hundred employees. Never mind all the retired employees, too."

"I see your point," Colton said. "But it's what my gut is telling me."

"There has to be a common denominator then that we're missing," Diaz said. "But what is it?"

"I don't know," Colton said. "But we better find out before the killer strikes again."

Just then, Colton's phone rang. He answered it.

"Detective Baker?" the voice asked.

"Yes."

"This is Detective Scott Hampton with the Canton Police Department."

"What can I do for you, Detective?" Colton said.

"Well … I have a body over here with your name on it," Hampton said.

Colton sat up straight. "What? Where?"

"Eliot Tower," Hampton said.

"Where's that?" Colton asked.

"At the top of Blue Hills Reservation."

"I'm on my way," Colton said and hung up.

Colton told Diaz. They bolted out into the parking lot.

Chapter 100

Romano Sand & Gravel
Stoughton, Massachusetts

Wolf and Barnes sat staking out Nino and Gino. They posted the FBI stakeout van back in the same spot. They'd hit Dunkin's right when they opened and got fresh coffee and donuts. Boredom was the enemy during a stakeout, but caffeine helped them stay wired and focused. Wolf had his camera resting on the dashboard along with a notebook to jot down all the arrival and departure times of the two suspects. They had a clear line-of-sight right into the gravel yard and the entire trailer that they used as an office.

Gino arrived early. He pulled into the yard at 5:45 am, followed by a trickle of employees. The yard opened at 6:00 am. Soon the scale house and asphalt plant lights came on. Steam rose from the plant as it heated up. Like magic, the pit came to life. Dump trucks poured in and out. Front-end loaders worked tirelessly loading dump trucks.

Barnes had gotten the records of all the state road work scheduled for today. They were easy to get. The Massachusetts State Police oversaw all the state road work. They provided the details to the police. There were several resurface jobs taking place in the area. Wolf and Barnes documented all the dump truck license plates. They'd match them with the logs submitted to the state. Wolf guaranteed that the Romanos were skimping on the asphalt and pocketing the money. Now they just had to match the scale house logs with the bid submitted. The bid they had obtained through intimidation.

All day, Wolf talked about nabbing a mob boss. How great it would be. Especially before retirement. He'd go out on top.

Barnes sat there thinking about what Colton had said. *How did this tie into the murders? Was Wolf more interested in catching a mob boss than the killer?*

Chapter 101

Eliot Tower – Atop Great Blue Hill
Stoughton, Massachusetts

Colton shot up Route 138 with Diaz right behind him. They crossed over into Canton and passed over I-95. Up ahead was Blue Hills.

Blue Hills Reservation is a seven-thousand-acre State Park. It's a large hill south of Boston and is a favorite hiking spot for the locals. Parking areas are located all around the base of the reservation. Each spot has at least one or more trails. The average trail length is just under two miles, up and back. They can usually be traversed in less than an hour.

They took a right onto Summit Road. It was steep and windy. The road ascended to the top of the park. Elm and pine trees lined the side of the road. At the top was the Great Blue Hill Weather Observatory. It's the oldest weather observatory in the country. They crested the top and spotted several Canton and State Police cruisers parked at the Great Blue Hill Weather Observatory.

Detective Scott Hampton met Colton and Diaz in the parking lot.

"The body's at the top of Eliot Tower," Detective Hampton said. "Some hikers found it. The tower is a couple hundred yards up this trail."

Hampton led the way.

They arrived at the tower. It was a thirty-five-foot stone tower that was built back in 1933. The tower provided a magnificent view of the Boston skyline.

They made their way up the tight stairwell. When they reached the top the body was hard to miss.

A man's body sat in an old school chair. The kind with the writing area attached on one side. He appeared to be in his mid-fifties. A cardboard sign hung from the man's neck. It read:

Call Detective Colton Baker (Norm)

The victim's arm was raised midpoint with its index finger pointing straight out.

Diaz turned. She looked in the direction the finger was pointing. Her eyes widened. She'd never been to the top of Blue Hill before.

"Oh!" Diaz said, looking out at the beautiful skyline of Boston.

It was a beautiful day. Not a cloud in the sky. The Prudential Center, the tallest building in Boston, pierced the horizon.

Colton walked around the body and stopped. He gazed upon the Boston skyline.

He squatted down next to the victim. He tilted his head and looked down the man's arm. It was like Colton was sighting down a weapon's barrel. *What are you pointing at?*

The skyline was vast. There was no way to tell.

"Binoculars!" Colton said. "Does anyone have a pair of binoculars?"

A Canton officer shouted, "I do, in my cruiser." The officer ran and retrieved them, and brought them back to Colton.

Colton used the binoculars and looked down the length of the man's arm. Concrete buildings and glass windows came into view. Slowly, Colton searched the skyline.

"What do you see?" Diaz asked.

"Nothing, just buildings," Colton said.

"Maybe the killer is telling us he's going into Boston," Diaz said.

"Or maybe he's telling us he's watching us," Colton said.

"See?" Colton said under his breath.

"See what?" Diaz asked.

"I don't know," Colton said. "What does he want us to see?"

Colton sighted in on the city and slowly adjusted the focus. A second later, the city was crystal clear.

"Come on!" Colton said. "Where are you?"

Then he saw it. The white church steeple.

"Not see. S-E-E, but sea. S-E-A."

Chapter 102

Eliot Tower – Atop Great Blue Hill
Stoughton, Massachusetts

Colton called Barnes. He told him about the body discovered at the top of Blue Hills and told him the arm was pointing into Boston.

Wolf and Barnes left the stakeout and headed to the top of Blue Hills.

McCormack and Harbor arrived just before Wolf and Barnes.

"Well," Colton said. "Our killer went to a lot of work to prove a point."

"How so?" Special Agent Wolf asked.

"He propped the victim here and pointed his arm straight out and waited for rigor mortis to set in. If you pick up those binoculars and sight down the victim's arm, you'll notice a church steeple off in the distance."

Wolf picked up the binoculars and looked. "Big deal, it's a church."

"Not just any church, Special Agent Wolf, but the Old North Church."

Wolf looked at Barnes. Then back to Colton.

"You have heard of Paul Revere's famous ride?" Colton asked. "One if by land. Two if by sea. That's the church the lanterns hung from."

"What is it he wants us to see?" Barnes asked.

"I've been looking into the symbols with a historian," Colton said. "He told me about a founding father who turned traitor. Supposedly he used those symbols to send encrypted messages to the British."

"I think you're starting to see what you want to see," Wolf said.

"It's where the evidence points, literally!" Colton said.

"I think you're interpreting it to see it your way," Wolf said. "I think you're regurgitating history."

"But why?" Barnes asked Colton.

"I don't know," Colton said. "But I can tell you we're dealing with a sick and deranged individual. They brought a school desk chair up here and murdered someone. Do you really expect a rational thought from them?"

"That's true," Barnes said.

"We need to get over to the Old North Church," Colton said.

"Why?" Wolf asked.

"I believe the killer left something there?" Colton said.

"What?" Wolf asked, sounding annoyed.

"I don't know," Colton said. "My gut instinct is telling me we need to go over there."

Wolf looked at Barnes.

"The kid's gut has usually been right," Barnes said.

"Fine," Wolf said. He pulled out his phone and placed a call. After a minute, he hung up.

"I have agents responding now," Wolf said.

"I have Troopers responding," Barnes said, hanging up his phone. "My office put a call into the Park Ranger's Office as well. They're responding too."

"Do you wanna tell me what's really going on?" Wolf asked.

"It's a hunch," Colton said.

"A hunch," Wolf said. "I'm wasting resources on a hunch."

Wolf's phone rang. He held it up to his ear. "They just arrived."

Two FBI SUVs screeched to a halt in front of the Old North Church. The agents exited the vehicles and ran inside.

"Where's the steps to the steeple?" the Lead Agent asked.

"Steeple access is closed to the public," the employee said.

The Lead Agent flashed his badge.

"Straight through that door," the employee said. She pointed towards the back of the church.

State Troopers and Park Rangers arrived.

"Steeple?" the first Trooper asked.

The employee pointed.

"What's going on?" she asked.

The Agents and Troopers climbed to the top.

"Wolf," the Lead Agent said into his phone. "What the hell are we looking for?"

"Detective Baker," Wolf said. "What are they looking for?"

"A body?" Colton said.

Wolf relayed the message.

"Yeah, there's no body up here," the Lead Agent said.

"No body," Wolf said.

"What the hell would he leave up there?" Colton asked himself out loud.

"False alarm," Wolf told the Lead Agent.

"No, wait," Colton said. "Ask them if they see any strange symbols?"

"Are you serious?" Wolf asked.

"Just ask, please," Colton said.

"How about strange symbols?" Wolf said to the Lead Agent on the phone.

"Look for some sort of symbols," the agent said relaying the message.

"Over here," an agent yelled.

"Hold on, Wolf," the Lead Agent said over the phone.

"Did you find something?" Wolf asked.

"How did you know there'd be symbols?" the Lead Agent asked.

"What?" Wolf said. "You found something?"

There was a pause.

"Yes, sir," the agent said. "We found a piece of paper taped to the wall up here. It's got a bunch of weird symbols on it."

Chapter 103

**Eliot Tower – Atop Great Blue Hill
Stoughton, Massachusetts**

"Now, do you want to tell me what's going on?" Wolf asked.

"I believe the killer is trying to communicate with us," Colton said. "He's trying to show us something."

"What?" Wolf asked.

"I don't know," Colton said. "I need the killer's cypher to decipher his messages."

"Let me guess," Wolf said. "You don't have it."

"No," Colton said. "But I've been speaking with a historian about the symbols. He told me about Dr. Benjamin Church, Jr., a surgeon from Boston back in 1774. Church was one of America's first founding fathers who turned traitor. Church supposedly used those symbols to send encrypted messages to the British. The historian believes he has a book which details the symbols and what they represent. But he hasn't been able to locate the book."

"How does that tie into our murders?" Wolf asked.

"This Dr. Church was a member of the Boston Sons of Liberty," Colton said.

"Like the medallions found on the victims' eyes," Diaz said.

"I understand that, Agent Diaz," Wolf said.

"The members of the Sons of Liberty wore the medallions around their neck," Colton said. "It was a way to identify members."

"Why place them over their eyes?" Wolf asked.

"I believe the killer is using them as a symbol," Colton said. "He's placing them over the victims' eyes to say, *look*."

"Anything else?" Wolf asked.

"Yes," Colton said. "I think he's trying to say the victims were all part of a secret group."

"A secret group?" Wolf said. "What kind of secret group?"

"I don't know," Colton said. "I think he's telling us via the symbols, but we need the cypher to understand his messages."

"The FBI lab is processing the paper found in the Old North Church," Wolf said. "Hopefully we can get a fingerprint. They sent me a picture of the paper and symbols. Now we just need the cypher."

Just then, Colton's phone rang. It was Stan at the Historical Society.

"Detective Baker," Stan said. "You're never gonna believe what I found."

Chapter 104

Stoughton Historical Society
Stoughton, Massachusetts

Colton and Diaz responded back to Stoughton and headed straight for the Historical Society. They parked and ran inside.

Stan sat at his desk with a smile a mile wide. "I found the book!"

"Does it have the symbols?" Colton asked.

"Not only that," Stan said. "But it has the cypher too!"

"Incredible," Colton said.

"The book also has Church's last encrypted letter that was intercepted," Stan said. "Apparently, he used prostitutes to deliver his letters."

"Ew … gross," Diaz said.

"The prostitute was caught delivering it and ratted out Church," Stan said. "In the deciphered letter Church sent, Church wrote that he had sent something here to Stoughton where the resolves were written. Whatever it was, he said he sent it here for safekeeping."

"I wonder what it was?" Diaz asked.

"Now here's the interesting part," Stan said. "I found out that George Washington sent a captain and forty soldiers to find and arrest Church."

"Forty soldiers to capture a doctor?" Diaz said.

"Seems a little overkill, don't you think?" Stan asked.

"Not if Church had something of value," Colton said.

Diaz and Colton looked at each other.

"The coins," they both said at the same time.

"I read somewhere that certain individuals were given new currency to pass out. They were trying to get it into circulation. Church was the first Surgeon General of the Army. He would have travelled to military camps checking on the soldiers. Maybe he was supposed to hand them out. But kept them instead. It's no secret Church was a ladies' man. Maybe he paid the prostitutes with the coins to deliver his encrypted messages to the British."

"Does it say in your book if whatever Church sent to Stoughton made it or not?" Colton asked.

"No, it doesn't," Stan said.

"What are you thinking?" Diaz asked Colton.

"I'm thinking those coins made it here to Stoughton," Colton said. "I think someone discovered them. We need to decipher the killer's message to find out more."

"Do you think they were passed down through the generations and someone discovered them?" Diaz asked.

"They're worth millions, which means they're worth killing over," Colton said.

"Do you think Larry Fuller found them?" Diaz asked.

"Or stole them," Colton said.

"Could explain the brutality perpetrated on Larry," Diaz said.

"It makes the most logical sense yet," Colton said.

"I found something that said Church's father used to frequent taverns and would leave envelopes of money for him after his reported death," Stan said.

"That's odd," Colton said. "I thought he went down on that ship in the West Indies."

"Who's to say he even boarded the ship?" Stan said. "Or got off before it left port."

"Okay," Colton said. "Let's just say Church never boarded the ship and that he reclaimed whatever it was of value he had sent to Stoughton, according to his letter."

"Maybe he assumed a new name," Diaz said.

"He was a ladies' man," Stan said. "Maybe he married and had another child. Maybe the coins were passed down?"

"If he had another child," Diaz said. "We'd have no way of knowing. Hell, we wouldn't even be able to trace it back."

"All we've done is open more possibilities," Colton said. "What we need to do is decipher the killer's messages."

"Here, Detective," Stan said and handed him copies of the cipher.

Chapter 105

Stoughton Police Headquarters
Stoughton, Massachusetts

They all met back at the station.

Colton went into his office and pulled out several large index cards. He wrote down the symbols found on each of the bodies. Then he used the book Stan gave him and deciphered the messages. Once done, he went to share his findings.

"Nice work, Detective," Harbor said, walking into the office. "I'm glad you stuck to your guns."

"Thank you," Colton said.

"Have you been able to find a connection between the victims?" Harbor asked.

"Not yet," Diaz said. "Other than the obvious."

"Walk me through it," Harbor said. "Maybe it will jar something loose."

"Well, they all live or once lived in Stoughton," Diaz said.

"And they all work or worked for the town, too," Colton said.

"Keep going," Harbor said.

"That's it. That's all we have," Diaz said.

Colton stood up and walked over to the whiteboard. He pointed to the pictures of the victims.

Bill McDonald

Larry Fuller

Alex Torres

Graziele Alves

"We used the cypher from the book the historian provided."

"Here's the messages the killer left on each victim," Colton said. He picked up index cards and taped them beneath each picture. Each index card listed the victim's name, profession, and the killer's message.

Bill McDonald - Firefighter - I Am Lies
Larry Fuller - Bank CEO - I Am Embezzlement
Alex Torres – Mechanic - I Am Concealment
Graziele Alves - Town Clerk - I Am Corruption

"We're still waiting for confirmation on the last victim found up on Blue Hill," Colton said.

Next, Colton put up pictures of the Sons of Liberty medallions.

"The killer placed them over the victims' eyes," Colton said. "We didn't find them on McDonald as a bum had taken them and pawned them."

"Why leave them on their eyes?" Harbor asked.

Before Colton could answer, Wolf spoke.

"Let me guess," Wolf said. "You're still on the Church thing, aren't you?"

"Yeah," Colton said. "I am."

"I've heard some really far gone ideas before," Wolf said. "But this takes the cake."

"You think the Romanos conducted these murders?" Colton asked.

"Yeah," Wolf said. "I do."

"Then you're dumber than you look," Colton said.

"Detective Baker!" McCormack shouted angrily.

Wolf put his hand up, signaling McCormack that he could handle it.

"No," Wolf said. "Let the wet behind the ear detective tell us how we're wrong. We only have decades of experience in law enforcement. But by all means, enlighten us, Detective."

"Have you ever met Nino Romano before?" Colton asked.

Wolf said nothing. He just stood there.

"I'll take your silence as no," Colton said. "Because I have. He's dumb. There's no way that inept idiot pulled off those murders. No chance."

"To throw us off," Wolf said. "But let's hear your wild idea."

Colton walked over to the whiteboard and spun it around.

On it were pictures of the Sons of Liberty Medallons, the Continental Coins and pictures of the victims' thumbs.

"I think it's a combination of things," Colton said. "First, the Sons of Liberty medallions ties it back to 1774 when Church lived."

Colton pointed to the Sons of Liberty medallions.

"Members of the Sons of Liberty, of which Church was a member, wore these medallions around their neck to identify themselves as part of the secret group. I believe the killer is telling us the victims belonged to a secret group. His placing them over their eyes was symbolic. He's saying: *look*."

Next, Colton pointed to the coins.

"Who makes someone eat forty-seven-million-dollars' worth of coins?" Colton asked, looking at Wolf. "Nino Romano would have stolen them."

"Wait. What?" Wolf asked.

Colton pointed to the coins again.

"These are rare Continental Coins created by the Continental Congress," Colton said. "They needed to have a currency. Each one of these coins is worth over one million dollars now."

"Holy shit," Diaz said.

"Is this true?" Wolf asked.

"Detective Barnes and I brought them to a coin expert who verified that they are real and also appraised them," Colton said.

Wolf looked at Barnes.

"It's true," Barnes said.

Colton then pointed to each picture of the thumbs.

"You see this right here?" Colton said. He pointed to the pictures of the thumbs. "You see, the *W* tattooed on each thumb."

They all nodded.

"Wrong," Colton said.

Colton pulled the pin from the first photo and turned it one-hundred-and-eighty-degrees and pushed the pin back in. He did it to all the photos.

"It's not a *W*," Colton said. "It's an *M* for Murderer."

"You see, Church was a surgeon and a pretty good one," Colton said. "He tended to the wounded from the Boston Massacre. He even helped conduct the autopsy on one victim and was called to testify as an expert witness at the trial of the British soldiers who shot the colonialists. Several soldiers were found guilty and sent back to England. But before they left, they were in the Sheriff's custody. He had an M tattooed on their thumb. M for murderer."

"Why?" Harbor asked.

"To deny them clergy," Colton said. "The church frowned on murder. They weren't as forgiving back then."

"Anything else?" Harbor asked.

"Yes," Colton said. "Back in 1774, John Malcolm, the Customs Commissioner in Boston, was tarred and feathered by the Sons of Liberty. He was then taken to the Liberty Tree and forced to drink tea until he puked. Obviously, you all learned about the Boston Tea Party. Our third victim, Graziele Alves, a tax collector, was tarred and feathered."

"Damn," Barnes said.

"Then we have the symbols," Colton said. "Church was a delegate to the Massachusetts Provincial Congress. He was also a member of the Committee of Safety which oversaw the preparation and collection of weapons to fight the British. You remember the Battles of Lexington and Concord? Well, Church was a spy. He sent encrypted messages to British General Thomas Gage. According to Gage's diary, Church sent him an encrypted message warning him about the colonists' stockpiling weapons. It was Church's message that kicked off the Battles of Lexington and Concord and thrust the country into the Revolutionary War."

Colton walked over to the table and held up the book Stan had given to him.

"In this book is the last message Church sent to General Gage. At the time, Church was the first Surgeon General of the Army. He used that position to travel to our different military camps to tend to the troops. He used that position to send troop levels and movements to Gage. One letter was intercepted, and Church was arrested. In that letter, Church states he sent something here to Stoughton to be kept safe. Not only that, when George Washington issued the order for the arrest of Church, he sent forty soldiers to capture him. Whatever Church sent to Stoughton was important."

"Why would Church have something sent here?" McCormack asked.

"Well," Colton said. "Back then Stoughton went from Dorchester down to Attleboro. It was named after Judge William Stoughton who presided over the Salem Witch Trials. It wasn't until after the Revolutionary War that the area was divided up. Now you need to remember that Church was friends with both John and Samuel Adams, along with Paul Revere, John Hancock and Joseph Warren. Joseph Warren wrote the Suffolk Resolves, supposedly with Church's help, in response to Britain's Coercive Acts, also known as the Intolerable Acts."

"The what?" Barnes asked.

"They were a series of acts by Parliament designed to punish Boston after the Boston Tea Party. They were the Boston Port Act, which closed the port of Boston. Then there was the Massachusetts Government Act. It stripped the state of its right to govern itself. It was followed by the Administration of Justice Act, which allowed accused individuals to be tried in England. And then came the Quartering Act, which allowed British soldiers to be housed in private homes. The Suffolk Resolves were Massachusetts' response to Parliament. Those same resolves were taken on horseback by Paul Revere down to the Continental Congress in Pennsylvania and given to John Adams, where they became the foundation for the Declaration of Independence."

Harbor turned to McCormack. "Thoughts?"

"Geez," McCormack said. "Lots of connections there."

"I know," Harbor said. "Makes plausible sense too."

Wolf stood there for a moment. "I still believe it's the Romanos."

"Fine," Harbor said. "You can continue looking into the Romanos. But Detective Baker is following up on his theory." Harbor turned to McCormack. "Are you okay with that?"

McCormack looked at Colton. "Do your thing, Detective."

Chapter 106

Stoughton Police Headquarters
Stoughton, Massachusetts

Diaz arrived at the station and met Colton in his office.

"You look chipper today," Diaz said.

Colton lifted his chin and pointed to his neck.

"What?" Diaz said. "You shaved this morning?"

"Well, yes," Colton said. "But I'm free. No more leash. Harbor and McCormack told me to run my investigation. Care to join me and catch the killer, or would you rather sit on the Romanos with your boss while the bodies pile up?"

"You're gonna follow your Church theory, aren't you?" Diaz asked.

"The symbols. The town history," Colton said. "I can feel it in my bones. The killer is leaving us clues which your boss has chosen to ignore. There's more to this. I know there is."

"But can you prove it?" Diaz asked.

"I have a hunch," Colton said.

"A hunch?" Diaz asked.

"Well … more of a theory. But it needs to be investigated," Colton said.

"What is it?" Diaz asked.

"I believe the victims all knew one another," Colton said.

"But we've found nothing to support that," Diaz said.

"Hence the investigation part," Colton said sarcastically.

"Let's do it," Diaz said. "Your hunches have been right so far."

"Let's work backwards," Colton said. "Start with Graziele Alves."

They drove over to Graziele's house and they cut the seal left after the forensic team processed the house.

"Is there anything in particular we should look for?" Diaz asked, walking into the house.

"Yes," Colton said. "Old photos."

It didn't take long to find what they were looking for. Graziele had an old shoebox full of pictures. Colton dumped the box onto the bed.

"Sort the pictures by who's in them," Colton said.

They each stood on a side of the bed and started making piles. Then they compared and sorted the piles. A pattern emerged.

First, there weren't many pictures. Most were from high school and college. There were some after, but not many. Second, there were no recent pictures. Well, not within the last twenty years. Third, most were of Graziele and the other victims.

They kept sorting until they found a group photo. In it were all the victims, plus five others. Colton recognized one of the others. The other four he did not.

Next, they drove down to Taunton and searched Alex Torres' house. They had no luck there. He had no pictures of any kind. Not even on the walls.

They drove back to Stoughton and searched Larry Fuller's home. Nothing. Colton remembered he and Barnes had searched the house and found nothing. There was just furniture.

They left and checked Larry's office at the bank again. Nothing.

"Let's go talk to Wendy," Colton said.

Wendy was home when they arrived. She let them in.

"How can I help you, Detective?" Wendy asked.

Colton removed the group photo from his clipboard. He handed it to Wendy.

"Oh, wow," Wendy said. "I haven't seen this in forever."

"Do you recognize this man?" Colton asked. He pointed to the man on the left.

Wendy looked at the picture. "I'm not sure who he is," she said. "But he was creepy."

"Creepy? How?" Colton asked, looking at the picture. The man wore a black trench coat. He had a long pointy chin with jet black hair.

"I don't know how to describe it," Wendy said. "But he gave me the creeps. I had just started dating Bill when that picture was taken. I only met that guy that day."

Colton looked over her shoulder at the picture. "I don't see you."

"That's because I'm the one who took the picture," Wendy said. "I was new to the group."

"And who are these two people?" Colton asked. He pointed to a couple hugging.

"Oh," Wendy said. "That's Richard and Samantha. I wonder whatever happened to them?"

"What do you mean?" Colton asked.

"Well, Samantha got pregnant our sophomore year in high school. After we graduated, they had another baby, a girl I think."

"Where are they now?" Colton asked.

"I don't know?" Wendy said. "One day they just dropped off the face of the earth. We never saw them again."

"Do they have a last name?" Colton asked.

"Yes," Wendy said. "They got married right after high school. Their last name was Church."

Colton and Diaz exchanged glances.

"Church. Are you sure?" Colton asked.

"Positive," Wendy said. "We used to joke that the Church's didn't get married in a church. They had a backyard wedding."

"Do you remember where they used to live?" Colton asked.

Wendy thought for a moment. "Somewhere off Turnpike Street. I don't think the house is there anymore."

They thanked Wendy for her time and left.

"Jesus!" Diaz said. "What are the chances their last name is Church?"

Chapter 107

Medical Examiner's Office
Boston, Massachusetts

Colton and Diaz were leaving Wendy's house when Colton received word that the Medical Examiner was ready to see them. Colton called Barnes, who spoke with Wolf. Barnes told Colton he and Wolf were still sitting on the Romanos. He said to head into the Medical Examiner's office without them. Barnes told Colton he could give them the details later.

Colton and Diaz headed into Boston.

Hurst was waiting for them when they walked in.

"Good morning," Hurst said. "Meet Brian Andrews, victim number five. This was quite the device your killer devised."

He turned and pointed to the desk they found Andrews sitting in atop Blue Hill.

"Your killer drilled a hole up through the desk and into the victim's arm. He used a tap to create threads inside the ulna bone. Then he slid a bolt up through the desk and screwed it into the victim's arms. Next, he did the seat and screwed a bolt into both femurs."

"Jesus!" Diaz said. "He anchored him to the seat."

"Probably easier to get him up the hill," Colton said. "Maybe he used a dolly or something."

"That's my guess too," Hurst said.

"I found traces of propofol in Andrews' system," Hurst said. "My guess is the killer put him under to secure him to the seat."

"You mean he was alive when the killer attached him to the chair?" Diaz asked.

"Yes," Hurst said.

"What's the official cause of death?" Colton asked.

"Asphyxiation," Hurst said. "I didn't find any ligature marks or signs of strangulation."

"How then?" Diaz asked.

"I can't be sure. But I think the killer put a plastic bag over his head," Hurst said. "He was bolted down so he wasn't able to struggle."

"Horrible way to die," Diaz said.

"That's not all," Hurst said. "The killer superglued his eyelids open. And he used rubber bands on his hands. That's how he got the three fingers to stay down and he put a finger splint on the index finger to keep it pointing straight until rigor set in. Then the killer removed them. I found marks on the hand consistent with those created by elastic bands."

"Did you find any markings on him?" Colton asked.

"I did," Hurst said, pointing to Andrew's hand. "They're carved into the palm of the pointing hand. The three fingers were covering them. I took pictures for you." Hurst handed Colton a folder containing the pictures.

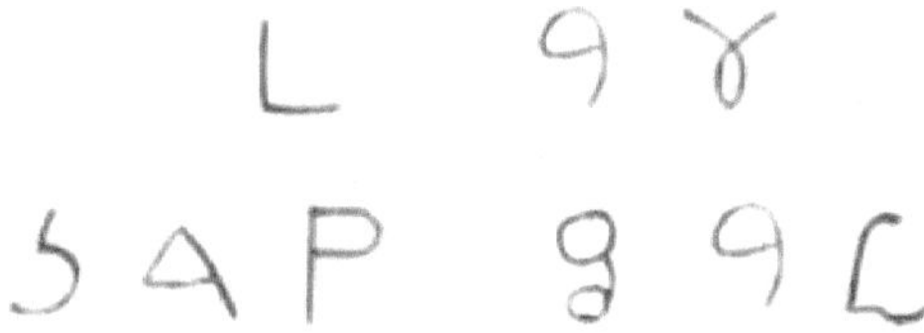

Colton had a picture of the cypher on his phone. He used a piece of paper and translated the killer's message.

I AM THE WAY

"Well, that's just weird," Diaz said. "Andrews is literally pointing the way."

"I think the killer is telling us we're on the right path," Colton said.

Chapter 108

David Monteiro's House
Stoughton, Massachusetts

Laynie and Dan were busy looking into the victims' past. She called the station and requested to speak with Colton. The dispatcher told her Colton wasn't in. She asked the dispatcher to text Colton and ask him to call her. She left her number and said it was urgent.

A few minutes later, Colton called. Laynie told him she had information she wanted to share and asked if they could meet.

Colton and Diaz drove over to her house.

"What's so important?" Colton asked, walking in.

Laynie told Colton about her meeting with Spanky. How he had provided Charlie's number and how she had taken a tour of the new Communications Center. Colton knew Charlie. He was a good man.

"So I did some digging," Laynie said. She told them about Frank Langer and Larry Fuller. How Larry had foreclosed on the bar and sold the land to Gino Romano. Then Gino had turned around and sold it to the town with Frank's help. Now the town was building a new fire station on the property.

"How does this connect the other victims?" Colton asked. "I'm not gonna lie. You kinda sound like Special Agent Wolf going on about the Romanos."

"Well, maybe you're just overlooking it," Laynie said, clearly upset.

"Listen," Colton said. "I appreciate your help. We already knew about that. The District Attorney's office is working with the Bank. They've provided a list of all the properties Larry forced into foreclosure. Tell you what. Take a look at this photo. Tell me what you think." Colton took out the group photo he had found at Graziele Alves' house.

Laynie looked at it.

"Are all five victims in this photo?"

"Yes," Colton said. "We just came back from the Medical Examiner's office. The fifth victim is…"

Before Colton could finish, Laynie cut him off.

"Brian Andrews," Laynie said.

"How did you know that?" Colton asked.

"Because he was my father's best friend, and he's standing next to my dad in this picture," Laynie said.

"What?" Diaz asked.

"Let me see that," Colton said, taking the photo from Laynie.

"Is that your dad?" Colton said, pointing to David.

"Yes," she said. "Let me call him."

Laynie called her father. He said he was at the grocery store and would be home shortly.

David arrived home and everyone went out to help carry in the groceries.

Laynie introduced Colton and Diaz to her father, David.

Laynie showed David the picture.

"I remember that day," David said.

"Why?" Laynie asked. "Because your best friend Bill McDonald stole Wendy away from you?"

"What?" Colton asked.

"It was a long time ago, Detective," David said, putting away groceries. "Wendy and I dated throughout high school. It was never going to last. Laynie's upset to find out I dated other people besides her mother."

"Because you never told me," Laynie said.

David finished putting the groceries away and asked to see the photo.

"Speaking of Wendy," Colton said. "We spoke with her this morning and showed her the picture. She knew who the couple was but didn't know this guy." Colton pointed to the pointy-chin man.

"That's Max McMullen," David said. "He's the Funeral Home Director over at McMullen Funeral Home."

"Wendy said he was creepy," Diaz said.

"No kidding," David said. "The guy owns a funeral home."

"And what about the Church's?" Colton asked. "What can you tell us about them?"

"Not much," David said. "They had just started hanging out with us before they moved down south. They had a baby together in high school and they were pregnant again when they left."

"Do you know where the Church's moved to?" Diaz asked.

"No," David said. "I hardly saw them. They had a young child, so they didn't hang out with us much."

"And you're positive they moved down south?" Colton asked.

"Well, that's what Frank Langer told me anyway," David said.

"Obviously, that's Frank Langer," Colton said, pointing at the picture.

"Dad," Laynie said. "You were friends with Frank Langer?"

"He wasn't my friend," David said. "We just had mutual friends."

"Speaking of friends, Dad," Laynie said. "I have some bad news. The latest victim was Brian Andrews."

"What?" David said, taking a seat. The news seemed to hit him hard.

"I'm sorry," Colton said.

"That can't be," David said. "I just had dinner with him last week."

Chapter 109

David Monteiro's House
Stoughton, Massachusetts

Laynie grew up in Stoughton. She remembered being a little girl and working at her father's paper.

Laynie was upset at what she had learned. How can those elected to represent us lie and steal from us instead? She called and spoke with Hank. He'd watched the daily reels Dan had sent. The story was coming along. Hank had been releasing highlight reels to get viewers excited for the exclusive story Laynie was getting. WTFH was getting good feedback.

"How are you?" Hank asked. "You seem tense. I figured you'd be more relaxed being back home."

"That's just it," Laynie said. "I'm not happy. I'm pissed off. The elected officials here are so easily bribed. I can't believe it."

"Uh oh," Hank said. "I love it when you're fired up. You bring me the best stories."

"The town officials just allow a bank, the same bank the town banks with, to foreclose on people's houses. Then they allow those houses to be sold for profit. It's disgusting. People work hard to buy their homes. It's not always easy either. It's the American Dream. Then to have some politician steal it. Oh, hell no! They're not getting away with it on my watch."

"Didn't you tell me that, as a child, you wrote stories for your dad's paper?" Hank asked.

"I did," she said. "It was called Laynie's Corner. Why are you asking?"

"How about you do a side piece?" Hank asked. "It can be on the foreclosure scheme. Maybe I can pitch it to the bosses and get you a spot on our Sunday morning show. People love your passion and search for the truth."

"Do you think they'll go for it?" Laynie asked.

"Tell you what," Hank said. "Do a piece on the foreclosure scam and I'll bring it upstairs. Most of our audience lives in a small community. They can relate to small town politics. I bet it'll be a hit."

"I'll get started on it today," Laynie said. "And thanks, Hank. I feel better."

After she hung up, she told Dan the news. "That would be great," Dan said.

Laynie had already done most of her research. Now it was just putting the story together.

Dan spent most of the day editing and splicing film together on his laptop.

A couple of hours had passed. They'd almost finished when David walked in. "Hey, there's a press conference in about an hour."

They hopped in David's car and headed down to the police station. The podium was set up outside again.

Laynie wasn't in the mood for the same bullshit they'd been feeding the press. She had questions, and she wanted answers.

Only McCormack, Wolf, and Harbor came out. They walked up to the podium together.

Wolf gave a brief statement regarding the body found atop Blue Hill. McCormack spoke next. She had little to add. The body was not found in Stoughton. Harbor spoke last. He didn't provide much detail except to say they were processing the scene. Harbor made the mistake of asking if anyone had questions.

Laynie's hand shot straight up. She started asking her question before she was even called.

"WTFH News has uncovered a foreclosure scheme here in Stoughton," Laynie said. "We've learned that the Town Manager, Frank Langer, was working with the deceased Larry Fuller. Through our investigation, we've learned that Great Blue Hill Bank has been foreclosing on properties here in town. Then, the Romanos, a local mob family, have been buying the properties, stripping them and selling them to the town. We've obtained documents that confirm this. My question is, did the Town know about this? And if so, are they investigating?"

Harbor stood there for a moment. He looked perplexed. It appeared the question had caught him off guard. He finally answered. "We too have recently discovered this. I can assure you that it's being looked into."

"Larry Fuller was the second victim killed, and he was the CEO of Great Blue Hill Bank. One property that he foreclosed on was the bar where the new fire station is currently being built. Again, we discovered Gino Romano bought that property. He then sold the land to the town. Then, Frank Langer gave the contract to Romano Sand and Gravel to not only clear the land, but to demolish the bar and dig the foundation for the fire station. The first victim, Bill McDonald, was a Stoughton fire fighter. Do you think Larry Fuller's and Bill McDonald's death had anything to do with the foreclosure scheme conducted by the Town Manager?"

"Again," Harbor said. "That's something that is being investigated."

"For days now, we've heard from those at the podium that there's no connection between the victims. Yet, WTFH has discovered the victims' are friends. Have been for years. How can you account for not knowing?" Laynie asked.

Harbor's face turned beet red. "That's something we've recently discovered. We're in the process of looking back into the victims' past. In some cases, not all. The victims haven't had contact with each other in almost twenty years. As you can imagine, digging that far back into someone's life takes time. I think you'd agree with that since you just discovered it as well."

Harbor turned and stepped away. McCormack announced there'd be no more questions. She followed Harbor and Wolf back inside the station.

Back at home, Laynie received a call from Hank.

"That was incredible, Laynie," Hank said. "You tore into that DA. You didn't let go until you got your pound of flesh.

Great job! The footage is going viral. I spoke with the bosses and they're prepared to give you your own show on Sunday."

"I sense a but coming," Laynie said.

"Just bring home this murder story and the show is all yours," Hank said.

Chapter 110

Stoughton Police Headquarters
Stoughton, Massachusetts

"Have you seen the news?" Harbor asked as he was, walking in the next morning. "The drilling I took from Laynie Monteiro was the top story on every channel. I want charges brought up against Frank Langer, and I want him arrested. I want his ass in cuffs and paraded in front of the media today. Barnes, you and Colton draft up the affidavit. We have enough probable cause from the paperwork provided by Great Blue Hill's bank attorneys to go after Frank Langer. Plus, the sales of the foreclosed properties for the town have Frank's name all over them."

When Harbor finished his rant, McCormack asked to see Colton. They stepped into her office. She had six words for him. "Find that son of a bitch!"

"Yes, Chief," Colton said.

Barnes and Colton drafted the affidavit. Once completed, they drove over to the house of the judge on call. The judge was out back in his pool when they arrived. After drying off, the judge reviewed the paperwork and signed it. Colton and Barnes now had their arrest warrant for Frank Langer.

"When we get Frank in the interview room," Barnes said. "We start out questioning him about the foreclosures. Once we get him scared enough, we work our way into the Romanos. Let's see if he'll flip on them in exchange for his testimony."

Colton agreed.

They headed over to Frank's house first. He wasn't home. They checked his office at Town Hall. He wasn't there either.

"Should we ruffle some feathers," Barnes asked. Head over to the Romanos. See if he's there. If so, cuff him right there in front of his buddies. Let them think he's gonna flip."

"Sure," Colton said. "Wolf is gonna flip when we arrive with an arrest warrant."

They arrived at the trailer at Romano Sand and Gravel. There were no cars in the lot and the door was locked. They left.

When they turned onto Turnpike Street, Wolf pulled out behind them. He hit his lights. Barnes pulled over.

"What are you boys doing here at the Romanos?" Wolf asked.

Barnes told Wolf that they had an arrest warrant for Frank.

"When you find him," Wolf said. "Let me know. I'd like to sit in on the interrogation."

Barnes promised to call once they picked up Frank.

They spent the rest of the day searching for Frank. No luck.

When the judge signed the affidavit, he agreed to let the police ping Frank's phone. Colton contacted Frank's phone company. They pinged Frank's phone.

"Sorry, Detective," the phone representative said. "It appears his phone is off."

Later that evening, the task force met back at the station, including Harbor and McCormack.

"I hate to say it," Harbor said. "But I think Frank Langer skipped town."

"I agree," McCormack said.

"What if we're looking at it wrong?" Colton asked.

"I don't think so," Harbor said. "That man is as crooked as they come."

"Right, that's my point," Colton said. "If he's so crooked, maybe he's tied into these murders as well."

"Wait a minute," Wolf said. "I thought you said you didn't believe the Romanos were part of the murders."

"That's right," Colton said. "I did, and I still believe it."

"Then what the hell are you talking about?" Wolf asked.

"Show them the picture," Diaz said.

"What picture?" Wolf asked. "What are you talking about?"

Colton retrieved the picture from his office and showed it to them.

"What am I looking at here?" Harbor asked.

"That is a picture of Frank Langer," Colton said. "With Bill McDonald, Larry Fuller, Alex Torres, Graziele Alves, Brian Andrews, David Monteiro, Max McMullen, and Richard and Samantha Church."

"Holy shit," Barnes said. "Do you mean to tell me you think the killer snatched up Frank?"

"Given most of the people in this photo are dead," Colton said. "Yeah, that's what I'm telling you."

"Jesus!" Harbor said.

"It would definitely explain why he kept showing up," Colton said, looking at Wolf. "He wasn't covering up for the Romanos. He was concerned about himself."

"I highly doubt that," Wolf said. "Whatever Frank Langer was into, the Romanos were into, too."

"I don't think so," Colton said.

"And why's that?" asked Harbor.

"Because the Romanos have only been around for the what … past ten years?" Colton asked.

"Give or take," McCormack said.

"Each victim has worked for or in this town for well over twenty years," Colton said.

"McDonald … twenty-five years," Diaz said, holding up his file.

"Town manager for twenty-two years," Chief McCormack said. "We both started working for the town the same year."

"So, whatever happened, happened before the Romanos arrived in town?" Colton asked.

They looked around the room at one another.

"Maybe we're not looking far enough back," Colton said. "This picture is over twenty years old."

Chapter 111

Romano Sand & Gravel
Stoughton, Massachusetts

Wolf and Barnes sat on the Romanos again.

"Do you really think the Romanos had anything to do with these murders?" Barnes asked.

"Not you too," Wolf said.

"Well, we've been sitting on them for days," Barnes said. "We can account for their whereabouts when the body was dropped up on Blue hill."

"I know that," Wolf said. "Let's sit on them one more day."

"One more day," Barnes said. "Then we jump on Colton's theory."

"Do you really trust him after that debacle with the gun?" Wolf asked.

"Like you've never made a mistake before," Barnes said. "Please."

Wolf's phone rang. He answered it.

He sat listening to the person on the other end of the phone. He sat up.

"Pen!" Wolf said excitedly. He pointed to Barnes' clipboard. "Pen!"

Barnes handed Wolf his clipboard.

"Are you sure?" Wolf asked. "Address?"

He wrote it down and hung up.

"A tip just came into the FBI hotline," Wolf said.

"What?" Barnes asked.

"Caller reports he saw his neighbor bringing out what looked like a body last night," Wolf said. "Caller swears they hear screaming coming from the house right now."

"Where?" Barnes asked.

"Right here in Stoughton," Wolf said.

"Isn't Frank Langer missing?" Barnes asked. "Think it could be him getting tortured?"

"I don't know," Wolf said. "This might be the break we've been waiting for."

"Let's go," Barnes said. "I'll call Colton for backup."

Chapter 112

627 Park Street
Stoughton, Massachusetts

Colton and Diaz sat in his office reviewing the case files. They compared the victims' pasts trying to find the connection that linked them to the killer.

They went through old photos from high school and college. They wrote down names of people they hung out with back then. Then they cross-referenced the list of names, looking for anyone that overlapped.

Colton's phone rang. It was Barnes.

"We found him!" Barnes said. "A tip came through the FBI hotline."

"Are you serious?" Colton asked. "Where?"

"Over off Park Street," Barnes said.

"627 Park Street," Wolf said in the background.

"You catch that?" Barnes asked.

"Yes."

"We'll meet you over there," Barnes said, then clicked off.

Three minutes later, Colton pulled up and parked in front of the house. Colton and Diaz got out.

Colton spotted Wolf and Barnes stacked up on the front porch.

"Shit!" Colton said. "They're making entry."

"Why aren't we waiting for backup?" Diaz asked.

"Wolf wants all the glory," Colton said.

Colton looked at the house and did a double take.

The back yard dropped off and went down a hundred yards to where it met the tree line.

Diaz sprinted past Colton and stacked up on Barnes. She put her hand on his shoulder like she was taught at the academy.

"They're here," Barnes whispered to Wolf.

Wolf kicked in the front door and made entry. Barnes and Diaz followed him in.

Outside on the porch, Colton heard Wolf barking commands and furniture being overturned inside the house.

Colton entered the house. As soon as he stepped inside, there was a volley of gunshots. There was a brief pause, followed by the sound of footsteps running on the stairs.

"Officer down! Officer Down!" Wolf shouted, clutching his chest.

Diaz ran to Barnes, who was lying on the ground. She knelt down and took a protective posture, her weapon out in front, ready to defend the downed officer. She pulled out her radio. "Officer down! Officer down!"

Wolf chased the suspect down the stairs.

Out of the corner of her eye, Diaz spotted Colton bolt outside the house.

Wolf shouted from downstairs that the suspect was heading out back.

Barnes looked up at Diaz.

"I'm good," Barnes said. "Go!"

Diaz ran for the front door.

As she exited, she saw Colton hopping into his SUV.

"Where are you going?" Diaz shouted.

Colton started the vehicle and stepped on the gas. The SUV went soaring down the driveway.

Barnes hobbled from the house out of breath. Blood ran down his arm and dripped from his fingers. He watched Colton's SUV go down the hill and screaming into the backyard.

Diaz and Barnes ran to the driveway. They watched Colton's SUV fly across the backyard, tearing up grass as it went.

"What the hell is he doing?" Wolf yelled, bent over with his hands on his knees, sucking air.

A moment later, Colton skidded to a halt, the front end in the tree line.

Colton exited the vehicle with his weapon drawn.

Suddenly, shots rang out from inside the tree line.

Colton's windshield exploded, as did the driver's side mirror.

Colton returned fire.

Diaz took off running. She sprinted down the driveway into the backyard.

Barnes grabbed his radio and shouted, "Shots fired! Shots fired! Officer needs assistance!"

Chapter 113

627 Park Street
Stoughton, Massachusetts

The cavalry arrived. Park Street was flooded with Stoughton cruisers along with State Police and multiple other agencies' vehicles.

News choppers circled overhead.

The suspect had been shot twice. But he was still alive. Both he and Barnes had been transported to local hospitals. Barnes was wounded in the shoulder. It was just a graze. Deep, but still just a graze. He was lucky to be alive.

Wolf had taken a direct hit, center mass. Thankfully, he had his vest on. The bruising would last for days. As would the pain.

A search of the house determined the suspect was not the killer. Based upon the amount of fentanyl found on the premises, he was just a drug dealer.

Wolf received a call from the FBI's Boston Field Office. They told him it appeared the tip came in from a rival drug dealer. Apparently, the suspect was moving in on his territory. After seeing the news, he decided to drop a dime.

"How'd you know?" Diaz asked. "Where the shooter would come out?"

"Yeah, I'd like to know too," Wolf said.

"I grew up in this town," Colton said. "I used to party in that house back when I was in high school and college. Some parties got out of hand. Some of us knew about the tunnel. We'd run when the cops showed up."

"To be honest." Diaz said. "I thought you turned chicken and ran when the bullets started flying."

"Thanks for the vote of confidence," Colton said.

"I'm glad I was wrong," Diaz said.

A man in a suit arrived and spoke with Wolf privately. Then they spoke with the State Police Colonel who was on scene.

McCormack and Harbor showed up shortly after. McCormack asked Colton for his service piece. He needed to be placed on leave pending an investigation.

Wolf, the man in the suit and the Colonel approached McCormack and Harbor.

"That won't be necessary," Wolf said to McCormack. "The suspect shot both a Federal Agent and a decorated Massachusetts State Police Homicide Detective. Detective Baker fired in defense of his fellow law enforcement officers."

"Are you sure?" Harbor asked Wolf.

Wolf looked at the man in the suit. The man nodded.

"Yes," Wolf said, rubbing his chest. "Both the FBI and the Massachusetts State Police stand behind Detective Baker's actions."

"The Federal Government is taking full responsibility," the man in the suit said.

"Alright then," Harbor said.

McCormack handed Colton back his gun.

The man in the suit walked away. Wolf and the Colonel followed. Colton watched the man in the suit leave.

"I wasn't expecting that from him," McCormack said. "Especially towards you, Colton."

"Probably because he knows an investigation will show he entered the house illegally," Colton said. "He had no search warrant or backup. He just went in."

"Well, if the feds are taking credit for the bust," Harbor said. "It's all theirs."

Chapter 114

Stoughton Police Headquarters
Stoughton, Massachusetts

Diaz arrived at the station.

"Where's your fearless leader?" Colton asked.

"Wolf was called to Washington," Diaz said.

"Was he expecting a promotion?" Colton asked.

"Not that I'm aware of," Diaz said. "Why?"

"Usually, you only get called to Washington if you're getting promoted or if you screw up," Colton said. "I'm going with the latter."

"He's a good agent," Diaz said. "He's taught me a lot."

They sat in silence for a moment.

"What were you working on?" Colton asked. "Why'd Wolf have such a hardon for the Romanos?"

"We had a wire up on them," Diaz said. "We caught them trying to bribe a state official to get highway resurfacing contracts."

"That's it?" Colton said. "Bribery?"

"When the official wouldn't take the bribe, they threatened the official and his family," Diaz said.

Colton looked at her for a minute, like he wanted to ask her something.

"Just ask," Diaz said.

"How did you not see the killer dump Alex Torres at Romanos Sand and Gravel?" Colton asked. "Didn't you have cameras up?"

Diaz was silent.

"Come on," Colton said. "We're working together."

"Fine," Diaz said. "Because our cameras and mics stopped working. Same with the surveillance cameras when you found Graziele Alves."

"Really," Colton said.

"That really got Wolf going," Diaz said. "And, as you know from Laynie, Wolf used to be assigned to the counter-terrorism task force. He assumed someone had used a jammer. When he found out the jammers were used again with Graziele, well … that pushed Wolf over the edge. He suspected the Romanos got their hands on some jammers and were using them for their criminal enterprise. He thought he had hit the mother lode. All he talked about was bagging a mob boss and going out on top."

Colton's phone rang. It was his sister, Cindy.

Chapter 115

Stoughton Police Headquarters
Stoughton, Massachusetts

"Hey sis," Colton said. "You talk to Mom yet?"

"No," Cindy said. "I haven't. Everything okay?"

"Not really," Colton said. "Dad got out of the house the other day while Mom was showering."

"That's not good," Cindy said. "What happened? Is he okay?"

"He's fine," Colton said. "I found him not far from home. He said he was going to see Aunt Marie."

"She lives in Florida," Cindy said.

"Well, Dad thought she still lived up the street."

"Hey, listen," Cindy said. "There's something I need to talk to you about. You brought it up the other day."

"Let me guess," Colton said. "The jammers?"

"Bingo," Cindy said. "That and the Romanos."

"What the hell is the CIA doing with the Romanos?" Colton asked.

"You can't repeat this to anyone," Cindy said.

"Dur!"

"I know. I know," Cindy said. "You've never said anything before that I've told you."

"Guns or drugs?" Colton asked.

"Both," Cindy said. "Gino used to move some serious weight. He got busted and turned snitch. The U.S. Attorney let him slide because the information he provided ended up stopping a terrorist ring in Boston."

"No shit!" Colton said. "Are they working for you?"

"Yes."

"And the use of the Wi-Fi and GPS jammers sent you guys into a tizzy," Colton said.

"There's a reason they're illegal," Cindy said. "In the wrong hands, they can be deadly."

"And I guess you heard about the shooting, then?" Colton asked.

"When a state trooper and FBI agent are shot, it hits the interagency news pretty quickly," Cindy said.

"I bet that put it over the top."

"Right again, little brother."

"I figured as much. A mysterious man in a suit showed up today," Colton said. "He said the Federal Government was taking responsibility for the shooting. They cleared me on the spot."

"They want full autonomy," Cindy said. "Spin the narrative how they want it spun."

"Should I stand down?" Colton asked.

"No," Cindy said. "Keep hunting for your killer. Just don't be surprised if a tactical team arrives."

"And what about the FBI?" Colton asked. "Special Agent Wolf has a hardon for the Romanos."

"Don't worry about him," Cindy said. "He's been called to Washington."

"I just heard," Colton said. "It's that serious?"

"There's been lots of chatter lately," Cindy said. "Pre 911 chatter levels."

"Jesus," Colton said. "Are they targeting Stoughton?"

"Were not sure," Cindy said. "All I know is the Romanos were supposed to move and broker the sale. Given the location, I'd say either Boston or New York City would be an intended target. But with those jammers already being used, combined with the increased chatter, it set off all kinds of red flags."

"Is that common knowledge about the Romanos?" Colton asked.

"I'm not sure," Cindy said. "Why?"

"Because, like I said. A certain FBI agent has a hardon for the Romanos," Colton said.

"The Romanos are under constant watch by other three-letter agencies. There's no way they're letting Wolf interfere."

"Why is the FBI gunning for them?" Colton asked.

"I bet Wolf wasn't read-in. If he gets too close, they'll stop him. Hence the man in the suit today," Cindy said. "Gino is a big fish under lock and key. He knows too much. They'll defend him just to keep him in play. Hell, the government allows the Romanos to meddle in road construction, because it keeps them in the game. In fact, word is they're grooming the son to take over."

"Nino!" Colton said. "That guy's an asshole on two legs."

"You guys best friends or something?" Cindy said with a laugh.

"It's good to hear you laugh, sis," Colton said.

"Listen Colton," Cindy said. "I wouldn't go chasing the Romanos for the murders. Like I said, they're under lock and key. And another thing ..."

"What's that?" Colton asked.

"Wolf could be pretending," Cindy said. "He could be sitting the Romanos to keep you away. Stop you from finding out. Trying to control the narrative. Or it could be multiple things."

"Like what?"

"Like the FBI is sitting on him in case he's your killer's intended target."

"You think?" Colton asked.

"I wouldn't doubt it," Cindy said. "The Romanos have made a lot of enemies."

"But why put Agent Diaz with me?"

"To help you find the actual killer," Cindy said. "They'd still get credit with the assist and keep you from snooping around the Romanos."

Colton's cell phone beeped. It was the station calling.

"Hey sis, I gotta let you go. I appreciate the heads up."

"Keep your head on a swivel, little brother," Cindy said. "Especially with those three letter agencies running around."

"Will do!" Colton said and hung up.

He took the other call.

"Hello?"

"Hi Detective," the dispatcher said. "We have another body."

Chapter 116

FBI Director's Office
Washington D.C.

Wolf was called and told to report to the FBI Director's Office. He caught a redeye out of Logan Airport and arrived in Dulles in less than two hours.

He'd never been to the Director's Office before, let alone met the Director.

After several minutes of waiting, the secretary told Wolf he could proceed into the Director's office.

"How are you feeling?" the FBI Director asked, shaking Wolf's hand. "Heard you took one center mass."

"I'm fine," Wolf said. "Not gonna lie. It hurt like a son-of-a-bitch."

"I bet," the Director said. "We're not getting any younger. Nice to see the vest worked. Glad you're okay."

"Please, take a seat," the Director said, sitting down.

Wolf sat down.

"I suppose you're wondering why you're here," the Director said.

"Yes sir, I am," Wolf said.

"You need to drop the Romano case," the Director said.

"With all due respect, sir, why?"

"Let's just say because of a three-letter agency,"

"DEA?" Wolf asked. "The Romanos are moving drugs?"

"No, the Director said. "The other three-letter agency."

"The CIA?" Wolf asked. "Terrorism? Are you serious? But why?"

"Do I have to spell it out for you?" the Director said.

"No sir," Wolf said. "It's the jammers. Even the local rookie detective figured it out."

"Detective Baker is smart as a whip," the Director said. "Both the FBI and CIA tried to recruit him."

"Are you serious?" Wolf said. "I knew he was smart, but damn."

"Is this going to be a problem?"

"No," Wolf said. "But how do I keep him off the Romanos?"

"Detective Baker is aware," the Director said.

"How the hell does he know?" Wolf asked.

"I just told you. Both the FBI and CIA tried to recruit him," the Director said. "Plus, his sister is CIA."

"And because she's from Stoughton. Right?" Wolf asked.

"You're getting an accommodation for the drug bust in Stoughton," the Director said. "And once the killer's caught, you'll get another accommodation for that as well."

"The man in the suit," Wolf said. "The one who just showed up today. Said the Federal Government was taking control of the scene after the shooting. I'm guessing he was CIA?"

"You and I both know the CIA is not allowed to operate on U.S. soil," the Director said.

"Oh, that's right sir," Wolf said. "I forgot. Must have been a different agency."

"This conversation is over," the Director said. "I'm glad to see you're a team player, though. You've had a hell of a career, Doug. Take the win and go out on top."

Wolf nodded.

"Yes, sir. Thank you."

Chapter 117

Stoughton Police Headquarters
Stoughton, Massachusetts

The next morning McCormack was taking flak from all sides. Her phone wouldn't stop ringing. Reporters were camped outside her home.

Laynie had released her story. She went in-depth with her findings into Great Blue Hill Bank, Larry Fuller, Frank Langer and the Romanos. She provided documents to quell the naysayers.

The murders, combined with Laynie's story and questions at the press brief the other day, brought the public to the brink. Residents took to social media posting about their experiences with Great Blue Hill Bank's foreclosure scheme. One woman even said her husband had committed suicide because of it.

Then, to add fuel to the already intense fire, throw two officers being shot into the mix. A firestorm was brewing.

Protestors had gathered outside the police station. They held signs that called for the arrest of Frank Langer.

McCormack called Colton into her office. She wanted to know where the murder investigation stood. Colton told her he felt they were getting close.

"Good," McCormack said. "Find him and fast. Last thing we need is another body."

Just then, a call came over the radio asking Colton to call Dispatch.

"You jinxed us," Colton said, hanging up the phone.

"Don't even tell me," McCormack said, putting her face into her hands.

Colton responded over to the First Parish Church.

He pulled in and saw it. Parked in the middle of the church parking lot was the McMullen Funeral Home hearse. Behind it was a casket sitting on the cart used to move it. The church was located directly in the center of town and the parking lot faced Washington Street. Everyone passing by had a clear view of both the hearse and the casket.

Lt. Bonnett and Officer O'Sullivan were first on the scene. They met Colton as he stepped out of his cruiser.

"Don't even tell me," Colton said.

"We got a call from the church staff," O'Sullivan said. "They said they don't have a funeral scheduled today."

"And it's too early for Halloween," Lt. Bonnett said.

"You open it yet?" Colton asked.

"Yeah," Lt. Bonnett said. "Hence us calling you. Looks like the same guy. He left his calling card."

Colton walked over to the casket and opened it. Inside was Max McMullen. Colton recognized the pointy chin from the group photo. Sons of Liberty Medallions covered each eye.

McMullen's hands were in his lap, palms up. The killer had branded each palm.

Colton checked McMullen's right thumb. There was an M tattooed on it.

He took pictures of the symbols with his department-issued phone. Then he pulled up the picture of the cypher. He translated it.

I Am Shroud

Colton looked up to find a group of onlookers had formed on the sidewalk.

Chapter 118

Holy Sepulchre Cemetery
Stoughton, Massachusetts

Colton was back at the station. The Medical Examiner had taken the body of Max McMullen away. The State Police Forensic Team had the hearse towed to their lab.

Colton sat at his desk, looking into Richard and Samantha Church's background. No one knew where or when they moved. They were last seen twenty-plus years ago. Finding someone today was easy. Trying to locate someone last seen or heard from two decades ago was tricky.

But Colton wouldn't have to look much further.

His phone rang. It was Lt. Bonnett.

Colton answered.

"Hey Detective," Lt. Bonnett said. "Can you come down to the Holy Sepulchre Cemetery? It's the one behind CVS."

"Sure," Colton said. "What's going on?"

"Well," Lt. Bonnett said. "This is a first for me. We received a call from the cemetery workers down here. Someone dug up a body. And … they left a note for you."

Colton sat straight up.

"What does the note say?" Colton asked.

"It says, *Detective Baker: Look here,*" Lt. Bonnett said.

"John," Colton said, using the Lieutenant's first name. "Is there just one body?"

"Hold on," Lt. Bonnett said.

Colton heard him ask the cemetery workers how many bodies were in the grave.

"They think three," Lt. Bonnett said.

"Is it two adults and a child?" Colton asked.

"Let me check," Lt. Bonnett said.

Colton waited.

"Yes," Lt. Bonnett said. "Two adults and a child. How did you know that?"

"Call it a hunch," Colton said. "I'll be right down."

Colton responded down to the cemetery.

Lt. Bonnett and Officer O'Sulllivan had taped off the area.

As Colton walked over, he noticed there weren't any tombstones around the grave.

"Where are the headstones?" Colton asked the cemetery workers.

"There are none," the man said. "This part of the cemetery isn't being used. Not yet, anyway."

"Does this cemetery have a Potter's Field?" Colton asked the cemetery worker.

"No," the worker said. "The only one around is in Boston."

"I need to view the bodies," Colton said.

"We can lower you down using the backhoe and a strap," the man said.

The workers retrieved the backhoe and lowered Colton into the grave.

There were no caskets. Just three skeletal remains side by side. All three had holes in their foreheads.

Now Colton had nine bodies.

Chapter 119

Old Maple Street
Stoughton, Massachusetts

Colton left the cemetery and headed for the Town Hall. He pulled all the records he could find on Richard and Samantha Church.

He went back to the station.

On the way to his office, he ran into McCormack. She wasn't happy that there were three new bodies. Barnes was at home resting after being shot, and Wolf was still in Washington. Diaz was keeping an eye on the Romanos, which left Colton solo.

Colton asked her to hold off releasing that information. He told her he was following up on something. She gave him twenty-four hours.

Colton sorted through the records. He found something.

He called Diaz and asked her for her help. He told her he thought he had cracked the case.

Colton walked over to McCormack's office. She was sitting behind her desk.

"Anything?" McCormack asked.

He handed her a piece of paper.

She read it.

"Are you serious?" she asked.

"Yes," Colton said. "I need to confirm something first. Can you meet me at that address later if need be?"

"I sure hope you know what you're doing, Detective," McCormack said.

Colton left and headed over to Old Maple Street. It was a dead-end street with just a few houses on it. The sun was setting when he arrived. He parked down the road and walked to the last house on the left. There was one light on in the back room of the house.

Diaz arrived a few minutes later. She parked behind Colton and made her way down the darkened street.

"You think he's in there?" Diaz whispered.

"I know he is," Colton said.

Chapter 120

Old Maple Street
Stoughton, Massachusetts

Standing on the front porch, Colton and Diaz heard muffled screams coming from inside the house.

They stacked up on the front door.

Once ready, Diaz squeezed his shoulder.

Colton moved into position to kick the door open. He leaned back and booted the door as hard as he could.

The door flung open. Shards of wood went sailing across the floor. The metal door latch plate bounced with a twang and slid to a halt.

Colton rushed inside, his weapon at the ready.

Colton spotted a man in a black hooded sweatshirt. He stood over someone in a folding chair. The man turned and looked at Colton. They locked eyes for a split second. Then the man bolted from the room.

Colton swept the room with his weapon, searching for other threats. It was clear. He moved further into the room.

Sitting in the chair was David Monteiro. His hands were bound behind his back with Duct Tape. His head hung low, and his face was bruised and bleeding. Blood ran down his chin and dripped onto his lap.

"Check on him," Colton said to Diaz, pointing at David.

Colton peered into the next room. It was pitch black except for a sliver of light from the door beyond.

Colton had his pistol out in front of him, ready to fire. He made his way into the room.

Suddenly, the man lunged from the darkness and tackled Colton. The impact sent Colton's pistol skidding across the floor further into the darkness.

Colton found himself flat on his back with the man on top of him. He punched Colton in the stomach, knocking the wind out of him. Then he punched Colton in the face.

Colton's training kicked in. He used his legs and wrapped them around the assailant. Colton jerked quickly. The move sent the man crashing onto the floor. The man screamed out in pain. In the blink of an eye, Colton had reversed the tides. Now he was on top. Colton used his fist and elbows to deliver powerful blows onto the man's head and face. Few people can withstand such a barrage. Instantly, the man's body went limp. He was out cold.

Diaz found the light switch. The darkness disappeared. Colton rolled the man over and cuffed him. Once secure, Colton rolled the man onto his side into the recovery position.

"Are you okay?" Diaz asked.

"I'm fine," Colton said, winded, crawling to his gun.

Diaz cleared the rest of the house. There was no one else.

Colton got to his feet and called McCormack.

"I found him," Colton told her. "Send an ambulance."

Chapter 121

Stoughton Police Headquarters
Stoughton, Massachusetts

Backup arrived, along with an ambulance.

They untied David Monteiro and took him out to the ambulance.

Laynie had been listening to the scanner and rushed over to cover the story. She appeared shocked when she found out her dad was going to be the next victim. She thanked Colton for saving her father. Colton told her to go with her father and that he'd fill her in later. Laynie climbed into the ambulance.

The Paramedics had brought the suspect out. He was groggy and had a busted nose and fat lip but denied medical treatment.

Lt. Bonnett placed him in his cruiser and brought him to the station for booking.

Once booked, they placed him in the interview room.

Colton let him sweat it out. Harbor was on his way. He wanted to witness the interrogation. Once Harbor arrived, he and McCormack watched from the other room.

Colton and Diaz walked into the interview room.

"I remember you," Colton said, walking in. "You're Barry Knight. The kid who was with Gino Romano the day I pulled him over. You'd just started working for them."

"Keep your friends close, and your enemies closer," Barry said.

Diaz sat down.

"Why didn't you kill the Romano's," Colton asked, taking a seat next to Diaz.

"They're assholes," Barry said. "But that's all they are. They had nothing to do with the death of my parents. Frank and Larry killed my parents. The others helped cover it up."

"Why don't you tell me about them?" Colton said.

"You're a smart guy. I followed you. You know why," Barry said.

"I need you to say it," Colton said. "For the camera." Colton pointed up at the corner.

"They killed my family," Barry said.

"The three bodies you dug up, correct?" Colton asked.

"That's right," Barry said. "They killed my family for money."

"You mean the coins, correct?" Colton asked.

"Yes," Barry said.

"Walk me through it," Colton said. "From the beginning."

"Twenty-two years ago, my parents befriended the wrong group of people," Barry said. "It took me years to track them down."

"Just to be clear," Colton said. "You used a fake ID. Your last name isn't Knight. It's Church, correct?"

"Yes," Barry said. "My last name is Church."

"And are you a descendant of Dr. Benjamin Church, Jr?" Colton asked.

"Supposedly," Barry said. "That's how my parents had the stash of Continental Coins. They'd been passed down through the family. My family never knew how much they were worth. Just that they were valuable. Money is a great motivator for wrongdoing."

"I can't argue with that," Colton said. "Please continue."

"I found an old picture of my parents with their friends. It was around the time they died. I went to see Larry Fuller. I asked him about my parents. He got mad. The next day, Frank Langer showed up at my door. He told me it was best if I left town. Told me not to come back."

"How did he know where you lived?" Colton asked.

"I lived with my grandma," Barry said. "She was watching me the night my parents disappeared. When Frank showed up mad, I knew. I knew he and Larry had something to do with their disappearance."

"What did you do next?"

"I looked into Larry Fuller," Barry said. "I found out he was running a foreclosure scam. That got me thinking about the house my parents owned. So I asked my grandma. She said that after my parents disappeared, the bank took the house back. I looked into the property. I learned the mortgage was through Great Blue Hill Bank. Larry Fuller's bank. So, I went and paid Larry another visit."

"What happened when you talked to Larry?" Colton asked.

"He kept threatening to call the police if I didn't leave," Barry said.

"Did he call the police?" Colton asked.

"No," Barry said. "I punched him in his face. I broke his nose. He started crying like a little baby. He said Frank forced him to do it."

"Do what?" Colton asked.

"Kill my parents," Barry said.

"He sent my parents over to Frank's house to discuss selling their coins," Barry said. "Larry said my parents wouldn't sell them. Said Frank started arguing with my parents and an altercation took place. Said my parents left. Larry said Frank forced him and Brian to go with him and they chased my parents. They caught up to them and forced them off the road. Said my parents wrecked pretty badly, and they died."

"Then what happened?" Colton asked.

"I asked him how they covered it up," Barry said.

"What did Larry say?" Colton asked.

"Larry said they called Firefighter Bill McDonald," Barry said. "McDonald was on duty that night. He came down. Said McDonald filled out a report that said my family died in the accident."

Colton opened his folder and pulled out a piece of paper. He slid it over to Barry.

"What's that?" Barry asked.

"I searched through the town's records," Colton said. "I found the run report Bill McDonald filed. It states your parents died due to traumatic injury sustained in the accident. But we know that's not true."

"Oh, I know, Detective. McDonald lied," Barry said. "I saw the holes in my parents' heads. They even shot my sister. His job was to save people. He covered up what really happened to them."

"How did you kill McDonald?" Colton asked.

"I called McDonald from Larry's house," Barry said. "He came over and I tied him up. I've read about my family's history. I knew Dr. Benjamin Church, Jr. was a traitor and that he sent encrypted messages. That's when I came up with the idea to mark McDonald's body. I used to dabble in tattooing, so I had the tattoo gun and ink. I figured if I made it gruesome enough and public, Frank wouldn't be able to cover it up."

"Continue," Colton said.

"Larry said they called Max McMullen to come get the bodies," Barry said. "Then they had Alex Torres tow the car and get rid of it."

Diaz sat there and shook her head in disbelief.

"How did you kill Alex Torres?" Colton asked.

"I called him," Barry said. "I told him I had a vintage car I wanted him to look at. When he arrived, I tortured and killed him."

"And then what?" Colton asked.

"Larry said Frank got Graziele Alves to forge the land and deed documents," Barry said. "Larry and Graziele made it look like Frank bought my parents' property. If anyone asked, they'd say my parents sold the house and land to him and then they moved away. Who does that? She just changed the names, and it was no longer my parents' property.

"Geez..." Diaz said.

"Growing up, I studied the Revolutionary War because of my family history," Barry said. "I knew several Tax Collectors and Customs Officials were tarred and feathered. So, I thought it appropriate for Graziele Alves. I forged contest documents, making it look like she won a trip to France. I even bought her airline tickets."

"What about Brian Andrews?" Colton asked. "What did he do?"

"He lured my parents over to Frank's house," Barry said.

"How do you know that?" Colton asked.

"Larry told me," Barry said.

"Why did you leave him up on Blue Hill?" Colton asked.

"Well, I'd been following you," Barry said. "I followed you into the Historical Society. I listened to you talking to Stan. You asked him about Dr. Benjamin Church, Jr. I knew you took the bait. So, I used Andrews to confirm it. It was apropos. Andrews led my parents to their death, and I led you to the truth."

"And Max McMullen?" Colton asked.

"Max buried my family in an unmarked grave," Barry said. "He disgraced their remains."

"Is that why you put him on display in the town center?" Colton asked.

"You're damn right I did," Barry said. "Showed him off to the whole town. He never gave my family a proper burial. He just put them in an unmarked grave. But I found them! I tortured Max. I promised to let him live. Once I confirmed where he buried my parents, I dug them up. Then I forced Max to drink embalming fluid. He died a grueling death."

"What about David Monteiro?" Colton asked. "What did he do?"

"He never covered the story," Barry said.

"You were going to kill him because he didn't cover the story?" Diaz asked.

"He was friends with them," Barry said.

"You do know that Wendy broke up with David and started dating his best friend?" Colton asked.

"Wait, what?" Barry said.

"David stopped hanging around with them," Colton said. "David had no way of knowing about what happened to your parents."

"Why didn't you come to us?" Colton asked. "We would have helped you."

"I did," Barry said. "I went to Detective Peterson. He was looking into my family. He told me he was meeting with Frank the night he died. Frank killed him."

Colton's eyes widened. He looked up at the camera.

"What did you do with Frank?" Colton asked.

"I haven't found that snake in the grass," Barry said. "I think he caught onto me and took off."

Colton looked up at the camera again.

"Just to clarify," Colton said. "The Romanos had nothing to do with the murder of your parents, correct?"

"No," Barry said. "Frank sold the land to the Romanos ten years later."

"One night I was searching through the paperwork in the Romanos trailer," Barry said. "I was trying to see if they were involved. That's when I found the paperwork from when Frank sold them the property. I also found a box of jammers at the bottom of the file cabinet."

Diaz perked up.

"Tell me about the jammers?" Colton asked.

"One day, I overheard Gino talking about the jammers," Barry said. "They received them from the Middle East. I also overheard Nino threaten to kill someone if they didn't play ball with the highway contract. When I found the jammers, I thought I could use one to mask my movements. But when I saw the FBI show up with you the day you found Alex Torres, I stopped using them. I figured if they got caught, who'd care. They were aiding and abetting terrorists."

"So you admit to using the jammer?" Diaz asked.

Suddenly, there was a knock on the interview room door.

Colton got up and answered it.

Wolf and the Man in the Suit were standing there with Harbor and McCormack.

Colton looked at Diaz, who stood up.

"We need to talk," Wolf said.

Chapter 122

Stoughton Police Headquarters
Stoughton, Massachusetts

They all met in Chief McCormack's office.

The Man in the Suit stood quietly in the corner.

Wolf explained that this was now a federal case. Federal charges were being sought against Barry Church.

Two FBI Agents escorted Barry from the police station out to a waiting black SUV.

"Can they do this?" Colton asked.

"I just got off the phone with the Attorney General," Harbor said. "The Federal Government is taking over the investigation. Barry Church is now in the custody of the U.S. Government."

"On what charge?" Diaz asked.

Wolf looked at Diaz. "It's a federal offense to use jammers."

"You did a great job, Colton." McCormack said. "You should be proud."

"What about the victims' families?" Diaz asked. "They expect us to arrest and convict someone."

"Find Frank Langer," the Man in the Suit said. "Find and charge him with the murders."

McCormack dismissed Colton, who went back to his office with Diaz.

"Who was the Man in the Suit?" Diaz asked. "Is this really about the jammers?"

"What if I told you the Romanos were working with the CIA?" Colton said.

"Really?" Diaz asked. "Are you serious?"

"Yes," Colton said. "The Romanos are part of the mafia. One thing they're good at is smuggling things into the country. The southern border is too hot. Plus, there's no way of knowing where they'd end up. Or in whose hands. Using the mafia in the states made it easier. Direct shipment. Hand to hand."

"But why would they work with the CIA?" Diaz asked.

"Criminal enterprise," Colton said. "People know they sell and trade illegal things. Therefore, they're trusted by other criminal enterprises."

"You mean terrorists?" Diaz asked.

"Yes," Colton said.

"But why would Gino Romano agree to work with terrorists?" Diaz asked. "I thought the mafia had standards."

"Nino wasn't Gino's only son," Colton said.

"Wasn't?" Diaz asked.

"I did some digging into the Romanos," Colton said. "Gino had another son, Mario, who served in the Marines. Mario was killed in combat in Afghanistan. That's why I think he agreed to help the CIA. His son died fighting terrorists."

"Oh," Diaz said. "I kinda feel bad for Gino. But the mafia kills people too."

"But they don't usually target or kill civilians," Colton said. "It's typically people inside the mafia. It's business. I don't think Gino wanted to see the jammers used to kill civilians. And when the government asked, Gino agreed."

"What do you think about charging Frank Langer?" Diaz asked. "Like the Man in the Suit suggested."

"Yeah, we should," Colton said.

"Why?" Diaz asked.

"I think we had it wrong," Colton said. "This whole time we thought Gino was using Frank. I think it's the other way around. Frank was using Gino to cover his tracks. If someone looked into the property or disappearance of Richard and Samantha Church..."

"They'd see the mafia owned the land and assume they killed the Church's," Diaz said.

"Bingo," Colton said.

"Now we need to find Frank Langer," Diaz said.

"Easier said than done," Colton said.

Chapter 123

Stoughton Bakery
Stoughton, Massachusetts

David was recovering at home. He was sore but getting better. Laynie made a good nurse.

Colton met Laynie at the Stoughton Bakery.

"I talked to my dad," Laynie said. "He filled me in on how he knew all the victims."

"They were all friends from high school," Colton said.

"Oh, by the way. My dad said to say hi," Laynie said. "He would have been dead if you hadn't shown up when you did."

"Glad he's okay," Colton said.

"Agent Wolf and a man in a suit showed up at the house," Laynie said. "They spoke to my dad in private. Now he claims he doesn't remember anything about that night. Do you know what they said to him?"

"No," Colton said. "I'm sorry. I don't."

"So, how did you crack the case?" Laynie asked, changing the subject.

"That picture I found," Colton said. "I started tracing all of their lives, seeing if their paths recently crossed. There were two people I couldn't locate. I spoke with Wendy McDonald and she provided me with their names. She said they were married and had two children. There was no recent record of them. I went to the Town Hall and pulled their records. I found their marriage license. Samantha's maiden name was Bailey. I found the birth certificate for their two children. Stacey and Barry. But there was nothing after that. They just disappeared."

"That's odd," Laynie said.

"I looked into their property to see if they sold their house," Colton said. "I found out that Great Blue Hill Bank foreclosed on their property."

"And that's where Larry Fuller comes in," Laynie said.

"Exactly," Colton said. "A few months after Richard and Samantha Church disappeared, Larry sold Frank the land. Years later, Frank sold it to Gino Romano."

"That's where Romano Sand and Gravel is now, correct?" Laynie asked.

"Yes," Colton said. "Off of Turnpike Street."

"Did Frank kill them?" Laynie asked.

"Yes," Colton said.

"Why?" Laynie asked.

"Continental Coins," Colton said. "Frank discovered they had them. He killed them and stole the coins."

"Hence you going to Roy's Stamps and Coin Shop," Laynie said.

"Correct," Colton said.

"Detective Peterson started looking into the disappearance of the Church's," Colton said. "Apparently, he was getting close."

"Did the others know about the murders?" Laynie asked.

"Worse," Colton said. "They helped cover them up."

"And Frank started killing them," Laynie said.

"And we believe he killed Detective Peterson, too," Colton said. "The Medical Examiner looked at the case and determined that Peterson had a higher than normal amount of antidepressant in his system. A dose that high can trigger cardiac arrest."

"That's unbelievable," Laynie said.

"We found a map of a cemetery at Larry Fuller's house," Colton said. "Larry had circled an area on the map."

"No way," Laynie said. "It's where Frank buried the Church's."

"Bingo," Colton said.

"After Detective Peterson died, Frank promoted me to detective because of my inexperience. He made the murders look like the work of a serial killer. He thought I'd never solve the case."

"Wow," Laynie said. "He was wrong."

Laynie had her story.
She sent it to Hank.

Chapter 124

Nancy and Paul Baker's House
Stoughton, Massachusetts

Colton stopped by his parents' house. His mom was sitting at the table. Her face was in her hands. The telephone was on the table.

"Are you okay, Mom?" Colton asked.

"Yes," Nancy said, wiping away her tears. "I just got off the phone with your sister."

"Oh boy," Colton said.

"No," Nancy said. "It wasn't like that. It was probably one of the best conversations Cindy and I have ever had. She supports my decision to put your father in a nursing home."

"That's great, Mom," Colton said. "What did Cindy say?"

"She made some great points," Nancy said. "Cindy said she understood. She agreed that if I couldn't take care of him anymore, then he needed to go into a home. And that it's not like I wouldn't visit. She said now I can spend time with him instead of taking care of him."

"I'm glad she called," Colton said.

"It was great to hear her voice," Nancy said. "She told me she loved me. She hasn't said that in years."

Tears streamed down Nancy's face.

"I wish I didn't have to do it," Nancy said. "But he's becoming too much to handle. It's like having a toddler at home. At my age, I just can't do it."

Colton hugged his mom as she cried.

Chapter 125

Corner Cafe
Stoughton, Massachusetts

Colton and Diaz sat in a booth at the Corner Cafe.

Wolf and Barnes walked in. Barnes sat down to join them for breakfast. His arm was still in a sling.

"I got to hand it to you, kid," Wolf said. "Your hunch was right. You're one hell of a detective."

"Thank you, sir," Colton replied. "It means a lot coming from you."

"I can't stay," Wolf said. "I'm heading back to Washington for my new assignment. But I wanted to say congrats."

Just then, Laynie and Dan walked in.

"That's my cue to leave," Wolf said and headed for the door.

Laynie passed Wolf on his way out. He gave Laynie the stink eye.

Laynie smiled and waved. They walked over to the table and sat down.

"Look," Colton said. He pointed to the TV in the corner. "You're just in time."

Laynie's final report was airing on the local news.

Colton, Diaz, Laynie and Dan sat and enjoyed their breakfast.

"What time is your flight out?" Diaz asked Laynie.

"Noon," Laynie said.

"How about you?" Laynie asked. "When are you heading back to Washington?"

"I'm not," Diaz said. "They offered me a position here in the Lakeville office, which I accepted."

"That's great news," Laynie said.

Colton looked at Diaz and smiled. Diaz smiled back.

"I saw that," Laynie said, getting up.

Laynie said her goodbyes and left.
"What now?" Colton asked.
"How about we grab that drink?" Diaz asked.
Colton smiled from ear to ear. "Sure!"

Epilogue

Nancy made arrangements and had Paul moved into a long-term care facility.

Colton received an anonymous tip regarding the whereabouts of Frank Langer. He was arrested in Rhode Island trying to catch a flight out of T. F. Green Airport.

District Attorney Steve Harbor charged Frank with murder, racketeering, and money laundering.

The Romanos brokered the deal on the jammers to a terrorist group on Cape Cod. They planned on blowing up both the Sagamore and Bourne bridges. Then using the jammers to block communication on Cape Cod while committing an attack like what Hamas did to Isreal. The FBI Director kept his promise. Wolf hit the mother lode. He swooped in and made the bust.

The Romanos continued their resurfacing scheme and kept the Sand & Gravel pit open. The government hoped they could be useful again in the future.

The town of Stoughton transitioned over to the new Dispatch Center. Everything went well and is still going smoothly. There were no more staffing issues.

The construction of the new state-of-the-art fire station went forward.

Colton investigated the home invasion on Elizabeth Street. There'd been heavy storms that week causing the landscapers to change their schedule. A new member of the crew had conducted the break-ins. He was caught trying to pawn the stolen silverware set.

Colton and Diaz had that drink and hit it off.

If you enjoyed this book,
please feel free to leave a review on Goodreads:

https://www.goodreads.com/book/show/211426213-murder-by-symbols

Visit me at:

www.emkellythrillers.com

Or drop me an email at:
emkelly@emkellythrillers.com

Coming Soon!

Two Lefts

A Detective Colton Baker Thriller

Available Now!

Pestilence

Book 1

A Drew Murphy Post-Apocalyptic Thriller

&

War

Book 2

A Drew Murphy Post-Apocalyptic Thriller

Coming Soon!

Famine

Book 3

A Drew Murphy Post-Apocalyptic Thriller

E.M. Kelly

A Detective Colton Baker Thriller

ABOUT THE AUTHOR

E.M. Kelly lives with his wife and daughter.